Also by Greg Gilmartin:
Crew

SPY
ISLAND

RUN. HIDE. SPY.

Make no mistake, they are coming for you.

GREG GILMARTIN

LifeRich Publishing is a registered trademark of The Reader's Digest Association, Inc.

LifeRich Publishing books may be ordered through booksellers or by contacting:

LifeRich Publishing
1663 Liberty Drive
Bloomington, IN 47403
www.liferichpublishing.com
1 (888) 238-8637

ISBN: 978-1-4897-2457-1 (sc)
ISBN: 978-1-4897-2456-4 (hc)
ISBN: 978-1-4897-2455-7 (e)

Library of Congress Control Number: 2019914925

Print information available on the last page.

LifeRich Publishing rev. date: 09/30/2019

Dedicated to
the truth seekers,
the lie breakers,
the spy makers.

ACKNOWLEDGEMENTS:

Heartfelt thanks to my friends who put up with my stories, pick apart my ideas and correct most of my spelling errors. And to those who shared a part of themselves, knowingly or unknowingly, to help build the characters I hope will find their way off the page into your world. Special thanks to Courtney, Hatsie, Tony, Jay, Billmo, Bob and Andy for their technical and spiritual counsel. Finally, to Kristin and Pat for their unconditional support. Now, read on!

Greg Gilmartin
October 2019

PROLOGUE

The brewing chaos of a storm drove the water before her, the random pattern of nature appeared so regular from up here, she thought. No beginning, no end, only infinite strips of white foam stretching across the blue green sea, rolling relentlessly to the rocky beach below, depleting their power in a thunderous crash then meekly sliding back into the churning sea with a bucket of sand. Was the sole purpose of this display to return the land to the sea? She wondered.

The wind tugged at the blonde strands encircling her cherub face, spilling them across her blue eyes. She reacted slowly, pushing the hair to the side while her eyes continued to dance across the whitecaps two hundred feet below her feet.

The weapon in her hand was heavy, more from strangeness than weight. She knew how to hold a gun, but it tugged on her shoulder, threatened to upset her balance and send her tumbling down the sandy cliff. The feeling was real, even as her feet stood firmly on the grassy edge.

She couldn't believe he was gone.

Her fingers tightened in her other hand, grasping the cool plastic cylinder that was to blame for it all. She didn't want anything to do with it, but she clung to it firmly.

His smile was still clear in her mind, a loving signature

that softened his hard jaw when he flashed it, which was frequent, but, no more.

Two gulls launched from the beach with a few flaps of their wings and climbed into the building breeze, turning lazy circles and climbing higher on the cooling air until they were above the cliffs, above her head. They gave her no notice as they effortlessly landed on the top of the nearby lighthouse.

The light glowed in the dusk, alternating white and green on its continuous sweep of the horizon. The comfort the beacon gave yachtsmen each night was not for her this evening. Rather, it was a ghostly splash across her sorrow. And the weight in her hands.

She absently moved the hair from her face again. Then a tear from her cheek, the back of her hand pressing harder as if the cure for her pain was buried somewhere beneath her skin. If she could only reach it.

She was not used to crying.

The colors of the sky were majestic, in gray and black, edged by orange. They defined another Block Island summer sunset slashing under the approaching storm. She stood there alone as the steel blue darkness overwhelmed the fire on the horizon.

one

THE BEACH VIEW BAR

Thursday Early June 1800 hrs.

"Everybody spies. We don't always know how well they do it." –SpyhakrF

They met at the Beach View Bar on Block Island only a day ago. She waited tables and tended bar there, serving the locals and transient sailors who preferred cheap drinks, good burgers and two pool tables. She had not noticed him come in Thursday afternoon, but suddenly he was there, sitting on a stool, next to old Francois, staring at the dunes across the street through the broad windows behind the bar.

His hair was jet black, his shoulders bare and glistened from under his tank top. They were broad and tanned and drew her eye immediately. The especially large bruise over his shoulder blade made him appear more manly. She caught herself letting out an involuntary sigh and was glad she was on the other side of the room.

"Hey, Pet, could we have two more here!" came a shout from the pool tables in back.

"Hold water, Freddy," she shot back in her accented voice, not even bothering to look his way. Freddy, the local pool hustler, always asked for more. She was a good waitress, but he made it a difficult job. She thought of him with disgust. His roaming hands and foul moods had drawn out her dark opinion of him from day one, which was only two weeks ago.

She continued to clean off tables, yet her eyes roamed back to the man at the bar. Suddenly, he swiveled on his stool, beer in hand and looked right at her. Their eyes met across the room and it caused him to pause. His were blue, like hers, and she felt a flush, as if caught in an intimate act.

He smiled, slipped off the stool and walked toward her, his eyes and smile unwavering.

"Hi," he nodded casually and walked on by. He actually sounded cheery.

"Hello," she returned, smiling back at him. He was a head taller than she, with a square jaw and a friendly aura. He passed within a foot and she detected the smell of a mixture of earth, cologne and sweat. She liked it immediately.

She watched him walk to the pool tables and place a stack of quarters on the nearest one, then take a seat to watch the game in progress. He didn't look back, just easily leaned against the wall in his chair, balanced on two legs, sipping his beer.

Quickly, she went up to the bar with the dirty glasses and ordered two beers. Sally Wren, the owner of the Beach View Bar, gave her a big grin from behind the bar.

"You're drooling, Petrika," she laughed, grabbing the two beers from the ice locker.

"You would not?" Petrika responded. "I like the way he smells!"

"I'll bet he tastes good, too," Sally giggled, giving Petrika a wicked grin. She blushed in return, then joined in the off-color moment, licking her lips in an exaggerated manner. She always thought it funny how her new friend Sally seemed to know what she was thinking when it came to men.

"He's not regular," Pet managed through her smile.

"Ha! That I don't know, dear!" Sally laughed sharply, turning toward the two thirsty looking men at the other end of the bar. Petrika just looked at her back and wondered what was so funny.

"Oh...*A* regular. Ha!" she laughed at herself, recognizing the missing article. English was not so easy to learn as it was to hear.

She brought the two beers to Freddy, setting them down at his table while consciously not looking at the new man. Without warning, she felt a hand on her ass and turned quickly to see Freddy's leering face.

"Stop it, you crap!" she shouted, swatting his hand away. She tried to move past him, but he blocked her momentarily with his pool cue. She had grown tired of this game long ago and pushed the stick aside. She moved to the other side of the table, but Freddy moved to cut her off.

"Freddy, you a prick! Get out of way," she said in an even, bored voice, realizing she was standing right in front of the man who smelled of earth and sweat.

"What's the fuss, Pet?" Freddy protested, his horse shaped face lit up in a big smile, his arms out stretched. "You have such a mouth! I just want to pay you for the beers." He pulled a ten-dollar bill from his shirt pocket and held it up, as if showing it to everyone around the tables.

Two of Freddy's buddies laughed, while the third ignored them all and lined up his pool shot. The man in the tank top didn't move. He looked up at the blonde waitress and thin man named Freddy from his chair still balanced on two legs not three feet in front of them.

Petrika wrinkled up her mouth and held out her hand for the money. Freddy moved as if to place it in her blouse, but she grabbed the bill. Freddy didn't fight but folded his own hand around hers in a rough caress from which Petrika quickly escaped.

"Thanks," she shot at him and started to slip past, but Freddy hooked her jeans' waistband and pulled her back toward him, turning her around so her breasts were crushed up against his chest.

"You Russian bitch, I forgot your tip," he laughed and pressed his lips against hers, holding her tightly around the waist.

Petrika struggled, managed to swing her empty tray and smashed it against the side of Freddy's head. She swung it again.

"Stop it, you creep!"

Freddy blocked the second tray slap with the pool cue in his right hand and let her go, but only for an instant. He grabbed her wrist before she could get far. He laughed, his grin a crooked leer, but his eyes betrayed the pain delivered by the tray.

"Don't you ever hit me!" His voice was a vicious gasp. And he slapped Petrika with the cue.

"Jeez, Freddy!" shouted his buddy shooting at the table. A few mumbles of protest could be heard among the scraping of a chair as the locals nearby focused their attention on the confrontation.

Petrika felt the wooden stick hit her in the ear, a glancing blow, but sharp enough to hurt. She redoubled her efforts to get free, realizing this game had gone too far. She kicked him in the shins, bringing a cry of pain. He let her go and she backed away holding her ear.

"Asshole!" she screamed. "*Osel!* You stupid, low life asshole!"

"Hey, bitch, come back here," Freddy answered, rubbing his left shin. He took a step to go after her, but that was as far as he got. He felt a sudden jerk backward as a hand on his collar lifted him off his feet and planted him on top of the pool table.

"Oh, man!" cried Freddy's buddy, his shot disrupted by the scattered balls and Freddy sprawled on the orange felt.

"What the flick!" Freddy exclaimed and turned to see the guy in the tank top who had been sitting against the wall now standing next to him wearing a big smile.

"I don't think she likes, friend, so leave her alone." The man's voice was calm, almost quiet. His teeth were so white, Freddy couldn't help but notice.

"Eff-off, man, you got nothing with me!" Freddy jumped off the table, rubbing his neck. He faced the new man.

"A man shouldn't be slapping a lady with a pool stick, Freeeeddee." He spoke the name with an exaggerated tone of sarcasm as if the name itself was a mockery to decent social behavior. The dark-haired man stood with his beer in hand, looking right at Freddy. He shook his head slowly, as if he was looking at a dumb ass child caught with his hand in the cookie jar. "You think?"

Freddy sized him up quickly. Broad shoulders, dusty pants and work boots. He was a formidable figure. Freddy grinned.

"Hey, man, we were just having some fun. She likes the rough stuff. We do it all the time, right guys?"

Two of his buddies were to the stranger's right, the third on the other side of the table, patiently waiting for his next shot.

They reluctantly nodded in unison, like a band of bobble heads. The stranger turned to them, convinced their bobbing was not as much a sign of support as it was fear of what Freddy might do to them. Freddy saw an advantage and grabbed the tip end of his stick with both hands and swung it like a baseball bat. The thick handle sliced toward the broad-shouldered man.

But the man saw it all the way and countered with the beer bottle in his left hand, the glass shattering into shards, absorbing much of the blow. The stick landed harmlessly on the man's arm and, in movements that others would later say were too quick to see, he grabbed it out of Freddy's hands and with a short return swipe, broke three thin fingers on his assailant's right hand.

The crack of the stick hitting the bones might have been the sound from the snapping of dry twigs on a fall afternoon. It was heard throughout the small bar. What had been loud talking was now a bar fight and the dozen patrons took notice. Most of them knew Freddy and felt little remorse when the horse faced bully's eyes went wide with more pain that drove him to his knees clutching his wrist and crying out in anguish.

"You broke my hand, goddam it! You broke my effin' hand!"

Freddy's buddies jumped at the unnamed man with the dark hair, but the wooden stick moved so quickly it seemed all three had been hit at the same time. Two to the side, one to the chest. They immediately backed off, holding their bruises, wanting no part of the fight.

It was over. The man dropped the pool cue on the table, picked up his stack of quarters and headed for the door. He stopped in front of Petrika who had watched him lay out four men in a matter of seconds.

"Are you all right?" he asked softly, his friendly smile cutting across angled jawbones. She noticed the smile softened the hard face and gave it an aura of friendliness.

"Yes, I'm fine," she nodded.

"You gave him a good smack with that tray," he laughed.

She looked into his blue eyes and saw a warmth she had not known before from any man. He didn't seem the same man of violence from a moment ago.

"Thank you. Freddy can be a real prick sometimes. How did you do that? You hit them so quick!" she asked with a wide look that showcased her blue eyes in the light from the bar entrance.

He smiled and shrugged his shoulders, as if it was not big thing.

"I did some martial arts as a kid, Shaolin Kung Fu. It's been hiding in there waiting for the right moment."

"I like the moment! For me!" She giggled.

"Bobby Jackson is on his way," Sally reported from behind the bar. "He'll take care of Freddy."

"Who is that?" the stranger asked Petrika, nodding toward Sally. "Bobby Jackson?"

"Bobby is the sheriff," she said, surprised this man didn't know Sheriff Bobby Jackson. The red and white Bronco, with his name emblazoned on the side, was as common a sight on the small island as sand and sailors.

"Welcome to the Block, stranger," she smiled and extended her hand. "I am new myself, last month ago. Petrika Inessova Rushevski. From the Ukraine."

He took her hand briefly, but she saw a shadow had passed over his face at the mention of the sheriff. The smile was replaced by a hard look in contrast to the warmth it had shown a second ago. Yet, his touch was still light, and he squeezed the back of her hand, just behind the thumb, and looked into her eyes. It felt good.

"I must go."

"Oh?" she asked, and he was gone, out the door, straight across the street into the grassy dunes that led down to Benson Beach on the east side of the island.

She wanted to call after him for his name, but his

purposeful strides struck a deep chord and she held back. It was as if he would be better off if she didn't know his name. She watched his tanned shoulders disappear into the tall grass and over the sandy dune just as Sheriff Jackson's Bronco turned the corner from Main Street with blue lights flashing.

As the Bronco slid to a sand crunching halt in front of the Beach View Bar, Petrika Inessova Rushevski stood still, coming to grips with an overwhelming desire to see the stranger again. She knew nothing of him but believed in her heart of hearts it would happen.

Sitting at the bar in his usual seat closest to the door, the elder gentleman with the floppy fishing hat sipped on his red wine and checked out the photos he had just taken with his cellphone. He was touched by the intensity of the young man and young woman right in front of him. He smiled to himself noting the obvious comfort they had standing so close together.

"Francois, you want another red wine?" Sally Wren interrupted his thoughts just as Sheriff Bobby Jackson walked through the front door. The Sheriff nodded at Francois in that familiar greeting shared with someone you know. Francois returned the nod and pointed with his thumb to the back. He then looked back at Sally as the Sheriff moved toward the pool tables. He was pretty sure he was going to need to ride with Win McGovern in his taxi to make it home tonight. He just couldn't hold his liquor like he used to!

"I will have another, thank you!" he nodded to her. "The hell with sobriety! It might be fun to watch what happens next!"

two

SHERIFF BOBBY JACKSON

Friday 0900

Ones and Zeros have changed the spy game. Not many busy with the same old same. Tricks and lies still rule the day but now, everyone likely knows what you say. —SpyhakrF

For one brief moment, Petrika thought she smelled him again. It came just an instant before she opened her eyes. The heat on her cheek felt like the touch of a human hand. Could it be? He had been swimming in her dreams all night. It was natural that her fondest hopes were to find him next to her. Instead, it was her mind playing more tricks.

It was the sunshine that filtered through her easterly window and warmed her face. It was the morning breeze that carried the smell of fresh earth from the garden next door. There was no one in the bed next to her. Only ghosts of a moment's memory.

She moaned from the disappointment, followed immediately by a laugh.

"I should be so much lucky!"

Stretching her body, she kicked aside the sheets to reveal her nakedness to the empty room.

A frugal woman, she grew up with the hardships of farm living and rough fabrics in the Ukraine, allowing herself the luxury of satin sheets shortly after arriving in America. The smooth, cool touch against her skin had turned her against pajamas forever. Her white body on the light blue background offered a vision made for those sexy art books, but it was lost in her solitude.

Her hands roamed lazily over her body, happy with the smooth skin. As cool as the sheets were, the warmth of her dreams lingered, and she let her hands linger as well. She was 25 and felt youthful. Her hands glided over skin that rivaled the hottest models who graced the magazine and television ads she watched every day.

She smiled at the thought of her grandmother, Inessa, a plump woman in a work dress and scarf, with bow legs and a permanent stoop. She carried the classic look of a Russian peasant woman that Petrika and her girlfriends fought hard to overcome.

But not the eyes. Petrika had inherited her grandmother's baby blues. They gave her the soulful look of a woman focused on something far away, so open they offered a standing invitation to gaze deeply into her being. It probably depended on who was looking at her. Or who she looked at. They never seemed to blink.

The roundness of her face came from her grandmother as well, but her grandfather's angular cheeks and jaw were lurking there. The effect was enhanced by a Grecian nose, narrow and straight with slightly upturned nostrils. It was a face that was well liked at her home along the coast where the southern edge of the Ukraine meets the Black Sea. Fishing and the military were the main industries, with tourism a solid third adding a hint of glamour only recently available in Russia. And a lure to the outside world.

While MTV was mesmerizing American teens, it dramatically enhanced the Coca-Cola Blue Jeans revolution of desires in the Soviet Union. The few whose families had acquired satellite receivers found they had many friends after school. Her friend Anna was one with the electronic device. While her father was doing his job as a politician, the teens would tune in the American station and enjoy it in the darkened living room of Anna's house. It was a secret no one kept. The music! The dancing! The clothing! The energy! They all had an immediate impact. The all immediately butted up against a communal life where chores were the family code. Play was way down the list.

She grew up in modest surroundings, with enough to eat and new jeans twice a year. Her family even had a car and a tractor, but there was little future for her here. Maybe working in one of the shops in Odessa where most Russians with money vacationed. Just being close to the glamour of sun and sand was a good hope for a young Russian girl. Maybe she would meet a man and live in Kiev. However, the first time she saw a David Lee Roth video, she knew America was where she really wanted to be.

Her hands drifted slowly over her flat stomach and down to her hips. Her body responded to the caresses, the warmth of her dreams simmering below her navel. The tangle of blonde hair was soft on her fingertips. She closed her eyes and saw the broad shoulders of her mystery man from yesterday. She remembered his touch and convinced herself again their connection had transcended a friendly handshake.

The earthy aroma borne on the morning breeze filtered through the window and mixed with her own scent. It was

11

a familiar smell of her Block Island mornings, but it took on new significance. Her hands became his and they explored slowly and freely, combing the ridges and valleys among the folds of her skin, sliding and gently probing. She had known the intimacy of only three men in her life, but they were long lost in the fog of her growing desire for the man in her mind. Her firm breasts heaved at his imagined touch, and she focused on a taut nipple. The sensations set her imagination into high gear and the fantasy grew with each breath.

She conjured up visions of his tanned back, her hands spread across the broad muscles. Then her head was resting on his stomach, her hands on his legs, his lips softly touching her. She felt the warmth of his skin even as her own fingers felt her own warmth. The pleasure was continuous, like surfing on a wave, only the steady movement of her fingertips necessary to stay on the crest. And she rode the wave easily, enveloped in the images of a man she did not know, but whose countenance, brief touch and violent defense of her honor were enough to fill her with a deep yearning. And that yearning was fulfilled as she imagined him become one with her in the lonely air of a morning tryst.

As the last shiver escaped, she curled into the fetal position, hands trapped between her legs and stillness all around. She lay there aglow, her ecstasy slowly receding like the tide until all that was left was sleep.

A sharp knock on the door brought her awake instantly. "Just a minute!" she called, rolling out of bed and into a summer dress hanging over the chair. She walked slowly through the living room to the door at the back of the kitchen.

She recognized Sheriff Bobby Jackson's uniformed back as he admired the view of the Salt Pond from the second-floor porch railing. He turned as she opened the door. His curly brown hair and stubbly chin awaited a morning mirror.

"*Dobray dyen, gahspeda Petrika*," he smiled in a genuine friendly manner, somewhat embarrassed by his Russian, but determined to make the effort for her.

"Hi, Bobby," she returned, with her own smile. Her mind was still simmering from her erotic exercise, but she liked the Sheriff and had taught him a few words of her language. His efforts helped focus her on the moment.

"Say 'doubrie…like dough, the bread, brie, the cheese," she corrected him. "It's masculine, dobrie d-yen."

"*Dobrie dyen*," he repeated.

"*Tak khoroshow*. That's good!"

"*Spasiba*," he nodded. He fiddled with his hat, shifting gears.

"Look, Petrika, ah, I'd like to ask you a few more questions about last night."

"Sure! Want to come in"" She pulled the door open wide and gestured to her kitchen table. Sheriff Jackson nodded and stepped into the tiny three-room apartment. He glanced again at the single photo hanging on the wall. She had told him it was her parents the only time he had been there before.

He sat at the table under it. Petrika sat opposite him, pushing a covered plate of brownies toward him. She saw his red-rimmed eyes and wondered what adventure had kept him awake all night.

He smiled and lifted the glass top, selecting a large chocolate snack. "I've been up all night, haven't had much time to eat. Thanks."

He took a large bite, drawing a short laugh from Petrika.

"Here, some milk?" she giggled and went to the refrigerator feeling very domestic. She poured him a tumbler full of the white liquid.

"Ma-la-ko."

"Mahlhakoo," he repeated, the word half lost in the mouthful of brownie. He washed it down with a big gulp. Petrika thought he looked comical with chunks of brownie on his teeth and a hint of white around his lips.

The brownie was devoured in silence as she watched from the other side of the table. A small smile crept across her mouth, her deep-set blue eyes twinkling at the sight of the Sheriff stuffing his face.

He finished with a big swallow of milk, momentarily looked for a napkin to wipe his mouth and accepted the one she held in anticipation.

"Whew! I guess I was hungrier than I thought," he smiled apologetically. "That was good!"

She laughed, a merry sharp sound, one that defined the word "mirth".

"Have another. I'm planning to bake a new batch after work tonight!"

"No, I've got to get back to business here." He paused, looking at her directly, his tongue still working slowly on his teeth in a search for pieces of brownie.

"Oh?" Petrika asked in surprise. "What more business do you need?"

"Actually, I do have a few questions. Can you tell me what time you left work?"

"It was about 7:00, just after you left with Freddie."

The Sheriff had pulled out a small pad and started to write.

"And you came here?" he asked without looking up.

"Yes. I took a shower, turned on the tube and baked those brownies," she answered with a smile.

"You didn't go out or speak to anyone"

"No. What is this about, Bobby?" She used his familiar

name and gave him that open, faraway look with her mouth slightly turned down.

He looked up and admired her for a moment, even though she only saw a thin line for lips and a very official manner. Her face was like an athletic cherub, he thought, hiding a smile in his mind. Then he backed his official face with official words.

"Petrika, Freddy is dead. We found his body this morning."

"Really? That prick! I hope the worms don't gag!" She spat out the words and sat back in her chair.

There was a momentary vision of piles of bodies in an open field near Chernobyl. It was a photo she saw just before she came to America. No one felt anything then, tear ducts drained of their reserves and only the dirty, dry tracks of their passing hinted at everyone's stress and sadness. Death had become another cruel reality check for her and her friends.

Except now, Freddy was on top of the pile, a shit eating grin on his face, his eyes wide open with that silly "undress you" look in his soul.

She had not cried then, and she didn't now. A lack of feeling not understood about Chernobyl, but fully accepted for Freddy.

Sheriff Jackson watched her carefully, surprised and intrigued by her answer.

"He was a lowlife, a shit, a A-1 asshole. A *naroosheetal!*" She spat the last, her eyes afire.

"Narasheetal?" he asked.

"Na-roo. Like t-oool. Naroo-sheet-el. A manmade disturbance, an offensive man who doesn't respect no one… anyone."

She felt a surge of energy and stood up, walking to the door, her back to him.

"He didn't know when to stop, Bobby. I thought he was vile."

"Did you kill him," he asked simply.

She turned and looked at him, surprised.

"He was killed?" Her eyebrows raised, the tiny birthmark between them moving in unison. It was the only sign of imperfection on a seamless face.

"Yes. He was stabbed. In the chest. He bled to death."

"Oh, my, he really pissed off someone, didn't he?"

"Did you do it?" he repeated.

"No, I did not do it. Silly man! Me?" She laughed, shaking her head. But it wasn't a happy laugh and she was quiet for a moment as she realized something that had been burning in her. "I did think about it. Him being dead. Wishing him dead."

"You did? When?"

"Every day for the last two weeks," she said quietly.

She let him know with her eyes that she understood what she was saying and to whom. She sat back down at the table across from the Sheriff.

"But I always saw him hit by a train, or maybe caught in one of those car crushers."

"That bad, huh? I wish you had come to me sooner," Bobby said after a moment, repressing a smile. "I could have done something about him. At least kept him away from you."

"I wasn't sure," she shrugged. "I kind of expected that was going to be a part of job, sexy comments and careless hands. There's a lot of horny guys who come to the Beach View. Girls, too. After it happens a few times, you keep working and just try to deal with it. It didn't make him any better for me, for sure."

He wanted to give her a hug, offering his chest as an escape pillow from the apparent fate to which she had resigned herself. Instead, he sat there, flipped his notebook shut and smiled.

"You didn't put him in jail after the fight?" she asked suddenly.

"No. He was bailed out by his buddies about 11. I had to let him go."

Sheriff looked sheepishly at her, almost embarrassed.

"He was a tough act, wasn't he? Not many people have good things to say about him." The Sheriff stood and made to leave.

"They are going to bury him tomorrow. Up on the West side."

"Where was he killed?" she asked, moving to open the door for him.

He paused for a moment before answering. "They found him up on Amy Dodge Lane."

That was less than half a mile from her apartment.

"Who do you think did it?" she asked.

"I don't know. Yet." He walked onto the porch and stood by the railing. She followed.

"You got one of the nicer spots here, Petrika." She thought she heard him sigh. "*Prekraznee, da?*"

"*Ochen prekraznee, da,*" she answered. "A friend of a friend of my family's. I was at the same time at the right time, yes?"

He laughed at her fractured phrasing. "Petrika, no one I know speaks English like you. You're good! But you were in the right place at the right time."

"Yes. Right place at right time. Thanks."

He started down the stairs then turned and paused.

"Say, did that guy from last night ever get in touch with you again?" he asked casually.

For a millisecond she felt a blush of the heat from his pretend touch a few moments ago. It passed quickly, but her white cheeks took on a slightly ruddy complexion. Enough for the Sheriff to notice.

"No. I haven't seen him since he walked through the dunes last night." She allowed herself an unthinkable thought.

"You don't think he did it, do you, Bobby?"

"Don't know, Pet. I certainly want to talk to him."

She remembered the flash of his hands as he slashed Freddy and his buddies with the pool cue. It was explosive, but she didn't for once believe he could kill someone. The touch she felt was too gentle.

"Actually, I have been thinking about him, kind of hoping he would be there this evening," she said.

"Did he say he would meet you at the Beach View tonight?" Sheriff Jackson asked surprised.

"No. No, he didn't say. I would just like to see him again." She shrugged her shoulders with a sheepish grin. "Like I told you last night, I don't even know his name."

"So you said. Well, if you should see him again, ask him to stop by the station. I'd like to talk to him." He waved and headed down the stairs. She yelled down at him just before he got into his Bronco.

"Bobby, he could have killed Freddy at the pool table! It was no contest. Why do it later?"

"So he wouldn't have a dozen witnesses," the Sheriff shouted back up to her, as if he had been thinking about that possibility. "Just tell him I want to ask him some questions. I'm not looking to arrest him."

With that he ducked into his vehicle and quickly backed away, disappearing in a dust cloud among the trees that kept most of the main road along the east coast of the island in the shade.

The sun felt good on the porch and she lingered for a few minutes, admiring the view. The afterglow of her meeting with the stranger had been disrupted by a sliver of doubt. She had to find him.

three

DR. ANDY'S DANDY

Late May

Detection is the game for ASW. Subs play it with stealth. New DNI with USN bosses getting out front from below. Initial reports indicate things will never be the same in the deep blue sea. All ears tuned; all eyes focused. The world's military waits and wants. –SpyhakrF

A few weeks before the young waitress from the Ukraine met her mystery man, an event occurred having nothing to do with beer, pool, bars or beaches. Instead, it changed the course of the coming summer and the future of submarine warfare.

The *USS Chorlton* was in the Veatch Canyon bearing 130 degrees magnetic out about 120 nautical miles from Block Island. She was 1200 feet down and moving in a southeasterly direction at 25 knots with a full payload of cruise missiles, torpedoes and a dozen Navy Seals.

"Shortstop, this is Century. Commence maneuvers,"

came the command in a digitally clear voice from the small speaker above the bank of monitors along the starboard wall of the sub's control room.

"Copy, Century," came the terse reply from Captain Vic Tennerman, listening through a wireless pair of headphones. He pressed a button on the arm of his upholstered chair, opening a channel to the ships 1 MC, the internal comm system reaching all departments in the boat.

"Commence exercise. Right turn, 3-5 degrees. Make new course 1-7-5. Depth 1-1-0-0." His calm voice filled the headsets of the helmsman and the dive plane operator to his left and the six other sailors sitting in front of their monitors. They were a dozen in all and from his raised chair he could swivel 360 degrees and see all the information from sensors around the ship filtered and displayed in the command center of the Navy's newest attack sub.

The boat turned hard to the right with a slight roll and seconds later leveled out on the new course. The veteran captain could feel the slight adjustment in pitch angle as the sub climbed the 100 feet to the requested new depth.

"Depth 1-1-0-0," came the confirmation from the dive plane operator through the headsets.

"Roger," was the captain's replay.

"Shortshop, this is Century. We'd like you to reverse course ASAP," came the clear voice from the speakers overhead.

"Copy, Century. Turning now," replied the Captain. He spoke again to his helmsman and the boat turned a half circle to the new course of 355.

For the next hour, Century commanded more maneuvers of the *Chorlton*, changing directions, adjusting speeds and depths. For the crew on board it was basic stuff. The commands were deliberate, the atmosphere was calm, the actions routine and necessary. The boat had been sitting in the Globallus Marine Boat Builders shipyard on the Thames River for an equipment refit and this was a chance to shake off any rust that might have developed during the crews' two-week shore leave.

The only sailor breaking new ground was a young woman controlling the SLACLONET 1000 at her console next to the sonar op. This was the whole reason for the exercise. Her job was to keep the ball in the circle on her screen, ensuring the laser beam emanating from the top of the sub's sail was hitting the designated satellite hovering 800 miles in space. Encoded in the beam of light molecules was the voice communication between Century and Shortstop.

At Sub Base New London, SUBCOMLANT HQ, rear Admiral Jason Conroy and his staff sat listening to the communications coming from the radio room next door. Sharing space around a large conference table were two high level assistants subbing for the Secretary of Defense, the newly appointed Director of National Intelligence Harold Miller and Dr. Andy Standord, the inventor of the SLACLONET 1000.

At depth and at speed, the voice communications were unprecedented. Since the Turtle, the original submarine designed in 1776, direct communication with subs below the surface was difficult. Radio waves do not penetrate salt water very well. Low Frequency radios had limited capacity, delivering words rather than sentences. Subs had to expose themselves to enemy surveillance by surfacing to talk to command. Trailing arrays of antennas near the surface limited maneuverability and increased the chance of detection from sonar.

Most of the time, submarine communication was a cumbersome procedure of verifying and interpreting blocks of letters and numbers. Thanks to Dr. Andy Standord's invention, subs would now be able to remain below the thermocline layers to avoid sonar detection and still communicate clearly with command.

Flying circles at 10,000 feet over the Atlantic in the general vicinity of the *Chorlton's* location was a twin-engine P-8 Poseidon from NSA with a Magnetic Anomaly Detector protruding from behind and a variety of antennas arrayed in the fuselage. Inside the cabin, a half dozen operators monitored a variety of radio bands that could pick up any signals on virtually any frequency. Radar and sonar operators shared the same space, scanning the waters below.

The MAD stick could detect any disruptions in the earth's magnetic field. Especially those caused by a large metallic object moving through the water. Like a submarine.

The P-8 was on Anti-Submarine Warfare patrol, simulating the latest known detection tactics and capabilities used by Russian and Chinese military forces.

"Redbird, this is Century. Report."

"Century, this is Redbird. All quiet. We hear nothing. We show no anomalies."

"Redbird, confirm. You have nothing."

"Copy, Century. Redbird has nothing."

Around the conference table, there were high fives and handshakes. Rear Admiral Conroy smiled brightly at everyone and gestured to the man in the white coat and glasses at the end of the table. "Well, I'll be dammed! Congrats, Doc. I think I'll call this Dr. Andy's Dandy!"

four

FOUND

Friday 1000

Waiting on tables put Petrika in the best seat to enjoy the theater of American society. It gave her a chance to dress up, even if only in the newest jeans. No need for the boots she wore in the muddy fields at home. Or the gloves that protected her hands from blisters doing farm work. Her boots now were made for dancing. Even if she only had one pair.

And she enjoyed being on stage, even if sharing it with the smell of beer and fried foods. She was a farm girl, who could have been a shop girl and now she was that girl. And she enjoyed the attention. With her soulful face and blonde hair and a knack of moving to the music, she made a lot of friends when she came to America.

Her visions of an idyllic summer on Block Island appeared out of the blue Ukrainian sky one day when her uncle showed up with a bunch of books in his suitcase. He had been out of touch for five years, but the knock on the door one afternoon brought the whole family running to the modest dining room in the five-room house they shared in the small village called Protopopivka, not far from Odessa on the Black Sea. The house sat on five acres of what was once a co-op from a communist mentality. Now a family farm, it was one of many lined up in orderly rectangles connected by dirt roads and fertile earth built around a small tributary feeding a huge lake called the *Khadzhybeis'byi*. Everyone ate what they grew and sold what they didn't.

The nearby historic city of Odessa was founded on a sandbar that separated the *Khadzhybeis'byi* from the Black Sea. It was a major port, a tourist destination and the center of the government in the region, just ten miles from Petrika's family farm.

Her father enjoyed being a farmer, especially one who owned his land. His brother had always been thought to be lazy until he showed up that day and dumped the books on the table in a proud display. Oversized and filled with photographs of churches, it was a compendium of architecture and people, costumes and customs, an homage to the spiritual side of Russian life. And her uncle's name was emblazoned under the title.

"Cathedrals in the Russian Sky" by Boryslav Rushevski was a best seller on the international market finding its way into many homes in America and Europe where it sat on top of coffee tables or on the bottom shelves of fancy bookcases.

"Five years, Boryslav!" Petrika remembers her father mumbling over and over, even as he lit up the room with his joy of seeing his long-lost brother.

And soon Petrika was smiling broadly as Boryslav presented her with an amazing opportunity for her 25th birthday. A trip to America.

Landing in Boston, she had worked her way during the spring to Block Island, grabbing waitress jobs at taverns in Providence and Newport along the way. It was a couple of months of meeting people, letting her ear absorb the

25

language and learning about the theater of society. It allowed her to hear English as it is really spoken in the neighborhoods. Then on to Block Island, a one-hour ferry ride to another world.

Block Island had a history, a busy summer and wind. She had never heard of it, but suddenly she had a trip and a place to stay. Her uncle's literary agent made a good living selling foreign authors in America, translating and distributing pieces of other worlds to those who wanted to know more about the planet's peoples. And the agent let Petrika stay in his island summer home. Actually, a three-room apartment above a barn behind a rambling clapboard house. With spectacular views.

"Stay as long as you like," he had said. "I will be working on the continent."

It was an easy choice and her timing was ideal, arriving at the Beach View Bar the day Sally Wren was thinking about gearing up for the summer.

She felt happy and free with her existence serving drinks on a small island. The summer was said to be warm, and she immediately felt a familiarity to the Black Sea she had left only a few weeks before. And the people were nice to her, most of the time.

Except Freddy. For him, she was not a real person, only a play thing. She was again comfortable with the thought of feeling happy he was dead. The dark cloud had passed, a threat no more.

Sheriff Bobby Jackson's visit hung in the air as she changed her clothes, deciding against a shower until after her bike ride. She had already planned a good workout this morning and decided to target the lighthouse the long way. The building was only a half mile south of her driveway, but she planned to bike north, following the pork chop shaped island's perimeter road counter clockwise and arrive at the lighthouse at the end of her workout. A 12-mile bike ride.

She pedaled slowly downhill away from her apartment toward Old Harbor, helmeted, wearing bike shorts and a Billy Joel Live in Russia t-shirt over her top. She had gone to that concert in Leningrad and wore it a lot.

Amy Dodge Road quickly passed by and she thought how hard it must be to kill someone and have to live with it. There was no sign that anything unusual had happened there, just the same old dirt ruts leading uphill to a bunch of new houses built on the hillside to catch the view of the water.

It was mid-morning now as she coasted into town and passed Ernie's breakfast joint. She waved at her boss, Sally walking with her dog, Elvis.

"Did you hear about Freddy?" Sally yelled across the street.

Petrika just nodded and kept going with a wave. She would talk to Sally at work later. The street ahead was crowded with a ferry full of visitors just unloading from the Anna C. Three hundred strong surged off the boat and up the short slope to Water Street. She was forced to slowly weave her way through the sea of humanity.

The dozen taxis on the island had all arrived at the same place and the right time to take the New Yorkers, Rhode Islanders and Connecticutians to their vacation digs. They clogged the street and forced the cars coming off the boat to slowly thread their way through the jammed intersection.

It was an oft repeated spectacle during the day, best viewed from the porch of the National Hotel with a cool, green bottle in hand. It didn't last long, however, as the people dispersed quickly. Many just crossed the street and climbed the steps to enjoy that cool, green bottle and wait for the next ferry. Or the one after that.

Petrika was busy balancing her slow-moving bike when a white jeep swept up the slope and found a gap in the people to accelerate through. She looked up in time to see him.

He was driving the jeep and he had a passenger. She had a good look at his shoulders again, exposed by the same tank top he wore the day before. She noticed his black hair was neatly squared across the back of his neck. He turned and looked right at her, only a quick glance, but they made eye contact.

The crowd closed in again and he was gone.

She felt his gaze as surely as if he had reached out and touched her shoulder. However, something about it wasn't like last night. It was as intense, but she sensed he was viewing her from a place he didn't want to be.

Was it a plea for help? She shook her head as if to climb out of the rabbit hole into which his existence had immersed her mind. "I don't know shit about this guy!" she murmured out loud. Help for what?

She pedaled away slowly and then picked up speed as the crowd thinned near the Post Office. She decided to take Corn Neck Road to Cow Cove and had shifted smoothly into cruising mode by the time she passed the Beach View Bar.

Who was the dark-skinned man sitting next to her mysterious guy? Did they have anything to do with Freddy's death? His murder! She could not believe the broad-shouldered man would kill anyone. He was too vulnerable. It gnawed at her for a mile or so until all speculation faded away, replaced by that focused energy burn of an athlete breathing for high rpms.

She did not pause at Cow Cove but made a smooth U-turn and retraced her ride as far as the Beach View and then turned toward Salt Pond and the West side road. She whizzed past The Oar and then Champlin's was behind by a bend. Suddenly, she was alone savoring the rush of air, the ticking of her wheel bearings. She made the easterly turn along the winding stretch of road that follows the southern coast of the island and give it one last spurt toward the finish.

A quarter of a mile from the lighthouse, the white jeep appeared again and nearly sideswiped her off the road. She took evasive action along the shoulder. Her mysterious man was not driving now, but someone else. The same dark-skinned man from the passenger seat. And he was alone.

If the man saw her, he gave no notice, not even a glance as he roared past. She thought about taking his license plate number, but he was around a corner and gone.

"Hooyla!" she shouted after him, loosely translated for "dickhead".

She pedaled on and soon the lighthouse tower appeared in the distance over the trees in line with the road. She noticed a cloud of dust that lingered near the parking lot where the stairway to the beach started and she immediately guessed the jeep had come from there. She ducked into the small lot, but it was empty. She knew that would change as soon as the tourists started touring for the day. It was a popular stop to access the cliffs and dunes, the sea and the rocky beach. The long stairway to the water was 141 steps down. An enticing romp one way followed by a challenging climb the other. A platform provided spectacular views of the Southeast Lighthouse and put viewers right on the edge of the harsh spines of the Mohegan Bluffs.

The Block Island Southeast Light had served for over a hundred and thirty years and would be a museum someday, but not this summer. Funding since the historic brick building was moved back from the cliffs had mysteriously dried up. The interior reconstruction had yet to start. The light was hooked up to provide a beacon for sailors, but the building itself was closed and fenced off.

Petrika pedaled back onto the road and a minute later pulled up to the chain link fence surrounding the lighthouse property. Curious as hell, she stopped and admired the classic Gothic Revival brick building. It normally occupied the Southeast corner of Block Island sitting near the edge of a 200-foot sand cliff. It signaled ships to stay away from the rocky shoreline with a Fresnel lensed green light first flashed in 1875. The entire building stood three stories tall, with a peaked roof and the light tower at the southern end standing another story taller with every brick in place.

Today, it was an odd sight sitting on what appeared to be a trailer. The scaffold of iron beams and railroad ties with dozens of tank-like wheels supported the granite base and gave the impression the national treasure had been hauled there and left for overnight parking.

Which is almost what happened. The lighthouse had been moved away from the cliffs to eliminate the chance of it tumbling down the eroding dunes. It was an amazing engineering feat. Three hundred tons of brick and wood crept along on wheels for ten days. Sadly, the treasure now sat seemingly abandoned, though not forgotten.

A classy looking sign on the other side of the fence advertised the "Historic Southeast Light" and "Museum Coming Soon!" There was a plea for support at the bottom of the sign to preserve the heritage of the site. "Donate at southeastlighthouse.org" it read. However, right there in the real world in front of her, an imposing chain fence with a large lock secured the park entrance.

The barrier extended both ways from where Petrika stood. One end disappeared in the heavy brush backed up against the property of a large home to the northeast and extended toward the easterly cliffs. The other end extended to the bushes on the south edge of the cliffs where the 200-foot drop of the Mohegan Bluffs provided inaccessibility.

She pressed her face against the metal and peered at the building about 100 yards away.

Nothing moved. Scaffolding was stacked nearby in neat piles of boards and iron supports, waiting for the workmen who went home one day and never came back. A dirt trail showed the path the structure had taken from its original location only 30 feet from the cliffs. The ocean was blue green and far away behind the lighthouse, an indication of how high up the cliffs rose.

Then she saw it. A rope was tied around the front tire of a box truck that sat like it had not been moved for months. The tire was flat, and the truck looked like it was sprouting roots. Crates were piled up around it, boards leaned against it and the rope disappeared over the ledge. She walked her bike closer along the fence and could make out a shiny piece of metal. It was a carabiner with a doubled loop of line.

She left her bike against a tree and worked her way into thickening bushes further along the fence. She could not find an opening, even underneath. She pushed on through the bushes and in a moment came to the edge and peered over at the sandy dunes leading to the rocky beach below. The ocean was alive down there and an extra section of fence cut off any safe way of getting around it.

The crashing of the waves far below was soothing. Then she heard something else. A sharp metallic sound hitting sand as if someone was shoveling. She listened for a minute or two and realized it was coming from along the cliff wall, but the bushes prevented her from seeing anything. She moved back along the fence line to a clearer spot and, with only a moment's hesitation, climbed over.

She threaded her way through the thick foliage on the other side for several yards but was soon out in the open, crossing over the flat field to the truck near the edge. She couldn't help but feel like she was violating some taboo considering the lock on the gate, but her curiosity was fully in charge.

The rope was taut under a strain and she got down on her hands and knees, crawled to the edge and poked her head over the lip. The slope was near vertical and hanging about 15 feet below her was the man from the Beach View Bar.

He hung suspended in a boson's harness; a step-in webbed affair attached to the rope. His tanned legs spread against the side of the wall and his broad shoulders worked a shovel against the sand. Everything he wore, the shorts, tank top and his boots were sandy colored with dirt, matching the cliff wall.

She couldn't help but notice how comfortably he stood nearly perpendicular to the wall. The harness allowed him to defy gravity which beckoned from the rocks 200 feet below. And how good his shorts fit.

"Hey, what'ya doing?" she called out in a friendly tone.

He looked up sharply, the shovel stopped in mid-air.

"You!" he said.

"Hi," she waved, backing it up with a wide grin. He just looked at her.

"You shouldn't be here!"

"You, too. Shouldn't be here," she answered back. Behind him straight down, she saw rocks and ocean.

He laughed, shaking his head. She was right about that, he thought. Damn, damn, damn!

"Move back from the edge, I'm coming up," he ordered, trying to sound annoyed.

Petrika backed away and stood up near the truck, her eyes focused on the line where it ran over the lip. It was a full minute before the line wound through the carabiner started to move. Suddenly his head appeared, then a leg swung over the top and he stepped onto level ground.

She noticed immediately that a container was dangling

from his belt. It looked like a travel mug for coffee. The folding shovel hung alongside.

He moved quickly toward her, coiling the line expertly.

"We can't stay here," he said simply as he bent and untied the line. He pulled them up over the lip and she saw it was actually two lines tied together.

He finished coiling the rope and started walking toward the lighthouse.

"Where are we going?" she asked as she fell in step behind him.

"Just over here," he answered with a wave of his hand.

He walked swiftly to the structured chaos around the building until they were behind it and obscured from the road. The ground was dug up, marking the path it took during the recent move.

He stopped at a pile of lumber and what looked like rubble leftovers. He reached under a broken railroad tie and pulled a rope lanyard that lifted a trap door in the form of a 4 x 8 slab of plywood revealing an opening in the ground.

"Get in," he said sharply.

"Ah, really? I don't think so," she said, coming up short, but still peered into the hole in the ground, overcome with curiosity. A narrow stone stairway extended steeply into the darkness.

"You go first," she smiled at him. God, what wonderfully deep blue eyes, she thought!

"We can't be seen here," he said impatiently, waving her to move but, she refused to budge. He sighed and stepped into the opening and turned to go down the stairway backwards.

"Hold this," he ordered, his shoulders and head sticking out of the ground. She took the rope lanyard from him and then held the door upright as she perched on the top step, took a breath and backed down the stairs, pulling the hatch closed behind her, leaving only a sliver of daylight shining through a crack in the opening. The smell of the earth enveloped her. She giggled, thinking that her grandmother would never have approved.

five

QUESTIONS

Tuesday 0900

*Dr. Andy has broken through the deep blue sea.
Or is it the deep green sea? New comm system for
USN subs in works right now at GMBB. Speed
and depth opens door to the magic kingdom of
command and control. Whole world is curious
and hunting. They want some of that!* –SpyhakrF

The precision of repetition sent security guard Antoine
Barskow deep into the rabbit hole of boredom and he
struggled to keep his mind on his relatively simple task
of checking security badges for the workers coming and
going at Globallus Marine Boat Builders' main facility on
the Thames River in Groton, Connecticut.

The plastic laminated tags crossed the scanner one at a
time, revealing the face and key ID information about the
bearer, a green light showing a match followed by a slight
nod or grunt in greeting from the young guard, allowing
the worker entrance to the plant. The rare hiccup displayed

with a red light accompanied by a beep was usually solved by a re-scan to produce a green light.

The workers were welders, electricians, draftsmen, pipe fitters, wrench wranglers, tool and tie makers, metal fabricators, assemblers, civilians and navy personnel who collectively built the boats that comprised the United States Navy's submarine force. Business was booming and the current workforce of over 8,000 was about to double.

For Antoine, that idea left him cold. He had bigger plans. He was going to catch spies.

Childhood dreams have a way of setting the path adults take when it comes time to choose a career. Antoine was immersed in spy lore growing up, building a fantasy world ignited by Mad Magazine's Spy vs. Spy cartoons, then fueled by the celluloid images of James Bond, George Smiley and Jack Ryan. It became obsessive when he discovered the real-life stories of the KGB vs. CIA vs. FBI as the Cold War slipped into history. Their shoes on the ground spy craft held his interest rather than the rapidly overtaking world of "D", as he liked to joke. Digital. No heroes there for him. Give him invisible ink, microdots and a good tail any day. However, saddled with bad SAT scores and a need to find a job after high school, Antoine joined the Army and became an MP. Four years later he found his calling in a guard shack.

It wasn't spy work. Not yet. He had bigger plans.

"Barskow, can I see you for a minute?" came the voice of the chief of the uniformed security team at the plant. Sgt. Ben Canfield's head poked in the doorway, followed by his hand, waving Antoine toward the main security office a few yards from the gate. "Need to see you now!" he commanded. "Barnes will cover you."

Antoine looked up, surprised. He immediately felt that familiar pang when the boss called. Like being dragged to the principal's office. Something he put up with in high school, definitely in the Army and something he continued to put up with through most of his working life. Never good enough for the boss! They had been experiencing a "rough patch" of late and he dreaded more of the same.

"Right away, chief!"

Antoine looked at his companion Barnes, nodded and slipped off his guard stool.

"You're the lucky one," Barnes muttered under his breath, his face cracked in a toothy grin.

"F-you, Barnesy. I'm good."

Antoine slid around the security counter and followed the chief out the door.

The warm air hit him thickly after the air-conditioned shack. It was filled with the staccato of a faraway rivet gun and the beeping of the massive North Yard crane as it slowly moved on its track alongside Dock A. His eyes blinked in the bright sunshine and the soon to be summer views of the Thames River. The city of New London sat placidly half a mile across the river, the slope of State Street rising to the west giving the impression the buildings lining the downtown streets were taller.

Ironically, the perceived image of the small city in Southeastern Connecticut was actually smaller than its real place in American history.

"The outward appearance of New London, down to a period considerably within the precincts of the present century, was homely and uninviting."

Antoine knew that quote by heart from historian Francis Manwaring Caulkins, penned in 1895 and read by him for a grade school history assignment. It always made him laugh. He had grown up in the shadow of the Governor Winthrop statue on Hempstead Avenue, a symbol of one of the area's first leaders plopped in a part of town that was at the lower ends of power in Connecticut society. It wasn't easy living there, but he grew up in a world filled with stories of the past that created a sense of importance for a young boy trying to find his way when even his parents weren't so sure of what was going to happen next.

If cities have redeeming graces that separate them from others, New London's was the deep water that allowed large ships to find refuge at the mouth of the Thames River. Once home to a half dozen tribes of Native Americans, the old world came calling after Dutch explorer Adrian Block sailed up the river in the 17th century.

Fur trapping and fishing along the river was the natural tendency, but so was the art of boat building. From canoes to clipper ships, steamers to PT boats and eventually submarines, the art became an industry and the number one employer in Southeastern Connecticut. This was the sense of purpose that surrounded Antoine's life now and he used it as a starting block to push himself forward every day.

He breathed in the hot air and paused a moment to savor the view. A Virginia class sub sat alongside Dock A and a tug was heading down river to the South, likely to meet another sub at the New London Approach. Since the US Navy commandant had issued an order to retrofit all subs in the fleet with a new piece of equipment, the boatyard had seen twice the normal traffic. Not only did Globallus Marine Boat Builders build the subs, but they repaired them and in this case, retrofitted any new equipment that came down the pipe from the dozens of contractors who were always upgrading and improving the thousands of individual systems and pieces of equipment that maintained America's leadership among the nations of the submarine world.

"Antoine, you are planning on joining us today, right?" came the sarcastic call from Sgt. Canfield standing with his arms crossed at the front door of his office.

"Hey, chief. Just enjoying the view." Antoine slowly looked over at his boss, easing his daydreaming to the back burner and turning toward the door with a sheepish grin. "Here we go," he muttered to himself.

"Son, we have some important things to talk about here, so sit down and tune in!" Canfield directed.

For the next five minutes, Antoine sat, quiet and uncomfortable, as Sgt. Canfield paced behind his desk reading him the riot act about overtime, filling out forms, clocking into work late and reading non training material on the job. He went off about the importance of security and how the actions of the staff reflected directly on him, the boss, and didn't he understand the important task they were all charged with in protecting the submarine force of the most powerful nation in the world. Antoine had heard it all before.

"Chief," he protested weakly, but was cut off as Canfield went on about the pressure he was getting from the front office. "Especially now!"

And then a brief moment of silence while Canfield's final retort echoed in Antoine's brain, loudly interrupted by the door opening and two suits sweeping into the office. A tall man and a short woman. One black haired, the other blonde. Both had gold badges hanging around their neck.

"Good, you're back!" Canfield said. He gestured toward Antoine for the two newcomers. "This is Barskow," he said simply and sat down in his chair, relieved to turn over the show to the newcomers.

He's been killing time just until these folks showed up, thought Antoine! Maybe he wasn't going to get written up about his sloppy paperwork. A moment of relief passed over him.

"Antoine Barskow?" the dark-haired man asked brusquely. Antoine nodded slowly, the moment passing.

"I'm Agent Martin, NCIS. This is Agent Vanallison. We'd like to ask you a few questions about your friend Luke Parmelian. You know Luke, right?"

Antoine immediately noticed the canvas blazer worn by Martin. It was unstructured and hung well off his athletic shoulders and trim waist. Antoine imagined a Glock 17 under the breast pocket. The white collarless shirt gave him a casual business look, sharp, but ready for action.

"Luke, yea, sure, I know Luke. What about him?"

"When was the last time you saw him?" Martin asked.

"I don't know, a few days ago," Antoine answered. He remembered them sitting at the Ocean Pony just down river built precariously on the rock formation known as Latham's Chair.

"Friday night it was." He nodded, convinced he had remembered correctly.

"This past Friday?"

Antoine nodded again.

"What did you talk about?"

"I don't know. We had a couple of beers, talked about the Sox and Yanks, sailing shit, ah...stuff. The usual."

"The usual, hmm? Did you talk about work?"

"Nah, we don't talk about work. We talked about the upcoming summer racing schedule. We race sailboats, every weekend practically. Not about work." Antoine thought for a moment. "I remember he was pissed about missing Off Soundings, the Spring Series."

"Did he tell you where he was going? Was he planning a trip somewhere?" asked Agent Vanallison, speaking for the first time since the two NCIS cops had walked into the room. Antoine admired her one button gray blazer over skinny pants and practical flats. She looked like she would and could chase you down if you ran. No sign of a gun, but Antoine guessed it was in the small of her back.

"Going? He wasn't going anywhere...that he told me." Antoine looked over at Sgt. Canfield. "He said he had to work."

Antoine shrugged his shoulders.

"Sarge, what's going on here. What's up with Luke?"

Canfield just gestured at the agents as if to say it was their gig. Pay attention to them. Not his call.

"Antoine, listen carefully to me," Agent Martin spoke again. "Your buddy, Luke, could be in big trouble, so I need you to think carefully. Do you know where he is right now?"

"Jeez, agent Martin, I would expect he's in his office or rooting around in some computer system somewhere. I don't know. This is a big place and I rarely see him here." Antoine shifted in his seat. "Except when he clocks in or out."

Antoine suddenly realized he had not seen Luke clock in or out at the shipyard since Monday.

"What did he do? What makes you think he went somewhere?"

"Antoine, we're just need to ask him a few questions. Would you call me if you hear from him or remember any chat about a trip or anything beyond the Sox and Yanks?" Agent Martin handed him a card with his contact info and turned to leave.

"Chief, fill him in on the details if you would."

The agents left and Antoine turned to Sgt. Canfield. "What gives, boss? What going on?"

"There was apparently a NISPOM breach in the Loops Building. That Dr. Andy guy caught it last night. A file dump of a *sensitive* nature," Canfield said with a sotto voice. "Your buddy was logged on at the time of the breach and he hasn't been seen since."

Antoine just stood there with mouth open, not believing. NISPOM stood for National Industrial Security Procedure

Operations Manual. It was the first manual he was asked to read when he was hired. It explained how every employee at GMBB was to protect classified information.

"He called in sick this morning, and no word since," Canfield went on. "So, he's MIA, right after a breach he was logged on for and there's a bit of a buzz rattling around my cage, god damn it!"

"How serious is the breach? What info?" Antoine asked.

"They haven't told me exactly. I believe it has something to do with all these subs coming home for emergency retrofitting. It's all Navy now, they're leading the investigation."

Canfield paused and riffled through the papers on his desk.

"All this shit means nothing! The focus now is going be on finding Parmelian. The frigging FBI will be here soon, I bet!"

"What can I do?" Antoine asked. He truly had no idea where Luke could be or that he was thinking of doing anything as crazy as stealing files from the boatyard, especially with the latest goings on. His mind raced through their last few get togethers and nothing out of the usual popped up.

Then he remembered the card game in Brooklyn.

"Oh, shit," he muttered under his breath.

"Shit, what?" Canfield asked, looking up from his desk.

"Shit, nothing. Just wondering what's up." Antoine immediately decided not to mention anything about their gambling trip.

"Yea, well…do nothing but listen and keep an eye out for him," Canfield said, as he picked up a pile of papers and held them out for Antoine. "NCIS is handling the lead. The feds will take care of it. I'm sure we'll be neck high in alphabet soup before this is over. FBI, DNI, DOD. Christ! I don't need this!"

"Okay, ah, what do you want me to do with these papers?" Antoine asked, taking them from the Sargent.

"Damn it, fill them out! That's what I brought you in here for, the stuffs got to be complete, correct and on my desk by Monday. It's shit, but that's what I have to deal with!"

Antoine said nothing and walked out with the folder of hourly worksheets, classification reports and weekly summaries. His mind, however, was focused on finding Luke's girlfriend, Rene'.

six

SOUTHEAST LIGHTHOUSE

Friday 1030

"What is this place?" Petrika asked when she got to the bottom of the stairway leading underground where her mysterious companion had led her. She counted six steps down and waited a moment for her eyes to adjust to the near total darkness.

She could sense he was nearby and then heard him moving further into the darkness. The smell of earth filled her nostrils and she couldn't help but smile. So, this is the place he came from! It smelled just like he did.

Suddenly, the darkness was replaced by the dim glow from a portable battery powered camping lantern on the wooden floor. She saw him adjust a dial and the room filled with light.

"Five bucks for this beauty!" he said proudly. "Probably should have bought a couple." It's LED casts a white light on the walls.

He was standing right there, not six feet in front of her. The light wrapped spookily onto a low ceiling only a couple of inches above his six-foot frame. The walls were bare blocks of blue-black stone that looked like they were carved out of a quarry and had been unattended for years. She could make out thick wooden beams overhead supporting flat boards. Cracks of light filtered through as if the roof would leak should it start raining. Looking around, she guessed the room was only 10 feet wide, but extended beyond the lantern into more darkness.

"What is this place?" she repeated.

He turned and looked at her for a long moment. His face was dimly lit by the reflected light off the dirty, dark walls, but she saw enough to tell he was thinking hard about his answer. Or if he was going to answer at all.

"Are you hiding from somebody?" she asked.

He suddenly laughed and his serious face broke into a big grin. He shook his head again.

"You are something!" he muttered and turned, picked up the lantern and started walking deeper into the underground cellar.

"Follow me this way," he said softly and started to walk.

"Whoa, dirt man," she called out, holding her ground at the foot of the stairs. "I am not following you any more until you tell me what this place is."

He stopped and looked back at her. "It's my home... right now."

"You live here?" she responded with disbelief.

"For now. Follow me this way. We can sit. I promise I won't hurt you."

He smiled again and she looked in his eyes. Damn it, so trusting, so open. He slowly reached out his hand, silently entreating her to take it.

"Ok, lead the way." She exhaled and placed her hand in his and followed him as he turned and walked further into the room. His hand was warm and smooth and fit firmly but gently around hers.

A few steps later, they came to an opening leading to another room off to the right and went into a slightly larger area with gear strewn around the floor. Petrika saw a bedroll opened along one wall, a small cooler, a backpack and a one burner stove sitting on three skinny legs. A canister of propane hung between them. A wooden box sat against the near wall. More beams were visible overhead and the bare dirty, dark walls.

"Come furnished?" she joked, glancing around at the sparseness. A couple of empty beer bottles sat alone on the floor.

"Rent-A-Center," he laughed as he let her hand go and set the lantern down on the wooden box. He unhooked the silver travel mug and set it there as well.

The mystery man set down the shovel next to the box and pulled out a folding camp seat and opened it for her. It was more like a stool, about a foot and a half high.

"Sit," he said simply. "But don't get too comfortable."

She laughed this time and flashed him a big smile.

"I'm sure not to."

He folded his lithe body easily into a cross legged siting position on the bedroll and looked at Petrika a moment.

"This used to be the cellar for the lighthouse when it was sitting right overhead. They moved it, the lighthouse obviously, and covered up the overhead, but they didn't bother to fill it in. I don't know why not, maybe lazy, too expensive, whatever. So, I'm hanging out here for a short time. It's cozy and no one knows I'm here. You get used to the smell."

"I like the smell," she answered. "I can smell it on you." She wondered if he could make out in the dim light that her cheeks were flushed.

"Like home." She flashed a memory of sitting on the

fender of her father's tractor as they plowed the black earth of the *Khadzhybeis'byi Estuary*.

"And where did you say is home yesterday?" he asked.

"Ukraine. Protopopovika. Near Odessa. You know it?"

"Odessa's the Black Sea, right? I've been on Google Earth. Never actually been *there*."

"I've never actually been here!" she said with a giggle.

"So, you're Russian," he said after a moment, curious about this new woman.

"Ukrainian. Different country."

"Okay. I think we see it like from the south or the north. In the end, all the same...but, different. I get it."

"Americans try to make everything simple," she said with a small laugh.

"Things aren't so simple, always, are they?" he said in a pensive tone.

"Unless you live here!" she said seriously, looking around. She laughed at her own joke.

"That's funny!" he laughed with her. They laughed and smiled and enjoyed the moment as if they were on a picnic in some park.

Then they fell silent, the stone walls giving off their own silence. She wondered idly to herself if the absence of sound was in itself a sound. Metaphysically probably not, she deduced, since sound was heard by pressure of air waves on the eardrum. So, no pressure, no sound. However, no sound was in the least a presence that maybe fell into the category of sound.

"So, look, I'm sorry I dragged you into this," he said after a while, most of which was spent staring at her. He was captivated by the fact she was not afraid of eye contact and had been staring right back.

"Don't drag me!" She protested half kidding. "Just tell me where we are going? I will likely follow."

It was a command that put more emphasis on an attitude she embraced, rather than wanting to know what "this" involved. She smiled after a minute, aware that she was taking center stage, not him. She knew he was hiding something and wanted to know more.

"Ok. Got it. I'll be gentle," he smiled at her.

"Wait one moment," she interrupted him, a new thought popping into her head. "Your name! Please tell me."

"Luke," he answered. "Luke Parmelian. I come from Connecticut. I'm 30 years old and I was bred, trained, work and play just 20 odd miles over there in New London. And I've gotten myself into a spot of trouble and I'm here to solve it. I hope."

She listened intently, surprised but delighted by his openness.

"Hello, Luke Parmelian. I am Petrika Inessova Rushevski. I am 25 from Ukraine. Ah, I guess maybe 8000 odd kilometers over there." She pointed to her right, even though not sure where the east was. She gave him a big smile.

"I am here for vacation and work and to learn about America." She paused for a moment.

"And to meet new people and have adventure," she added.

Luke Parmelian never knew when an adventure began in his life. Most of the time he was already into it before he realized he was actually on an adventure. More often than not, there was a stiff drink, usually rum, with beer never a stranger. This particular adventure he realized, started a few weeks ago and included an element of chance.

"Well, Petrika, welcome to my adventure." He gave her a big grin. She didn't take it to mean he was very happy. He pointed to the silver coffee mug cylinder sitting next to the light on the wooden box.

seven

LUKE'S ADVENTURE BEGINS

Two weeks ago

The new naval threat assessment shifting USN to shoot and scoot. Boomers alive, but more Seals deployed next to missiles. Stealthy within 100 miles, not thousands. Eyeball intel still reigns in digital world of who is doing what. —SpyhakrF

The cards looked good and Luke was sitting pretty. Three Queens and a pair of Jacks. The uneven pile of money in the center of the table amounted to about $500. He took a sip from the glass in front of him loaded with McCoy Rum on the rocks. He looked at the four men around the table, all focused on him. Their cards all held in front of them, not a hint of concern showing, like students waiting for the teacher to finish the lesson.

"I'll call," Luke said simply and tossed in a few bills. The tall man who sat a head above the rest, sitting to Luke's left, with the wiry hair, let out a muffled groan and dropped his cards face up on the green felt. He closed one eye and grimaced, already convinced that his three nines were not enough.

"Figg city!" spit the man to Tall Boy's left. He tossed his cards face down on the table, resigned as well to losing.

"Straight to the 10!" the third man, Antoine Barskow, said simply, spreading his cards in front of him. He looked at Luke with that sly smile he often flashed at his best friend and he waited.

"Hmmm. Sorry, boys. My house is full and so are my pockets!"

Luke dropped his cards on the table in a flashy spread. Antoine and the Tall Boy sat back in their chairs disgusted.

"Fill this, Luke!" Antoine blurted. "Lucky bastard!"

The fourth guy seated across from Luke sat motionless, already thinking about skipping the next hand. His name was Bailey and he watched Luke pick up his bills, leaving twenty dollars behind to start the next pot.

"I'm out for tonight, boys," Bailey said in his straight forward tone. He pushed back from the table and got up to leave.

"See you next time, Bailey" said Tall Boy and they shook hands briefly. "Better luck then!"

"I'm sure," Bailey answered. He turned to Luke.

"You got a minute?"

Luke looked up from counting his stash and nodded. "Sure, what's up?"

Bailey gestured with his head, as if to say, follow me out.

Luke could see the others were going for a reboot on drinks and grimaced with annoyance. Sometimes he just lost his patience when the cards were flowing right. Never take a moment when the moments are good, he thought.

He sighed, got up and followed Bailey to the front room.

The two of them had only known each other for a short time and only around the felt of the gamblers' green field. Bailey was a machinist at GMBB, but the two never saw each other at work, just the local friendly games, where the pots were never over a few hundred dollars. Tonight's stakes had gotten out of hand quickly, much to Luke's delight.

"You interested in a real game?" he asked, keeping his voice just above a whisper.

"They're all real," Luke answered. He smiled and nodded. "How real you talking?"

"Thousand and up," Bailey whispered. "Often more. I've seen some big money plopped down...maybe 20,000. 30."

"Whoa! I'm not sure that's for me, but it does sound tasty."

Luke had a problem with gambling. For at least ten years it had captured his soul and never failed to bring a small tingle to the back of his throat when the games were on and the cards were dealt.

"These guys are for real," Bailey continued. "Different games, Stud, both 5 and 7, River, even Acey Duecey. It's a big-time operation, but you gotta know someone to get in."

"And you know someone?"

"I do. A friend of a friend. Been there a couple of times, they know me now. I walked out with $5000 in a progressive pot game a couple of weeks ago."

Luke looked at Bailey with a skeptical glare.

"Really?"

"Yes, shit, yes. Hottest night in my life!" Bailey smiled big time.

Luke's gambling problem didn't appear to be such an issue when he was winning, which was more often than not. Over the years of success, he had been able to manage his losses which kept him going. The dark cloud that he never saw was the growing attitude that his winning would win out and any losses were just a temporary diversion of his destined path of ultimately walking out of the game room with a pocket full of cash.

Who wouldn't keep going with that attitude? And Luke kept going, immersed in the games, fearless of the challenge, ready to play. Ready to wager.

"You want in?" Bailey laughed, knowing the answer.

"Sure. Sounds like it might be a fun adventure," Luke said.

Two weeks later Luke and Bailey with Antoine in the back seat drove to New York City's borough of Brooklyn to play some cards. They parked in a municipal lot nestled between Coney Island's famous Riegelmann Boardwalk and the 80-year-old brick high rises of Brighton Beach.

The neighborhood had the distinction of being the most densely populated community in the United States. Nearly 120,000 people per square mile. Half of them did not own cars. If anyone spent just a few minutes on the streets, one might think wheeled walkers, complete with handlebars and seats, were the main form of transportation.

Luke noticed a gathering of three elderly folks sitting on their walkers chatting at a street corner as soon as he stepped out of the car. There was a distinct aroma of stewed meats in the air, mixed with the metallic rumble of the "EL" train running overhead Brighton Beach Avenue just a block away. The flash of the subway cars 50 feet over the street caught his eye down the canyon of buildings.

The shrill cry of a seagull drew his attention in the opposite direction where the boardwalk provided a pleasant promenade for visitors and residents who flocked to the sandy beach that extended 150 yards to the ocean.

He stood between the busiest city in the world and the gentle lap of the Atlantic. This cusp of man and nature was a destination for thousands every day. The three young gamblers from Connecticut walked up onto the wooden planks that bordered the beach for two and a half miles and turned east.

The proximity of sand and city gave Luke the feeling he had landed in a strange country and that was hammered home when he heard a tall man walking along the boardwalk speaking Russian into his cell phone. They passed a souvenir shop with the sign in English and Cyrillic, the 36 lettered Russian alphabet. "Памяти" it read. Translated to "Memories".

The boardwalk was busy with strollers, couples holding hands, moms herding kids, men on benches arguing, tourists and locals, basking in the long shadows cast by the pending sunset. Summer was still a few weeks away, but beachgoers sat on canvas chairs, bare toes burrowed into the sand, sweaters draped around their shoulders.

Luke looked down the boardwalk to the west and could see the golden rails of a roller coaster, half the profile of a Ferris wheel and two tall towers that hinted at one of the many thrill rides awaiting the "school's out" chaos of summer that made Coney Island famous since the late 19th century.

Towering over it all was the 250-foot-high cantilevered tower that looked like a long-stemmed mushroom of iron. Once a functioning parachute drop amusement ride, it stood as the iconic symbol of the fun that was Coney Island.

Luke had never been to Coney Island, but he knew the structure.

He suddenly had a hankering for a hot dog.

"In here, guys," waved Bailey as they reached the Avianka Restaurant. Like most shops on the boardwalk, the restaurant's front opened to the fresh salt air. Wherever you sat, you felt like you were on the boardwalk. But the boys weren't sitting. Bailey spoke briefly with a bulldog of a guy wearing a fedora, a blue and white checked shirt with a flared collar and baggy pants. He looked more a gadfly hang about than a maitre d', but he acted quite civil in directing the trio around the far side of the bar. The arcade-like façade of the restaurant joined a brick wall that was actually the ocean side of an apartment building. Down a hallway they went, around a corner, passed by an office and into an elevator run by a thin, older man.

He smiled as they entered, pushed a button and up they went. Thirty seconds later they emptied out into a dimly lit hallway with a view of the distant city through venetian blinds at one end and a nondescript door at the other. The elevator operator pointed to the door and smiled.

"Two knocks. *Provodit!*" he said in a thick Russian accent, flashing two fingers as if giving the peace sign. They walked over and two knocks later, the door opened into a brightly lit room with floor to ceiling windows letting in the view of the Atlantic Ocean from twelve stories up.

Luke let out a slow, quiet "whew" as he took in the scene. Green felt topped tables everywhere. Round tables, oval tables, square tables with men and cards and chips. He counted a dozen tables, eight of them active with players. A low murmur and the rattling of plastic chips were the only sounds, punctuated by an occasional laugh or chuckle. The atmosphere was friendly, but intense.

A bartender presided over a mahogany bar in one corner. Four guys were spread around the room, standing and watching, moving and shifting, changing focus from table to table. They quietly melted into the atmosphere of the room, ever present but not obvious. Like furniture. Like bodyguards.

Bailey shook hands with a burly guy in his 50's with a tan, shiny, summer shirt that looked like it would be perfect for a family barbecue and he was the happy uncle.

"Misha, good to see you again!" Bailey gushed.

"Good to see you, Mr. B," Misha responded deliberately in a thick Russian accent.

Luke and Antoine looked at each other in amazement. Antoine mouthed "Mr. B?" silently and they both grinned. Was this a joke or what?

"I am hoping you bring more good luck to our humble games," Misha continued and then turned to look right at Luke. "Are these your friends you told me about? Welcome to Misha's real House of Cards."

He extended his hand to the pair.

"I am Misha Yanovich Yevtechnov. Call me Misha."

"Luke. Luke Parmelian. Born in New London, raised in Groton." They shook hands.

"Groton? Where they make submarines. I know it. Still revolutionary?" Misha added with a smile, repeating Connecticut's tourism slogan with a satirical tone.

"Yea, GMBB. Not so revolutionary, though. I work there. I play there. I live there. It's just there."

"Ah, but you travel for a game? I like that." Misha laughed, patting Luke on the shoulder.

"That's why we're here," Luke responded with a laugh.

"Good. I cannot promise you luck, Luke, but I can promise you games." Misha spoke with great confidence. Luke presumed he had played this polite welcoming patter many times as he watched him shake hands with Antoine, greeting him with an affirming smile. If there was a picture in the dictionary for *disarming,* Luke imagined Misha's picture would be there. He smiled to himself as he wondered if it would be a Russian dictionary.

The Russian in the party shirt turned with a grand gesture to the sun dappled room as if the tour guide to a fantasy yet to be lived.

"So, gentlemen, what shall it be? Draw, Hold'em, Chicago,

Stud...maybe some Acey Duecey? What is your passion or, how you say, poison?"

"Texas for me," Antoine piped up immediately and Misha nodded with another broad smile. He gently placed his hand on Antoine's back and guided him to the right side of the room toward a table with an empty chair where the river card was just coming out in a game of Texas Hold'em.

"Well, look at that, Antoine. A seat beckons. Let your games begin!"

Antoine wasted no time and within minutes was seated with five strangers and the cards began to come his way.

Bailey headed to a table on the other side of the room, recognizing a couple of the players from his previous trips to Misha's real House of Cards. Luke decided to head to the bar before jumping in.

"I think I'll start with the poison," he smiled at Misha. He received a slight nod of understanding in return and Misha turned abruptly away and headed to a table to watch the proceedings.

When Luke had to decide between drink and game, he usually chose drink. He didn't allow himself to think that was a problem. He ordered a McCoy on the rocks at the bar and turned to allow the room to settle over him before choosing his passion.

Not what he had expected for an underground, obviously unlicensed gaming venue. Instead, he saw a pleasant room, utilitarian but clean and classy with plenty of bright lights and focused customers, all who seemed to be enjoying themselves. He didn't sense the tense, foreboding, atmosphere he had experienced before in massive game rooms at the legit casinos in Atlantic City, Yonkers, Uncasville and even Las Vegas.

The desperate drive to win money seemed to be lacking. Just the quiet enjoyment of cards sliding across the table, chips clinking and players going in or out. Half the tables had dealers, dictated by the nature of the games. The others seemed to be running themselves as players took turns dealing Seven card Stud, straight poker and a game he didn't recognize at the table closest to him.

And strangely, no smoke clogging the air.

Misha's men hovered in and around. He counted five women among the 40 or so players at the tables. One of the ladies stood up, picked up her drink and excused herself. Misha was right by her side helping with her chair and smoothly gestured halfway across the room to Luke with an open invitation to take up the seat.

Luke recognized the game at the table was Seven card stud game and immediately went for it. His favorite game. He sauntered over, smiling at the woman who looked straight past him with a tight smile.

"Warmed and ready, Mr. Parmelian," Misha gushed, and Luke sat down, passed over five one-hundred-dollar bills to the table cashier and spread his hands over the green felt.

"Ready as ever," he said to no one in particular. He looked up and scanned the four men sitting around him and nodded. "Call me Luke. Nice to be here."

And the cards began to come, and a new game began.

It has been suggested that poker started with card sharks in the 1800's somewhere between New Orleans and St. Louis on the Mississippi riverboats that took advantage of tourist, called "pokes" back then. Seven Card Stud was popular and for over a century was d'riguer when folks would sit down for a friendly game.

It's a game of wishing and hoping for some. Card counting and bluffing for others and with an ante up front and as many as five rounds of betting, it became an expensive game for the losers and a windfall experience for those lucky and good or both.

Luke loved the game because it required some smarts. It required a touch of cool and a sharp eye. With half the cards visible and half hidden, you could only count on the expression of your opponent, their betting styles and the luck of the draw. You could also count the cards. And there were many chances to bet and build the pot. Many "streets" to travel as you drive your opponents to fold city.

Luke was a bit of a computer geek, but his love of card games was based in felt and cardboard. The outbreak of on-line poker and the birth of variations of the original game, even the casinos opening on Native American land across the nation in the last 30 years, in his mind, had cheapened the poker experience, even as it spread the game to every mobile phone and tablet. But he wasn't lamenting much over the next two hours because he killed it at the table. He quickly determined that one of the four sitting around him had some skill, but the others were ripe for the picking. And he picked.

Tells were rampant to his skilled eyes. The cards flowed miraculously into his hands. Blind draws were coming way too often, defying statistics. More hands than not went to fifth street and he capitalized. He felt like he had been delivered to a freshman card player's training class and he was the graduate assistant.

His pile of chips was embarrassing, reaching nearly $5,000. Luke saw Misha conferring with one of his table watchers as the money piled up in front of him. He didn't care. The cards were right, he was winning, and the world seemed on a perfect axis.

And then he did something he never thought he would. He picked up his chips and left. "You impulsive fool!" he admonished himself as he stood up.

It may have been the unusual streak of good fortune that allowed him to see through the haze of his gambling addiction that normally would keep him playing. In fact, to leave defied all logic. Defied all previous experience when he regularly rationalized how much he could afford to lose, kept accepting a larger amount, kept telling himself things would change on the next hand and he would, more than once, end up flat broke.

In a flash he wondered if his efforts of the past had been because he was addicted to losing. He had certainly done enough of that and when he got on a losing streak, he inevitably forced his way downward by playing more and losing more. But, tonight! His addiction was winning!

And for the first time that he could remember, the mere fact he had won so easily set off a warning light flashing at the end of his gambling tunnel. Walk away. This cannot last! This will not last.

"Leaving so soon, Mr. Luke?" came the somber voice from behind as he gathered up his windfall in $100 bills. It was Misha Yanovich Yevtechnov.

Luke turned to the smiling man and couldn't help noticing more than a few of the patrons had turned their attention to the two men standing by the cashier desk.

"I'm thinking it is best to leave now so I have something to comeback to," Luke smiled as he stuffed the bills in his pocket.

"You appear to have done well," Misha laughed and patted him on the shoulder. "I am hoping you return soon. You are welcome anytime."

Misha handed him a card. It simply had a drawing of an owl face and a phone number. Luke immediately recognized the same image tattooed on the back of the bartender's hand. And it was on the wrist of one of the players he had just faced at the Stud table.

"Please call and we can make sure we have a good, competitive game ready for you."

He reached out to shake Luke's hand and Luke grasped it strongly, only to be met with a weak grip from Misha. Like a young boy, Luke relished a moment of superiority. The wad of bills in his pocket surely helped as he flashed a big smile at the Russian. I don't deserve this, he thought, as he turned and walked out of Misha's real House of Cards.

eight

EASY MONEY

"**What did you do with all that money?**" **Petrika Rushevski** asked, a big smile on her face. She loved a good story and was totally smitten with Luke's carefree telling of it. He seemed lost in the words, the images, the memories. She wanted to know everything.

"Bought some new shoes," he laughed. "Papa needed them! Cowboy boots! Never had a pair, now I got a good pair. Cost me over $400 bucks."

"What else?" It had become a game to Petrika. She never had $400 to spend on shoes.

Luke thought about the leather jacket he bought for Rene', but that didn't turn out so well. He decided not to mention it to this young blonde girl sitting in front of him in the abandoned dirt cellar. He liked her and he didn't want thinking of Rene' getting in the way. At least, not yet.

He stared at the lantern for a few moments before he picked up the story. What the hell was he doing in this hole?

"I paid off some bills. Put a lot of it away. I knew I needed it next time I went to play."

"You went back to this Misha's place?" Petrika asked.

"Of course, how could I stay away? Easy play, easy money."

Petrika shook her head sadly.

"I don't know about easy money."

"Yea, well, it doesn't come along that often."

"And when it does, you keep going, yes?"

"Yes, I did and that's why I'm right here, right now."

"This place, right time?"

Luke looked at her with a grin. He didn't know what she meant by that. He flashed back to a moment one week ago and grimaced.

"Well, let's just say it turned into a bad time at the wrong place."

nine

CONEY ISLAND'

Friday One Week Ago

Brits drop China chip from 5G net plans. MI5 sites intel from deep cover in MSS. Meanwhile, ZITiS arrest AISE ops with pinched BMW electric motor plans. Ferrari plug and play? Any one stealing recipes anymore? –SpyhakrF

Rene' Sanderson was a sexy blonde with long hair, alluring curves and a fetching personality. She never met a mirror she didn't like. She met Luke at the craps table at Casino in the Woods just north of Mystic and seemed to like him right away. Luke didn't play craps much, but he saw her commanding the table one night and joined the spectacle.

He even won some money riding her string of five box cars to a nice little pocket bonanza. He was standing close enough to her around the table that twice she offered her open palm and had him blow on her dice for good luck. They ended up at the bar for a drink and he fell under her spell.

The next morning, he watched her sleeping in his bed. A sudden wave of "the loves" passed over him. A common ailment among men, often dreamt about in anticipation with no fore knowledge of the next emotion... confusion. Such a sweet night of passion and tenderness filled with orgasmic satisfaction and no care bliss! Only to be replaced with "now what?" the next morning. Can't have one without the other, can you?

And Rene' liked to be pampered. Her physicality became his reward. At first, he relished doing the pampering and reveled in his buddies' compliments, jealously offered, on his good fortune to have her, to be able to experience her. You don't deserve her! They laughed in delight. Jealous fools for sure, he knew!

But as insatiable as he thought his appetite to be, Rene's was equal if not greater. A few weeks in to their closeness, he was sure they were not exclusive. He saw the way men watched her in public and the way she responded. After a while, he knew. She was just to be another chapter in his life, such as it existed. His struggle. His saga!

He bought her a leather coat because it seemed like the right gesture to keep her close and to keep her warm. He wanted to see that 1000-watt open fetching smile again, as if it would soften her heart and she might pamper him a bit outside of the bedroom.

"Feel like an adventure?" he asked her innocently one late morning, the sun shining across her shoulders as she stirred from sleep. He had taken the Friday off and was ready for a long weekend with no interruptions in their time together. Immerse yourself! Let her know I am the one! He needed to know that she understood, believed, wanted him only.

"Always," she smiled, opening her eyes and reaching for him.

And three and a half hours later, freshly fucked, fed and looking fabulous, the two of them were on the boardwalk at Coney Island. The afternoon traffic on I-95 was unusually light and they made good time to Brooklyn. Halfway down the pike, Luke fished out the card he had been handed by Misha Yevtechnov during his first visit to the House of Cards and dialed the number.

"I want you to hear this guy," Luke smiled as he punched up the number on his speaker phone.

"This is Misha," answered Yevtechnov. Luke recognized the friendly voice with the Russian accent.

"Misha, Luke Parmelian from Groton. We met last week."

"Yes, Luke. The big winner from Groton. Are you good?" Misha sounded happy to hear from him.

"Feeling great! Look, just wanted to let you know I'm heading to Brooklyn with a friend and she and I are looking forward to some fun tonight. I hope you are open."

"Ah, Luke, we are always open. Please, come and enjoy. I will set aside some, how you say, 'poison', for you and your lady friend."

"That's terrific. She is a player and is very excited to meet you."

"I'm always ready to play a good game!" Rene' offered with a laugh.

"And I you," Misha laughed back, obviously please by her voice. "A good game I can promise! Be sure to ask for me if I am not there when you arrive."

"He sounds pleasant," Rene' mused after Luke hung up.

"Just a warning, my dear. He will charm your pants off if you are not too careful," Luke smiled.

"Hmmm…I like him even more!" She bit her lip after she said it and looked at Luke, who had lost his smile. "Oh, silly, stop being so sensitive! I was just kidding!"

She laughed and playfully caressed his inner thigh.

"I know," Luke said sheepishly. He cursed himself for showing that weak side of his "manhood". Where the hell was 'Mr. Powerful - I got the woman so shut up asshole!'? He searched in silence as they drove on, fighting through darkness, looking for the brightness that always seemed to elude him in moments of sorting out his confidence around Rene'. Her hand helped him focus.

And then they turned onto Coney Island Avenue.

Whatever doubts Luke felt about his relationship with Rene' receded in a quickly enveloping cloud of enjoyment. The old amusement park couldn't help but brighten the day of even the most morose fellow. This was Coney Island, famed in song and story, a legacy of laughter and thrills. Of carefree moments where the innocence of children pushed the bounds of excitement, tickled the edges of frightening, only to end in joy and smiles. No consequences except the price of admission.

They stepped out of the car and, as if on cue, the first thing they heard were screams. The unique mix of terror and joy. Fear and release. They turned as a chain of plastic and steel horses clattered overhead on iron rails, a dozen steeds two by two, carrying young teens on a twisty turvy zoom into the history of the Steeplechase. A hint of a time when rickety horses straddled spindly rails and shakily rattled around the old Steeplechase building where New York learned about amusement parks.

That building was long gone, replaced by the open air spread of rides nestled against the boardwalk. Rides that sent thrill seekers soaring like eagles or super beings, lying flat on their bellies, side by side, encased in a cocoon of safety, flung up and around and upside down, screaming all the way.

The old Thunderbolt roller coaster, the barf inducing

wooden sleigh ride of old, always the step child to the legendary Cyclone, had been replaced by an open-air carriage that looked like movie theater seats on wheels. Four across, four deep, the riders secured by padded chest guards that locked them into their contoured chariot. And then a vertical climb up a superstructure of steel and cogs to pause at the top for only a moment, the anticipation building to the inevitable release as the car peaked and went over, falling down a vertical track that turned into a series of loop da loops, inverted twists and gravity bending turns.

And more screams, more hormones released from teenagers who will forever seek their rite of passage by having the bejesus scared out of them on some adult concocted defier of gravity designed to pop your eyeballs, snap your head, flip your stomach and pound your heart. Twists, turns, and slides right out of sync.

"Better than drugs," laughed Luke watching a spinning circle of what looked like easy chairs strapped around a central shaft reaching 150 feet into the air. A dozen screamers went up the shaft sitting on the spinning seats, then suddenly down, then up real high, then down real low, each movement offering no hint when it was to end and reverse in the opposite direction.

There were the usual other attractions they passed as they headed east along the Riegelmann Boardwalk. The go karts seemed tame after their excursion down I-95. The kiddie swings and carousels were thrilling enough for the very young and the gigantic Wonder Wheel seemed better tuned for romantic fantasies.

The games of toss, spray, shoot and whack were sprinkled among the rides and attracted their own world of wonder. Teddy bears and stuffed sharks shared the open-air arcade with minion dolls held under arms of the game winners or hung at random angles above the water pistols and basketball hoops, awaiting a new winner and a new home.

But you gotta play first! Anybody can win! And the barkers barked, the tickets ripped, and everybody had a good time!

Standing guard over it all at the west end of the boardwalk was the legendary Parachute Drop, the 256-foot-tall mushroom shaped skeleton of steel that was once the ultimate death-defying ride. Luke had only seen it from a distance the last time he was there, but this time they stood right under it and imagined what it was like in the 50's and early 60's.

Strapped to a bench, patrons rode to the top under a canopy of loose hanging cloth. Once there, with little warning, the canopy released and the parachute went to work, holding the air to slow the descent. For those who remember, it looked like a Lili flower popping open upside down.

The Drop was designed to train Army soldiers in the 1930's and was moved to the boardwalk after the 1938 World's Fair in Queens. For a few moments everyone could experience the thrill of free fall. The occasional wind gusts kept it interesting. Of course, the six wires that were attached to each chute kept the descent under control, and virtually every time the bench come to a spine jerking halt a few feet about the ground, the riders returned to their feet laughing about defying that age old adage, "The fall won't kill you, it's the sudden stop at the end!"

No one was killed, according to official records. There were a handful of incidents when wires broke, and the parachutes crashed into the tower. But what good is an amusement ride if it can't induce a bit of real terror?

While standing there next to Rene', Luke convinced himself he would ride the drop if it was still operational.

He found himself wondering about the choices he made through his life, aware of his doubts, ignoring the worst-case scenarios, going forward knowing full well the slightest hesitation could easily put him on another path.

He wasn't sure what he was doing all the time, but knew simple acts often were the way to find the way. He slipped his hand onto the small of Rene's back, touching her bare skin under the loosely fitting blouse she wore, and reached down her pants to touch the smooth crack of her ass. He pulled her close and kissed her passionately, their lips and tongues instantly responding in a naturally sexy way that stirred both of them. It was a full minute before they parted, and he looked in her eyes.

"I need this time with you," he said softly.

"An adventure," she smiled back and kissed him again, then grabbed his hand and led him away along the boardwalk. The sun was low in the sky, the crowds were moving every which way and a solid warm breeze kept the flags, banners and floppy signs flapping.

A ripple in the crowd ahead turned into a troupe of jugglers, clowns and mermaids heading in the opposite direction. The sudden intrusion on an already eclectic scene stopped Luke and Rene' in their tracks. The traveling gaggle of troubadours was escorted by two park rangers in a golf cart and a dozen children moving in and around the scene. A balloon artist was weaving heads and arms and tails of rabbits and dogs, walking along with the golf cart that was carrying his bottle of compressed air. The kids were laughing and yelping and jumping up and down with joyful exuberance. The whole scene lasted but three minutes and it moved on down the boardwalk toward the main carousel under the Parachute Drop tower. Luke and Rene' resumed their stroll with ear to ear grins on their faces.

"Such innocence lives in the heart of Coney Island!"

Luke practically gushed. She just looked at him, surprised by his childlike innocence.

"Clowns at work!" she laughed.

A moment later they came to the end of the amusements and were surprised by the emptiness of one ride area.

"What is that?" Rene' asked, looking at the open space around a slightly raised platform with a ball like metal cage sitting in the middle. Two seats sat empty in anticipation; the padded seat belt bar raised up. Nothing was happening around the cage. The omnipresent worker bees that attended to every other ride were conspicuously absent.

"It's the Astro Sling Cage," Luke answered after surveying the contraption and confirming its name by reading the sign on the ticket booth. "A bungee jump in reverse. A bungee cage!" He gestured with his hands, starting low and arcing upward. The cage was attached to a triple wrapped bungee cord on each side, with the other ends attached to the top of two towers that looked to be 250 feet high.

"Oooohhh," Rene' nodded slowly, understanding what happened when the cage was released from the platform with the bungees under tension. "Like a sling shot. Zoooom!"

"Zoom is right. Into the night!" They both laughed, looked at each other and spoke in unison. "Let's play some cards!"

And they walked off down the boardwalk.

ten

Sova' Golovi'

Friday One Week Ago 1600

Only a few yards away from Rene' and Luke, James Michael Joseph McSamarlie sat on the white sand listening to the gentle lap of the tiny waves that ended their long trip from the southern hemisphere onto the shores of Brighton Beach. He cut an odd figure sitting in one of those canvas beach chairs that barely kept his butt off the sand. On top of his head sat a leather cowboy hat cocked proudly with a pinched crown. The sharply rolled brims formed a point with the front dip not unlike the bow of a ship ready to plunge through the waves.

Since settling in Brooklyn, a couple of years back, he felt the need to reinvent himself. He had taken a shine to the great outdoors, cast in images of the great American west. Fully aware of his station on the sands of Brighton Beach, his dreams thrived under his hat and he wore it proudly. Defiantly.

Distinctive as was the hat, the gym shorts and soccer style shirt he wore, emblazoned with the yellow and green *Dun n'Gall* crest from his favorite Irish hurling team, were equally unique. The black running shoes also seemed out of place.

By his side was a worn but sturdy Hurley, in Gaelic, a *"caman"*, used to play the ancient Irish sport. The three-foot rounded shaft, hand carved from ash, extended from a smooth angled grip to a flat paddle or *"bas"*. It too was oddly out of place lying peacefully on the sand. Hurling was often referred to as the fastest game on grass. It followed the pattern of similar games where 15 players a side ran, passed and whacked a ball through uprights and into nets.

Lacrosse with a long-armed ping pong paddle.

A strong player could whack a ball, called a sliotar, 100 yards with a full swing, zipping it through the air at more than 100 miles an hour. The nature of the game often saw that swing interrupted by the closeness of a competitor who constantly balanced good defense with a smack in the head.

McSamarlie never went anywhere without it and relished the image of Uncle JMJ from Faraway, the only Irish thug in the Russian mob. While most of the crew had an owl head tattooed on their wrist, McSamarlie was also known as that guy with the stick.

From that game played with rage.

Even though he never actually played the game.

McSamarlie had experienced the rage of storms in the North Atlantic as a merchant marine, but that too was transferred to a passion for using the Hurley. It was a thread to a heritage he had not really lived but took a shine to anyway. It was the outright toughness it took to play the game that appealed to him. The same kind of toughness it took to stay upright on a tossing ship in the middle of the ocean.

He was an odd fit, for sure, born to Irish parents, raised by them around the world. His father, a wildcat oil rigger and his mom, a hard-working cook. They worked the wells and fed the crews. Most of his parent's work was in the North Sea, inside the Arctic Circle and off the coast of Sakhalin Island. That's when James Michael Joseph McSamarlie hooked into a Russian culture that stayed with him to this day. As a teenager who had seen the world's most remote places, he had never felt rooted to any until he found a penchant for beating up people who were intent on hurting him in the ramshackle towns of wooden shacks and outhouses on the edges of the frozen tundra.

He didn't think himself a bully, and he tired of bullies quickly. In a world with nothing but knuckle-breaking work and endless cold, men easily turned to drink and savagery. He learned how to defend himself. He had no choice. The hard life was distinctly Russian gulag stuff, except he had three squares a day, loving parents and a satellite TV connection.

He eventually tried the oil rigs himself but, after a year opted for the open oceans. He signed on as a lowly deckhand on an oil tanker out of *Prigorodnoye* when he was 19 and continued to travel the world. His hands were as calloused as his mind was hardened. He did what he was told by the bosses but, took no shit from nobody.

Nikogo ne vzyal!

The quiet, powerless, pond like waves along the sandy shore of Brooklyn soothed his savage soul. Not six inches high, the waves curled rather than broke and ran out in a foamy spread along the nearly flat beach. The angle was gentle, yet the inertia was enough to push the water 30 yards up the flat sands before the momentum died and gravity sucked the frothy mix of saltwater and sand back to the ocean.

On this Friday, a dozen bathers were scattered about wading in the cool calmness. First timers were always surprised by how far out they actually had to go for the water to cover their knees. He saw mostly adults trying to cool off, their flabby skin and bargain rack bathing suits making it an easy choice for Uncle JMJ between napping and gawking. This was not the French Riviera.

It was hardly the Russian Riviera either, even though it bordered the Brighton Beach neighborhood. A neighborhood no stranger to the Cyrillic alphabet. Turn onto Surf Avenue and you would think you were along the Black Sea. It was on display in business signs and on store fronts. Add the smell of pelmeni and boiled potatoes, mix in a touch of freshly baked breads and the chatter of a foreign language older than the history of the United States. All this a few miles from Times Square, yet a world apart from anywhere else.

It was home for James because he had a bed and three squares a day. There was no home he was going to return to, only places he hadn't been yet. The calmness was a treat, because he knew the savagery was never far away.

A rustling noise close by brought him awake, but he forced himself not to open his eyes. He could smell the cologne and knew who it was. The darkness was his escape and he let it linger.

"I never liked this beach," said the voice next to him. He could hear the man settling into the empty chair alongside. "Too much sand. Not enough women. Ha! You agree, my Irish friend?"

"I like the sand, Misha. It reminds me of fresh snow, but warmer." He opened his eyes behind his sunglasses, a big smile on his face, but he didn't move his head for a full ten seconds. Then he turned to the man next to him.

"It is my escape."

Misha Yanovich Yevtechnov was a bald, burly man with wrinkles across his brow that extended above his ears on both sides of his head. He had a pleasant smile, dark eyes and a broken nose prominent on a round face with a hint of sagging jowls. Some would call it a "bulldog" face but, not to his face.

Some also didn't call him *lagooshka*. Russian for frog. Not to his face. That was reserved for moments among the crew when they were alone, and he was out of earshot.

Normally, they just called him *shef*. Or Boss. That's who he was. The boss. The leader of the gang, the chief of the crew that was known as the Owl Heads. *Sova' Golovi'*. Silent in flight, sharp eyes able to see in two directions and patient in the night. The FBI saw him as the head of the Russian mob in Brighton Beach. At least for now, because the competition simmered but, had yet to challenge him. There was only respect when he was in the room. And fear.

"Mr. J, listen to me now," Misha spoke seriously, refusing to call him Uncle JMJ. McSamarlie focused on his boss and listened.

"Tonight, I have a frog in the pot. I think we can get a big result, if we just do our jobs as we all know how."

McSamarlie nodded his head. "So, it is tonight? Finally! I'll make sure the boys are ready."

"We'll start in the House, but I think we will end up here," he said, nodding his head to the other side of the boardwalk where faint screams mixed in with the late afternoon sounds of the beach carried by the onshore breeze.

"This is for our friends on 91st Street," Misha added. "We are working this plan to its end. We must make an impression."

"The cage, yes? I see," McSamarlie nodded. He knew 91st Street meant the Russian Consulate on the East Side of Manhattan. He realized they were heading for another big score. Or another big mess to clean up.

He sat for a second, staring out at the water and the beach, reluctant to leave the view, but well aware of what lay ahead. "I'll make things ready," he exhaled and jumped up, grabbed his Hurley and beach chair in a sweeping move and headed off across the sand to the boardwalk without looking back.

Misha let him go without a word and sat back to take in the view himself. He saw so many creatures idling away their lives, devoid of any thoughts of the impending doom they all faced. They clung to hopes that would rarely be fulfilled. They lived through the classic misery of a day to day existence as darkness swirled in from the edges. The bright sunshine and white sand blinded their eyes.

He was determined not to be the frog in the pot of boiling water, ignoring their inevitable fate. He was determined to own the pot and control the temperature. It was the least he could do to honor his father's legacy.

In a land of haves and have nots, where peasants and czars, workers and secret police, farmers and oligarchs battled for centuries for the riches of society, the have nots smashed the niceties of following the rules, whatever they might be at the time. They stole food they didn't have. They extorted money they didn't have, to buy the food they didn't have. They killed those who didn't give them the money. They put fear in their hearts and minds and souls of those who they didn't kill, even after they gave up the money. They battled in a harsh world for their own brand of justice. Which became their own brand of truth.

And someone had to be the *shef.*

Misha Yanovich Yevtechnov had a special place in the underbelly of America, this nation of laws, with its network of law enforcement, a spider web controlling behavior established by generations of high priests, lowly teachers and lying politicians who spouted the social norms and engrained the moral standards. The lines of this web strengthened by the constables, sheriffs and street cops and on up the ranks to the State and Federal task forces established to find the evidence that built the cases against the individuals who violated the norms. A cast of judges and juries decided if the laws were broken. Cages were built to store the violators.

Each day the people went forth as a society expecting things to be a certain way. They learned early that disruption is bad and shall be punished.

The Russian mob was different. History taught them there is nothing to lose if you have nothing. Evolved in a society where the bosses had it all and the workers had nothing, the workers learned to take what they wanted and fought to keep it.

They traded in their morality as they lessened their respect for decency and responsibility for one's own actions. We have nothing. We don't care. Thugs and Thieves. Assassins and Spies. *Vory v zakone – thieves in law.* Trust no one but yourself. Hunger shapes the day of decisions. If you have something I want, it's mine because I can take it. The only way to fight is to fight back.

Misha smiled to himself sitting on the sand. Of course, he was not starving. His childhood was son of a *shef.* Yan Illyanovich Yevtechnov had established a ruthless reputation as a thug, confidant and eventual *shef* of a crew with a long history in Brighton Beach.

His father arrived with a wave of Russian Jews in the 70's, twenty somethings with nothing much to live for in Kiev, but a whole new world of promise in America. His arrival in Brooklyn was followed quickly by sex, drugs and rock n'roll. He met a girl, got married, had a child named Misha and joined a crew.

He found his calling and was quickly up to his eyeballs in petty theft, extortion and bribery and by the ripe old age of 32, he controlled all the fruit stands along Brighton Beach Avenue under the "El". There were six of them, one on every corner. If you bought fresh fruit and vegetables, you bought them from Yevtechnov.

He bought a high-rise apartment building on Bridgewater Court that faced the famed Riegelmann Boardwalk. The owner was reluctant to sell at the price Yan Illyanovich was offering. However, the owner's wife agreed to sell after her husband met a tragic death. He was found one morning hanging from the vacant Parachute Drop on the West end. No one knew how he got up there.

The neighbors all suggested the dead man was a peaceful man, quiet and reserved, who seemed to get along well with his wife. And he was a friendly landlord to boot. The wife was not much of a negotiator and settled quickly. She passed away in her sleep within a year, but by then, Yan Illyanovich Yevtechnov was the new owner of the building.

The rumors about Yon started at the community center and helped build his legend as a "ruthless thug". Yon himself did little to dispel them.

Misha at ten years of age, remembered standing in the crowd of curiosity seekers watching the fire department retrieve the body of the recalcitrant landlord from the 250-foot-tall tower. Misha had been there the night before and understood better what his father was capable of doing.

Yon ruled with violence and fear, avoided the cops with payoffs and multi layers of players who did a lot of the dirty work. But Yon knew how to take care of himself and wasn't afraid to bloody his hands. He was said to have shot a man once just to check if his gun was working. The victim was suspected of shorting him on weekly collections. Tributes of respect as they were called. He was comfortable with a blade, too, as adept at carving up a thug as he was carving a brisket for lunch.

Upon the death of his father, the victim of a late night stabbing himself during a friendly game of poker, Misha took over the reins of the dominant crew of thugs under the EL. A few feathers were ruffled by those who had served his father and thought they had earned the power. They were dealt with swiftly and surprisingly by the young man of 33 who had never shown a bent for violence.

Misha carried on his father's reputation as one of the most vicious Russian mobsters to ever settle in Brighton Beach.

But it was his father's reputation, not his. Misha as a child lived in fear of the violence spewed by his father. But he was inexorably tied to a life of crime. A code started in the gulags of Stalin, evolved through Perestroika and the Russian emigration to America and was now adapted for Misha's reign over the family business.

His only solace was to be less brutal, even as his resolve to be an enforcer was strong. He knew it was part of the job of being the *shef*.

And as the years went on, he was drawn to the rides and games of the old amusement park on the edge of the neighborhood. The screams and the laughter. The freaks and the fun. His fascination grew like the weeds that had sprouted among the rides during periods of neglect. He began investing his profits from gas scams, extortion and stolen medical equipment. He parlayed his legitimate business reputation as the Russian fruit guy into connections with the city of New York. Before long he joined a line of dreamers over the 100 plus years of Coney Island's history who controlled the attractions known variously as Luna Park, Dreamland, Steeplechase Park and Astro Land.

Local economic conditions saw the resort's fortunes fluctuate through storms, depression, booms and busts. But the beach never changed, and people kept coming and the rides continued to scare and delight. Misha took control and renamed it ScreamTown at Coney Island. And he struggled with his childhood fascination and his criminal legacy.

eleven

VLAD MEETS MISHA

Thursday Last Month 1300

Yasen Project 990 delayed by saboteurs at Sevmash boat builders in Severodvinsk on White Sea. More delays for rebirth of Russia Fed sub fleet. FSB blames Ukrainian Nationalists. Arrests pending. Glory days return of Russian fleet still miles to go. –SpyhakrF

Vlad knew he was being followed but didn't care. The young woman had been there before. Average height, average build. A girl next door type with changing hair color, different clothing, nicely attired, but occasionally in casual jeans and a jacket over a blouse. Sometimes glasses, sometimes not.

He had seen her so much in the last month, he was actually beginning to think she didn't exist. Maybe he was paranoid, which was a strange thing for him since his job was to trust no one. Was every woman behind him a tail?

He was especially concerned now because the

information he had recently cultivated could lead to one of the best projects of his career. He was filled with the excitement of seeing it through to success. It was another opportunity to gain points with his boss and take a step closer to his retirement somewhere "upstate".

He took one more look around and stepped out into the street. She was wearing a silky scarf today, with black streaks running through it. Odd for an early spring morning in New York City, he thought.

Vladimir Vladovich Chemenko worked in a five-story renaissance style building built of limestone and cornices on East 91st Street, on a lot once owned by Andrew Carnegie, America's iconic industrialist and philanthropist from the late 19th century. The entire neighborhood on the upper East Side was a bastion of wealth and since 1994, the town house at number 9 had been the home of the Consulate General of Russia in New York City.

Vlad was officially listed as the deputy assistant trade minister, a job that required him to travel, mostly on the East Coast, connecting with importers and exporters who bought from and sold to the Russian Federation. In reality, he traveled but, he could not care less about Russian products beyond his slowly diminishing pride for his mother country.

His travels were at the direction of Konstantin Diasovich, the assistant trade minister. Both worked for the Main Directorate of the General Staff of the Armed Forces of the Russian Federation, abbreviated to the GRU. In Russian, it was named *Glavnoye Razvedyvatel'noye Upravleniye,* and it meant Foreign Military Intelligence. The acronym descended from the world of Russian government agencies that started with the Expedition of Secret Affairs in 1810. It evolved into a series of Directorates called variously RSVR, GKO and KGB. The KGB became the iconic reference to Soviet secret agencies, but Vlad was paid by the GRU and his job was to spy and manage spies.

In the grand scope of things, very little had changed in the last 70 years. The Russians and the Americans were always nose to nose, snooping and sniffing on each other, planning for the ultimate confrontation. Vlad never understood why Russia would want the problems of governing a city like New York.

Konstantin, his boss, was the number one spymaster for the Russians in the United States. Vlad was his right-hand man, number one recruiter and go to guy. He didn't carry a gun, except on special occasions, but he was well trained in old school tradecraft. He went through the motions because that was his job. For now.

That is why Vlad walked north on 5th Avenue for six blocks, then jumped on the M4 bus southbound and rode it to 42nd Street. He walked east for a block, then south and then four blocks back west to Bryant Park to meet Misha Yevtechnov. The woman in the scarf was no longer behind him when he arrived at the park entrance.

Bryant Park provided a graceful respite in midtown, covering half a square block in front of the New York City Library. Vlad liked it for its unusual style of offering no fixed park benches. Instead, small, round tables and metal chairs with wooden seats and backs allowed groups of time killers to sit together or apart, anywhere they wished. A small token of free choice for the citizenry, possibly to keep them from revolting, thought Vlad with an internal smile.

He always insisted Misha meet him there the many times they had made contact. He considered him a primary source of things Russian in America and things American for Russians. And he had lots of connections.

They playfully opened each conversation with barbs

about who had to travel the farthest to get there. Misha came from Brooklyn, a 40-minute subway ride on the B train.

"It was 35 minutes for me today! I had to walk slow to meet you," Vlad boasted. They made a game of arriving at their favorite spot at the same time.

Vlad wore his usual snap brimmed beret and green windbreaker. Misha wore his usual tracksuit with the red, white and blue stripes down the pant leg and over the shoulders. He relished the stereotype.

"Тот, кто носит Adidas сегодня, завтра будет продавать Родину!" Vlad greeted him.

"He who wears Adidas today, sells the Motherland tomorrow!" Misha translated proudly. They both laughed.

"My friend," Vlad said as he gave him a manly hand shake and hug. "It is amazing how much I have learned since we last met." They grabbed a couple of chairs and moved them to an empty table by the patio steps next to the guard shack that looked like a phone booth from London. The guard was more an usher, helping keep the park in order during its daily chaotic ritual of freedom to gather.

"Does that mean you are smarter now, or have I grown dumber?" Misha answered with a laugh.

"We shall see. Maybe we both become smarter with what I have learned. And richer!" Vlad raised his eyebrows with delight, clearly excited about what he was about to tell his friend.

Misha reached into the small bag he carried and pulled out a thermos of coffee and two cups. He patiently filled each cup with the black liquid, still steaming. When he was finished, he returned the thermos to the bag. Vlad reached into his jacket pocket and pulled out a small bottle of clear liquid and added a shot into each cup.

Silently, in a ritual they performed often at these meetings, they toasted one another.

"So, tell me. How can we get richer?" Misha smiled, savoring the vodka flavored coffee sliding over his tongue.

"For two hundred years we have been stealing information from our American friends and we have infiltrated them on so many levels," Vlad began. "But so much can be learned by just reading what is on the open market."

Vlad told Misha about the chatter in the intelligence world, both from intercepted communications and open sources. Like defense industry magazines that were reporting new contracts with the US Navy. He was almost giddy telling him about the emails he had subscribed to that were like a warning alert to fulfill his Christmas shopping list.

"I can almost buy them on line!" he laughed loud enough that Misha looked around suddenly to see who was within ear shot. Anyone within fifty feet could hear the commotion his friend was making.

Vlad calmed down and explained how he was interested in all things Navy.

"We have had some setbacks, Misha," Vlad continued quietly. "We are 10 years behind the President's plan to rebuild our sub force. We need a boost!"

New technology was the holy grail, no matter where it came from.

"And I have found just such a thing! It's a new communication system using lasers underwater. It's very exciting, a game changer!"

"Lasers?" said Misha, slightly confused. "What do I know from lasers?"

"You know about cards, so I'm sending you a card player."

"A frog, you mean. Someone I can slowly boil and then trade for information, yes?"

"Well, maybe not him exactly, but he knows people. In Connecticut, where they build the submarines. Some who have access to certain types of information." Vlad looked around at the young couple sitting across from them on the other side of the walk. They were fully into each other. The traffic noise was constant though dulled by the many leafy branches hanging from the trees, showing the first blooms of springtime.

"In my business, I must be patient and careful," Vlad continued, his voice lowered ever so slightly. "This situation has been pushed forward by Konstantin. I need access as soon as possible."

"What do I get out of this?" Misha asked. As usual, he thought, Vlad was throwing a general proposition his way, and the outcome was clearly in doubt, if not the method used to get the hoped-for results. The more energy he put into it, the more resources required, the more value he expected in return.

"100," Vlad smiled.

Misha looked at him for a moment, letting the number sink in. He was impressed and pleased. $100,000 would go a long way to help his enterprise.

"That important, eh?" he laughed. He was interested. "Does our card player have a name?"

"Bailey," answered Vlad. "He comes from New London. He knows people and he is willing to help. He's ready to help. Let's say he has no choice but to help."

"Of course," Misha nodded, well aware of his friend's techniques of persuasion.

"I will send him to you," Vlad nodded.

Misha pulled out a business card and handed it to Vlad. It simply said Misha Y. with the image of an Owl's face on it. It matched the small tattoo on Misha's wrist.

"Have your man show me this when he visits. I will begin to plan immediately. Let's catch a frog and boil him!"

They shook hands, chatted for a few more minutes about their love of living in America and then parted ways. Vlad walked to the bus stop for the M4 to head back to the consulate. As he was about to get on the bus, he saw a woman with large sunglasses and a hooded sweatshirt. He swore to himself she was looking at him and he turned away from the bus doorway and started walking north.

Misha walked the other way to the 6th Avenue subway station and got on the B train heading to Brighton Beach. He never looked behind him, oblivious to the man in the tie and fleece vest who stepped into the same car at the other end.

Misha split his riding time on the train thinking about the design of a plan to force someone he hadn't met yet to do something they most likely would never do, unless they were forced by circumstances they could not yet conceive.

And the rest of the time he pondered about the new ride he would build with this unexpected influx of cash to replace the go-cart track that had lost its scream-ability.

"It is time to start the water boiling," he said to himself with a smile.

twelve

MISHA'S REAL HOUSE OF CARDS

Friday One Week Ago 2200

The world continues to teeter on a slippery slope, dark and secret, filled with danger and the guns are out. Ayatollah not happy after surprise murder of prized acolyte, mayor of Kashan. Led efforts to suppress local opposition protests. Resistance economy to blame. MI6 fingerprints all over. Oil payments issue still? —SpyhakrF

Friday night at Misha's real House of Cards was like any other night, except more players enjoyed the offerings of the secret club on the 15th floor of the Brighton Court apartments. When Luke and Rene' arrived, he noticed immediately more cocktail waitresses wandering about with trays of colorful drinks. The room was nearly full compared to the last time and Luke immediately noticed a second room open and active off to the right beyond the curved mahogany bar.

The two of them settled in on stools at the end and ordered two rums. Luke felt the eyes of the room looking at them and realized he would be looking too at the attractive blonde by his side. She didn't pay much attention but could clearly see herself and the rest of the room in the bar mirror. Luke smiled to himself and understood this was his fate by her side.

He thought about the games and shifted focus. There was not a hint of formality with the players in the room. No Friday night dress code that you might see in Monte Carlo. But the crowd was younger than the last time he was there and the noise level higher.

Still only cards in the main room, but the shouts from the new room beyond the bar indicated table games with dice and roulette wheels were in action.

"Black Jack," Rene' answered when a hostess in a sleeveless dress came up to them and asked what they were interested in playing. The young woman smiled and nodded in the direction of the noisier room.

"You want to be in here," she said and took Rene' gently by the hand and led her away. "I have a table for you." Rene' smiled at Luke, as if to say, "I like this." And they were gone, leaving Luke with his McCoy on the rocks and the sound of chips moving around the tables in front of him.

"Don't worry, she's in good hands," said a voice behind Luke and he turned to see a man dressed nattily in a western cut tuxedo sport coat that came down over his hips. The string tie and the cowboy dress shirt made him look like Brett Maverick. But, no hat.

Luke took him in and smiled.

"You think so?"

"I do. I'm McSamarlie. James Michael Joseph McSamarlie. A friend of Misha's." He raised his class in greeting and Luke returned the toast.

"I'm Luke. That's Rene'. I know she can take care of herself."

"I bet she can!" McSamarlie laughed with a nod of his head. "So, what do you like, Luke? Word is you're partial to Seven-card?"

Luke was surprised.

"Word? I've only been here once."

"Yes, you have, but you did well. Misha always remembers the good players," McSamarlie answered with a smile. "In fact, he asked me to make sure you got in a good competitive game. Shall I seat you?" He pointed to an open seat at a table in the middle of the room.

Luke looked at the table, then at the room where Rene' had disappeared and finally back at his new cowboy friend.

"Sure, let's do it."

Luke got up and followed him across the room. He was surprised to see McSamarlie carrying a paddle of some sort by his side.

"What is that?" Luke asked.

McSamarlie turned and held it up with a big grin.

"That's my frog swatter! They're everywhere!"

"Frogs?" Luke asked, more than a little confused.

"Yes sir, you never know when they are going get a little crazy!"

With that, he turned and tapped the empty chair at the Seven-card Stud table and announced with a grand gesture to the five folks sitting around it, loud enough for most of the room to hear, "Friends, this here is Luke! And he loves the game! Treat him right into the night!"

Luke chuckled at the introduction and felt the eyes on him again. He soaked it in, waved and sat down, passing over ten $100 bills to the dealer and collected his chips.

"He's a little whacked, man, but he's whacked in a good way."

The man sitting to Luke's left laughed as he stuck out his hand.

"Ted Lumber."

Luke shook his hand.

"There's no frogs here, right?" he asked, playing along.

"We are all frogs, man. Just some smarter than others."

What the hell are these people talking about? Luke thought. Then the cards started coming and Luke put frogs out of his mind.

"Okay, folks. Let's play a game."

An hour and a half later, Luke was hung out to dry on 7th street with a pair of 7's in the hole and a third 7 down and dirty. The King, Jack, Queen, nine were showing pretty on the table and it came down to him and two other players for the showdown. A pair of 5's exposed to his left and a low inside straight threatened to his right. He raised on his 7's by $500, hoping his own inside straight would scare them off. But they hung in and called.

"Sheeettt" came the cry from Ted to his left when he saw Luke flip his buried 7s. His own buried 5 was useless.

"Oh, yea!" came the cry from across the table, as the player called "Loosey" showed a 3 and a 4 to complete the low straight.

Luke said nothing, but sat back in his chair, stunned by the realization that he had been losing a lot more than he had been winning this night. He had already blown through his $1000 stake and in fact was now down about $2500 with only $500 in his left pocket.

He waved to the waitress nearby for another McCoy on the rocks, handing her his empty glass. "This table sucks!" he said to no one in particular.

And then he stood up and excused himself, losing his balance for a second.

"You gonna be okay, Lukey boy?" said Ted as he reached

out with a hand to steady him. "Or should I say, "no Luckey boy!"? Ted laughed at his own comedy.

"I need to shiff gears," Luke slurred and wandered his way toward the bar.

"Don't give up, sweetie," cooed the waitress as she held his fresh McCoy on the tray in front of him. "I've seen things turn around in minutes. You'll do fine." She swung on her high heels and did a fashion runaway walk back toward the tables with a playful glance over her shoulder.

Luke felt nothing. His mind focused on the left pocket with his remaining cash. He would have to work it carefully to get back into the evening groove he had imagined while driving down earlier that afternoon. He knew the cards would even out for him and maybe more. They always had.

He questioned if he had ever been in a groove tonight. If so, it certainly hadn't been a good one. He wandered into the other room and checked out Rene'. She was not visible at first, lost behind a crowd of a dozen spectators who were watching her amass a pile of chips at the Black Jack table.

As he approached, he saw the tuxedo cowboy with the stick standing close by, at her elbow, fully involved with the game. They were trading glances and comments as the cards slide from the dealer's shoe. His hand touched her arm, tapped her wrists and his left arm was on the back of her chair. Luke stopped in his tracks.

"She doesn't need to see me," he thought and turned back into the card room. He understood how a person can get so wrapped up in what they are doing that the world just stops and all that matters is that moment. Luke knew that feeling all too well, but he realized he didn't like it when he was the one being shut out.

To hell with her, it's time for me to get back on the horse, he thought and went back to the bar to refresh his drink.

"Looks like that blondie is doing real good," came the

voice he immediately recognized as Misha's. The Russian plopped on the stool next to him. Luke turned to see a big smile on his face.

"She's taking that money from the house, right? From you?" Luke asked, trying to figure out the big man's game. "I suspect you would be worried."

"Worried? Ha, do you see the crowd around her? She's got their juices flowing."

Misha sipped his drink, something tall and dark.

"When the juices flow, the money goes," he laughed. "They all want a piece of the action." He looked directly at Luke without a smile.

"I am not worried, my friend," Misha continued in a steady voice. He took a sip and continued staring at Luke.

"You, on the other hand, do look worried."

"How do you mean?" Luke asked staring straight ahead. He was focused on the vision of Rene' surrounded by men at the Black Jack table. Misha settled on his seat as if a batter digging into the batter's box, but he was shuffling his butt cheeks against the stool. Getting comfortable. Ready for the next pitch, but one that he was making. He turned to Luke and started talking in a quiet voice. Almost fatherly.

"You think they all want a piece of her, too. Right? So what? Focus, my friend. You are one of the lucky ones, aren't you? You've been with her and you can't get rid of the sights, the smells, the sounds. She captivated you and you find yourself completely under her spell. This is true, no?"

Luke was at first taken aback by Misha's familiarity, but he listened, and he had to admit the truth. He was under her spell and it was destroying his game. Or so he thought. So he blamed. He sipped. He worried about his left pocket.

"You cannot let her spoil your night. She is a shooting star! Her brightness draws you in, her heat keeps you close, but she burns with a fire that no man can control. You have to accept what you have. What you had. You have to find your own brightness."

Misha paused in his soliloquy to let his words sink in. He smiled ever so slightly as he watched Luke listen quietly, offering no protest, no rebuttal.

"Look at the men in this room. None of them have touched what you have touched. Your fingers burn, your brain burns with that touch. It is yours and no one can take that from you. Sure, maybe others have experienced it, but even they cannot take it away from you."

Luke's brain was aroused by the memory of his intimacy with Rene'. He looked at his hands and smiled. He did know her. He could feel the satisfaction of fulfilling his wildest dreams born as a young teen, sexual fantasies about girls and women, the mystery swirling through his savage blood lizard brain response to overcoming the admonitions of the nuns, the warnings of his parents and the pure freedom of immersing himself in the realm of freedom that came with ignoring it all and feeding the feeling from a woman as beautiful as Rene'. She wasn't the first, but she was the best. So far, he allowed.

Could there be more? Was there ever finality? He wanted her like some goddess, but she was not an object. She was a chalice of emotion, passion and pure pleasure that fulfilled his animal instinct, honed by his human intellect. There was nothing wrong with enjoying it! But, was there anything wrong with letting it rule him?

"You may not be alone, but you are alone because it was you and her," Misha continued. He moved closer, his voice low and urgent. "Forget those other men. They don't exist between you and her. They don't change you and her."

"You want monogamy? You want exclusivity? Please, my friend, wake the F up! I also wish to be the emperor, but I know how to dress each morning and put the clothes only on myself. I know when I am naked. What others do does not change what I have done."

Luke slowly turned and looked at Misha. "I sometimes want it so much I can't think of it not being there. The feeling."

Misha stared back at him. "Women and passion and, dare I say it, "love" can only carry you so far. Power? Is that what's it all about? In the end, you will need to be who you really are. A Lothario? A "playboy"? God's gift to women? No! That is not what you can be! Or all you should be. You need to be what you really are. What you come here for."

Luke swallowed the remains of his McCoy on the rocks, sucking in the last two ice cubes. A big smile creased his face, as if to signal he understood what his new found muse was pushing.

"I'm a player, aren't I? A frigging, pot busting card player! Aren't I?"

Misha sat back and laughed.

"I knew you knew," he said, nodding his head with slow satisfaction

"The cards will not lie to you. They are not capable of cheating on you. They are only what they are. They don't care who you are. They don't know you. They only fall when you call."

Misha put his hand on Luke's shoulder, surprising him with the strength of the grip.

"Get your head out from between her legs and get your head into the next game. This is where you can excel, where you make a difference. No one can take that away from you."

"Except for the obvious. My left pocket is kind of thin right now." Luke's confident smile took a slight down turn at the corners. He cocked his head toward Misha with what can only be described as a wry look. He shrugged his shoulders. Held out his hands palms up as if to say, this is what I really am. This is what I have to play with. Nothing.

Misha stood up from his stool and tapped the bar.

"Mr. Luke, you are a friend of Misha's real House of Cards. Take my confidence in you and be the player you are destined to be!"

A man like Misha has a quiet power that might go unnoticed by those who are not familiar with his methods. He was, after all, a well-known figure in his community who owned many businesses and played many angles. He was also a noted Russian mobster who kept himself under the radar, if not above the law. A slight tap on the bar was an unmistakable power sign that had the bartender appearing with a leather-bound portfolio, about the size of the check book in which a waiter might bring your bill after a pleasant dinner.

This portfolio held a piece of paper with a typewritten note.

"Line of Credit: $20,000."

Luke was surprised by the amount but did not hesitate to take the pen offered by the bartender and sign.

"Sometimes you must go deep before you can fly high," Misha said simply raising his glass to Luke.

Luke picked up the fresh McCoy that the bartender had conveniently placed on the bar next to the credit voucher and returned the toast.

"To going high," Luke said.

thirteen

SATAN DEALS

Friday One Week Ago 2300

Gas bomb traced to GU Syria via DGSE deep cover. Photos in hands of NCIA. Palace on high alert re: deep cover rumors. Termination? US or Mossad? —SpyhakrF

If going high is a goal to strive for, being high doesn't always help you get there. After two more hours, Luke was drunk, and it was getting worse. He had blown through most of his 20,000 dollars credit, was desperate for salvation and refused to believe he was finished for the night. Many of the players close to the action seemed surprised that Misha and his men allowed Luke to continue to play. They said nothing, took his chips when they won, and played on.

Those average onlookers weren't aware of the real story. Except for a table of players in the far corner who had been hooting and hollering for the last half hour, exclaiming the excitement of winning for several lucky players.

At one point, James Michael Joseph McSamarlie came

over and pulled Luke aside, not to slow him down, but to direct him toward that noisy table. Luke was all for it. When he heard the winning shouts, he wanted part of that action. His gambling dopamine dump was in full flow. The pretty waitress swung by on cue and handed him another McCoy and McSamarlie sat him down to the right of the dealer.

The room was spinning, as much from the liquor as it was from Luke's confusion about his mounting losses. This wasn't like him. He knew he was a winner.

The game was Acey Duecey, as simple a card game as it gets. Two cards dealt face up, player bets against the pot on the hope the next card is somewhere between the first two. There were a few specific rules, but nothing is wild, everyone gets to win big and everyone gets to lose big. You bet a minimum or you bet the pot and on it goes until someone takes it all.

"Pot's $500 per, Mr. Luke," said the dealer. He tapped the shoe as he watched Luke drop his chips in the pile in the middle. "No splits. Bet high or low on pairs and first ace is always player's choice. You know the game, and here come the cards."

The history of Acey Duecey is foggy. Luke tried to open his mind to all he knew or had heard about the game. Hints of a Chinese ancestry, legends of American GIs in the South Pacific playing between battles in the Great War, even a sun drenched weekend locked in a day room with a Turkish desert panorama outside and a rickety table of dog eared cards and payday stakes inside, relayed as one of Luke's father's great stories of killing time in the US Air Force in the 60's.

Luke himself likened the game to a field goal kicker trying to split the uprights on a football field. Don't hit the post!

And it continued...Luke's blurry ride down a card

shuffling rabbit hole. Luke loved the lingo of the games on the green felt from the earliest days he could remember learning to play. The Gretzkys and gorillas, ladies and jaybirds, tension and candy canes, flipped or buried, sliding on the green, playing the rush, fighting the Rocks, looking for paint, hoping for the Four Horseman.

But with Acey Duecey the last thing he wanted to see was two of a kind. And for some time, Luke didn't see a pair. He chipped away at the pot, $500 here, $700 there. The cards were sliding in between just right. His pile of chips began to grow.

There was no strategy built on counting cards or looking for tells from the other players. Instead, Luke played conservatively, betting strong with a spread of eight or more. Less so for the smaller spreads. And more than once the minimum.

It was almost boring, and Luke tuned in to the chatter among the strangers at the table. He was convinced they were all locals. One was a grocer, handling fruit all day, another sold medical supplies to the dying populace living out their days in the Brighton Beach neighborhood of high rises. Luke laughed to himself thinking of his first visit to the area when he saw retirees sitting on their walker chairs on a street corner, like a town meeting.

The youngest player was studying business at City College between waiting tables at a local tavern. He had an owl tattoo on the back of his wrist same as Luke had seen on the bartender. The oldest guy didn't say what he did for a living, he just fingered his stacks of chips and darted his eyes around the table. Luke thought him kind of creepy, but what did he know.

The betting continued, the pots went up and down and Luke was feeling confident.

He allowed the thought into his brain. "Misha was right. I am here because I'm a player!"

And he was drinking. The McCoy rums continued to flow from Anastasia, the pretty hostess who seemed to have attached herself to him as his personal server.

Then the cards took a turn. The spreads looked good, but pairs started to show up. Like a snowball from hell, in a matter of minutes the pot started to grow. The grocer bet bravely with a risky spread between the 4 and the 10 and was slammed with a Jaybird arriving. $4000 added to the pot. Another Jack posted the medical supplier, crashing his deuce and Jack. $2000 in.

The business man to be from City College also posted on an Acey – Duecey and the pot grew suddenly, doubling to $20,000.

"I can't f-ing believe this crap!" he shouted when the second deuce slid from the deck. With each losing card, the moans and groans built around the table. The buzz was attracting some of the players at tables nearby.

The creepy quiet one with the shifty eyes broke the streak with a $1000 low ball call on his 9 - Queen, drawing a 10. He pulled his chips leaving the pot at $19,000 and then it was Luke's turn.

There was a leftover buzz around the table as the cards were dealt from the shoe. A pair of sixes slid face up in front of Luke wallowing in his own buzz. He blew a sigh of relief. He could make the minimum bet and get on.

Or should he split the cards and double up his chances?

He looked at the dealer for a second, threw in $500 as the minimum bet and called "high", betting the third card would be more than a six.

It wasn't. Instead, another six.

The leftover buzz turned to a collective "Whooaa!"

"Holy sixes, Batman!" came from the college boy.

"Satan Sixes!" said a spectator. "You are F-ed!"

Somebody in the crowd mumbled to the person next to them, "The water is boiling!"

Luke sat back in his chair and suddenly everything churned in slow motion. He drifted as if hanging over the table on a rope, seeing the cards from far away. This was not his reality now because he could, no, would not believe the stir around the table was about him. He refused to believe the three sixes sitting face up in front of his place at the green felt were actually his cards. He was in complete denial as the full awareness set in that one of the obscure rules in this simple, ancient game called Acey Duecey, also known as In-Between, Between the Sheets, Maverick and Red Dog, was trip sixes paid six times the pot!

Satan Sixes. Some idle card playing guru making shit up to make the game more interesting! 666.

"Mr. Luke, the call is $114,000." The dealer's voice cut into Luke's fog.

The room rippled with a mix of shock, marvel, surprise, amazement and awe. No one had ever seen Satan 6s. Many had not even been aware of the rule. Certainly, it was a unique event for Misha's House of Cards. The buzz was loud, but Luke heard nothing. He was frozen in time, his brain wondered how he could suddenly disappear.

Luke looked at the dealer and around the table at all the faces focused on him.

"I don't have it," was all he could manage. Then he turned as the reality of the situation hit him fully. The cacophony of noise filled his ears and the faces showed disappointment, some sadness and others seemed to smile in joy, as if to celebrate his plight was not theirs.

Luke looked around for Misha's round face but did not see him in the crowd.

He stood up with such sudden force he knocked over

his chair and stepped back from the table. The effects of the McCoys mixed with sitting so long left him disoriented and he stumbled his way toward the bar, pushing through the three deep crowd that had gathered around the sudden turn of the cards.

A few steps later and he was at the bar, a refuge in the storm of disbelief that swallowed him up. The bartender dropped another McCoy on the rocks in front of him and gave him a look of sympathy and disbelief.

"That was a tough one," he said and turned away.

Luke's friend Bailey, the card player who had brought him to Misha's real House of Cards two weeks ago, suddenly appeared and whispered in Luke's ear.

"I'm sorry, Luke. I had to do it."

"Had to do what?" Luke asked but, Bailey was gone, hurrying into the other room.

Luke jumped up after him, but there was no sign of him by the time he turned the corner and looked in. The Black Jack table was busy, but Rene' wasn't anywhere to be seen. Luke stumbled around aimlessly, not knowing whether to look for Bailey or Rene' or just run away. No one seemed to notice him, all focused on their own passion plays at the tables.

He saw a far door and started heading that way, but he suddenly felt the sting of a hard object that came in from his right and landed on his chest. It was the tuxedo cowboy, Misha's enforcer, James Michael Joseph McSamarlie, wielding his Hurley like a cop's nightstick. The force of the ash blow surely had left a mark on his breastbone, Luke thought.

"Owww. Hey, what the fuck!" Luke shouted.

"Mr. Luke, Misha would like to see you now," McSamarlie smiled tightly. Polite and forceful, he expertly pushed Luke backward with the Hurley. Luke's first reaction was to grab the stick and fight it off, but he was surprised at the strength of the Irishman. He was forced back two more steps.

"Hey, easy, Maverick! Okay, cool it. I'm not running away." Luke pulled his hands away from the stick and held them up. He felt out of his element and wasn't ready to cause more of a scene. The magnitude of his loss was settling in and the odds didn't look so good if he tried to take on the tuxedo cowboy in front of him.

McSamarlie eased the pressure on his weapon and jerked his thumb back toward the main card room. Luke nodded his head and started walking that way.

Two other men were suddenly there to escort him. The fruit grocer and the young college kid from the Acey Duecey table.

"What the hell?" Luke wondered as the Hurley pressed into him again, this time at his back as McSamarlie urged the procession forward.

The four of them walked through the main card room and Luke could feel the stares of just about everyone. It felt like a perp walk without the cuffs. It lasted only a brief moment, and as he turned toward the main entrance, the noise of the card room returned to its green felt paradise self.

The small entourage continued into the hall and the Hurley again poked Luke, pushing him to the right. They went down two doors, into a stairwell and up one flight of stairs and immediately into another room with a desk and a couple of wooden office chairs. The grocer and the college boy stayed at the door and Luke was roughly directed into one of the chairs by the Hurley in the hands of McSamarlie and landed with a plop.

"Really, is this necessary?" he asked innocently as he turned to McSamarlie. But he was met by the flat paddle end of the stick that landed on his left shoulder and with a flick of the Irishman's wrist, pushed his cheekbone forcing his head to swivel forward.

"Face the desk, shut up and sit here. Don't move. Lagooshka will be right here." There was a strange mix of mirth and danger in McSamarlie's voice. He clearly was enjoying being the strong arm.

"Lagooshka? Who the hell is Lagooshka?" Luke asked, even as he turned to face the desk. He looked around the room and was surprised to see a dozen pieces of art, photos and posters on the walls. Each one depicted a historic moment in the life of Coney Island.

The largest was a dramatic painting of revelers on horses in a pure display of fun and freedom. The center focus was a woman with her skirt hiked up high on her thigh, holding the reins of her horse in full gallop. The cigar smoking man sitting close behind her had his feet secured in metal stirrups just below the woman's high heeled boots, also in a stirrup. Luke realized the horses were not real, but an amusement ride, carved from wood and frozen in the height of a gallop. Other riders were close behind, each enjoying the moment.

Luke was struck by the contrast of the horse's expression, mouth open, head up as if in full stride, while the woman and man were tightlipped and calm, as if bored by the ride. Maybe, he thought, they had ridden it enough. The initial joy of discovery and fun was gone. And yet, they rode on, caught in the moment, pressed together for all the world to see.

Freak shows, water slides and the Wonder Wheel were displayed in other photos and paintings. Behind the desk hung the face that Luke had seen over the front gate of Scream Town. The long-time image of the Coney Island amusement world, Luke could only grimace at the wicked, toothy grin, the freckled face and the hair parted in the middle and combed out like a huge mustache on top of his head. Howdy Doody's freak show uncle.

Then the door opened and in walked Misha Yanovich Yevtechnov.

He came around the desk, dropped a folder on it and kept on walking to the other side and sat on the edge right in front of Luke. He looked up at his cowboy with the Hurley and nodded.

"You boys can leave us for the moment. Mr. Luke isn't going to do anything silly...are you Mr. Luke." Misha's expression came from a side that Luke had yet to see in his short acquaintance with the man. The genial host of a couple of weeks ago was not smiling and not at all fatherly as he had been earlier in the evening.

Then they were alone.

"I am worried about the children, Mr. Luke."

"The children? What children?" Luke was confused. He was sobering up as the seriousness of his situation settled around him like a dark cloud. "Worried" left him wondering if he had heard right.

"The young boys and girls who enjoy my rides, of course. You must know we are doing wonderful things over on the boardwalk. They are expecting new and thrilling games, whirly gigs and scary chariots in my amusement park."

Luke could see Misha was wrapped up in telling his plans, proud in fact. He could hardly believe this was all about rides at Coney Island.

"Hey, Misha, I've never seen cards like that! I was doing okay, I had things under control, I still had half my credit line available, but three 6s? What the fuck, man! Who could see that coming?"

"Yes, it's a devilish game, isn't it?" he mocked and then shook his head as if commiserating. He stood up and walked back around behind the desk and sat down. Exaggerating every move, he opened the ledger and studied the figures as if adding up the totals. He looked up at Luke.

"So, bottom line, my friend. Looks like $110,000 plus the 20 on your credit line, a cool $130,000. I don't expect you have it tonight considering all we've been through, so I'll give you until Wednesday to deliver the funds here."

Misha smiled ever so slightly.

"And that's without interest for the first few days. That will kick in if I don't see the money."

"Jeez, there is no way I can have that money by Wednesday! I just don't have that. Maybe a few thousand, but man, I am not that guy. I can't do it! I'm sorry, I'm just a working geek...."

"Luke," Misha interrupted hm. "I took a chance on you and now I'm counting on you coming through with the money you owe to help make that happen for the kids." Misha's tone was soft, almost a whisper. He sounded reasonable, like it was the most obvious thing you could imagine. Come on, we're all in this together!

Luke heard the sound of an angry banker controlling his temper.

"This is crazy. You're crazy!" Luke started yelling. He jumped up and started pacing the room. "I can't believe you loaned me money in the first place. There is no way I can repay you by Wednesday! Not in five years of Wednesdays."

"You did sign the credit slip, yes? You did lose the hand, yes? You do owe the money, yes?"

Luke said nothing. He stared at Misha wide eyed, begging for sympathy with his eyes, but there was nothing offered from the Russian but a grim return stare. Then Luke panicked and decided to run. He threw open the door.

That was a stupid idea because McSamarlie was right there, string tie and all, with a silly grin on his face. The

Hurley in his hand came up and whacked Luke right in the chest, sending him stumbling back into the room.

"There's no place to run, lucky Lukey boy!" seethed McSamarlie. The grocer and the college kid were right behind him and filled the doorway. Luke's adrenalin kicked in and he grabbed one of the office chairs and swung it toward McSamarlie, but the Irishman deftly parried it with his Hurley, then landed a vicious blow to Luke's left knee.

Luke went down in pain. He tried to get up but, he couldn't get his left leg to co-operate. McSamarlie loomed over him and the two other guys stepped in, grabbed him and spun him around, throwing him back into the remaining chair.

Misha was suddenly in Luke's face, his finger pointing like an angry dad telling his kid that enough was enough. "Luke, stop this! You are in deep trouble. Deeper than you know. I don't want to hurt you, but I will. Mr. J will. So, shut up, sit and listen. I think I have a solution."

Misha stood upright, slowly walked back behind the desk and sat down. He opened up the folder sitting there and glanced at it for a moment.

"Your friend Bailey has told me about your work at GMBB up there in Groton."

"Bailey? What did he tell you?" Luke asked. He remembered what Bailey had said to him just before Misha's goons hauled him out of the card room. He didn't know him very well. He was more Antoine's friend than Luke's. He was the one that got them into the House of Cards.

"Oh, shit!" Luke whispered to himself. Like a curtain pulled open behind door number 4, the full realization hit him. He looked at the grocer and college kid who had played Acey-Duecey at the same table. The owl tattoo on the kid. The grocer's rolled up sleeves revealed his own copy of the owl face. He looked at the slight grin on Misha's face sitting behind the desk, watching the light bulb go on in Luke's eyes.

"I am a fool!" he blurted. He shook his head, devastated by the obvious. "You set this whole thing up! I've been set up! From the beginning!"

Misha sat at the desk, his chin resting on his folded hands, as he watched Luke go through the machinations of revelation. He shook his head and removed a slip of paper from the folder.

"Mr. Luke, I am going to ask you nicely one time. Acknowledging you owe me over $100,000 from your card playing riskiness, I am offering you a simple option. In fact, it is your only option. On this slip of paper is the name of a new piece of equipment that the US Navy is installing on their submarines, right now at the Globallus Marine Boat Builders in Groton."

He slid the paper from the folder in front of Luke. It has one word on it. "SLACLONET1000".

"I am not a traitor, Misha." Luke pushed the paper back at Misha.

"Oh, I don't want you to be traitor, Mr. Luke. Think of it more like a trader. T-R-A-D-E-R. Get it. You trade me this information, I forgive your debt."

"Impossible! Security is so tight there in the Loops building! I can't get my hands on this device. It's too big, for one thing. I'd never get it out of the yard! You're asking the impossible."

"Not for the IT guy, no? You have access to files. That's all I want. Files."

Misha sat on the front of the desk again, grabbing the arms of Luke's chair.

"Luke, you don't have a choice here! Find a way or else." Misha stood up.

"Or else what?" Luke asked, instantly regretting his brashness.

"You don't understand, do you? Who do you think you are dealing with here? This is not some three-card monte on the street corner, my friend. This is Misha's real House of Cards. I am Yevtechnov! That name means something around here!" Misha was agitated and nodded to his three henchmen in the room.

"I will show you what else!"

Then everything went dark as Luke felt a cloth bag go over his head. His arms were pinned by two pairs of strong hands and he felt tie wraps go around his wrists. That was followed by a sharp pain in his belly that doubled him over, delivered courtesy of McSamarlie and his Hurley stick.

Then he was lifted and dragged out of the room, down the hallway and into an elevator where the grocer and college kid administered a series of blows to his back and belly. The Hurley stick contributed painful shots to the thighs and the backs of his knees. Painful but not debilitating, each one eliciting a cry of anguish when it landed.

Once on the street, Luke was thrown into a car and it sped away for only a couple of minutes before coming to a stop where he was dragged out and stood up. The bag was ripped off and Luke saw the same outrageously grotesque face from behind Misha's desk, staring right back at him. The image of Howdy Doody filled his brain again, this time on steroids as if seen through an LSD haze.

It was a haze from his leftover drunk, mixed with his stupid, dopamine filled, card crazed addiction that drove him deep into gambling hell. All edged with the swelling that began to show on his bruised body.

The amusement park was quiet and dark, only work lights illuminated the shadows of metal roller coaster tracks, whack-a-mole booths and the Wonder Wheel off to his left.

Misha appeared to his right and spoke with a smile on his face.

"Even deserted at night, I hear the screams in the air. The joy of fear. Amazing how many will pay me to scare the daylights out of them."

He turned to Luke and said thoughtfully, "Don't worry. We won't mess up your face."

The grocer and the college kid dragged him across the sidewalk and through the gate and brought him to a round metal mesh cage sitting on a low platform, with twin towers rising up into the night sky over 250 feet. The cage door slid open and Luke was lifted up and tossed like a sack of cement into the sitting area.

Luke crashed into the hard, plastic seats, unable to cushion his blow with his hands still tied behind his back. His cheekbone took most of the contact and he shouted in pain again as he lay crumpled half on the side by side seats and half on the floor of the cage. He could hear a slow whirring sound as if a line was being tightened around a drum. The tension actuator was winding up and the cage rolled back and locked into place as the powerful magnet under the platform was turned on.

He knew this was the Astro Sling Cage that he and Rene' saw earlier in the day. There was something missing. The over the head shoulder harness that kept the two occupants in place was missing. Not good, he thought.

Then the sliding metal cage door closed with a clang and Luke thought of Rene'.

"Rene'? Where is she?" he asked McSamarlie standing three feet away, his hand on the switch that controlled the ride. The guy with the stick made a crude gesture, grabbing his crotch with his free hand.

"I got your Rene' right here!"

Yevtechnov was behind him with the grocer and the

college kid off to the side. McSamarlie smiled and then spoke in a soft voice, just enough for only Luke to hear.

"Welcome to Lagooshka's Cage! The water is boiling!"

He pressed the switch and the cage launched straight up in the air powered by the thick, tensioned bungee cords attached to each side. The sudden release of pent up energy overcame inertia and pressed Luke down on the mesh floor, helpless against the pressure.

He let out a scream involuntarily because even the best visualization of what is going to happen can't prepare your body for the edges of consciousness when your blood rushes away from your head on the rocket launch ride up.

About 400 feet in the air, the energy generated by the bungee was all used up and the cage reached the top of its flight. Unfortunately for Luke, with his hands tied behind his back and nothing to hold onto, he continued to travel upward and slammed into the top of the cage, his shoulders taking the force of the blow.

Immediately, the cage went into free fall, returning to the pull of gravity, not unlike falling off a cliff.

One of the unique aspects of this ride is the free rolling attachment points which allow the cage to rotate. As it fell it spun and Luke's tied arms were thrown against the latch that held the sliding cage door shut, unlocking it. Even as he cursed the pain in his elbow, the cage rolled upside down and he was thrown back up on the inside of the roof and away from the door. Then the cage reached the bottom of its fall and the bungee spring it back skyward, spinning as it rose and bashing Luke all about.

He lost his bearings but instinctively spread his legs as far apart as he could, pressing his feet against both sides of the cage, even as it reached a peak again, rolled over and threw him toward the sliding door which was moving on its track. Now the reversal of direction on the descent allowed gravity to pull the door shut just before Luke slammed into it with the back of his head, knocking him unconscious.

When he awoke, he was sitting behind the wheel of his car with the sun lighting up a deserted West 12th Street right where he had parked it the day before, next to the boardwalk between the Wonder Wheel and The Thunderbolt.

fourteen

STOLEN HEARTS

Friday 1100

The silence in the cellar was complete as Luke paused in the telling of his adventure leaving Petrika sitting there in amazement. The stone walls of the 150-year-old hole in the ground gave dimension to where they were sitting, but Petrika felt like she had been taken to another world.

"What happened to your girlfriend, Rene'?" she asked innocently.

Luke looked at her for a moment, thinking about his answer. Just the mention of her name pissed him off. He pushed that feeling out of his mind and focused on the stranger in front of him. He liked her and felt comfortable with her, as if she were sent from somewhere to be his confessor.

"Ex-girlfriend," he finally said, feeling a need to clarify himself. He paused again looking at her.

"I was ready to leave her there," he said finally.

"Leave her?! No, you can't do that!" she protested.

"I know!" he retorted, embarrassed by the fact he

certainly had been ready to leave her in the shadow of *Lagooshka's Cage.*

"She didn't answer her phone. I had seen her having a good time, surrounded by guys," he ranted. "I know she can take care of herself. No, she *likes* to take care of herself. And I was pretty shaken up."

He knew the excuses sounded lame.

"You didn't, did you?" she asked hopefully. He thought it weird how girls seemed to stick up for girls when it came to guys, even if the girls didn't deserve their support.

"No. Well, yes and no. I started the car and was ready to pull out when she appeared on the arm of that Irish asshole cowboy wannabe McSamarlie with the stupid stick." Just talking about it made his mind bounce around to the pains in his back, legs and arms.

"He walked her up to the car, kissed her on the lips and shoved her in!"

"Oh, Luke. That is terrible!" Petrika said shaking her head.

"I can tell you the ride home was pretty bad. She was all pissed at me for getting her involved with a bunch of thugs. I was pissed at her for spending the night with those thugs. I know she slept with at least one of them, maybe more. She can be such a slut sometimes."

Petrika watched him change before her eyes. His broad shoulders slumped, his chin dropped to his chest and he slumped down in a sitting position on the sleeping bag spread out on the dusty floor. She didn't know what to do. He was suddenly so vulnerable, the antithesis of the man she watched beat up four guys at the Beach View Bar just the night before.

"I told her I was done with her," he managed to say. She couldn't tell if it was anger or sadness that choked his words.

"And that's the least of my problems now." He looked at her and all she could see was a man lost.

She did not know this man before her, but she felt for him, she believed his story was real. He was clearly affected by what had happened in the last few days. She slid across the floor and knelt next to him, gently touching his bruised, bare shoulder showing through his dirty tee shirt. His muscles felt good to her touch.

"Hey, Luke, things work out. They always do, yes?" she said gently, laughing to herself how much of a platitude that sounded like. She remembered something her mother used to say.

"*Zima – ne leto, proydyot e eto,*" she said in her most soothing voice. She echoed her words in English.

"Winter is not summer, it will pass"

Then she thought of another Russian proverb. "*Poshivyom – yvidim.* We will live. We will see."

She had no idea what was going to happen, but it seemed like the thing to say. She genuinely felt bad for him. She continued to rub his shoulder tenderly.

"Ha!" he laughed. "You are full of wisdom, aren't you?" Her hand was warm on his skin and felt good.

She gingerly traced a large bruise on his bicep that extended under his armpit and down his side. He opened his eyes and looked at her and whispered, "Who are you, Petrika Rushevski?"

"I am girl you protected, Luke...Parmeely?" she spoke slowly, unsure of her pronunciation. She looked right back at him, seeing an open, hurting man.

"Parmelian. Par-mell-ee-an," he gently corrected her with a smile. Her eyes were so blue even in the dim light from the lantern. Her lips were full, but in such an innocent way that made them even more appealing to him. He realized he was looking at her closely for the first time since their brief encounter the night before. She was a vision.

"Wait one minute, Luke Parmelian," she said suddenly with confidence, her mind filled with a major question. She stood up and moved away.

She blushed thinking of how his mere physical presence had distracted her from the whole reason she had set out to look for him this morning.

"Did you kill Freddy?" she asked bluntly.

"Freddy? Who is Freddy? Oh, the guy from last night?" Luke's eyes opened wide showing his surprise. He moved easily upright and faced her. "That guy is dead?"

"He was stabbed by somebody and the sheriff is looking for you," Petrika said pointing her index finger at his chest. She described her visit with Sheriff Bobby Jackson just a couple of hours ago.

"He just wants to talk," she finished.

"Great! More shit to wade through!" Luke moaned helplessly, as if another rock had piled on his life.

"Well?"

"Well what?"

"Did you stab him?" Petrika grabbed his arm and Luke winced at the pain. She looked him right in the eye, waiting for the answer she wanted.

Luke looked right back. He took her hand gently and pried if off his arm, holding it between his hands. He was acutely aware of her skin and the warmth she was giving off.

"No, I did not kill that guy Freddy. I just broke his fingers because he deserved to be taught a lesson. You don't deserve to be treated like that. No one does. Nevertheless, I don't think he deserved to die."

She liked the sincere sound of his voice. She also liked the way his hands held her. Strong but gentle.

"*Khorosho.* Good. Then we can be friends," she said

and joined her other hand over his and squeezed it. Luke responded by slowly pulling her closer, only their clasped hands separating them.

"That would be nice," he said with a slight smile. "Although I am not so sure you want to be friends with me."

"Yes, I am doubtful too. You seem to be much trouble."

"Well, I don't know how much trouble I am," he smiled. "I'm certainly "in" trouble."

"Yes, I meant that. What can I help?"

They stood there for a moment, her eyes wide and openly searching his. She could feel him against her, their noses inches apart. His hands tenderly holding hers between them.

At that moment, both of them felt no pretense with the other. Whatever walls society ruled should be built between the sexes did not exist. Their paths had crossed by accident and their baggage was inexorably a part of their selves, but across the open stare into each other's eyes they felt a sense of newness. An open door to an immediate moment. One with no fear of the past and no care about the future.

"I want to kiss you," Luke said softly, succumbing to the physicality of her body, the sweetness of her breath and her delightfully alluring nose. And those damn eyes!

"Yes," was all she whispered in response and offered her lips to him. Their kiss was soft and long and passionate. And in the dusty confines of a forgotten hideaway, they caressed and explored each other, sharing a mutually satisfying encounter that had no connection to anything but the safety of sharing vulnerability and trust as if they were the only two people on earth.

fifteen

DR. STANDORD,
I PRESUME

Monday 0800

Chatter continues over lost Borey-class boomer missing north of Gdansk Basin. Search and rescue underway. Swedish and Finnish naval help rejected by Admiral Chesney Rudamenka of Maritime Fleet of Russia (MMFR). "Stay away!" is the command as hope fades for missing sub. Weapons malfunction the buzz for cause of sinking. 104 souls on board. –SpyhakrF

Dr. Andrew Standord set them more than lived up to them. Standards that is. A brilliant student at M.I.T., as soon as he graduated in the late 90's he found his way inside the technology beltway along I-495 circling the city of Boston. Then he got into lasers and he found he could shine. The mere concept of information traveling along light beams made up of unimaginably small light particles at similarly unimaginable speeds posed little problem for him.

One's life choices are often driven by happenstance. Dr. Andy, the nickname he picked up while sailboat racing, connected up with PJ McDonough of Mystic, Connecticut. McDonough was an entrepreneur who built carbon fiber engines that ran on methane gas produced from rotting garbage. He put them into carbon fiber cars. He also dabbled in flying boats.

Dr. Andy built him a laser guidance system that was accurate and reliable. It was a simple collaboration that started as a conversation on PJ's race boat one afternoon during a race postponement.

"You know sailboat racing," PJ used to say. "Sometimes it blows and sometimes it sucks!"

Idle times, idle conversation and the two of them talked themselves into a business relationship that allowed Dr. Andy to expand his research and make an extraordinary breakthrough in laser technology.

Financed by McDonough and profits from the commercially successful laser guidance system, Dr. Andy dove deep into nanophotons, Fourier optics, Quantum Key Distribution and orthogonal frequency division multiplexing. He also figured out a way to rearrange water molecules and built a device that came to be known as the SLACLONET 1000. It took five years, thousands of man hours and only four million dollars, but he succeeded with astonishing results. In another year, his device was under contract with the US Navy and he began building and installing them in American submarines.

This green light "GLASER" device had nothing to do with navigation. Instead, it allowed data and voice communication at depth and speed underwater.

Free Space Optics is a term that had been bandied about

for decades by engineers striving to replace copper wire. Dr. Andy was a strong believer in the 40 principles of the Russian TRIZ system. *Theoria Resheneyva Isobretatelskehuh Zadach* or translated as the "theory of the resolution of invention-based tasks". The concept was simple. Someone at some time had previously solved part of the problem. It was the researcher's job to find the parts that work with the immediately required solution. Dr. Andy did that and took the best of the research and carved out a dramatic shift in military capability.

Not only did the laser comm system allow up to 300 Mbs of information to be transmitted through water, it was virtually impossible to intercept and decode because of QKD.

Secure comms at speed and depth. The holy grail of submarine warfare.

Some considered this as big a breakthrough as the efforts of Admiral Hyman Rickover in the mid-1950's. Rickover and his team crammed a nuclear reactor into the *USS Nautilus* along the Thames River in Groton and submarines could now disappear for months without surfacing to replenish their batteries.

Stealth has been the raison d'etre of submarines since the American Revolutionary war when a submersible was tested at the mouth of the Connecticut River. The legend suggests *the Turtle* was designed by David Bushnell of Westbrook and built by a New Haven clockmaker named Doolittle. They attempted to attach underwater bombs to the hulls of British ships anchored in New York and Philadelphia harbors late in the war. While the Bushnell's *Turtle* failed, the concept changed the path of naval warfare innovations.

Today the US fleet of over 70 submarines projects the strength of America's military might in a variety of packages from nuclear missiles and littoral defense to inflatables filled with SEAL Teams. Submarines play a major intelligence role keeping an eye on the rest of the world's fleets and are the ace in the hole when all the other land-based cards have been played out on the global landscape of deterrence and nuclear annihilation.

Who needs ICBMs launched out of Wyoming, when there's enough firepower submerged around the world to destroy the world? The power of the Silent Service was never under estimated even if its importance was under reported. And now, with subs retrofitted with the SLACLONET 1000, they don't have to expose themselves to enemy surveillance by coming to the surface to get their orders.

Dr. Andy's breakthrough worked in conjunction with the government's partnership with private corporations to launch a network of low earth orbit satellites that facilitated world-wide communication between command and soldier. The combination was a game changer for all warfare.

With hundreds of subs spread among a dozen nations around the world, the enemies and friends of America now had something else to think about. And covet.

sixteen

WORRIES, RANTS
AND PLOTS

Monday AM

US Navy mum on fleet deployment with refit program underway in Groton. NATO sources express worries about "holes in force effect" with several US subs heading to port. Brits and French doubling patrols. –SpyhakrF

When Luke woke up on Monday morning, bruised and battered from the beating he took at the hands of Misha's thugs, he wasn't thinking about Dr. Andrew Standord so much. His first thought was a wave of anger and hatred toward his card playing buddy Bailey. Followed by a feeling of shame for playing the role of idiot so well. A classic stupid pawn in another man's game! He was set up and fell hook, line and sinker.

He was in debt for over $100,000, money he didn't have a prayer of delivering by Wednesday. That was his salary for an entire year! What salary? He was about to jump into a rabbit hole that would surely cost him his job. Job? Job? How about his freedom? He feared for his life and fully expected further physical harm if he didn't deliver.

By Wednesday? Impossible!

Rene' was history, too. He didn't want anything more to do with her and was sure she felt the same.

And he was now faced with betraying his security clearance and his country, by stealing the plans for the SLACLONET 1000. He knew full well that opened him up to charges of treason and imprisonment. Embarrassment! End of life as he knew it! He had read all the security notices, watched the videos and heard the warnings of the GMBB security chief about "getting caught in compromising situations".

He tried to come to grips with betrayal but, he could only muster a halfhearted effort. He really never thought much about patriotism while going about his daily life. Who did? As much as the flag was pushed on society, how many folks actually felt the power of that symbol? He thought of it more of a marketing scheme, like selling cars or beer.

He blamed the lack of leadership in America. The politicians who ran the government had done very little to bolster a sense of respect for the country. The White House was the ultimate seat of power, but it seemed ultimate power always attracted ultimate crooks, liars and cheats. He truly believed demanding respect wasn't the same as letting it brew a natural way. They lied and pedaled their influence and platitudes for the sole purpose of lining their own pockets, boosting their own ratings, maintaining their own place at the government trough. They didn't give a crap about this country beyond their own popularity! Why should he?

Stealing secret files wasn't as big a deal as getting your

head bashed in. Or your life ended. And we've been at peace so long…the warnings about the enemies of our country fell on so many deaf ears, especially when they came from the bloviating clowns in charge. Their brand of patriotism was as empty and worthless as the rest of their blather.

Sure, men and women have died while fighting, but in whose wars? Soldiering was a noble profession until you have to kill someone. Then who do you answer to? Where is the real threat? It's not who do we have to die for, it's who gets paid? The military-industrial complex! The defense contractors! The damn politicians! The policy makers! The whole charade depressed him as much as his impending doom at the hands of the Russian mob!

He had to sit down on the edge of his bed to calm down.

"Your life is over, Luke ass!" he shouted.

After a few moments, he stood up and walked to the window of his third story downtown New London apartment with a view of the Amtrak swing bridge that opened at the entrance to Shaw's Cove on the West side of the Thames River. Fort Trumbull sat to the south, another bastion of patriotism built to defend from threats long ago. On the other side of the half mile wide, deep water port, sat Globallus Marine Boat Builders with her wharves and cranes and a warren of green and white work barns where the subs were built to defend tomorrow.

Great decision often required great rationalizations, built in the depths of misperceptions, the heights of hopes, or the foolishness of wishful thinking. Luke experienced a moment like that gazing out his window upon the future.

"I am doomed!" he thought aloud. "Unless I can get away with it."

seventeen

YOUNG EYES

Monday 1000

The world is sub happy. Thailand, Philippines, Vietnam and Bangladesh latest powers building littoral defense underwater with pre-owned subs. (Special Pricing This Week Only!) PeepsRepubChina training Bangladesh Navy personnel in Ming class. Kutabdie Island site of new base with 3 subs in water within 12 months. —SpyhakrF

The young man called Tad weaved his way against the traffic on Bank Street in New London heading south out of the center city on the bike he had "found" the month before. He had become a familiar face along the narrow roadway that had recently gone to one lane so the city fathers could proudly brag about the new bike lane. No one seemed to care except the folks in cars who had to slow down even more than before to navigate passed those parked on both sides, the bikers in their own lane and folks who just crossed where they wanted.

Tad waved to the shopkeepers he knew and some shoppers even as he dodged them because he didn't always stay in the bike lane and, in fact, frequently found the sidewalk more to his liking.

Once out of town, he turned left on Howard, then onto Walbach which took him under the railroad tracks and finally the short pedal on East Street to the entrance of Fort Trumbull State Park.

The granite fortress dominated the waterfront from the west side directly across the river from the GMBB boatyard. Built in the 18th century, the fort protected New London from the British, although there were never any shots fired. The British Navy coveted the deep waters of the Thames River. It wasn't until after the War of 1812 they were finally convinced this land was now America and they were not wanted.

The first home of the US Coast Guard Academy, the imposing structure now provided the citizens of the region a wide open hillside to picnic with a view of the river traffic, to enjoy a day of fishing from the pier as well as offering one of the best vantage points for the annual Sailfest Fireworks display celebrating Independence Day.

It was also a great spot for Tad to read his weekly adventure story acquired from Sarges' Comics on State Street, and count the submarines sitting at the 13 docks available in the GMBB yard.

And if he was lucky, he would catch the subs moving up and down the river to the Navy Sub Base New London positioned conveniently just 2.7 miles up-river from where they were built. He would count them as well when they steamed through.

"I'll pay you 25 dollars a week to do this," said the

gray bearded man in the green windbreaker and the snap brimmed beret who approached Tad while he was fishing off the pier one spring afternoon. He left him a card with an email address and a $50 bill. VCHEN@gmail.com it read.

"Once a week, no more than twice," he said. "It's for an environmental study my group is doing."

"$25 a week, once or twice?" Tad clarified. That was good money for an unemployed 19-year-old without a driver's license and no hopes visible in his immediate future.

"Sure. One payment, in cash. You go fishing say Monday and Thursday. That simple. Count the boats you see, send me a text message before you leave. You'll be helping our study and your country."

That was two months ago and since then the cash had arrived by mail in an unmarked envelope on Wednesdays like clockwork and he had sent his texts each day he counted boats. Sometimes he sent two texts if there was more activity.

Tad felt good about what he was doing. He was told he was part of a nationwide effort to count boats. They were part of solving the "pollution problem". There was a team of folks like him at "all the big rivers and harbors" the man had said. And the money was good because it kept him in comic books all week.

It was easy and pretty boring for the first several weeks, but Tad noticed one day that three submarines had sailed into the river on the same day and there were already three in docks. That was a busy day.

On this particular Monday in June, Tad noticed a tug heading south to the mouth of the river as he sat on a bench and opened his latest edition of "Son of Batman". That usually meant a sub was coming in. Another tug was opening a gate to the lagoon by the southernmost pier, something he had never seen happen during his short tenure as a "green watchdog".

He counted seven boats in the morning, but two left before lunch time. And another came up river, making a total of six at the docks. He made his notes on a sheet of paper and stuck it in the back of his comic. He sent his text that afternoon and wondered what was going on in the world.

The last time the river had seen that many subs moving was a mass exodus from the sub base the week after the 9/11 terrorist attacks on New York City and Washington, DC.

eighteen

TCSAPB-24

Monday 1030

Space Spy vs. Space Spy. French accuse Russians of spying against French-Italian comm satellite with a Luch-Olymp satellite. "It passed by very close attempting to intercept signals," says French Defence official. Source say French building laser weapon to shoot down nosey satellites. Nearly $.75BEuro on Space Defence. Not in Kansas anymore, Dorothy! —SpyhakrF

Meanwhile, across the river, Luke Parmelian wasn't counting subs. He was counting on routine to accomplish his pending task.

"Morning, Mr. Bond," Luke laughed as he greeted his friend Antoine behind the security counter at GMBB's main entrance. He slid one of the paper coffee cups he carried toward Antoine, who grabbed it smoothly as he did pretty much every morning.

"Thank you, N. That's N for Nerd! What's the

password?" Antoine smiled as he flipped the top off and took a healthy sip.

Antoine was a James Bond freak. He knew the movies, knew the dialog and they liked to play a two-sentence game. If one starts the other finishes with some Bond movie trivia or note.

"Moneypenny," Luke responded as he passed his badge under the security scanner followed by the familiar chirp of acceptance.

"Ocean Pony tonight?" Antoine asked, hoping they would grab a drink at their favorite tavern down river. "Sox on at 7:05."

"I don't think so tonight, Antoine. I'll "C" you on the way out."

Luke flashed him a smile as if, "got the last one in!" and walked out of the Security building, down the newly enclosed walkway that crossed the lawn to the ten-story admin building at the South end of the yard. The angle of the walkway was such that in the winter the Northwest breezes would whip right across the river and up the lawn making the 75 yard walk a bone chilling affair.

Enough to get the attention of the new CEO of GMBB who had to make the same walk and the glass enclosure was quickly installed, keeping the admin workers out of the elements. A small concession from management that all appreciated.

The other workers who entered with Luke went down another path off to the right towards the main work complex by the docks. Those guys and girls were tougher, being the welders, pipe fitters and construction engineers who actually got their fingernails dirty building the 7000-ton steel wrapped floating bomb carriers.

Luke glanced around the yard, relishing in the same view he had seen for several weeks now. The yard was busy.

The *USS Chorlton* was partially visible sticking out of the North Barn, scheduled to return to patrol that week. The other boats in for their refitting of the new SLACLONET system were berthed at various angles, taking up more than half the docks available.

Everyone was off to work and the only thing missing was Snow White and the Seven Dwarfs singing their way down the path.

Luke's office was on the first floor. The bottom floor actually. He considered it the basement. No windows, just three cubicles in a 20 x 20 room with two other Information System Technicians, or ISTs, sharing the space. Matt and Sheila were already at their workstations.

His boss, Dave Frezooly, the Chief Information System Technician or CIST, worked out of an office at the end of the room. Luke could see him behind the glass door. His office had a small window, about four feet up from the floor that looked at the HVAC equipment for the whole building in a small courtyard accessible down the hallway near the rest rooms.

"Morning, Luke," Sheila greeted him with a tip of her coffee cup. He nodded in return and slipped into the comfortable chair in front of his workstation. He turned on the two 30-inch screens and booted up both his computers under the desk, stashed his small computer bag in the corner and sat back, watching the green lines of text begin to appear.

"Have a good weekend, Luke?" came Sheila's voice from behind the cubical wall, followed by her head appearing as she slid around on her chair.

She was a small, thin woman with black hair and fine features and an oversized pair of glasses tilted back on her head.

"Saw Rene' yesterday," she said seriously looking into

her coffee cup. She enjoyed the morning ritual of gossip and gab, often not caring who was listening. "She looked a little tired. Have you been riding her hard and putting her away wet?! Ha!"

She laughed and Luke could hear Matt laughing on the other side from his cubical. They had been teasing him mercilessly about Rene' for several weeks.

"Hey, easy, Sheels!" Luke responded with a look of feigned disgust on his face.

"Come to think of it, you look a bit ragged yourself, Lukey boy!" She persisted. Mark laughed louder.

Luke gave her another serious look, then shook his head.

"The Red Sox lost again. We're all taking it pretty hard."

Sheila laughed as Luke turned away. Then he looked back.

"Did she say anything?" he asked, trying not to sound too concerned. Inside, he feared the worst that she had spilled the story of their weekend adventure.

"No, I just waved to her across the aisle. She was buying veggies."

Life back to normal for a moment? Luke wondered, then turned his attention to his desk.

He unlocked his security drawer with a three-digit combo and pulled out a plain brown folder with the GMBB logo. An atom with a constellation of electrons flying around the nucleus and a bolt of lightning piercing the center. The company may be under new ownership, Luke thought, but it carried on the century old traditions of its original owner, who started the whole thing by putting electric engines in little luxury boats for pastoral Sunday afternoons on a quiet lake.

Luke opened the folder, found the eight-digit number for the date and entered it into his righthand computer. In five-seconds, the computer returned a twelve-digit line of asterisks which Luke copied and pasted onto his second screen on the left in a small blinking window in the lower corner.

Ten-seconds later, both screens flashed the GMBB logo and then the home screen for the GMBB Information Systems department popped up and displayed the agenda for Monday's work load.

Luke did a quick scan and found what he was looking for. A third of the way down the list, between replacing two printers in the payroll department and a new employee change of passwords for the marketing office was a line item that read:

TI-32 update. TCSAPB-24.

Just as he expected, the weekly routine was exactly that. Routine. Software and informational updates on the Technology Insertions number 32 for the Tactical Control System under the Advanced Processing Build number 24. Luke knew that was the SLACLONET 1000 laser comm installation project. GMBB was up to its eyeballs in retrofitting the new system into the Navy's Virginia class attack subs.

"Luke! In my office now!" came the cry from Frezooly at the end of the room. "Mark and Sheila. You, too! It's Monday, let's get it rolling!"

The three assembled in their boss's office and he quickly ran down what he hoped they would accomplish today and for the rest of the week. The daily session often turned into a bull and bitch session, but today, no one was in the mood to bitch and moan. The agenda was lengthy, and it appeared that it was to be another week of being understaffed with not enough time to get everything done.

"Luke, payroll is driving me static about those printers you supposedly fixed last week. So, replace them with brand new ones," Frezooly ordered.

"Mark, I want you to do the TI updates in the Loops Building. We've got 6 subs in port right now and they need to be out of here ASAP. They need the digital tablets updated before they can go forward."

"Really? I hate dealing with that Dr. Andy. He's such a stickler for detail, procedure...precision!" Mark complained.

"Mark, he's dealing with lasers," Sheila jumped in with a big laugh. "I suspect precision is a part of the job!"

"He drives me crazy. And he's a low talker, you know?"

"Boss, I'll do the Loops building," Luke interjected. He turned to Mark with a big grin. "Mark, why don't you go see Harriet in payroll and get those printers working. I know she'll be happy to see you and we'll all be happy to get a paycheck this week."

"Yea, that's good for me!" Mark said.

"Jiggle a wire or two," Sheila joked.

Frezooly nodded agreement then added, "Sheila, you keep working on the new email protocol for compliance. The tenth floor wants it ready for review by Friday before they install it system wide."

"I'm on it."

"And folks, remember, I'll be gone Tuesday through Thursday at the Cyber Security Conference in DC," Frezooly finished.

"Midweek vacation, boss?" laughed Luke.

"Right! Two days of gobbly-gook and hacker-speak. It's a whole new military-industrial, secret society, cyber-sanctity psycho world! It's keeping me in the game, I guess."

"Total game," Mark added as he grabbed two printers from the stack next to Frezooly's desk. The meeting broke up and the three walked out of the office and back to their workstations.

Luke locked up the security folder in his desk after grabbing the security dongle he needed to get into the

Loops Building computers. He threw his Password Manager manual into his bag and left the building.

Building submarines takes a few million manhours from design to launch for each one. The first one floated into the Thames River in 1943. Over 200 had been built since and the boatyard that spread out before Luke today was as busy as ever.

In the last few years, a dramatic change in production techniques had set a new era in motion. Called COTS in the acronym world of conglomerate-speak, the letters stood for Commercial-Off-The-Shelf. While subs were still built from the keel up, the parts were built by thousands of outside contractors, delivered to the boatyard and assembled.

It usually took a year to finish a modern sub and the process kept 8,000 workers busy around the clock at GMBB. Luke never ceased to be amazed by the numbers. At 7000 tons, they were the most sophisticated vessels in the world, able to travel around 30 knots, at 800 feet deep and more, filled with sensors and weapons that could detect enemy ships, torpedoes to send those ships to the bottom and literally enough nuclear firepower to turn the earth to radioactive dust.

Plus, the cruise missiles that had shifted emphasis from first strike nuclear annihilation to coastline defense and pinpoint target elimination without dusting the rest of the world.

And now TCSAPB-24 had come along and the work load increased. The new laser communications system had been approved and the boats were returning ahead of their normal repair and retrofit schedules for a two-week installation.

That work was happening with a crew of 20 men and 4 women who had set up shop in the Loops Building, right next to the South Barn right on the river. The building could hold two subs floating side by side or on a dry dock lifted out of the water. Each boat went inside for one of their two-week scheduled stay.

The rest of the time was spent fine tuning the lasers at dockside. All of this with the crew of a 135 or so sailors hanging around. That put over 700 extra sailors in the area, which was good for the local bars but not so good for traffic around the docks.

The new addition to the Tactical Controls System involved modifications to the LPPM, or Low Profile Periscope Mast, and a super high tech coating of optical receptors that were attached to the front of the sub's sail or what used to be called the conning tower.

Back in the day, the "Conn" where the captain ran the boat was positioned right under the conning tower because that's where the periscope optics were located, a straight tube with glass mirrors. Today, submarines have glass conns, fed by digital sensors through fiber optics. Command and control are positioned further aft behind the sail. X-box controllers manipulate the information on multiple flat screen TV monitors. The sub maneuvers at the hands of a young crew brought up on video games. And the savings were in the millions of dollars, since the Navy could literally buy gear off the shelf.

Luke stepped into the Loops building annex, flashed his security badge at the two guards, then waited for the locked door to open. Access was severely limited here. It was a specifically designed Top Secret Specialized Compartmental Information Facility, called a SCIF. The door buzzed open and Luke entered a cavernous hangar bigger than four football fields sitting side by side, two by two, with a roof 100 feet high. The black hull of the *USS Colorado* floated right in front of him not 30 feet away, blocking his view. Unseen on the other side in its own slip was the *USS New Hampshire*.

On the river side, the dual sets of huge barn doors were closed. Luke knew that armed guards were patrolling outside along the wharf. Not to mention a patrol boat working the river 24 hours a day.

Sparks were flying from the scaffolding encasing the sail of the nearest boat. Three men worked at the top of the catwalks partially obscuring the SSN 788 that identified the 377-foot-long attack sub. The sound of grinding was sporadic and loud as if someone was sanding metal. Luke could see a series of periscope like masts sticking up from the sail, with the attention focused on the most forward device that looked like a telephoto camera lens on top of a foot-wide pole. The front edge of the sail had a shiny tinge to it, as if it had been freshly painted.

Luke allowed a sliver of pride to slip through his chest as he realized he was right in the middle of important work. That sliver quickly went to dust as he contemplated his next move.

He stepped into an office enclosure along the North wall and closed the door, shutting out most of the sound. A man in a white lab coat was sitting at one of the computers in the middle where four desks were crammed together, back to back. Two tables were shoved together in the corner, surrounded by chairs to form an impromptu conference space.

A bulletin board carried the usual OSHA and US Navy notices about safety and security. There was even a poster about an upcoming concert at a local pub. Luke recognized the guitarist as one of the workmen on the project.

Two security cameras mounted high in opposite corners blinked red. Below one was a picture window of thick glass that faced the inside dock. It was filled with the tail section of the *Colorado.*

He saw the familiar line up of blue mobile tablets

plugged into a charging station connected to a separate computer that sat along the far wall. The computer was the server for the LAN that was isolated to only this room. It fed the four computers and the rack of tablets. He noticed ten tablets sat in place plugged in and two chargers sat empty. Everything was hardwired to the computer in the middle where the man in the white coat was working.

"I'm really going to do this," he thought silently. It wasn't a question. It was an affirmation to himself.

Suddenly, the man in the white coat turned from the square of workstations and looked at Luke.

"What!" he shouted, as if Luke had come in to scold him.

"Hello! Dr. Andy!" Luke responded, recognizing the lead guy on the project. He put his hands up as if to show he meant no harm. "I.S.T. here for the updates on the APB - 24. I'm Luke."

Dr. Andrew Standard looked at Luke for a moment, then his badge, assessing him to confirm that either he wasn't in any danger or he was who he said he was.

"Okay, set up over there. The server is on. There's a couple of tabs out in the barn, so you'll have to swap them out. Make sure the new pages on the Los Angeles class are included. We expect to have a couple of those boats in here next week. The master file is marked with tomorrow's date, so don't get confused."

"No, problem, Doc. I got it. Not my first time," Luke responded in a friendly tone. He was kind of pissed that Dr. Andy didn't seem to recognize him from the initial set up session when Luke and Mark had worked directly with him to set up the whole system back when the project began. Or from the dozen other times he had updated the system. Not to mention they were both sailors who raced against each other out on Long Island Sound.

While the actual details of the device were never

discussed, they had talked a lot about how to get the information to the work crews while maintaining security. What was logical, what was possible and what was within the guidelines of corporate policy, all complicated by the sale of the company in the lead up.

It was not like they didn't know each other.

Luke chalked it up to a Brainiac mentality on the part of Dr. Andy. There was clearly a lot on his mind, and he was famous for going deep into his own rabbit hole at times.

The problem with any new installation was determining how to teach workers how exactly it all went together. The days of pulling out hard bound manuals onto the work floor were over. You would be better off standing by your mailbox waiting for a catalog from Sears. That just wasn't going to fly anymore.

The world was digital, even in the boatyard. The 100 gigabits of data that comprised the Operating and Installation Manual for the SLACLONET 1000 were dropped onto a microchip and installed in the dozen off the shelf tablets with hard plastic shells, slip-your-hand-in holders on the back and a protective plastic coating on the screen, with a cover. One tablet for each two-worker team. Flip out keyboards attached. $700 off the shelf from Best Buy. In a world not too long ago, Navy hammers had cost more!

They were using the same tablets NFL coaches used to figure out what defenses to call on the sidelines.

Electronics, optics, metal fittings, fiber cable runs and connections were all explained in detail with pictures, videos and text. Operational procedures and nanophotonic calibration techniques were included. SLACLONET stood for Submarine Laser Communication Low Orbit Network and was part of the growing constellation of low earth orbit satellites that were being launched by the dozens for use by all government agencies, primarily the military.

The work of Dr. Andy, born from the TRIZ methodology through the years, was all on those tablets.

Luke walked over to the rack, sat down at the server and plugged in his dongle that provided access to the file directory. A second layer of protection required a daily password which he read from a card inside a drawer under the server. He easily beat the 30 second countdown between passwords before the computer could lock up. That would require a super password to unlock it. Luke wasn't even sure who had that password today. Probably Dr. Andy.

In a matter of minutes, he found the directories and files needed and began the download that would update the 10 tablets sitting in their chargers. He was pleased with his design of the unit. The tablets were all plugged into a hub connected to the main server in the room and the data flowed quickly and seamlessly. It only took ten minutes.

"So, Dr. Andy," Luke turned to the man busy at his computer. "Shall I go swap the two tablets or...?"

Just then, one of the workers walked in with a tablet in her hand. She nodded at Luke with a friendly smile as she showed Dr. Andy her tablet screen.

"Doc, section 54 here. The c clamps on the orthogonal multiplexer don't fit. We made it work with a d clamp. That a problem?"

Dr. Andy looked at the screen in her hand, then turned to his own larger screen on the desktop and quickly found the section she was worried about. After a moment of study, he nodded.

"Make sure the torque is the same and the vibrational tolerances are less than .5. Let's take a look at the new periscope mast for the New Hampshire and see it that's going to be the same. It's still in the shipping rack on the dock, right? Come on." He logged out of his computer while already on the move and waved at her to follow out the door.

"Ah, Rosanne?" Luke called after the worker. He recognized her from an earlier meeting and could see the name on her badge. "Want to swap tablets? I've just updated this one?"

She hesitated for a moment, knowing full well Dr. Andy didn't like to be kept waiting when he was on a mission. Then she shrugged and handed the tablet in her hand to Luke and took the new one.

"I'll sign you out for number seven, right? Number four in," Luke smiled.

"Thanks!" she nodded, turned and left.

Luke took the tablet from her and as he turned to the bank of recharging tablets, he deftly flipped open the fold down key board on the back revealing the microchip slot in the tablet. He pushed slightly on the partially exposed chip with his fingernail, causing it to spring outward so he could slide it from the tablet into his palm. With his right hand, he grabbed the USB cable in the docking bay and plugged it into its connection. Simultaneously he slipped a new microchip from between his fingers and pushed it into the vacated slot, flipped down the keyboard and settled the tablet into its cradle.

His body blocked the two cameras blinking in opposite corners. He was pleased he had manipulated the two chips in one hand and felt a sense of relief as he slipped back into his computer chair and repeated the keystrokes to update the new tablet. He casually removed a folder from his bag, letting the chip he had removed from the tablet fall between the pages of the manual at the bottom.

A moment later Dr. Andy returned with another tablet, the final one that needed updating, and handed it over to him.

"Last one," Dr. Andy smiled in relief. "They will all be in use tomorrow! We have a busy day coming."

Luke plugged the last tablet in and repeated the update process. A few moments later, as he grabbed his bag to leave, Dr. Andy suddenly asked Luke if he was racing that weekend in the Off Soundings regatta on Block Island.

"Ah, can't do Friday, but maybe Saturday. Have to work, but you should have decent conditions from what I've seen."

"Hey, it's only Monday, I haven't even looked at the weather. Good luck, we'll probably see you out there."

Luke smiled to himself, strangely satisfied that Dr. Andy apparently did remember him.

"See ya."

The project leader never looked up, already lost in his computer screen. Luke left the office walking through the Loops building security shack with a wave to the guard. His heart was beating pretty good as he strode up the hill heading for the marketing office and his next assignment. The microchip was near weightless but, it burned a hole in his mind as it sat benignly in the bottom of his computer bag stuck between the pages of the Administration Password Master manual. He expected a shout from someone, calling him back, but none came.

nineteen

AFTER GLOW

Friday 1130

Petrika felt a slight draft on her cheek and opened her eyes to see the man who smelled like earth an inch away from her. He was lightly blowing on her face, his eyes wide open. His name was Luke and she had just shared a true moment of passion with him.

"Did you fuck me to sleep?" she asked quietly and then broke out in a happy laugh.

"I've heard it called 'petite mort'," Luke responded with a smile. He kissed her and they held it long and soft, then slowly nibbled their way apart. He couldn't believe how wonderful she felt to his touch and how she had taken his mind to another level.

She sat up, her hand over his on her naked thigh. She felt his wetness on her belly and playfully ran her fingers through it, then brought them up to his mouth. She kissed him with her fingers between their lips and inhaled deeply one last moment of passionate freedom.

"Wow, you are something!" Luke said when they parted.

"You died too!" she laughed, spreading his release over

her. Then she pulled up her panties and bike shorts and pulled her Billy Joel t-shirt down over her breasts.

"We never got to my bra!" she laughed again, realizing it was still clasped. She was giggly like a little girl, still glowing from their passionate embrace, wallowing in the release. So much better than the self-play when she awoke this morning. Their lovemaking had been real, on a shared wavelength. She wanted to keep going.

She reached over and picked up his jeans lying in a pile on the cement floor. She handed them to him with one hand, while reached down to touch his groin with her other, fondling him briefly, enjoying one last touch before they were covered up.

Luke slowly wiggled into his pants, still on the sleeping bag they had completely abused for their lovemaking. He couldn't take his eyes off her as she wandered in a little circle, her hips moving ever so slightly as if tuned to a song in her head. She ran her hands on the stone walls and then returned to the small camp stool where she had first sat down.

Luke's mind was laser focused by her physicality and he was only thinking of the next second. He didn't have a past beyond meeting her, he didn't have a future without her. He felt as if in a trance, at the most forward edge of his life. Whatever he thought was going to happen before, he didn't care now. He was only going forward with her.

"Who else knows you are here?" she asked innocently.

twenty

WHAT HAS LUKE
WROUGHT?

Mon 1800

*Open sources reveal Chinese technology developed
with US tech giants for passive surveillance on
grand scale. Suitcase sized device can record all cell
chat & text within 2 miles. Deployment active in
MENA dictator nations. Saudi Arabia, Morocco
and Sudan among users. OpenPower Foundation
denies direct involvement. Careful what you say.
They are listening. –SpyhakrF*

Luke's Jeep was parked three blocks up the hill from the
main exit gate at GMBB and he felt like he was walking
in mud to get there. He fully understood that much of
the strength of the security system at the boat yard was
centered on the belief that the folks who worked there were
not traitors.

That's why the vetting process to secure a gate pass

included a 127-page background application and a multi-month process of review by the FBI and other government agencies. Not to mention the security force at the yard whose simple presence kept the concept of security on the front burner.

The biggest fear among all security chiefs is the simple moment when someone with a clearance violates that trust. Passwords be dammed, we're in! And there was a ton of violation weighing on Luke's mind as he slipped into his car, laid his computer bag on the seat and drove home across the river to his condo in New London.

He couldn't help but check the rearview mirror every few seconds and imagined the winged devil of guilt about to appear and carry him off the Gold Star Bridge that spanned the Thames River. By the time he got home and shut the engine off on the third floor of his building's parking garage he was fighting panic because the chip was so small, smaller than his thumb nail, he kept forgetting where he had stashed it!

He was a mess.

"What am I worrying about," he thought and laughed to himself. "I'm good. I'm out. No one knows."

He stuck the key in his door, turned the lock and pushed, realizing in a millisecond that the lock turned really easy because it wasn't actually locked. Too late. As he swung open the door in one routine motion, he saw someone was in his condo.

Sitting right in his easy chair, facing the door, dressed in a worn leather jacket, a cowboy hat with a sharply curled brim, pointy toed boots and a Hurley stick casually laying across his knees was the enforcer.

"Maverick!" Luke blurted out and froze with his hand on the door knob. "Whiskey Tango Foxtrot!"

"Lukey Lucky Boy, good afternoon!" James Michael

Joseph McSamarlie boomed. "Come, sit down and join me!"
He gestured to the couch with his Hurley, all friendly like
except the stick immediately triggered the pains in Luke's
arm, back and leg.

"I thought I had 'til Wednesday," Luke said as he closed
the door and slipped onto the couch. McSamarlie tapped
Luke's knee with the Hurley, still all friendly like. Luke slide
another foot away, out of reach.

"Well, that was the deal with Misha, yes it was, but I
figured if you had the chance, I'd take the chance that you
have it for me today." McSamarlie gave him a big smile.

"I don't have it," Luke lied, trying to sound casual. "The
moment wasn't right."

"Well, that's a shame, isn't it?"

"I thought I made the deal with Misha. What are you
here for?"

"Luke, I am *Lagooshka's* main man. Dealing with me is
just like dealing with Misha."

"Except for that frigging stick! What the hell, man!"

Luke sized him up and thought he could take him. He
saw the cowboy's arms and shoulders were big. Probably a
weight lifter, he thought. But, Luke had maybe an inch or
two on him, maybe 15 pounds. Plus 10 years younger, at
least. but that damn stick made it tough to get close enough
to land a punch or two.

"You don't like the stick, Luke? Maybe you want to take
this to the ring, some bare-knuckle bravery?" McSamarlie
got up and pressed the stick toward Luke's chest. Luke
pushed it away with his right hand, but McSamarlie kept
coming.

Another thrust and the Hurley connected right to the
breastbone, already bruised from their one-way altercation
on Saturday night in Brighton Beach. Luke fought back.
He pushed off the couch and stood up, then grabbed the

stick with his left hand as McSamarlie pressed it toward him. Pulling on the Hurley brought McSamarlie closer and Luke cocked his right hand for a big haymaker aimed at the left side of the Irishman's face. It connected and drove him backward, his cowboy hat flying off his head.

McSamarlie responded quickly, built on the momentum from Luke's punch and spun around to his right, pulled the Hurley out of Luke's hand and swung it in an arc clockwise, like a left-handed batter, smashing it into Luke's right shoulder.

"Aaagghhh!" Luke moaned taking the full force of the flat end. The blow sent him stumbling onto the couch but, he kept moving forward, used his hands to fend off and rolled back upright on his feet. He backpedaled and McSamarlie came after him with the Hurley.

"All right, hold it!" Luke held up his arms as if surrendering.

"Not in the face, man! I still got to look good for work!"

McSamarlie stopped his advance with the stick poised to smash into Luke again.

"Well, maybe a whack in the balls will keep you thinking right!" he said and moved a step closer, the Hurley poised. And then his cell phone went off.

"Whooo. Whooo. Whooo."

The digital sound of an owl hooting, thought Luke, as he took another step back, keeping his eye on the Hurley.

McSamarlie held the stick up, warning Luke not to move.

"I have to take this," he said. "You stand there and keep your mouth shut!"

He reached into his pocket, looked at the caller ID and rolled his eyes.

"Sheeett!"

"Yes, I'm here." He spoke into the phone, his eyes on Luke, the Hurley pointed at his chest.

"No, not yet," McSamarlie shook his head after a moment. Luke detected a hint of impatience, not with him but with the phone call. Suddenly, McSamarlie handed him the phone.

"Misha would like to speak to you."

"Misha? Jeez. Hello?"

"Mr. Luke, how are you today? Are we on schedule?" The Russian mobster sounded cheery as if they were ready to go golfing.

"Ah, Misha, ah, I don't have it yet. Tomorrow I expect things to work out."

"Good, good! I'm delighted you are helping me, Mr. Luke."

"Yea, well, delighted is not a word I would use right now. You man here is a nut case and you need to call him off!" Luke surprised himself but, he figured he still had some standing at least until he delivered the file.

"Luke, I apologize if Mr. J has misbehaved. You understand, I cannot have you misinterpreting how serious is the situation. You owe me and I expect you to deliver by Wednesday. That is clear, yes?"

Luke said nothing. He felt angry, rebellious and hopeless, all at the same time. He looked at McSamarlie who stared back with a confident grin on his lips. He heard Misha's faint breathing in his ear. He thought, if he had a gun, he would shoot the Irish cowboy in the face, something he never thought he could do before today. And he wished he could melt the mean little man breathing in his ear on the phone.

But, he couldn't.

"Luke?" came the questioning voice of Misha on the line, as if he had any other choice.

"Yes, it's clear," he said finally.

"Excellent, my friend! Then, it is settled. We shall meet

on Wednesday at noon at the New Haven train station. I will be there personally to see you. Have the package and we will be square."

"New Haven?" Luke asked. It was a 40-minute ride from New London, but as good a place as any to hide in a crowd.

"It is almost halfway, yes?" Misha responded. "I will wear a Yankees cap and you will bring me the package. Now, I would like to speak to my man."

Luke handed the phone to McSamarlie. "He says get the hell out of here! Leave me alone, let me get the job done I promised!"

McSamarlie laughed and flipped him the bird as he took the phone and turned away into the open kitchen.

Luke moved quickly to his bedroom right off the living room and into his closet, rummaging in the far corner next to his golf bag. He found what he was looking for and returned to the living room.

McSamarlie got off the phone with Misha and looked up to see Luke standing quietly in the middle of the living room with a baseball bat over his shoulder. The Irishman took a step forward, his Hurley resting on his own shoulder but, he stopped about six feet in front of Luke and smiled at the younger man.

"Okay, you want to go knuckle to knuckle, fist to fist, stick to stick?"

Luke shook his head and stood his ground.

"My dad gave me this souvenir a hundred years ago it seems. It's a Jackie Robinson special from Spaulding. A toy, really, but the wood is real. I'd just like you to know that if you want go, the next time it should be a fair fight."

McSamarlie slowly lower the Hurley to his side in a non-aggressive movement, and walked right up to Luke, who did not move.

"Okay, Lucky Lukey. I hear you. I see you. Cool your

jets...or your bats...until Wednesday. Get the file and then we will worry about how this little thing plays out between us two." He paused for effect. "I'd suggest you bring more than the Little League!"

He laughed and waggled his finger between them and then tapped his Hurley on the floor with a thunk. Then he turned and walked toward the door where he stopped and looked back at Luke before he walked out.

"Rene' lives nearby, doesn't she?" He gave Luke another smile, saluted with his Hurley and closed the door behind him.

Luke stood there and watched him go. The bruises on his body fueled his anger, as did the mention of Rene's name but, he kept it inside, happy McSamarlie was gone. For the moment.

Luke collapsed into his easy chair, the weight of his world crushing him deep into its cushions. After a moment, he reached into his sock and pulled out the microchip. He held it up between his fingertips and tried to come to grips with what he had done. And what he was going to do.

twenty-one

Nipom Breach

Monday 1900

Smuggled photos reveal frienemies play nice with Syrian battle lines drawn in gold. Pro regime Russian ISR UAV shot down in Syria by Israelis was actually designed by Israel. Meanwhile, Russia turns its back on Israeli attacks against Iranian backed pro-Syrian forces. Who's your daddy? –SpyhakrF

Dr. Andy almost missed it. The metadata were part of the usual scenery he scanned during his end of shift review of the computer activity of the day. Lines of code and file info that clarified what had happened when humans sat down to work the keyboard and execute the software that controlled the actions of the computerized process. Much of it was complex, most of it mundane. A perfectionist by nature and bearing the full weight of the project, he did the work. And he rarely missed any of it.

The dates didn't match up.

The files that comprised the Operational Manual and Installation Guide of the SLACLONET 1000 stored on the

12 blue tablets were all modified that afternoon by the technician with user name "lukep" from IST. However, while tablet number four indicated the proper date for "Last Modified", it showed the same date for "Creation". Both dates were today.

"That's not right," Dr. Andy said out loud to himself. He was alone in the Loops Building office, looking forward to getting home after a 12-hour day.

He knew the files were created originally on the microchips a month ago, uploaded for the first time to each tablet. He had loaded them himself. He quickly rechecked the directories of the other 11 tablets and found the different but correct date of creation from last month and today's date for modified. Tablet number four showed the same date for creation and modified.

The only way that could happen, he knew, was if the update earlier in the day was loaded onto a new chip. A blank chip. A chip that was reading the files for the first time. A quick cross reference of serial numbers from GMBB inventory control confirmed the fact the microchip in Tablet Four was not the one originally assigned. In fact, was not even listed from GMBB inventory.

"That son of a bitch!" Dr. Andy whistled. He picked up the phone and dialed the direct line to Security Chief Ben Canfield. The call went directly to voice mail and he left a message.

"Ben, this is Dr. Standord in the Loops. I need to speak to you as soon as possible. I have a procedural breach."

He hung up the phone and sat back in his chair, surveying the room. There was a bottle of wine and a dear friend he had not seen in several days waiting for him with dinner at her home. There were two submarines floating outside his office waiting to rejoin the fleet. And a third on Dock A scheduled to ship out on Friday. And three more waiting to begin their refit. Now this monkey wrench, the size of a thumbnail, was dropped into his daily challenge of balancing his life with his labor.

The red blink of one of the cameras in the corner of the office caught his eye and he pushed back from the desk, realizing the wine would have to wait. He walked out to the security desk and nodded to the guard.

"Prescott," he read off the guard's nameplate. "We have a problem."

twenty-two

Runaway

Tuesday 0700

After a nightly bender Luke enjoyed nothing better than a tasty andouille sausage scramble prepared with tomatoes, onions and smoked gouda, all served up by Doreen at The No Yolk Cafe in New London. Owner, head chef and renown marshmallow marksman, Doreen reigned supreme six mornings a week with generous portions, a constant vibe of chatter often served with a cacophony of chaos. The crowd was a mix of students from nearby Mitchell College, lineman from the county, lusters lost in love and loners looking for a friendly face and a hot cup of coffee.

If Doreen wasn't shooting you with tiny marshmallows from her pipe gun, then Teresa and Cindy were pouring the black elixir and making sure you got what you wanted. As long as you ate what you ordered. On the warm days, the friendly atmosphere spilled onto the sidewalk where a half dozen tables accommodated twice the crowd – plus a dog or two.

A short dozen offerings were written on the specials board and a surprising selection of Australian wine was available for breakfast or lunch. Unique bottles that literally told a story when you scanned the bottle with the right app on your phone.

On this particular Tuesday morning, the crowd was thin, and Luke was one of the loners. He sat at the counter pushing his eggs around his plate aimlessly, lost in a rum induced fog, coupled with a sizable headache and the soul crushing expectation that he was not handling his current situation very well. He had already called in sick at work and three phone calls back from work had gone unanswered. After the third, he silenced his phone.

McSamarlie's appearance at his condo the night before spooked him. The gravity of his problem was just taking hold. He was fearful that the world was about to fall in on him. What started out as a calming pour from his rum locker after McSamarlie left, turned into a need for a bar crawling binge. He packed an overnight bag, a small cooler, his laptop, the bat and left his home without a destination in mind.

He drove north to Norwich but couldn't get past the Harp and Dragon in the center of town. Two drinks later he was back on the road and worked his way back south and west, stopping at the Rustic Cafe in Lyme. Every drink came with glances over his shoulder. A couple of more stops at local joints along Route One did not help to quell the paranoia and at last call there was only one place left — a commuter lot where he spent the night, curled up in the back seat of his jeep alongside I-95.

He slipped into Doreen's early to talk, in hopes of finding some plan for his immediate future in a plate of eggs.

"Tortola is my dream right now," Doreen was saying. "Wanna sit on the beach by Sebastian's, see if the Bomba Shack is still standing and just devour a book or two and a few bottles of rum." She never paused in her cooking, flipping a pair of eggs expertly on top of extra crispy hash browns. Her hands moved quickly as she dolloped a big glob of butter into a bowl of grits and deftly swept the plates off the stove and onto the counter behind her.

"Terry, two's up!"

"And then there's Mexico, just outside of Cancun. Love the waves there. Good veggie meals, a sweet little hotel on the beach and Tequila. Love the Tequila."

Luke poked at his sausage and smiled. She suddenly turned to him and got right up in his face.

"I'm thinking I should just close the place up. Take off. Sit down my spatula and say now is the time for you, Doreen! Ha! How'd that go over in the summertime! Maybe Thailand? Love what I know about Thailand!"

"I'm looking for the same thing. To get away," he said wistfully.

"Then come with me!" she laughed as carefree as a wisp of wind. She turned to her grill and cracked two more eggs and shoved the potatoes around a bit. A handful of onions appeared from a bowl and some seasoning.

"No, I was thinking more of a cave. Someplace to lay low."

"You mean a hideout?"

"Yea, I guess that. Hide out." Luke looked around nervously. The two college girls at the far end of the counter were busy chatting and seemed not to hear him. Doreen moved back in close.

"What are you running from, Luke?" Her tone suddenly serious, as if she were a counselor and a session had begun. "Who?" she added with a tilt of her eyebrows.

He just shook his head and poked at his eggs. "Nothing. Stuff."

"Stuff? Ha!" she said skeptically. "Well, we all got stuff!"

They went quiet and she focused on her grill. Terry grabbed the two plates and hurried them off to a booth on the other side of the counter. The local radio station played the hits of the 80's and Cindy brought over a stack of clean plates, setting them down next to the stove. She gave Luke a smile and went to attend to the coffee maker.

"Hey, did you hear what they are doing to the Southeast Light at Block?" Doreen sudden opened up again. "They're moving the damn thing again! Moved the damn thing another 200 yards back from the cliffs! The damn thing was gonna fall into the ocean if it stood there much longer. Climate change or erosion, maybe those big storms last winter, waves from the Southeast smashing the cliffs. Hell, the island is getting smaller and the damn light was getting closer to the edge. Amazing, moving that brick thing. It must be 100 years old. Older! They just put it on tracks and moved it back! Amazing!"

"I know the light. Historic. Great views. What's going to happen to it now?" Luke had sailed around the island many times over the years. One night during a race, his sailboat tangled a spinnaker during a gybe right on the Southeast corner. While the crew battled with the flapping sail, the green light of the lighthouse swept the chaos on board in an eerie glow. The incident lasted only 15 minutes or so before they got control of the sail, but it had become an indelible memory, not to mention a must tell story when the booze broke out under the party tent after regattas.

"Nothing right now. Funding dried up, so it's sitting on stilts and rails right now. Doesn't look like much going to happen this year, but hopefully, they'll reopen the museum or something next season or maybe in two years," she explained. "But I'll tell you something."

She looked around, making a big deal as if what she was about to reveal was top secret.

"You wanna hide?" She moved close to him again.

"There's a sub-basement under where the original

lighthouse stood. Covered with wood and dirt now. You know Jennifer Reston? Used to run Landmarks in New London? She's running the foundation that is restoring the whole thing over there. She's a regular. Told me all about it."

"A sub-basement. Like a root cellar or bomb shelter?" Luke's curiosity was tweaked.

"Yea, I guess. The thing is 150 years old, I bet. 1875, I think. Who knows what they put in there?"

She got close enough to whisper. "Here's the thing. I bet you could hideout in that cellar and no one would know you were there. Hell, no one is allowed on the property now, so you could make it your own. Maybe bring in some carpet, a little stove, a camp bed." She was smiling big now.

"As long as you don't mind the dirt, dark and damp." Luke laughed. "Maybe some rat poison? Tortola sounds better," he said.

Doreen laughed out loud. "Yes, it does, my dear. Bring on the rum!"

Luke threw a twenty on the counter, adjusted his hat and got up to leave with a big smile on his face.

"What's going to happen to the light now?" he asked.

"Jennifer says they've run out of money," Doreen shook her head while shifting potatoes on the grill. "Work is at a dead stop. She's beating the bushes for funds, but this summer looks like a quiet one. Too damn bad!"

A visit to Doreen's always made him feel better. Even if just a little bit. He took a breath and switched gears to deal with his current problem.

"Luke, honey. Remember," Doreen looked at him over the high counter next to the grill by the doorway, covered in toys collected over the years. He wondered if they were gifts or items Doreen went looking for.

"You can't hide out forever." She waved her spatula at

him for emphasis. "Whatever or whomever you are running from."

"I know, Dor'. See you next time."

Luke drove the few blocks down to the Thames River and turned left toward the center of New London. He followed Bank Street, around the central square and passed the train station. He could see the cars lined up for the ferry to Long Island right next door. And next to it was the high-speed ferry to Block Island. Just like that, he knew what he had to do.

twenty-three

ANTOINE TAKES POINT

Tuesday 1200

GMBB abuzz with security breach. NCIS initiate investigation with security office at sub maker. Tech specs involved on top secret equipment. Subs being called back for refit at record rate. Somebody's got some splaining to do! –SpyhakrF

Antoine Barstow's knee jerk reaction to bust out of work after meeting with the NCIS agents at mid-morning on Tuesday was driven as much by his concern for his friend Luke as it was by his desire to have any excuse to see Rene'.

Luke and he had bonded over a friendly chat one day a few years back when both were new to the sub building icon of America's military industrial complex. A spilt cup of coffee at the main gate started it all and the two of them found they liked the same things when Luke showed up with a make good cup the next day.

Pretty soon they were facing off with each other on the basketball court, sharing season tickets at Coast Guard academy football games and raising stakes at the friendly poker games that became a Saturday night ritual at Luke's condo in New London.

Antoine soon learned they also shared an interest in Rene'. He had hovered on the periphery in their circle of friends, loyal to his buddy, but never lost sight that he was ready to take Rene' to that magical land of 'more than friends'. Yea, he was hot for her and, being the dreamer type, never let the hope die. Even as he stood quietly watching Luke woo her right into that place he wanted to be. Or was it her wooing him? Didn't matter. He wasn't going there. Unless given the chance.

So, Antoine was more than a little distracted and conflicted when he swung by Luke's only to find no one home and then went to Rene's to figure out what Luke was up to. If anything! He was taken aback when he saw the guy with the stick from Misha's real House of Cards striding out of Rene's apartment building just as he pulled into a parking spot in the complex's lot.

McSamarlie drove away in a late model blue Corvette as Antoine hunkered down in his seat watching in the rearview mirror.

"Whiskey Tango Foxtrot!" he muttered. "What is she doing?"

When the Corvette was out of sight, Antoine ran up to her door and rang the doorbell. He repeated it twice more before he heard the lock click and the door opened. Rene' stood there in a bathrobe with a towel on her head, obviously just out of the shower.

"Antoine!" she greeted him with surprise and a smile. "Come on in!"

She closed the door behind him and rushed past, holding her hand up as if to say, 'wait one minute'. He watched her trot off in the flowing robe only to return three minutes later in a colorful blouse and shorts. She walked right up to him and gave him a big hug.

"Look at you in that spiffy uniform. So good to see you!" she gushed, pressing her body against him. For a split-second Antoine forgot why he was there.

"Where's Luke?" he finally asked. "They're looking for him at work! He's in trouble!"

"Luke the drunk, you mean?" Rene' responded in mock surprise. "Why who would've believed!"

They sat next to each other on her couch. Rene' seemed genuinely pleased to see Antoine. She certainly was comfortable sitting with him while she ran a towel through her still wet hair.

"Have you seen him? Talked to him? He's not home and not answering his phone," Antoine asked her again.

"Not since Saturday morning," she answered. She stopped drying her hair and sighed. "Probably the last time."

"What happened?"

"We went to Brooklyn to play some cards, walk the boardwalk, see Coney Island. We drank, we played. He got tanked up and lost. I won. Ha! Then things went a bit sideways...," her voice trailed off.

"Sideways? You went to Misha's House of Cards? Then, that is the guy from Misha's I saw coming out of here?"

She looked at him, shrugged her shoulders and nodded. "Yep, that's him. Uncle JMJ from Faraway. We hooked up Friday night and he showed up last night by surprise." She smiled sheepishly, batted her eyes and sighed again.

"Oh, Rene'! Does Luke know?"

"Shit, yes, he knows! At least about Friday. Well, he fucked up! He got all goofy and went down a deep hole with those thugs. I think he's probably still in the hole a bunch and he has to deliver this week."

"How much?"

"I don't know. A hundred, 120."

"A hundred twenty-thousand dollars!" Antoine was shocked.

Rene' nodded slowly.

"And you hooked up with the bouncer?!"

She nodded again and couldn't hold back a smile creeping onto her lips. "What can I say, things got a bit... sideways. I think they're mobbed up or something. But, he's nice."

Antoine stood up and started pacing around the room.

"What was the guy with the stick, that cowboy from Misha's, doing here today?"

She struck a pose on the couch, showing off her body as if the answer was obvious.

"Well, he wanted to see me!"

Antoine looked at her and understood immediately what was happening. He felt it when they had first gone to the House of Cards a couple of weeks back. It was a mobbed-up joint for sure, but they had a great time. No harm, no foul. But, now, Luke owed them money. Shit, the guy with the stick was here to enforce the collection! Rene' was just frosting on the cake. And how the hell was Luke going to repay them?

"Crap, he stole something from work! That's what this is all about!" Antoine's heart started pumping. He shifted gears to investigation mode and sat down again. He was on the case. If he had a cape, he would have donned it.

"Who stole? Luke! Oh, shit!" Rene' asked, answering her own question as soon as it was out of her mouth.

"He's run off. Into hiding, I know it, I know him!" Antoine said. "Did the guy with the stick say anything about Luke? Where they going to meet somewhere? Did he talk about a time?"

Rene' just shook her head. "His name is James and he was all about me when he showed up."

She remembered how cute he looked with his Hurley stick, cowboy hat and range coat, suddenly standing on her stoop. He definitely appealed to her naughty side and they had spent the night together and shared a pleasant morning before he left. She didn't think about Luke at all. And JMJ said nothing about him.

"Where did he go?" Antoine mumbled, almost to himself.

"Who?" Rene' asked.

"Luke, dummy! Forget about your stick toting play toy. We're trying to find Luke!"

"Well, if he was looking for a place to stay, I bet he ran off to Boston, maybe Vermont, or Portsmouth. He's got a buddy in Portsmouth, New Hampshire." Rene' rattled off a few more locations.

"He's got friends in those spots?" Antoine asked. She nodded and he shook his head. "No, not where he knows people. They'll find him quick enough because you are probably going to have a visitor or two from the FBI or NCIS or even the local cops. You'll tell them where his friends live, and they'll quickly find him. I hope he's figured that out! I bet he's going to a place he might know but not know anyone there."

"Why do we want to find him?" she asked innocently.

"To warn him! To help him? I don't know, to protect him?" Antoine realized he was a bit confused himself about what he was feeling. Did Luke really steal a secret from GMBB? Like a traitor would do or a spy for some foreign government? The Russian mob probably did not have the best interests of the US government in their hearts.

"To bring him in?" he said quietly, shaking his head. "It has to be that GLASER thing, the new comm device they're installing on the subs." He looked at Rene' and smiled. "You didn't hear that from me."

The next thing they both heard was a sharp knock on the door.

"Is that J?" Rene' asked hopefully as she jumped up and went to the door.

"Rene', wait!" Antoine protested, but it was too late. She was at the door and threw it open. In an instant she jumped back and in walked Agents Martin and Vanallison, badges around their necks and guns drawn, aimed directly at Rene'.

Antoine couldn't help his reaction and grabbed her by the shoulders, pulled her close and swung her in a protective move so he was between her and the guns. He then raised his right hand to show the agents he meant no threat to them, even as the woman, Agent Vanallison put him in her sights.

"Hello, Antoine Barskow. NCIS. Again! We are looking for Luke Parmelian. Who is your friend?" It was Agent Martin. He was all business like and glanced to his partner and nodded for her to look around. She stepped behind Antoine and surveyed the apartment quickly and then headed for the hallway.

"This is Rene' Sanderson, she's a friend," Antoine answered.

"Mr. Barskow, I'm going to ask you to slowly put you weapon on the table there and the two of you sit on the couch," Martin said, gesturing with his gun. Antoine complied with his right hand, gingerly lifting his Glock 17 from his belt holster and then he pulled Rene' to the couch with him.

"Luke's not here," Antoine said. Agent Martin smiled at him and shook his head while putting his finger over his lips.

"All clear," came the voice of Agent Vanallison as she came out of the bedroom. "It's just us."

"Okay, good." Martin nodded and slipped his gun into his shoulder holster under his sport coat. Vanallison slipped hers into a belt holster in the small of her back and picked up Antoine's gun as she walked by the table. She emptied the clip expertly, slipping it into her jacket pocket and replaced the weapon on the table.

"So, you are Rene' Sanderson?" Martin asked. He was familiar with the name from their recent conversation with the co-workers Mark and Sheila in the IST office.

Rene' was still a bit shocked by their intrusion and just nodded her head.

"Do you have any idea where Luke is?" Martin asked.

Rene' shook her head sideways and said nothing.

Agent Martin turned his attention to Antoine.

"And Mr. Barskow, may I ask what the hell you are doing here?" The tone of his voice was clearly one of anger and confusion. "How are you involved with Ms. Sanderson? And by the way, you realize you have one pissed-off boss right now!"

Antoine looked at each of the NCIS agents, then at Rene'. He thought for a moment about what he was going to say, realizing he had put himself in a bad position.

"How did you know I was here?" he asked, his arms open, palms up, surprised and confused.

"What kind of a cop are you?" Martin asked in a sarcastic tone. "We followed you right out of Canfield's office. We thought you might lead us right to Luke."

He turned to Rene' and asked.

"And how long do you know Luke?"

"We dated for a few months," Rene' answered quietly.

"You're his girlfriend?" Vanallison asked. "When did you see him last?"

"*Was* his girlfriend," Rene' said with emphasis, as if she were trying to convince herself, as well as the two agents. "Was… as of Saturday."

"Oh, as of Saturday? What happened?" Vanallison asked as she pulled out a notebook.

"Well, things went a little sideways," Rene' started. She offered the agent a sheepish grin and told the story of how they went to Coney Island and gambled at the Russian mob place in Brighton Beach and Luke lost big time, but she won a bunch and she ended up with the bouncer and Luke was beat up and they drove home in silence and he didn't want to see her anymore.

"Shit!" muttered Agent Martin when she stopped talking. "How much did you say he lost?"

"A hundred twenty-thousand dollars," Rene' sighed.

"And the frigging bouncer was here today, this morning when I got here! Didn't you see him? Blue corvette?" Antoine blurted it out excitedly, wanting to help his fellow law enforcement brethren.

Martin looked at Vanallison with a question in his eyes

"I saw a Corvette go past," she nodded. "Didn't make note of the driver except his hat. Nice car. Weird cowboy hat."

"Well, that's the guy! He's the bouncer for Misha's House of Cards. He was visiting Rene'…right?" Antoine turned to Rene' and she returned his look with a cold hard stare, as if she wasn't interested in getting into that part of the story.

Agent Vanallison moved behind the couch and bent down between Antoine and Rene' and spoke softly into Rene's ear.

"Rene', why don't you come with me into the kitchen and we'll write down some information that we might need to help find your new ex-boyfriend."

She was all nice and polite, but there was an impatient edge in her voice that made Rene' sit up quickly and follow her to the kitchen counter where she sat and wrote down a page of info in response to guidance from Vanallison.

Agent Martin sat across from Antoine and continued to question him about Luke, Rene', his job and his intentions. After a few minutes he was convinced that Antoine was acting out of friendship and was not part of any master plan to steal secrets. However, he clearly was still a person of interest. He offered him some advice.

"Look, kid, we've seen your record at GMBB, it's mostly good! So, don't fuck it up by playing the lone ranger here. Go back to work and let us do our job."

Antoine nodded contritely outside, but inside his brain was racing through dozens of scenarios that Luke could be working. Going back to work was the last thing on his mind.

Agent Vanallison returned with Rene' in tow and the two agents said their goodbyes with a demand that they be notified if Luke or the cowboy bouncer or anyone relating to the case should pop up out of the bushes. Vanallison looked at Antoine with a small nod as she walked by the table and slipped his clip out of her pocket and placed it next to his Glock.

Walking back to the car, the sun had burned off the morning fog and a warming breeze was rolling up the river. They stopped at the back of the car and leaned on it for a moment, enjoying the view from the high ground where Rene's apartment overlooked the Thames River.

"BOLO on Parmelian, for sure. I'll call that in," Agent Vanallison said.

"Yep, for sure. Top secret clearance. Gambling. Russian mob. This one is a classic," Agent Ed Martin sighed. "Time to clue in Seamus downtown. I'm sure he'll be delighted to add this to his workload!"

"We can offer to help him. Although that probably means we won't be going away this weekend."

She had a slight frown on her face as she looked over at her partner of seven months working out of the Naval Submarine Base New London. She shook it off with a shrug. "We'll find time, won't we?"

"Hey, maybe we can offer to go to Coney Island and check out this cowboy bouncer," Martin answered hopefully with a smile. "Make it a beach day."

They looked at each other for a long moment and then broke off with a laugh and slipped into the car. As they backed out of the parking spot, he let his hand drift lightly to her thigh and squeezed it. After a moment, he pulled his hand back. He spun the wheel of their government issued sedan and turned it toward the resident office of the FBI on State Street in New London.

This case was about to become a blip on the national security radar.

twenty-four

SEAMUS MOORE

Tuesday 1400

The USIC is on full alert for stolen Top-Secret files from GMBB. Your spy hacker hears the ground rumbling with a BOLO for local suspect. FBI heading up the man hunt or is that a chip hunt? Special focus aimed at the Russian mob. Anyone surprised here? –SpyhakrF

FBI Special Agent in Charge Seamus Moore was a stickler for detail. And he was a firm believer in Executive Order 13388. Issued in response to the 9/11 terrorist attacks on the US, 13388 required wide dissemination of intelligence information to the US Intelligence Community (USIC), America's 17 agencies, the alphabet soup of gatherers, analysts and distributors of information for both domestic and foreign, commercial, private and military incidents that affect National Security.

It was a busy time for the USIC and despite a dramatic expansion of budgets in the years immediately after 2001, recent budget constraints had been instituted and every agency was struggling to keep up with the workload of gathering, analyzing, planning and predicting. There was a lot to know, there was more unknown and the daily task to find answers to real or imagined threats was the reason nearly 100 billion dollars had been allocated by Congress to get the job done. And it wasn't enough for some.

From human to human surveillance (HUMINT), to satellite recon and cell phone intercepts (SIGINT) and all that entailed, over 100,000 government workers toiled in a bureaucracy of effort designed to stop the enemies of the state from accomplishing their goals. They constantly straddled the borders between national security and private citizens' rights. There was no concrete wall to determine which side was which. It was more a floating point of attack that was often misrepresented by the media, misinterpreted by the public and sometimes, actually crossed the threshold of legality. Oh, *that* wall!

And then there was the time the President dismissed the results of the USIC efforts as "misguided", suggesting the IC "should go back to school."

"Are we wasting his time or is he wasting our time?" asked the DNI, Director of National Intelligence. It was a political minefield, even though the IC was supposed to be just an army of worker bees doing what was asked of them.

The IC bosses forever battled the perception of good and evil, taking the bruises when they failed to stop an event, or a bad actor. Conversely, they rarely received the praise when they succeeded. The simple revelation of success was often buried by the desire to not reveal sources.

As that same Director of National Intelligence testified before Congress, "They may know what we do, but not how well we do it. We hope."

Despite support by scholars and pundits who actually

studied in school the various elements of international threats, that quote was the last for the DNI in his official position.

A new leader was appointed and attempted to revive the dwindling spirit of interagency cooperation. Fortunately, the new DNI, Harold Miller, was a good old friend of Seamus Moore. While that might have eased the burden of fighting the forces in Washington, DC, the immediate problem of the stolen top-secret file had landed on Moore's desk in the tiny New London FBI office.

Moore was strapped for support. His downtown office only had Jennifer Parsons, a new multitasking whirlwind agent who played the role of secretary, techie and analyst as needed. Two more agents were promised, but he was forced to rely heavily on the Naval Criminal Investigative Service in the form of Agents Ed Martin and Valarie Vanallison, based at the Naval Station upriver. They were the first to connect to the theft and he was happy to have their assistance during his particularly busy workload.

A man in his mid 50's with a shock of white hair, wire rimmed glasses and a bum knee, Agent Moore worked at one of those adjustable desks that could be moved from sitting to standing position with a flip of his wrist. He couldn't stand or sit still for very long and if he wasn't adjusting his desk, he was pacing his office.

He was a voracious reader, as one might expect from someone trained to be a lawyer. There were a lot of rules to follow in the FBI and it wasn't unusual for him to express his frustration for the protocols with a snarky comment or two, even as he pushed himself and his small staff to follow them.

When Martin and Vanallison met him at the FBI office on State Street on Tuesday afternoon, he was surrounded by open files on his desk and one in his hand that he was studying. It was a transcript of a long deposition regarding his latest investigation. New London Mayor Roman Passimino was about to be charged with corruption and money laundering involving the awarding of contracts for street reconstruction in the city.

"You would think you could rebuild a city without trying to line your own pockets!" he shouted as Martin and Vanallison walked into his office. He threw the document on his desk and stood still, hands on hips and turned to the two NCIS agents. He smiled at them in welcome. The three had worked several cases together and he considered their inter agency co-operation a model for all government agencies.

"What have you got? I've got three minutes!" he laughed.

Agent Vanallison handed Agent Moore a folder and spoke up first.

"Someone stole a chip with the operations manual for a new submarine communication system called SLACLONET 1000 out of GMBB. We have a BOLO for a suspect named Luke Parmelian and a few names who know him."

"Someone stole a chip?" Moore asked, realizing how different the world had become since he joined the FBI 24 years earlier.

"A microSD card," Agent Martin specified. "Holds about 100 gigabits of data. How to install, calibrate and operate this laser communications system. Brand new stuff for subs. Clearly, Top Secret info."

"And where is this guy Luke Parmelian?" Moore asked as he scanned the sheets of paper in the case folder.

"In the wind right now. Last seen Monday afternoon leaving work. Called in sick this morning," said Vanallison. "He's not at his home in New London as of an hour ago."

"We've interviewed an ex-girlfriend and have reason to

believe this is a gambling debt issue. Likely extortion by the Russian mob out of Brighton Beach," said Martin.

"Russian mob? Great! And I'm sure a few navies might want to get their hands on this chip as well," Moore surmised. Both agents nodded. He scanned his desk and the files stacked heater-skelter. After a moment, he turned to them. "I'll open an investigation, let New Haven know we are active on it here. Jennifer!" he yelled towards the outer office.

"We are available to help track this down," Vanallison offered.

"Yea, I can use the extra eyeballs. You work the BOLO and let's find out what his phone has been up to. Check the ferries and airport, trains, etc. You know the drill. I'll alert USIC and get NSA on board."

"We can shoot down to Coney Island to check out this Misha character," offered Martin, glancing over at his partner.

"No, this guy Misha Yevtechnov is not a new name," he said remembering a recent report that had flowed through his daily briefings from New Haven. "I'll see about him. Get going on the phone and maybe set up intercepts on a couple of phones from this list of friends. Talk to them first."

Jennifer walked in and Seamus handed her the folder. "New case. Set it up!"

A quick mix of nods and the deal was sealed, as it had been many times before. He trusted them and they left him standing there debating to himself whether to return to the long deposition about the mayor or shift gears to national security.

Just before they exited his office, he shouted one more thing after them.

"Remember, everything comes through me. No lone ranger stuff, right?" And he waved them off to their tasks.

Special Agent in Charge Seamus Moore flipped his desk to the standing position and ripped off a quick email to the FBI Special Agent in Charge John Heslin of New York City's organized crime task force. Less than a half hour later the reply confirmed that Misha Yevtechnov was already the subject of a RICO investigation. New London was now added to the loop on that case.

Agent Moore sent off a second email, this one to Agent Ted Dixon in New Haven, his direct boss, and copied the National Security Branch of the FBI, advising them a new case was open, investigating one Luke Parmelian, suspected thief of National Security documents. He copied DNI as well, who would spread the word to the USIC.

Executive Order 13388 set up the protocols designed to ensure the word travels fast when national security is at the core of a law enforcement problem but, there are so many layers and so many problems, not everyone gets the word in a timely manner. All of it mitigated by the fact the criminal elements followed only the laws of human fallibility. The process was destined to evolve with each case. Finding clues, following clues and confronting wrong doers doesn't always play out the way the protocols lay it out. The few cracks that still existed, more often than not, are simply created by the humans who are the end users.

Moore, acutely aware investigations required patience, knew the waiting game had started. He knew little of this Luke Parmelian, but he did know Mr. Parmelian had no idea what was about to reign down on his life. If they could find him. He reached for the mayor's file and returned to the world of political corruption.

twenty-five

STOODUP

Wednesday 1200

"CSIC Naicho Japan evolving eyeballs on ground. Breakthrough photos of PLA Navy sub base at Yulin-East Hainan. Ballistic missiles being loaded aboard Jin Class nuclear sub confirm USIC worst fears. China ready for full time deterrent patrols? Missile range near 5000 miles with multi-warheads. Water beginning to boil in South China Sea? –SpyhakrF

Bob Smoot was a lucky guy in the macho world of Federal agents because he didn't need a nickname. Nicknames usually came with a touch of ribbing, a poke of friendship, a sprinkle of the intangible to create a *bon-homme* way to show affection, or a one-word clue to a specialty. "Smoot" stood on its own.

Bob Smoot wasn't sure who his relatives were, though most of them apparently came from Scotland and the first one to appear in the U.S. was as recent as 1920. That mattered little to him. Smoot was an expert in looking like other people and had found his calling with the FBI.

His target today was the Russian mobster Misha Yevtechnov who appeared to be on his way into Connecticut for some unknown purpose. Smoot and his partner Bob Smith, no relation, were following Yevtechnov on I-95 North five cars back from the two-car caravan of SUVs that had left the Avianka Restaurant in Brighton Beach 90 minutes ago. Three other men, presumed associates of Yevtechnov, were accompanying him.

Smoot and Smith were passing the time discussing the nuances of running the football in the NFL when the conversation ended abruptly as the two SUVs ahead turned off the highway in New Haven and pulled into the train station.

Smith drove a block beyond and parked on a side street while Smoot slipped out of their car and started walking toward the station. He had decided to start with his hirsute outfit, meaning a full beard with glasses and mutton chops. He carried a small leather briefcase and wore a light rain coat that reached mid-thigh. A college professor or a mad bomber, he hadn't decided which, but he felt invisible in the fairly light crowd that was entering the modern facility where Amtrak connected eastbound and northbound trains for Boston and Springfield.

Misha Yevtechnov sat in the SUV parked in the commuter lot and checked his watch. He had ten minutes before his schedule meeting with Luke Parmelian and the transfer of the coveted files on a microchip that was supposed to change the battle plans of Russia's rebuilding navy. Or whomever. Misha knew Vladimir Chemenko well and was open to the idea that Chemenko would sell the secrets to anyone for the right price. Misha only cared about the 100 large he was owed, once he had the file in his possession.

He slipped on a Yankee baseball cap and wandered casually toward the train terminal.

"Stay back, but keep me in sight," he told McSamarlie sitting in the driver's seat. "I don't want him to see you unless there's trouble."

"Got it," nodded McSamarlie.

Misha was uncomfortable on the front line of intrigue, but this operation was important enough that he was the only one to be trusted. Besides, he had already set the conditions on the phone with Luke two days ago. He tried to look like the casual traveler resigned to mass transit, waiting for his ride. He scanned the rack of magazines carefully, picking up a local issue of the New Haven Advocate and went to the back to check out the personal ads.

At 12 noon exactly, he put the issue back in its rack and walked toward the tracks. The southbound Acela had just pulled in and he expected Luke would be on that. He scanned the wide hallway looking for his target but did not see him. A dozen commuters of all shapes and sizes hurried on their way. A couple of young women caught his eye for a second as they bustled in the opposite direction.

When he arrived at the stairway down to the track, only two men were heading up. By the time he reached the platform on the lower level, the Acela had pulled out heading for New York City and there was no one else visible. He turned and climbed the stairs, wondering if Luke had arrived by car. He pulled out his phone and called the college kid who was sitting in the second car at street level.

"Anyone? Did you see him?" he asked impatiently.

"Nothing," he reported.

Misha saw McSamarlie sitting in the coffee shop in the main hall and caught his eye, getting a slight shake of the head in response. Misha smiled when he realized McSamarlie didn't have his Hurley next to him. A rare sight, he thought.

Then he cursed silently, focusing on the problem at hand, turned back to slowly walk the entire length of the concourse and then back again. He dialed Luke's number, but heard only a genial voice greeting promising to be in touch as soon as he could. The northbound train for Boston came and went, dumping and receiving a small crowd of travelers, but Misha did not find Luke among them. By 1230, he gave up.

"We got a no show, *shef,*" McSamarlie stated the obvious when they got back in the car. "Let me track him down!" JMJ gave him an intense look, backed by a gentle pat on his Hurley shaft that was stuck between the seats next to him.

Misha was angry. The one thing he hated more than anything was being played. He tossed his Yankee hat in the back seat and waved to his other two men in the second vehicle to come close by. The four of them stood in the parking lot and Misha laid out his plan.

"Mr. J, you take the car and go to Groton. Find this asshole and if you need to, let him know who he is dealing with." Misha pointed to the Hurley stick in the car. "Whatever it takes, but don't kill him, understand?"

McSamarlie smiled and nodded. He understood.

"I need that chip!" Misha barked. Then he waved them away and walked back into the station.

"Boss, you coming with us?" the young college kid yelled after him.

"I'm taking the train," he answered without looking back. "Need time to think."

Bob Smith watched the foursome from his SUV five rows away at the back of the commuter lot. He spoke briefly to Bob Smoot who was on the other end of his mobile communicator.

"Smoot, Misha's coming your way, back into the station!" Smith told Smoot.

"Got him!" was the response. "Grab my bag in the hall by restrooms. I'll stay with him."

"Copy," Bob Smith confirmed and shifted the SUV into gear. Their mission was to follow Yevtechnov where ever he went, so Smoot would take the lead. Smith kept his focus on the two Russian SUVs as they started moving toward the parking lot exit.

Bob Smoot had been watching from the inside of the double doors at the terminal side entrance and quickly turned down a short hallway as Misha approached. With practiced moves, he stripped his muttonchops, glasses and overcoat off and stashed them in his bag. He decided to add a hat, a fedora that gave him a slightly eccentric look, but no more so than an older Justin Timberlake. He left the bag at the end of the hall outside the men's room and walked casually into the concourse, ending up about 30 feet behind Yevtechnov.

"Penn Station," Misha commanded loudly at the ticket window and walked off toward Track One to wait for the 12:50 express. Bob Smoot stayed back until he was out of sight and then bought his own ticket to follow him back to New York City. He was winging it, but that was okay. It wouldn't be the first time.

Outside, Bob Smith watched the Russians leave the lot, one turning right, the other turning left. He slid quickly up to the side entrance, ran into the hallway, grabbed Bob Smoot's bag and returned to the tail. He followed the SUV that had gone right with the two crew on board. He caught them a few blocks later as they entered I-95 South and followed them back to Brighton Beach.

McSamarlie headed north on I-95 with mixed thoughts of what was going to be more fun - visiting Luke again or visiting Rene'. By force of habit, he checked the rearview mirror and was satisfied he was not being tailed.

twenty-six

NEED A FRIEND

Friday 1300

Luke couldn't take his eyes off her. Her skin was so smooth, her hair silky, haphazardly spilling around her deep-set eyes, as blue as the sky. Which he could only imagine since they were still in the hole in the ground that was once the cellar of the Southeast Lighthouse on Block Island, with only the portable lantern glowing on the cement floor.

He couldn't help smiling as he wondered about her strong forehead that conflicted perfectly with her sweet lips. She even looks Russian, he thought, and it stirred him enough to crawl the few feet to where she was sitting and brush against her again with his own lips. She responded softly.

"I don't care who knows we are here," he whispered, answering her innocent question, his focus lost on her. He relished the firm muscles of her back and held her close. But it didn't last because her question came back to the fore. He pulled back awakened to the fact he actually *didn't* want anyone to know where he was!

"What about you? Does anyone know you are here?".

She shook her head no. "No one knows I am in *this* place." Then she realized her bike was hidden in the bushes next to the fence. "Oh, my bike! It is out front but, hidden."

The mention of her bike brought the outside world crashing into their little cocoon of fresh passion. Luke stood up.

"Okay, we have to figure out what we are doing here. I have a date this afternoon," he said.

"Date?" she asked, cocking her head.

"A meet," he explained. "With Antoine, my friend. The guy in the jeep this morning? Wait, I mean with the Russian guy, Misha. Antoine set up the FBI to be there too. He thinks I should turn myself in. Says he has a plan."

"Turn yourself into what?"

Luke couldn't help but laugh. "I have no idea what I could turn into, no matter what I do!"

"I do have to go to work very soon," she smiled. "Got to go home and change. Clean up and show up."

"I guess I've done it again," he said. "Made things more complicated than I intended or wanted."

He felt like he needed to tell her everything. He wanted to. He couldn't fully understand why it happened so quickly, but his mind accepted it. Maybe it was the afterglow of their surprisingly wonderful lovemaking, but she was in his life, his heart, his mind, his body. She was everywhere. She needed to know everything. He needed to tell her. Or so he convinced himself. And so, he did.

Ever since Tuesday afternoon, 72 hours ago, Luke had been haunted by the reality of his running away and the magnitude of his theft. When he passed the ferry dock that morning, the urge to jump on board the Hi-Speed was easy and immediate. It was the instant answer to his problems, in the same way kids slam the door of their room on their mothers when she admonishes them for bad behavior. He had done that plenty of times when growing up. As if closing the door makes things different. What happened before was gone. Problem solved. Outside world doesn't matter.

He understood problems. He had plenty of them. He was a geek, a computer guy. He wasn't a spy. He wasn't a thief. Sure, he gambled, liked his drink and his job was easy... sitting at a computer terminal all day...moving from office to office.

No sense of duty...just make things work. For others.

He knew he couldn't take the jeep, but he had to go. Slam the door to the mainland! Trouble awaits there! Running on impulse, he jumped on the Tuesday morning ferry to Block Island. He made the boarding call, overnight bag and a soft cooler in hand, with two minutes to spare.

The Hi-Speed ferry was another fruit of the boat building trade in New London, assembled just a mile up river in the early 80's when matching jet engines to ferry boats was all the rage. Any hopes of a big market across the world were captured by other boat builders, but this jet ferry was still in operation locally. It made the 25-mile trip to Block Island a one-hour alternative to the one-hour drive to Pt. Judith and then the slow ferry to the island, another hour. Hey, every hour on the island is better than an hour traveling, folks liked to say!

About 15 minutes into the trip, while scrolling his Twitter account, he suddenly realized his cell phone was a beacon to the world. Stupid distraction! He knew better, if he only could think better! He jumped up and went to the rail and tossed the phone over board just as they were passing Ledge Light.

Now he was off the grid, alone and running. But, to where? A hole in the ground of which he knew very little?

"What did you think was going to happen?" Petrika asked, interrupting his verbal brain dump.

"I'm not sure," he said and laughed. How many times had he thought that in the last days? He sat down in front of her and took her hands.

"Right now, I feel like it was the right thing to do for no other reason than I now know you." He smiled.

"Yes, you do. A little bit," she laughed back at him and touched his cheek. She felt like a stream bed newly aware of the melting snow beginning to flow, a trickle destined to become a torrent through her veins.

"Block Island has always been a good spot for me," Luke continued. "It was always an escape, mostly for sailboat racing, but it was away, another place. Nothing bad can happen here...the bad stuff is all back there."

He looked around and laughed again.

"Of course, I've always had a nicer view. And no one wanted to kill me. Sitting here, I finally realized what I wasn't going to do. I wasn't going to betray my country by handing over the goods."

He picked up the travel mug and held it as if it was the holy grail. "I buried it right after I got here on Tuesday. Over the cliff. No one was going to find it, even if they found me!" Petrika edged closer to him so she could touch his leg as she listened to his continuing story.

"I'm glad I found you." She smiled at him as he jumped back into his story.

The waiting for the unknown was the worst part. Wednesday night after a day of restless tossing and turning on the hard cellar floor, wrapped in his thin bedroll and burdened by a tsunami of soul searching, accompanied by steady sipping on his bottle of McCoy, Luke slipped out of the cellar and walked the 1 1/2 miles to downtown Old Harbor. He was in need of a drink and he grabbed a six pack of beer at the Harbor Grocery. He carried it to a park bench along Water Street across from Chapel Street, popped a top and sat overlooking the Old Harbor drinking, fretting and looking for a plan.

The last remaining pay phone on the island was hanging in a small alley between the Novelty Department Store and the Mohegan Tavern. He laughed when he realized there was only one number he actually knew by heart thanks to the digital phone revolution. He finished the first beer and walked into the alley and dialed Antoine's cell, the simple alternative repetition of 4s and 2s leading to a connecting ring.

A band called Ragmen in Spades was in the middle of their first set at the Mohegan next door and their sound drifted onto the street as Luke waited for Antoine to pick up.

"Hello?" came the uncertain voice on the other end.

"I blew off Misha," Luke blurted.

"Luke, what the fuck are you doing!" Antoine responded, recognizing Luke's voice immediately.

"I'm didn't meet with Misha."

"Misha? The card guy? What does he have to do with anything?"

"I'm scared shitless of these guys and I don't believe paying them off is going to end things happily ever after."

Antoine was quiet for a full 30 seconds. He could hear the faint sounds of music in the background

"You heard me, right?" Luke broke the silence.

"Yea, I did. I don't know exactly what you're talking about, but my friend, you are fucked! They are looking for your ass right now. NCIS, the FBI, Canfield! The APB is out! They've questioned me and Rene' and I'm sure they are looking closely at everyone you know. Where the hell are you? Whose phone is this?"

Luke didn't answer right away. He was smart enough to

realize Antoine was a security guard at GMBB and might very well not be sympathetic to his plight. But he was a dear friend. The only one he would consider trusting.

"It's a pay phone. I'm hiding out for now. I need some gear. You've got to help me. I may be away longer than I thought."

"Rene' says you lost $120,000 the other night," Antoine pushed for information. He had to hear it from Luke himself.

"Yea, Satan Sixes. Acey Deucey. You ever hear of that?"

"Sixes, shit!" Antoine knew the game but had never seen the hand where three sixes showed up. He shook his head in amazement.

"I was set up, man! I was drunk! They beat the shit out of me, stuck me in a cage, shot me into the sky! I'm sure I got busted ribs. And I was supposed to turn over...." He stopped, trying to control the run of his mouth and wondering if he should say anymore. The light but steady sound of a guitar solo filled the silence.

"You stole the SLACLONET files didn't you, Luke, the chip?" Antoine asked after a moment. It sounded like he had resigned himself to that knowledge, that depth of trouble that was sure to follow.

"Antoine, these guys are gonna kill me! They already sent that cowboy asshole with the stick to my home. I didn't make the handoff today. I was supposed to meet Misha in New Haven. I haven't moved!"

"Moved from where?" Antoine asked again.

"I can't tell you that..."

"Alright, listen to me. You said you blew off Misha. What do you mean? Where were you supposed to meet?"

"Yes. At noon today in New Haven."

"You never went? For an exchange, right? To make good on your debt?"

"Yes." Luke answered quietly, almost a whisper. Antoine

felt like he had to talk him off the ledge. A ledge that was not going away.

Despite the years of training and the hours of lectures, videos and security warnings, it all became very real for the first time at that moment. There was no neat way to end it, even if you dumped a ton of secrets on the Russians. The Feds would always have your balls in a wringer.

"Luke, my friend, this is serious. The only people you can trust right now are the Feds. You have to come in from the cold. You still have the chip? No one's seen it? You can talk your way out of this! We'll call it a mistake, you forgot to put it...make, make a notation in the log. Tell them you've been sick. We can figure out something."

"I don't know, man. I'm not sure anyone will believe anything I say. And I've got to deal with Misha and his crew."

"Let me talk to someone here. I know this guy."

"There's always a guy, isn't there?" Luke managed a quiet laugh. The two of them had shared that private joke many times in the past.

"Luke, you know I'm *your* guy, right?"

"Yea, Antoine. Sure."

"Yea, good. Now listen to me. I'm gonna get you out of this."

twenty-seven

THE WORD GOES OUT

Wednesday 2100

The Coasties kill drone project but hold on to legacy - Eagle Eyes. Miniature tilt rotor project cost too much says USCG Bossman. When was last time you heard that from your government? Lone prototype remains for special search and surveillance thru NRO and USCGA training. –SpyhakrF

By the time Antoine hung up the phone with Luke on Wednesday night, the tentacles of the United States Intelligence Community (USIC) were abuzz with the theft of the top-secret file from the USA's top submarine manufacturer. Seventeen agencies and a baker's dozen more branches, directorates, and units, right down to the local patrolman doing the swing shift on the streets of New London, were advised to be on the lookout for one Luke Parmelian, an American computer programmer, suspected of violating the Espionage Act of 1917, under Title 18 US Code Section 798.

In short, there was a traitor on the loose!

Not everyone cared and most did not don their hunting caps and set out to sniff for his trail. Too much to do! That's the gig for someone else! Have you *seen* the list of bad guys we are tracking?!

It *was* the prime task for the NCIS and FBI. The Naval Criminal Investigative Service was the Navy's primary unit tasked to handle criminal investigations involving Navy and Marine tech secrets, service members, and affiliated civilian personnel. NCIS civilian Special Agents have the authority to investigate criminal acts in accordance with both the Uniform Code of Military Justice (UCMJ) and established criminal laws under the United States Code (USC) when there is a Department of the Navy nexus.

The FBI did the same for National Security. Since they had interviewed Antoine and Rene' the two NCIS agents and Special Agent Seamus Moore had worked the IC surveillance system and developed personal information about Luke Parmelian's background.

"We know he's a computer guy with a security clearance who apparently has gone off the tracks to pay a gambling debt from a Russian mobster," Agent Vanallison reminded everyone in the FBI ops office in New London viewing the large monitor where images of Luke's face, his driver's license and GMBB security badge were displayed.

Agent Martin stood a good head taller than his partner and had to make a conscious effort to move from behind her to the other side of the group because her mild perfume was totally distracting his thoughts from the presentation of case facts. Instead, his mind wandered toward a hoped-for future of carefree social encounters. No one but Agent Vanallison paid much notice to Martin's plight.

New to the group was assistant US Attorney Hadley Carlson from the Department of Justice office in New York City. She had been called to New London earlier in the day to assist and bring new information. Two faces shared a monitor in the ops center and added a digital context to the gathering. It was SAC Dixon and SAC Heslin from the New Haven and New York City FBI offices.

Agent Moore looked around the room slowly and realized this was another joint investigation with multiple agencies doing the work. He had the lead and expected no jurisdictional issues.

"We are all after the same thing here," he reminded the group. "We have a security breach and the suspect is our primary concern. I'm in the lead but we are all contributing. Got it?"

All nodded and Moore affirmed their acceptance and then nodded toward the Carlson. "What have you got, Hadley?"

"This mobster is one Misha Yevtechnov. They call him *Lagooshka*. He's under surveillance by the New York office following a different case," Carlson said, speaking up for the first time.

"Who calls him *Lagooshka*?" agent Martin asked.

"His crew. Runs a dozen guys out of Brighton Beach. They call themselves *Sova' Golovi'. Owl Heads*. New York is working a RICO case against him. Extortion, gas scams, medical supplies and, of all things, fruit."

"Fruit?" Moore repeated. "What is he doing with fruit?"

"He's selling it," interjected Agent Heslin on the TV screen. "May be legit. Or not. We suspect a money laundering front and are building paperwork on that. He owns the fruit stands in Brighton Beach. There's six of them! All on the same block." Carson nodded to confirm what Heslin explained.

"*Lagooshka*?" questioned Vanallison.

"Means 'frog' in Russian," Carlson explained, unable to suppress her smile as she looked at the three agents' quizzical expressions. "I have no idea."

"Frogs and owls? Whiskey Tango Foxtrot?" Agent Martin shook his head.

Vanallison clicked her remote and pointed toward the screen displaying Luke's photo as they all shared a chuckle.

"We're pretty sure Luke has left New London and probably headed out on the ferry. We found his jeep in the garage across from the terminal. The last hint of his whereabouts comes at 1027 on Tuesday morning when his phone suddenly drops off the grid."

She clicked again and a nautical chart appeared showing the marine approaches to New London. "That puts him about four nautical miles south of the city docks in Fishers Island Sound."

"In the water?" asked Carlson.

"He either removed the SIM card or dropped the phone in the water. We are getting no ping from it right now," Vanallison continued. She changed screens to show a wider view of Block Island and Long Island Sound.

"Unfortunately, two scheduled ferries departed New London within five minutes of each other. The phone drops off the grid just after the main channel ends, so he could have been on the car ferry that went southwest to Orient Point, but without his car, or the one that went southeast to Block Island. Definitely no car on the high speed."

"We are waiting on security footage from Orient Point," Agent Martin advised. "Block's cameras apparently are not working."

"If he went to Long Island, wouldn't he take his car?" Moore asked turning to Martin.

"Likely. You need a vehicle to get away from Orient

Point. Opens up the whole east coast. The ferry terminal is ten miles away from the nearest town, Greenport, where he might get a rental or a bus. Block Island, not so much. There's no place to get to from there. Would he put himself on an island?"

"He could grab a ferry from Block back to the mainland, Pt. Jude, Newport. Even Montauk and the South Fork of Long Island. But that doesn't make sense, does it? I say keep it simple." Agent Martin pointed to the map of Block Island on the screen for emphasis.

"Do we need Old Eagle Eyes out of Charlestown?" Vanallison asked.

"How do you know about that?" asked Agent Moore.

Vanallison looked at him for a moment. "SpyhakrF?" she said, as if she was providing information that wasn't quite official.

Moore nodded. "Yep, I've seen that story. From our spy friendly blogger who has eluded the FBI for a few years."

"He got the story right, that's for sure," smiled Vanallison.

The story goes that Techtron Conrols, one of the first military contractors to build drones in the 80's and still headquartered 50 miles up the road in Providence, had tested their earliest prototypes at Naval Air Station Charlestown, in southern Rhode Island.

The small airfield had an important past. Navy pilots used it to practice carrier landings during World War II on a short runway. There was a rocket launched from there as an astronomical experiment that reached 55 miles high. Drag racing and Lover's Lane-ing had been the other main activities after the military closed it in the 70's. The last 50 years had seen mother nature regain control and it was now a public park and nature preserve.

Under the guise of the Frosty Drew Observatory, a working telescope had become a popular draw for the elementary schools of the South County. Twice a week, mostly in winter, young children shared a glimpse of the stars in the early evening sky.

One section of what was left of the runways had been converted to a massive parking lot and paths for joggers and dog walkers were built around the edges of the property, helping to obscure the history. Sitting at the edge of old runway 34 was the original wooden barn that housed the first model of the drone that created a Teutonic shift in air warfare strategy. The barn appeared to be abandoned and rarely drew any attention since it was several hundred yards from the main pathways.

Unnoticed to the casual eye is a narrow path among the bushes and trees that cover the old runway. It ran right toward the edge of Ninigret Pond, wide enough for the 20-foot wingspan of the drone. It could literally taxi a few yards out of the barn, turn right and run a few hundred feet along the old runway before lifting off into the sky over Governor's Island, the nature preserves, and then offshore over Block Island Sound.

Twelve miles later it would be directly over the Block Island airport. The only living creatures who might notice were furry and protected.

"We actually tracked a petty officer who stole a boat a couple of years ago," Vanallison offered. "I think it's a special project with the Coast Guard working with NRO." She half smiled, wondering if she had revealed too much. "I know the Coastie who runs it. From the academy. It's low key, but still an eye in the sky."

"The National Reconnaissance Office has a special drone project through the Coast Guard in Charlestown?" asked Attorney Carlson in surprise. "I did not know that. I thought they just did satellites."

"A legacy contract, I guess," Vanallison offered with a shrug. "That's what the blog said."

"I thought everyone knew about it."

"Hmmm." Moore murmured, then shook his head. "I don't think we need it. Yet."

Agent Dixon chimed in from his side of the TV monitor. "He has a 36 hours head start. If he was leaving the country, we would have heard from the airports by now. Nothing has come in. He could be literally anywhere but...I like Agent Martin's theory. I'm betting Block Island."

In walked Jennifer, the young Jenn-of-all-trades, Moore requested from New Haven to help analyze the info they pulled from various SIGINT resources at NSA.

"We've grabbed a phone conversation from Barskow's phone! Parmelian talked to him. They want to make a deal!" she said with excitement, waving a couple of pages of transcript.

"They? The security guard? Are they working together now?' said Agent Moore, reaching for the report. "I thought you cleared the security guy," Moore asked pointedly to Martin.

"I think he's genuine. A friend. Seems like a pro, albeit young, unseasoned. Earnest before experienced," Martin responded, surprising himself with his enthusiasm.

"Sounds like he has a fan," Moore laughed. He quickly scanned the transcript without waiting for an explanation. He laughed when he got to one line.

"They actually used the phrase 'come in from the cold'." He shook his head in amusement. "Brando? No, Richard Burton! The Spy Who Came In From The Cold! 1965, right? I know my movies!"

"Who are these guys?" laughed Carlson.

Moore couldn't help himself and smiled broadly at

Carlson. "Butch Cassidy and the Sundance Kid! Most famous line from that movie!"

Vanallison, all of 28 years old, who had not seen either movie, listened and watched somewhat amused by her older companions riffing on movies.

"What cold is he coming in from?" she asked.

Martin's phone pinged at that moment with a text. "It's from Antoine, the security guard," he announced.

He read it aloud. "Talked to Luke. Need to see you ASAP!" Moore didn't hesitate. "Get him in here immediately. Like right now!"

Martin typed a response. "Get ass to FBI office ASAP. Now. State Street."

Fifteen minutes later, Antoine was sitting in Agent Moore's office with four Federal agents watching him intently.

He was flushed with excitement, balancing his concern for Luke with the idea he was now in the middle of a national security case. Like a real detective. Like a real intelligence operative. He dared himself to think of the word *espionage*. And he was with the good guys.

"Where is Parmelian?" were the first words out of Moore's mouth after introductions around.

"He wouldn't tell me, but I think he's on Block. He used a pay phone. He wants to make a deal!" Antoine told them excitedly.

"Ha, Block! I knew it!" It was Agent Martin, relishing his earlier hunch.

"Deal! A deal for what?" Moore scoffed.

"He wants to be a double agent. Trade his freedom for inside information on the Russian!

"Yevtechnov?" Agent Moore scoffed! "Is he planning to hand the chip off to him? If he goes through with the trade, we have Yevtechnov and we have Parmelian. It's cut and dried. This guy's a traitor. We arrest them both and case closed."

"But what if it goes deeper?" Antoine protested. "Luke could keep contact with Misha, promise him more info from GMBB. You could wire him up and maybe Misha leads you to something else, or someone else. I mean, he's a Russian mobster! I'm sure his fingers are in a lot of dirty pies!"

"I don't see the need for it going any deeper," Agent Vanallison added. She was with Moore. "Arrest them and it's over!"

Moore turned to Agent Martin.

"Ed, what do you think?"

"The primary thing is bringing this traitor to justice," Martin answered. "I say we set up a meet and wrap them both up."

"He's not a traitor!" Antoine protested. "He's a nerd in trouble with money. Coercion 101! It's classic leverage for the Russians. They set him up and now are forcing him under threat of bodily harm to do their deed. Can't we turn this into something to help our side? I know Luke would rather go there."

Carlson interjected. "You're right about classic leverage. R.I.C.E. Reward, Ideology, Coercion, Ego. I'm not sure Ideology is apparent here. They're not paying him - just forgiving his debt. Or so they say. But there is something else."

"What is that?" Moore asked.

"We know Yevtechnov met with a Russian operative from the consulate a couple weeks ago. Our tail noted the meeting, but it didn't seem to tie into anything we were looking at for the RICO case."

"When were you going to mention that?" a pissed Moore asked the DOJ rep.

"At the right time, which seems now!" Carlson defended, though a tad sheepishly.

"That's my fault, Seamus," came the voice of SAG Heslin on the TV. "I asked her to keep it quiet. Need to know."

"Well, need is now!" Agent Moore shot back, but let it go. "Parmelian says he didn't meet with Misha. What was that all about?" Moore asked waving the transcript file at Carlson.

"I'm guessing that was a blown meet in New Haven. Our guys tailed Yevtechnov there, but nothing happened." Carlson stood her ground looking Moore in the eye. "They were working the RICO case and didn't connect this Luke character with New Haven."

"Well, I'd say it's connected now, Hadley." Moore nodded.

"It has to go deeper!" Antoine piped in, standing up and entreating Agent Moore with his pitch. "What the hell does Misha Yevtechnov want with sub secrets! He's a gambling entrepreneur! He runs a House of Cards."

"He runs a racket," Carlson corrected. "He deals in making money, the old-fashioned way. He steals, coerces, intimidates, and tricks for it."

"So, you're suggesting we wire-up Parmelian, monitor the trade-off of the chip and then continue feeding this Misha character documents and watch where he goes with the secrets?" Moore threw the file onto his desk and struck his characteristic pose with hands on hips.

"This is crazy," said Martin. "Parmelian knows nothing about dealing with bad guys. He obviously got into this shit storm on his own. Who's going to keep it from going off the rails again?"

"I will!" Antoine raised his hand with a big smile. "I can handle him. With a little help from you guys," he added with a smile.

Agent Vanallison asked everyone. "We still don't know where he is, do we?"

"He's on Block Island!" Antoine said.

"How do you know that?" she asked.

"Summer Brain Drain," Antoine smiled like he had swallowed the canary and it was delicious.

"Brain Drain?" Vanallison scoffed.

"Summer Brain Drain. It's a song! It was playing in the background when Luke called me." Antoine looked at everyone, realizing they had no idea what he was talking about. He started to sing the song, surprising everyone with his baritone.

"Sky filled with a sudden rain, laying on the beach feeling no pain, starting to think it's all insane. Just another Summer Brain Drain…"

The Feds just looked at him with mouths agape. Antoine was animated and felt freed up to make his case.

"The Ragmen in Spades were playing at the Mohegan when he called me. On Block Island! The pay phone is only a few feet away outside the building. I know that pay phone. Hell, I've used it before. I could hear them! I know the song and sure enough, when I checked their web site, there was their schedule. They'll be on Block all week. Captain Nick's on Saturday."

Moore was quiet for a moment. He looked around at the assembled group of agents and the security guard who had suddenly been thrown into the middle of their manhunt.

"Anyone else have a notion about this Luke guy?" he asked. He got nothing but blank stares in return.

"Ok! Meeting over. Everyone out!" he commanded with a wave of his hand.

"I have to make a call." He turned and walked into his office.

A moment later Moore was chatting with his old friend

Harold Miller, the new Director of National Intelligence, on a secure line to Washington, DC.

"Is this business or personal?" Miller asked after the two traded pleasantries.

"I wanted to confirm our golf outing next week," Moore answered with a laugh. "And ask you about the Russians."

Miller laughed on the other end.

"Will they be playing with us?"

"Oh, they are playing, but I don't think you'll call it golf."

Law school at Georgetown had been the first phase of their long-time relationship. After graduation, Moore went the investigative route with the FBI while Miller worked his way through the Intelligence Community starting with the CIA, then the State Department, National Security Agency and finally the White House.

While Moore liked the down and dirty chase of criminals, Miller relished the chase of the men in high places misusing the people's trust - criminals of another caliber.

Miller gained a reputation as an honest man, welcomed at power parties and invited to mingle with the government's elite from political, bureaucratic and diplomatic circles. He often thought his nearness to the corrupt allowed them to believe they were more trustworthy than they deserved. Perception was everything in DC. Honesty was rare.

Miller attributed his strong moral compass as the reason he had survived three administrations, both Democratic and Republican. He liked to believe not all apples go bad when the rest are rotten.

More than a mover and shaker, he was an observer unafraid to point out corruption, misguided agendas and plain old stupidity when it reared its ugly head. He built his observations on facts which he believed always, in the end, trumped false perceptions. He had also learned where the good guys lived.

"So, what is happening on the street, Seamus?" he asked. "Your name popped up in one of my daily SITREPs."

"Just floating a balloon on this GMBB theft," Moore offered lightly. "We've zeroed in on the bad guy and may turn him to a cooperator to help us drill deeper."

"And the Russians are 'deeper', right?"

"Appears so. On one end it's amateur hour, but on the other, 91st Street could be involved."

"You've jumped a few links talking to me about this," Miller warned. "Heslin in New York will not be happy if he finds out."

"He knows we're buddies, right? I'm just chatting about work, Harold. Besides, he's holding up another side of the same deal with this Misha dude."

"Well, two things. Do not, under any circumstances, lose the football, the chip, to some unknown and second...." He paused as if formulating how to say it. "When you stop drilling, you better have rock solid evidence."

"Got it, Harold. Thanks."

"I'll drill down from this end and stir up the alphabet soup. Make sure everyone's got their ears up," Miller promised. He found his strongest influence from the top seat in the IC was to just remind folks to check their daily reports. "There is so much intelligence flowing in this DC cesspool, a nod from me often helps kick the stream in the right direction."

"Don't know if you have anything on the Russians at the consulate. Justice is aware, but I'm not sure if they are watching 91st Street on a regular basis. Any hint of what they are up to would be good to know," Seamus explained.

"Oh, yea, we're looking at them. I know a guy," Harold laughed. "And Seamus."

"Yea?"

"Yes, we are on for 10-hundred hours next Wednesday at Congressional in Bethesda."

"Great! I'll be there, assuming we wrap up this one by then."

"Bring your sand wedge and your wallet. In fact, you better bring two sand wedges!"

With that, Miller was gone. Agent Moore laughed at his old friend and took a deep breathe to refocus.

"Martin! Vanallison! Carlson! Jenn, you too! Let's go! We got some bad guys to catch!"

twenty-eight

FRANCOIS

Thursday 1000

The five eyes alliance has added a sixth eye. French Military Intelligence (DGSE) joined in discussions with the Canucks, Aussies, Kiwis, Brits and the 'mericans - sharing intel. "This means we have something to offer!" says one happy Frenchman sitting at the table. –SpyhakrF

The old man was just happy to be out of the house after three days of hacking away at several new sources. His interest sparked shortly after the BOLO for one Luke Parmelian showed up on his computer screen from the Rhode Island State Police "Cops Line", as he called it. That was the secure email network from HQ out of Providence used to notify state troopers of alerts and pending actions around the state.

It wasn't completely secure because he had hacked into it from his man cave in the Stone Tower where he lived on top of Beacon Hill on Block Island. He had a feeling in his bones that this Parmelian character was not far away. That excited him but, first things first. He had to replenish his food supply.

So, Francois Demuniez - the "z" is silent - found himself on this first Thursday in June enjoying the fresh southwesterly breeze and the dissipated fog as he walked down the hill intent on visiting Maggie at the BI Grocery. It was warm for an early June day and the two-mile walk would do him good. Ease the eye strain he endured from too many hours in front of a computer screen.

A wise old man once said the first spy was the wife of the first husband suspected of sleeping with a prostitute, thus making it the second oldest profession in the world. Then the government got involved.

Demuniez always liked that sentiment, or maybe it was a joke told at a cocktail party. Whatever and whenever, it was clear to him the level of mistrust continued rampant among humans who don't want others to know what they do but can't control their desire to know what everyone else is doing.

Of course, governments and corporations convinced themselves to spy for their own protection. They must prevent their neighbors from executing any plan that will debilitate their efforts to maintain control over the governed or just win the race to the marketplace.

Francois Demuniez was the world's ultimate spy. He spied on all the spies. A self-taught hacker, he tapped into the security networks of more than a dozen countries, agencies and individual agents to create the first and only true Spy Blog. He created a niche that let spies know what other spies were doing or had done. The town crier in a community of dark secrets.

Spying was in his blood by birth since his father parlayed a heroic career in the French Resistance during World War II to an equally courageous career with the *Direction Générale de la Sécurité Extérieure*, the DGSE, France's version of the CIA.

Demuniez followed his father into the French spy world until his career was interrupted by the *Rainbow Warrior* affair in the mid 80's. People died and fellow agents were charged by New Zealand authorities with murder and terrorism in the bombing of the ship that Greenpeace used to protest atomic weapon testing by France in the South Pacific. Demuniez escaped on a French submarine but fell out of favor with his superiors who publicly threw a lot of the blame his way. He dropped out of site for more than twenty years, but this Thursday afternoon found him walking toward Old Harbor in sunshine.

He survived off a modest pension from the DGSE and a fund created by his now late father who used stolen insider information while spying on French industries to create an endowment for his son. Most of Francois' time and money now went into hacking the web.

Demuniez worked the dark side, behind the public pages that sold the propaganda for the intelligence agencies around the world. The alphabet soup made him dizzy at first, but as he dug deeper, he unraveled a world of back channels, double secret alleyways of electrons and bits and bytes. After many years of keystrokes, books and articles and a few well-placed old friends, he was able to create an extraordinary reputation as *"SpyhakrF"*.

His audience was built from the men and women who did the spying. He had no clients and no agenda, only idle time that became a passion and soon overwhelmed his quiet life on the sandy chunk of glacial excess called Block Island that had been his home for the last 15 years. As long as he had electricity and an internet connection, he was king of the spy hack.

It started at DGSE with a backdoor password into the

French paymaster's database. That led to an operational local area network in Calais and soon he was reading the email of the Commandant of foreign operations in Paris. With no timetable in mind, but an endless curiosity, he tapped into a rich stream of information. And then he passed it on.

The acronyms were pervasive and covered so many layers of intelligence gathering. NCIA, NATO, FVEY, NCIS, NSB, FBI, CIA, MSS, DGSE and of course, LSMFT! He found the agencies who connected larger groups were easier because there were many countries involved and a need to keep it simple across software and hardware differences. NCIA connected NATO. FVEY connected the Five Eyes Alliance from Australia, New Zealand, Canada, US and UK. The hacks hit as diverse a culture as the Naval Criminal Investigation Service from the US and the Ministry of State Security from China. The National Security Branch of the FBI was just another target who used the internet to communicate with other agencies and each other. He was able to create legitimate accounts under the user name of RobMorr04 on many of the networks.

Francois hacked his way through code, line by line into each of these agencies. Like the man in the middle, he read the network communications without anyone knowing he was there. He grabbed tidbits that interested him. Like a reporter watching through an open window, he learned a lot about how these agencies worked, what they knew, who they told and who they didn't tell.

He stayed in the background, an observer not an abuser. He never attempted to change plans in motion, only noted their existence when he blogged about the ones most interesting.

Armed with a growing list of email addresses from these agencies, it didn't take long for his blog to become a favorite among the spies upon whom he spied. He used deeply encoded VPNs to keep the source of the blog hidden. He dabbled with X-agent from the Chinese and even wrote his own program that shifted the apparent original location of his blog each time it was broadcast. The recipients found it in their inbox and the true links would disappear or be rerouted down blind, what he called, 'ether alleys'.

The frustration of the agency counter-hackers grew during the first year of his reports. He was able to stay one or two links ahead. Eventually, they stopped tracking him and became fans. His blogs made him the beat reporter in a village square for deep state operatives. Hints, eyewitness accounts, maybe's and could be's became his staple.

When Francois wasn't culling the net for spy fodder, he was the village crier on Block Island, hanging at the Post Office, at the Boat Basin, at the Beach View Bar and town meetings, culling local information or dispensing it. He became master of the who's who and what do they do.

A lanky man of 70 years, his familiar fishing cap, pipe and cocker spaniel dog named "Frankie" were a fixture to the year-round residents of the island and a quaint attraction for the summer travelers. He appeared totally harmless and friendly, engaging at will with others and enticing everyone to talk about themselves. He was a man without an agenda, just a natural, friendly attitude.

Thousands of visitors came to Block Island weekly so one of his active connections was the police BOLO network. If the cops wanted to find you, they alerted everyone to "Be On the Lookout" for who you were, what you did and where you might hang out.

By Tuesday midday, Francois received the BOLO with a photo of one Luke Parmelian of New London. A computer technician suspected of stealing secrets from Globallus Marine Boat Builders. That was interesting news for his blog and promptly posted it for his followers. The thought that something as exciting as a national security manhunt was happening a couple of dozen miles away in Connecticut gave him a thrill.

He couldn't hide the fact from himself that he wished he could help find the guy. But first, he needed to resupply his refrigerator and maybe get a drink.

twenty-nine

LUCIUS LANDOW

Thursday Afternoon

MI6 and CIA chatter regards co-op with small band of Iranian dissidents near Bandar-e-Jask on Straits of Hormuz. Patrol boat sabotage reported, putting 15 Iranian boats out of commission for several weeks. Sugar in gas tanks does the deed! IRG not laughing. Shippers applauding. —SpyhakrF

It was raining hard in Boston and Lucius Landow needed one more stop before he started his American Taxi Tour. He pulled his custom restored English cab to the curb on a side street behind the modern office building three clicks from Harvard Square. Freshly retired from MI6 after 45 years in the British spy business, Lucius had big plans for the summer. He was going to add what he called a "Chekhov" to his bucket list. Amazingly, for a career that took him all over the world, from China to India to the Middle East, South Africa and Australia, he had never been to the United States.

Now he was about to embark on a tour of America in his 1972 Austin FX4 Taxi. The classic design, at one time ubiquitous on the streets of London, with the steering wheel on the right side, luggage space next to the driver and a wide open bench seat in back for passengers, designed with extra head room to accommodate top hats, was to be what he called, "my chariot of retire". He didn't have any plans for passengers, but he could take them if he so desired. What plan he did have was open ended, with hopes he could circumnavigate all 48 states before either the car gave up or his heart did.

But, first things first. "Chekhov" some old friends.

One of his dearest, Carl Lemon, had invited him to stop by when he was in town. Lucius dutifully followed Carl's directions from the Boston Autoport, where he picked up his freshly delivered taxi from England and found himself on the 5th floor in front of a doorway with the name Continental Importers Associates stenciled on the smoked glass. He immediately noticed the small camera in the ceiling and saw a door bell. He pressed it, smiled at the camera and the door unlocked with a click.

"Double Zero!" exclaimed the small, bald man in a friendly greeting. They shook hands, paused for a moment, sizing each other up and then shared a hug.

"Mr. C," Lucius responded warmly. The "C" stood for Carl and for cypher, because Carl Lemon was one of the top codebreakers in the CIA. They had worked closely together over the years on dozens of cases around the world, each representing the best intel the close allies had to offer, first by teletype, then emails, phone calls and more recently by skype and facetime. However, this was the first moment they were physically in the same room at the same time.

Over glasses of Scotch on the rocks, the two spy veterans sat in Lemon's office overlooking the Cambridge skyline to the right and Boston to the left with the Charles River between.

"You plan to travel the US in that thing!?" Carl laughed looking at Lucius' unique vehicle on the street below. "You've come out of the shadows, haven't you? You'll probably become a Facebook hero when folks start seeing that on the streets of America."

"Isn't that a thought?" Lucius responded, as if the idea hadn't crossed his mind before. "That might be fun, but I must admit, I'm looking to not have to deal with folks. This trip is an escape."

"And escape from this life, eh?" Carl smiled grimly. "You realize it will not be easy after decades of chasing down intel, matching faces, numbers, meets, photos. Looking, looking, looking and now suddenly, not looking? I know you. Not going to be easy."

"And what are you doing in Boston? I didn't know the CIA had satellite offices. Looking for something in particular?" Lucius couldn't help but be curious. Carl was right, information was what he thrived on.

"Lucius, we even have bad guys in Boston. I'm probably here for a few more weeks. Some phone trails to follow. I'm calling it Baku in Boston." He tossed him a folder and invited him to open it.

"Baku, as in Azerbaijan?" Lucius asked as he looked at the one-page list of names and places with phone numbers.

"Recognize anyone?" Carl nodded.

Lucius studied it for a moment and tossed it back with a smile.

"Got one there. Huseynova. Elvina Huseynova. Guns and heroin. She's been around a few years. Used to sleep with a man name Hamil. She took over his smuggling operation."

"What happened to him?" Carl asked.

"Oh, I shot him." Lucius said straight faced. "He was a very bad actor."

Carl looked at his friend for a moment and then raised his glass in toast. "And where might I find Elvina?"

"Old intel had her in Erzurum, I believe. Turkey. What is she up to?"

"Don't know yet. There's a buzz about a cell of Azeris chatting locally about guns, C-4, messing with the southern Caucasus pipeline, so we're just trying keep abreast of the latest. Connecting the dots of who is talking to whom. The pipe goes right through Erzurum. Who knows? Same old. Same old."

"You have anyone there?" Lucius asked.

"Hmm, probably. We'll try to find out why the folks here are talking to this Elvina. Might be a money connection. If she's there, that's a big dot to dot connect!" He laughed. "We try to be everywhere, you know! Can't always pull that off."

The phone rang on Carl's desk and he answered it. Lucius recognized the comm box that secured the line. He only heard one side of the conversation, a terse "Okay" from Carl after 30 seconds.

He then turned to his computer and opened a password protected file. He read the text that appeared on the screen and then closed the app.

"You following the security breach over on the Thames in Connecticut?" he asked Lucius.

"Not really. I did see mention of it a couple days ago on the spy blog." Lucius smiled inside about the mention of the Thames. He thought of his own apartment on the Thames in London awaiting his return. His curiosity regarding the British influence on the history of New London on the Thames in Connecticut had caused it to be included on his American Taxi Tour itinerary in the next day or so.

"Well, they think the guy who stole the files is on Block Island!" Carl announced. "Looks like the FBI is all over it."

"Oh, my! I had planned to see a friend who lives on Block Island." Lucius said, with a twinkle in his eye. "A busman's holiday, maybe?"

"Well, have at it, my friend! You're only a couple hours and a ferry ride away!"

Carl confirmed the directions as he knew them to get to Block from Boston and after another scotch and a few stories, laughs and warm goodbyes, Lucius was in his taxi with a sense of adventure ahead of him. First, the Red Sox game that night, followed by a stay at the Charles Street Hotel downtown and then a day trip to Block Island to see old Francois, another spy guy who he had not seen in over 20 years.

He felt like a kid with a week off from school with a strange desire to bring a math book with him.

thirty

ASIS

Thursday Lunch

Aussies see Chinese, Chinese see Aussies. Military growth for both. Aussies open with a dozen subs from India, designed by French. Chinese counter with six carriers in build. ASIS goes to DC hoping to share sub secrets with US Navy." —SpyhakrF

Jack Bangerman was built to play rugby, but he was far more comfortable chasing information. He loved the intrigue of Washington, DC where a person who loved chasing information could do well. There was so much to chase! A former Special Ops soldier in the Australian Army with two tours in Afghanistan and Iraq, he had put down his guns and turned to spy craft as a special agent for the Australian Secret Intelligence Service, known as ASIS.

ASIS was the eyes and ears of the Australian government out of country, interacting with allies and spying on enemies to stay on top of the intelligence wars that affected the politics at home.

And he was up to his bushy blonde eyebrows this week as he sat with his good friend, *Capitaine* Pierre Petit of the French Navy at the Oz Club in the heart of the Clarendon neighborhood, a ten-minute drive from Embassy Row, in the heart of the District of Columbia.

"Pierre, the kangaroo here is succulent. Give it a burl! Chef Marcus soaks it, then cooks it and that keeps the juices," Jack suggested earnestly, confident of his suggestion based on many meals of personal satisfaction. "Sure, some of my fellow countrymen are spewing about eating Kangaroo. They'll give you a gobfull about the sacrilege of devouring the favorite pet of the down under but, fuck that, I say! No one thinks twice about ordering rabbit, do they? If *any* animal rules Australia, it's rabbit!" He laughed loudly and doused the noise with a gulp of his beer.

"Jack, do your kangaroo swim? You know I'm a fish guy," grinned his companion. The former FSM submarine commander now spent his days and nights in DC trying to keep the French Navy brain trust up to speed on what the US Navy brain trust was thinking, planning and hiding. If he still wore his uniform, he would have 5 stripes on his shoulder boards.

He enjoyed the diplomatic work after a dozen years patrolling underwater. He once led a joint training mission in the Mediterranean that resulted in his sub, the *Casablanca*, infiltrating the US Navy's fleet perimeter and painting the USS *Dwight D. Eisenhower* aircraft carrier with torpedoes. That "training victory" stood him well over the years and landed him in Washington.

The two patriots from different cultures had only met two weeks prior at an opening night gala at the new Latvian embassy. It was quickly apparent their devil made care spirits were in tune. As was their love of spirits. They became drinking buds in a moment amidst the rarified air of the world's power players.

Jack invited Pierre to lunch at the famed Aussie eatery to chase down information. The Australians Pacific Step Up campaign was well underway as the ruling Labor party extended the point of the spear from down under with a major outlay of military dollars to build new aircraft carriers and submarines.

The French designed the subs and Pierre was a trusted ally who advised on operational tactics. He was scheduled to travel to Adelaide, Australia next month to help train the crews of the first boat hitting the water.

"I will try some of this Australian wine because I am a wine guy most of all," Pierre continued with mock seriousness then toasted his friend and swallowed what was left in his glass.

"Easy, Pierre! Aussie wine is meant to be sipped, so you can savor the blood, sweat and tears of our criminal roots."

"I don't know how you buggers can survive in all that heat and dirt!" the Frenchman joked, shaking his head. "Dry as a dead dingo's donger, right?"

"Not bad, mate. Keep listening, you'll pick up the lingo." Jack smiled at his friend. They fell silent for a moment.

"I've got to ask you something," Jack got serious.

Petit wasn't ready to shift the conversation just yet.

"You able to afford this lunch now that you've shot your wad?" They both knew he was referring to the $50 billion dollar contract the Aussies had signed with the French to build the dozen new submarines.

"No worries, mate. I've got the docket. There's big mobs of cash coming your way," Jack answered with a laugh. "But I need to know something."

Capitaine Petit looked at his friend in anticipation, all ears.

"What the fuck is wrong with the Americans?" Jack asked simply.

The unprecedented agreement between the French and Australian governments had thrust both countries out of the myopic view that the USA controlled all military decisions in the world.

The Indo-Pacific region was heating up. A growing Chinese military was the obvious concern. So was the level of uncertainty generated from the petulant American president about future support for decades old alliances. As the Aussie Defense Minister posed it when the agreement was signed, "...we are entering a very changed, dynamic strategic environment."

As she put it, the French had "equities" in the Pacific, while the Australians had "family". Yet, the long-term interests for security and stability were the same. Both countries felt a need to do it on their own.

It wasn't as if a dozen diesel-electric Barracuda class attack subs would suddenly make Adelaide the Submarine Capital of the World. That moniker was solidly stuck in Groton where GMBB was a century of war ship production ahead. Regardless, both soldiers turned diplomats were feeling pretty cocky, even if they were only the smaller cousins.

The US had something Jack's bosses wanted and that had become his main mission in DC. The laser communication system in the form of the SLACLONET 1000 designed by Dr. Andy and being installed on US subs was not being made available to the US Navy's allies around the world. Both governments felt left out, snubbed and demeaned by their bigger brother.

"I don't know," Petit responded. "They have shut us out as well. Either it doesn't work or, it works so well they want to keep their cards close to the vest. They may not trust us.

I mean, look at you blokes, busting out with a new fleet. Everyone's looking around a bit at the new playing field."

"Ya, but we've busted our hump, carried the water for a few decades, mate. In the jungle, the desert, the mountains of Afghanistan?" Jack complained.

"They are probably pissed at us," Pierre continued. "We haven't smacked down the Russians for their cyber antics. Maybe it's the gas pipeline we're building to connect Europe and Russia. They don't like anything or anyone making the Russkies stronger."

"Maybe they should look in their own closets, eh?" Jack said with distrain. "It's always 'follow the money'. We deserve to see the goodies, mate!"

"Well, somebodies gonna see them, because the Americans have got a spot of trouble right now, wouldn't you say?" Pierre gestured with his phone as if it held the answers.

"What trouble?"

"You don't know?" Petit looked around, eying the crowd sitting around them. It looked like a mix of business men, government officials and casual couples stealing a midweek afternoon. He lowered his voice and leaned in.

"Someone stole some files," he practically whispered. "Just happened this week. We call it *un probleme majuer!*" He quickly poked at his phone and went on line to the blogosphere, pulling up the latest notification from 'spyhakrF".

"You don't subscribe to spyhakrF?" Pierre asked as he showed his saved messages. Jack took the phone and read the blurb. It was dated two days ago on Tuesday evening.

"The USIC on full alert with reports of stolen top-secret files from GMBB. The ground is rumbling with BOLO for local geek. FBI heading up the

*man hunt or is that a chip hunt? Special focus
aimed at the Russian mob. Anyone surprised
here? –SpyhakrF*

"Well, holy crap, *Capitaine*, that's a big cock up! I'll bet
DNI Miller is mad as a cut snake!" Bangerman shook his
head. He had met Miller at the welcoming party all new US
agency heads throw and thought him a solid, straight shooter
with a worldly understanding of how allies should act.

"Who is this 'spyhakerF'?"

"Some gentleman out there wired into the spy world? I
don't know, but I've become a fan. He appears to be on top
of most of the shit that is happening!"

Capitaine Petit reached for the bottle of Australian wine
in front of him and poured himself another glass.

"You're a soldier of fortune, Jack. Maybe you can track
this geek down and get your own copy of the files," Petit
laughed. Jack didn't look up from the phone screen. He was
scrolling through past posts and the content surprised him.
He was especially intrigued to read one entry concerning a
Special Op in Borneo where he personally knew two of the
participants.

"Some of this stuff is classified!" Jack muttered as he
handed the phone back.

"That it is, my friend. That it is."

Jack took another swallow of his beer and looked at his
French friend.

"Are your folks doing anything about acquiring the laser
comm?" he asked, switching back to his main purpose.

"We've made our desires known to the Navy, but I think
we'll play the patience card. At some point it will pop up,
either from them, like a reward they'll give us for some trick
that helps their goals. You know, 'roll over, good boy!'." He

laughed. "Or maybe someone else will reveal it." He pointed to his phone.

"My DG is not a patient man. He wants it now!" Jack could see the sour, bespectacled face of his Director General the last time they met in his office at ASIS, practically scolding him for failing on the mission he hadn't begun yet. He was an ex-Brigadier in the Army and expected things to be done as he commanded them.

"Whatever it takes. That's what he said." Jack finished his beer and set the glass down with a thump and a big smile. "He knows I'm that guy!"

Pierre tipped his glass to Jack.

"Tu es l'homme. Etre l'homme."

"So, how do I subscribe to this hacker dude?" Jack asked, pulling out his phone. Pierre picked up his own phone and showed Jack how to subscribe to *SpyhakrF*. They looked like a couple of teenaged girls in the cafeteria, their eyes focused on their screens, but their intentions far more serious.

thirty-one

SHERIFF BOBBY
GETS INVOLVED

Friday 0600

Lukey P, he's the man, stole the secret, on the lam...
GMBB Groton on the scram with missing info on
the one-thous-and. FBI won't let it go, Block's the
place for IC BOLO. –SpyhakrF

Francois woke up Friday morning with the sudden realization that the person pictured in the BOLO from Tuesday was the same person in the fight with Freddy Thursday night. And the person's photo on the BOLO was the same person he photographed talking with Petrika at the Beach View Bar. He shook his head disgusted with getting old. He should have noticed that right away when he snapped the phone shots last night after the fight!

Probably shouldn't have had that last wine, he realized, vaguely remembering being helped to Win McGovern's cab at closing time after the Sheriff had wrapped up his questioning of the witnesses left over from the fight with Freddy.

He realized he owed Bobby Jackson a conversation.

So, the world was looking for Luke Parmelian and he was right here on Block Island!

"I knew it!" he shouted out loud and jumped out of bed, grabbed his phone and dialed Sheriff Bobby Jackson's direct number.

When the phone connected, Francois didn't even allow the sheriff to answer.

"Bobby, guess what? That guy in the BOLO is here, on Block, right now! He's the one in the fight with Freddy last night! I've got pictures! You better call the Feds!"

"Now, Francois, slow down. It's way too early to get your ticker going like this." The Sheriff was a mostly laid-back guy, tough but easy going, not one to get excited by events.

"I'm glad you are back with the living. You were in no shape last night!"

Bobby Jackson had seen a lot of things as a Providence policeman over the years and his 5-year stint as Block's number one cop had been good for his blood pressure.

"What time is it?" Francois asked, pacing around his bedroom.

"It's 630 in the morning, Francois."

"Oh, shit! I'm sorry. It hit me first thing and I figured you should know."

"Right. Got it. No problem. I was up already." The Sheriff took a breath. "Fact is, I haven't slept a wink."

"What's going on?" Francois asked, surprised.

"Well, seems Freddy met his match and ended up dead on Amy Dodge last night. Stabbed in the chest. The medical examiner is coming over today."

"Oh, man! Murdered?!" Francois shook his head.

"Appears so. Maybe we should get some breakfast and

talk," Sheriff Jackson suggested to his friend. They had hit it off right from the start of the Sheriff's tenure on the island and were used to bouncing ideas off each other when issues arose. Both of them had yet to deal with a murder on the island, so this was going to be new ground.

"Give me an hour, see you at Ernie's," Francois replied without skipping a beat.

"Better make it two," Bobby replied. "I've got some things to sort out here. I'll text you when it's time."

"Sounds like a plan," Francois answered.

"Francois, send me those photos, okay. Right now."

"On the way."

"Great. I'll call the FBI. See you later." The line went dead.

Francois hung up, pulled on some clothes and headed to his computer room in the tower. He forwarded the two snaps of Luke and Petrika talking. He looked again, wishing the lighting was better, but the guy's nose, chin and hair were clearly the same as the BOLO ID photo. He felt confident he was on the right track.

He then checked his digital sources and spotted an email from Naval Operations Command ordering two pilots to standby at Quonset Airport (OQU), making reference to REACT unit USN1715 and the slug line "OPS BI TBD". He composed a brief blog note and hit send, tickling the notification alerts on his fans' phones across the world. He felt like his years of distant spying had suddenly come home.

thirty-two

CHOCKA COOK

Friday AM

Circle drawing tighter, photos don't lie. Your SpyhakrF sees the face and it's on Block Island now. Feds making move, Russians, too. Everyone wants what LukeP's got. But where is he? —*SpyhakrF*

Jack Bangerman's Friday morning jog around the Washington monument ended abruptly when his phone bleeped an alert from the *SpyhakrF* blog he had only subscribed to the day before. Upon reading it, he made a typically bold and brash decision to stick his nose in where he was sure it wasn't wanted. He hadn't convinced himself yet that it wasn't needed.

Two hours later he was on a chartered Pilatus PC-12 flying from Dulles Airfield toward Block Island at 300 knots. The alert stated that Luke Parmelian was there, and he was suspected of stealing the plans for the US Navy's new laser communications device. The same device he had been sent to acquire for his Australian Navy. Jack offered his friend

Capitaine Pierre Petit a chance to travel with him on ASIS' dime, but the French sailor declined.

"Patience, Jack, patience," Pierre had coached. "Not going to get my hands dirty just yet. Don't want to piss off the Americans. Other battles to fight. Besides, I have a meeting this afternoon at the Pentagon."

"Well, send my regards, Pierre," Jack retorted through the phone. "The only patience I have are the ones I'll put in the hospital if they get in my way!"

"Be the man, Jack! Go take your Captain Cook!" Pierre laughed and hung up.

As Jack's flight flew through the clouds, he scrolled the web for information about the island and fought off any sense of doubt about his mission. He did admit he did not have a solid grip on the tactical situation on the ground. Just a dark image of a man named Luke and an island that covered 12 square miles.

He also had a terse text from his Director General in Canberra asking, "Broken any doors yet?" He laughed and considered that the full go ahead to follow his hunch.

Even the pilot could not stop Jack when he announced Block Island was socked in with fog and their only options were to divert to New London or maybe Montauk on the eastern end of Long Island.

"Which is closer to Block?" Jack asked.

"Montauk is about six miles closer. Still open and looks like weather is moving west to east. We could hole up there for an hour," the pilot answered.

"Land us there. I'll get a boat the rest of the way."

By the time they touched down, Jack had already secured an Axopar 37-foot motor yacht capable of 50 knots on a good day. It was floating at the Lake Montauk Marina, literally across the street from the end of the runway.

"You Jack?" he asked the young man in his 20's in the marina office.

"I'm Jack. And you're Jack, right?" responded the man with a smile, extending his hand. The Jacks shook hands.

"Nice to meet you, mate. Let's get a roll on."

"Need payment up front. $500."

Jack handed Jack his ASIS credit card, signed the receipt and in five minutes they slipped lines, the young Jack stepped behind the wheel, throttled up the twin 350 Mercury engines and they were off.

"Finnish design, you said?" Jack commented as the props dug in and the boat accelerated out of the narrow channel that connected Lake Montauk with Block Island Sound. The skinny, deep hulled vessel with a wraparound glass cabin took to the calm water easily and in a short time the speedo was reading 45 knots.

"Old Harbor in 30 minutes," Jack the younger proclaimed.

"This fog planning to slow you down any?" Jack the Aussie asked.

"No worries, mate! I'm not planning on slow." said Jack the younger. He punched on the radar and focused on keeping the throttles open and the boat on the GPS plotted course.

Jack Bangerman had no idea was he was rushing into but pressed on with confidence. He would handle it for his team on the other side of the planet.

thirty-three

HAE-TAE SE - DPRK

Thursday 1300

*Decrepit. Diesel. Deceptive. Still Dangerous?
45 DPRK subs missing from NoKorea ports.
South Korea Navy on alert. 2nd time in 3 years
DPRK Navy shakes status quo between North
and South. Ongoing negotiations come to halt.
US Navy deploys R-8 recon to help locate missing
subs. —SpyhakrF*

Hae-Tae Se awoke from a deep slumber filled with images of fairies and flowers, winged creatures in white and a robe flowing from her shoulders, complete with a frosty crown on her head. The taste of blood and semen was fresh on her tongue. She smiled, exposing a row of pearly white teeth, unseen in the darkness of the garage she had chosen for her bedroom.

It had been a tiring 24-hours but she was used to the simplicity of hardship and living moment to moment. Her training at the hands of the Democratic People's Republic of

Korea Secret Service had created a machine-like operative who was equally adept at the honeytrap as she was at assassination. In fact, the two were so often linked, that one frequently followed the other.

Murder often followed sex. Sex sometimes followed murder, though not with the same person, of course. She had yet to travel *that* road.

She was effective and the counter intelligence string pullers of the North Korean government, all the way up to the Supreme Leader, were aware of her talents and used them when they could.

She reached into her knapsack and retrieved a bottle of mouthwash, swished the tangy liquid around in her mouth and swallowed. Then a swig from a bottle of fresh water that she spit on the dirt floor. Next, she pulled her laptop from the bag, established a signal with her portable modem and began the secure upload of the data she had acquired the day before from the scientist at the Brookhaven National Lab on eastern Long Island.

The thumb drive contained the latest research on High Temperature Superconductors, knowns as HTS, capable of carrying 150 times the amount of electricity in a fraction of the space required by copper wire. Simple efficiency, more power, smaller wires, shorter runs. For a country trying to join the 22nd century, North Korea had ambitions of leapfrogging its enemies. Building a more efficient power grid was just one way to the dream. Literally, a power grab.

As she watched the progress bar move slowly but steadily, she thought of the slow and steady morning of love making with the older scientist before he balked at turning over the promised material. Her nakedness apparently not enough, she provided the final motivation with a knife in the neck. Men are so easy to manipulate with the proper tools, she thought, shaking her head. The thrill of power was satisfying.

The upload complete, she opened another file and created her report for the completed mission and sent it off to the clandestine control center in New York City. She watched the screen for several minutes until a reply appeared.

Shelter in place.

A small murmur escaped from her lips and she shut down her laptop, sat back and let her mind go idle for only a moment. Soon, the feeling of zipping across the water with a personal watercraft between her legs filled her mind. It was a fun trip from Connecticut necessitated by the sudden change in missions ordered by her handler after the Brookhaven job. She had been on her way to Canada, but now she was on Block Island.

Shelter in place.

She had been trained to never waste time. When inactive - sleep. When awake - exercise, explore, eat, execute.

She had slept. Now, she exercised. She stood up and began her 30-minute routine that kept her limber and balanced. She finished the workout and found the rental property's water main valve and turned it on. She slipped into the empty house to enjoy a cold shower.

She couldn't help but wonder about her motorcycle parked in the marina back in Charlestown 12 miles across Block Island Sound where she stole the Sea-Doo 500. The ride across on the water rocket had been thrilling, but she loved the ground hugging bike and the way it set her free in the wind, the vibration through her body and the speed, the danger, the need for careful and quick decisions. She smiled again, thinking the only thing missing was a white robe flowing from behind. Then she stopped worrying about the motorcycle.

Shelter in place. Or explore? She chose to explore.

thirty-four

FINAL CALL

Thursday Late

Cold War spies vs. Brain War spies? DNI Miller raises red flag over Chinese Comm Party funding educational efforts in US colleges. Playing long game, Confucius Institute pays to preach support for Party View. Covert influence, espionage or Chinese 101? NSC investigating. —SpyhakrF

Misha Yanovich Yevtechnov admired the painting of horses in full gallop, their mouths open, their teeth bared and the red, green and gold bits connecting rider and steed. The artist from the turn of the 20th century had only captured their heads in full gulping effort with a colorful expression of all its pain and joy. One could imagine what their legs looked like as they raced to some unseen finish line.

It was the horses' effort that drew Misha to the image. The physical exertion driven by the will to move at the highest levels. To overcome inertia, gravity and the limits of the body to reach the heights of performance. Or did the image show the sheer pain resulting from these same efforts?

If the painting could speak, would it shout in agony or in ecstasy? You can't have one without the other, he thought.

Misha always wondered if the horses weren't running from something, driven by fear to reach for the limits of their physical ability and, upon reaching that peak, experiencing the total joy of satisfaction. Somewhere in that mystical mishmash of interpretation was the nexus of why he loved his amusement park.

That the painting was not of real horses on a track, but of the original merry go round horses that he had restored, sitting on the boardwalk only a few feet below where he now sat, only helped sustain his magical world on Coney Island.

ScreamTown was built upon the thrills that drove the screams that ended in joy upon returning to earthly normalcy. The phone had rung three times before Misha broke from his musings to pick it up from his desk in the Brighton Beach apartments one floor above Misha's real House of Cards.

"This is Misha," he answered absently, his eyes focused on the splash of color hanging on his wall.

"Misha, this is Luke. Luke Parmelian," came the static laced voice on the other end. Misha's vision went red and he caught his breath.

"Luke! Luke, Luke, Luke," he said quietly at first.

"You miserable, son of a bitch, Luke!" he shouted into the phone.

"Yea, go ahead, I deserve it. I stood you up!"

"You stood me up! Luke, I am not sure you appreciate the situation you are in. You owe me money and I am not one you want to owe money! And I am not one to be stood up!"

Misha's voice had a wide range and high volume was not always the way he displayed his anger. When he started talking, he was shouting, then he softened his voice when he got to the part about owing money. By the end, he was talking in what can only be described as a vicious whisper.

"Misha, I understand," Luke answered meekly. He and Antoine had talked about how to approach Misha in this phone call and they expected he would have to ride a wave of anger. Luke, however, was a little unsettled by the viciousness and felt that fear for his life that had been a part of the whole mess from the beginning.

"Luke, I am not sure you understand me. How serious I am. I am wondering now that maybe this information I need from you, maybe this isn't enough for your present debt. What is it, $120,000? Maybe I will need something else from you."

In a nearby high-rise apartment building on Coney Island Avenue, Bob Smoot nudged his partner Bob Smith and smiled. "That's what we want to hear!" he said softly.

The two FBI agents assigned to case MX7234, code named The Fruit Seller, were monitoring Misha Yevtechnov's phone calls. The focus had been racketeering and money laundering, but the new angle included the theft of national secrets. Luke Parmelian was their newest cooperator and they needed his connection with Misha to extend beyond the immediate transfer of secret information. They wanted to follow the trail to Misha's eventual buyer of the missing chip and begin dismantling that network. They had been waiting for the call.

"Misha, I have nothing else to give."

"Luke, sure you do. A man in your position has access to many important things. Information is the game, my friend. It is very valuable."

"I may have burned my bridges there," Luke said with regret.

"Do they know it was you?" Misha asked.

"I'm on the list of access for sure, so I'm guessing they

suspect me along with others," Luke lied, knowing full well the FBI was aware of the theft and was expecting him to cooperate.

"I see," Misha said quietly. "You do have the package still, correct?" Misha was thinking more about the 100 large coming his way if he delivered to Vladimir.

"Yes, I have it and I *am* ready to give it to you. But it has to be on my terms."

"Oh, Lukey my friend, you are not in a position to bargain with me. I need that package. It is very important to me and I will come get it from you."

"I think I am in a position to bargain, Misha. I *do* have the package. If you want it, you will have to get it from me and no one else." Luke heard the silence on the line.

"Where are you now, Luke?" Misha asked after a full 30 seconds of quiet.

"Not yet! I'm nowhere. I'm everywhere. You have to meet me tomorrow at 330 pm on Block Island. Do you know The Oar?"

"The Oar? I have heard of this place. Best stocked bar in New England. Used to be a getaway place for wise guys from Providence, right? What is at The Oar?"

"That's where we meet. 330 pm. 1530 tomorrow. No questions, just be there. Wear your Yankee cap, if you like. I will meet you, you will get the package and my debt is paid. You will then leave me alone." Luke hung up the phone, breathing hard.

"You will not stand me up this time?" Misha asked sarcastically, but immediately realized the phone had clicked in his ear and the line was dead.

"Luke!? Luke? You son of a bitch!" Misha shouted at the top of his lungs and threw the phone across the room where it slammed into the wooden frame of the horse painting he had been admiring earlier. His anger at Luke was suddenly replaced by his concern for the painting. He rushed over and was relieved the phone had missed the actual canvas and had only left a minor blemish in the gilded frame's golden surface.

His anger at Luke resurfaced and simmered as he pondered what to do next. He needed the package because he had promised Vladimir and he needed the cash promised him. It was worth the risk, but he was not happy he had lost control of the circumstances of the transfer.

He picked up the phone from the corner of his office where it had landed in his fitful explosion and dialed McSamarlie's number. He was pleased to see the phone working but not pleased when it went direct to voicemail. He did not like being out of touch with his people, especially when he needed to get something done.

"Mr. J, where the fuck are you?" he whispered into the phone when prompted to leave a message. He tossed the phone on his desk and walked to the corner window to watch the final rays of sun setting over the Brighton Beach boardwalk. He could see the lights were on in ScreamTown two blocks away and people were coming out to enjoy the early days of summer. The Wonder Wheel turned, the Cyclone rattled, and the Cage went flying high in the air along with the attendant screams. That calmed him. His love was here, along the sand, the classic wooden boardwalk, the lights and the noise of thrills, the laughter and fear.

He was Misha Yanovich Yevtechnov, the *shef*. This was his world. He was not going to Block Island on Friday afternoon. He had people to do those things for him.

On Coney Island Avenue, FBI special agent Bob Smoot picked up his own phone and dialed his boss to relay the information from the phone call between Luke and Misha.

"Not sure what we can get out of these two down the

road, but the chip hand off is set for tomorrow afternoon," reported Smoot.

"Chip first, the rest later," Special Agent In Charge John Heslin responded. "You and Smith get going with a bug package," he ordered. "You can make the last ferry to Block if you move now."

thirty-five

GAME PLAN

Thursday Night

Block Island is center of universe for world's IC. Enemies and friends sharing the sand. Seek cataclysmic change in sub warfare. Lukey P's got it? Everyone wants it. Focus on The Oar to get the score. Afternoon tea anyone?" –SpyhakrF

In the end, Antoine convinced FBI Special Agent Seamus Moore that Luke wanted a way out and was ready to help capture Russian mobster Misha Yevtechnov.

"If that keeps him out of jail, he's ready to do whatever you want," Antoine argued. "He'll be a great cooperator!"

Vanallison objected again. She believed Luke had no business dealing with a mobster and would likely blow the deal, but Moore didn't agree. He directed his case to the talking heads of Agents Heslin in New York and Dixon in New Haven on TV monitors hooked by satellite to the New London office.

"We have no choice but to take the chance, draw

Yevtechnov in and then be ready to make the best move as it presents itself," he said. He also agreed to allow Antoine to handle Luke, including meeting him on Friday morning to rig a listening device so the handoff with Misha would be recorded live.

That decision was made over protests, but Moore believed two things. One, Luke was not going to deal with anyone else. He clearly had Antoine's confidence where no one else even knew him. Two, he saw something in Antoine that gave him confidence the young security guard may have a future in their business. He acted maturely, was respectful and seemed to have the USA's interests at heart.

"Antoine's has shown some good instincts, so far," he said definitively. "He's the handler on this one. He is closest to our subject."

US Attorney Carlson agreed but Agent Heslin interrupted. His focus had been the RICO cash against Yevtechnov.

"Can we bring charges against this guy yet?" Heslin asked. He was a lifelong cop, used to dealing with the bad guys and the lawyers. He knew they needed evidence to bring charges and they had to be line item specific. The generalized stuff got the story going, but the details were the blood and guts of any good case.

"Can we convince a body of his peers that he has violated the law?" Heslin added, with a touch of annoyance, realizing again how many times he had said the exact same thing.

Carlson was confident.

"We can prove the money laundering and the extortion," she said, holding up a stack of files with affidavits, witness testimony and bank records. "There is way too much money flowing through the fruit stands no matter how many apples and grapefruits he's selling. If he sold all his inventory each week it only would account for a third of the deposits."

"Where's the rest of the money coming from?" Dixon asked.

"We think it's both the Medicaid scam and the gas tax deal. He's over charging the government, bribing doctors for their information, setting up phony labs and we have a dozen witnesses ready to testify that he's running a good old protection racket with the restaurants along Sheepshead Bay."

"Pay or plunder, right? They pay or he plunders." Agent Moore chimed in.

"Well, that's the thing, he's smart about keeping his face and name away from the extortion game. But his crew is all over it."

Carlson reached for another folder.

"And there's the gas scam. He's apparently got a regular crew stealing gasoline tanker trucks from Virginia, Tennessee, as far as South Carolina. They sell the fuel locally, use it at his own string of gas stations, even sell the whole truck to clients in New Jersey and Pennsylvania."

"No taxes, no bulk rates, no nothing. Free gas to sell as the market allows."

"They can turn over 8000 gallons of gas in 24 hours. It's in the ground or in someone's gas tank before the cops start looking."

"There's a paper trail of phony companies, forged invoices and drop boxes, but we can trace about 30 million to the amusement park which Yevtechnov purchased 3 years ago." Carlson dropped the last folder on the pile and handed Moore a one sheet copy of the ownership certificate for ScreamTown at Coney Island.

Heslin looked wearily from the TV. He saw days if not years of court time. Witness testimony, headlines, paper trails and denials, not to mention the likelihood of some nasty business when the witness list was revealed.

"Hadley, nothing would be finer than a clear-cut case of theft, possession and distribution of national secrets. Slam, bam, thank you Misha Yevtechnov. Off the streets you go!"

Hadley agreed wholeheartedly.

"Seamus, do what you have to do to ring up Yevtechnov on possession. We'll couple that with at least the money laundering and the medical equipment scams."

Moore nodded, there was general agreement among the agents and the meeting broke up.

Moore made provisions that Antoine would not be alone. He ordered agents Martin and Vanallison to Block Island that night to stake out the island.

"Worse case, I want you two there to pick him up. He may be a cooperator, but he is still subject to arrest," Moore explained and added with emphasis.

"And we can't let the chip get away."

That seemed to satisfy the two NCIS agents and they shared a smile at the realization they were heading to Block Island that night.

Moore also used Vanallison's contact with the Coast Guard to order the drone in Charlestown on standby for Friday morning in case aerial surveillance of the island was required. He also directed Agent Martin to set up a REACT team out of NCIS office in Newport to also be on stand-by, ready to move at a moment's notice.

The Regional Enforcement Action Capability Team was NCIS's newest unit, their own version of a SWAT team, created after the mass shooting at the Washington Naval Yard in 2013. Recruited from active military and retired civilian units, The Navy took the stand they should be ready if their agents were forced into a dangerous tactical situation. The REACT unit was mobile, armed and trained to provide the necessary firepower for high stakes arrest and protection situations.

The newer unit was more flexible than the FBI's own SWAT team, if for no other reason than scheduling. Eagerness to get their feet wet was a key factor that put the REACT unit on the front burner for this mission. Moore didn't care where the guns came from as long as they were ready and delivered when called. The simple fact a helicopter was available out of Quonset Air Field on Friday that could deliver the unit secured the deal. New York's were already committed.

"Should we contact the local sheriff on Block," Agent Vanallison asked just before she and Agent Martin left the office.

"I'll take care of that in the morning," Moore responded. "Try to fit in quietly unless the bleep hits the fan."

Martin and Vanallison caught the last hi-speed ferry to Block on Thursday night and waited. They checked into the Surf Hotel in Old Harbor, enjoyed a meal on the porch and then a drink at the National overlooking the harbor.

"This is as perfect a romantic set up as we could have asked for, don't you think?" Agent Ed Martin asked his partner Valarie as they watched the last rays of the sunset touch the boats in the harbor.

"Ed, we are working tonight," she said, placing her hand on his and holding it there long enough for him to feel her warmth. Then she took it away. "The focus is the bad guy. It has to be."

Ed Martin looked into her eyes and understood. They were both pros. He also saw she was as interested as he in taking their partnership to another level and he filed away his desire for the moment.

"Next week I'd like to shift the focus to the bad girl," he said seriously. Valarie laughed and nodded. She sipped her iced tea and he turned back to the street to watch the few tourists on island wander by. They sat for another hour, their phones glowing in front of them with the photo of Luke Parmelian. The only thing they recognized was the unmarked van that drove off the final car ferry from Pt. Judith with Bob Smoot and Bob Smith on board, rushed in from Brooklyn by the FBI's New York office to man the surveillance gear for the planned meeting with Misha Yevtechnov on Friday afternoon.

The two of them had a busy night ahead with plans to install a surveillance camera after The Oar closed.

Back in New London, Seamus Moore called his wife to explain he had more work to do and would be spending the night on his office couch. A veteran wife of law enforcement, she wished him luck, offered a declaration of love and hung up, returning to a bed that had been half warm more nights than she cared to remember.

Moore picked up a folder marked New London Mayor, MX9233, Operation Streetscape, and resumed his research into the other pressing case on his agenda.

thirty-six

INTO THE LIGHT

Friday Afternoon

"At least, I won't have to spend the rest of my life in some jail cell," Luke surmised. Petrika touched his ear and slid her fingers gently through his hair, then pulled his head toward her and kissed him on the lips, slowly and passionately, pressing hard against him, then hovering her tongue close to his. She felt a sense of freedom and abandon. Again, like nothing mattered but the two of them right there in the dirty old cellar hidden on some island in America.

"If I cannot live in your cell, I will live in your mind," she smiled when they parted. She surprised herself to hear her own words. I only know this man for a few hours, she thought! Yet, the distance of time is only ahead. Behind is irrelevant. The feelings were right here and now. She trusted them.

"What do you have to do for your friend Antoine?" she asked.

"I have to meet with Misha, the mobster guy from Brooklyn. I have to wear a wire. Give him the chip."

"A wire?" she asked, unfamiliar with the expression.

"A microphone, so the FBI can listen in to me talking to Misha. For evidence," he explained.

"And this will make you free?" she asked again, trying to understand the concept.

"Yea, well, I guess so. It may not be that simple. I'm pretty sure I'm out of a job, but maybe they can set me up in a witness protection program they call it. New ID, new place to live, new life."

"You don't sound so certain," she laughed. "I don't mean to laugh, but is this a promise or is this a wish?"

He looked at her, raised his eyebrows and shrugged his shoulders, conveying an emotion he really didn't know.

"How would you like to come with me to South Bend, Indiana? We can live together, grow vegetables and raise a family." He smiled brightly with eyes wide open. He felt an innocence he didn't understand, an uncertainty that left him completely vulnerable, and yet, he knew if she said "yes", they would start tomorrow.

"Ha! I'm not sure I want to be a farmer again!" she laughed. "Besides, where is this place South Bend, Indiana?"

"I'm guessing it's a place you could go and get lost and no one would find you," Luke smiled. "I had a friend who said he drove past it by nine miles on the highway before he realized he had missed his destination."

"He must have been distracted!" she laughed.

"And I'm afraid that is exactly what you have become," he said to her, stepping closer and putting his arms around her waist and pulling her close to him. They kissed again and it was as good as before and they held it and found that this was something they really liked.

Petrika had never felt as comfortable as she did with this man. Luke's lips told him the same thing. South Bend or East Bend, if she was there, he would make it happy.

"When do you have to go?" Petrika asked after several moments of holding on to each other.

"Soon. My meeting is 330ish. I plan to be late."

"I, too, have to go. Will it be dangerous?" she asked. There was a look of concern on her face.

"Danger is my middle name," he laughed with false bravado.

"No, no, no! Talk. You talk, but this man does not like you, correct? You already left him in lurch, did you not?"

"I have what he needs, so I don't think he will do anything."

"Until they have what they want, no?" She looked at him intently, her eyebrows letting him know what was obvious.

He was silent for a moment, pondering the danger. The pains in his chest, shoulders and legs born from the Irishman's Hurley stick were easily retrieved if he allowed his mind to focus on them. However, he did not expect this meeting with Misha would be a physical confrontation. Just a quick transfer of the chip and it would be over.

Or would it? Antoine suggested the FBI would want to use him for future contacts if needed. Clearly, if Misha wasn't true to his word, and Luke had no reason to think he could trust him, then his life would be one of harassment balanced with close contact to gain more information to incriminate. The FBI would determine when they had enough to call it off and shut down the operation.

He trusted his friend Antoine, but he also was fully aware that the FBI was really controlling it all. He wondered how much Antoine was placing their friendship behind his own desires to get closer to law enforcement and the spy game. Luke was the guinea pig in this situation and if all worked out, Antoine would surely benefit.

He could only trust himself, and right now, he was

thinking going to jail was not an option. So, his choices were very limited. He took Petrika's hand and it felt good.

"I'll be okay. And I expect they'll be some back up nearby." He reached into his nearby bag and pulled out the wireless microphone transmitter, holding it up as if it was the life jacket he needed to keep from drowning in the whims of the mobsters. It was shaped like a pen with a wire thin antenna embedded in the barrel, powered by a triple A battery.

"The power of the pen, yes?" Petrika said, not convinced he would be safe. She found herself worrying about him, the man who had shown such quickness and agility when he defended her honor against the vile Freddy just the day before.

And then it was time for her to go. Work beckoned and she did not want to be late. Suddenly their little respite from the outside world was over. She stood in front of him, touched his cheek and kissed him. His hands held her close, and moved over her body, touching her in all the right places, sliding down the new slope they had traveled. She had to pull herself away or she would not leave.

"When will I see you?" she asked again.

"Soon," was all he said and touched her cheek. Then he slipped up the stairs and propped open the trap door an inch and looked across the field toward the tree line and the gate. Nothing moved, just the sea to his left and an open field ahead. He nodded and let her slip by him as he propped open the door enough for her to slip out.

She moved quickly across the field not looking back until she was alongside the metal fence by the tree line. When she did, she saw nothing. The trap door was closed and hidden. Luke was not in sight. She found her bike and slipped onto the road, coasting downhill to her apartment less than half a mile away.

Once home, she sat on her bed and tried to grasp what had just happened to her in the last four hours. She could smell him and feel him on her and in her. They had given themselves to each other completely. The physical and mental connection was effortless. It was a new experience and she loved it.

In the shower, she felt the tiniest tinge of regret as she cleansed herself of their togetherness. Work beckoned and she allowed that reality to seep its way back into her immediate actions. And when was she going to see him again? Not soon enough, she thought!

She dressed and prepared to leave but made another decision that had been swirling in her mind in the last hour. Under the sink she retrieved a small handgun that a one-time friend had given her as a gift when she worked at the HandleBar in Providence shortly after she arrived in America. It was a Springfield XD-S 9 mm, designed to fit into a woman's handbag.

"You should be safe when you walk home each night," the friend had told her. He had even taken her to a shooting range to show her how to shoot the gun. She kept it with her when she worked in Providence, but never had to use it. After finding a new job in Newport, in a nicer neighborhood, she stopped carrying it and stored it away. It never left storage after she moved to Block Island, until today.

Now, she slipped it into her knapsack and grabbed a loaded clip from behind the soup cans in the kitchen cabinet. She hoped she didn't need it, but something told her she was better off with it as she headed to work.

thirty-seven

STONEY RIDE

Friday 1300

France, Spain and Germany all in on AntiSubWarfare gear for H225M choppers. 4 more each to upgrade marine patrols. FCAS programme part of Europeanisation strategy response to uncertain support from USA. Airbus behind effort to get ahead. −SpyhakrF

Vlad Vladovich Chemenko had seen desperate times before and had been forced to make desperate decisions. This seemed to be one of those times, he thought, as he sped along I-95 North through Connecticut and turned south shortly after crossing the Rhode Island border heading for Route One.

He was not happy with the phone call from his friend Misha Yevtechnov. He felt left high and dry. He would deal with that later, but right now he needed the chip, he wanted the chip and decided only he could get the chip. He certainly didn't have any reason to trust Misha's second,

McSamarlie, so, his plan was to fly to Block Island and be there for the hand off. At least close enough to take matters into his own hands should the need arise. That's just the way he preferred to do things.

Westerly Airport was five minutes off the highway, and he knew he had to be there in less than ten minutes to make his flight. The rain that he had been blasting through at 85 miles per hour had not let up, and as he turned onto the entrance road to the small commuter airpark, the gray sky offered no hint of good flying weather.

He hated to rush things. He hated rushing to things, hated the feeling of being out of control when time tables and deadlines pushed him. Yet, he knew, nothing kills a plan like a missed deadline! Sure enough, after he parked his car and walked into the terminal of the one-horse airport and saw the dozen folks sitting around the waiting room, he realized his flight wasn't going to take off on time.

"Ceiling is only 500 feet, Mr. Chemenko," smiled the young woman ticket agent behind the counter, handing him back his ticket. "FAA regulations prohibit flights under certain limits for the safety of our passengers and crew. If you'll have a seat, grab a cup of coffee. We are expecting a break in the fog in an hour or so."

Vlad slammed his hand on the counter in frustration, startling the young woman. A young man with blue tie and white shirt festooned with faux epaulets looked up from his desk behind the counter.

"Excuse me, sir! Let's not have any of that!" He stood up and came to the counter, offering Vlad another smile.

"I've got to get to Block!" he demanded, pushing the ticket he had slammed on the counter. He was a grown man who had lived through many political upheavals and dangerous missions for his mother Russia and through most of that time he was known as the calm individual who thought carefully about his actions. But not when he felt rushed. And not when he felt stopped.

"God dammit!" he muttered and gave one last dirty scowl to the two behind the counter, who held fast with their apologetic smiles. "Are you the pilot?" he accused the man with the epaulets.

"Yes, sir, I am. I do not want to fly in this soup, you don't want me to fly in this soup and the FAA certainly won't allow me to fly in this soup."

The pilot continued smiling, working hard to maintain his customer relations demeanor.

"There is the ferry out of Pt. Judith, sir," the pilot continued in his friendly manner. "That's an hour drive from here, plus an hour ferry ride...probably get you there about 5 this afternoon. Time for happy hour!" He laughed lightly.

"Too late," Vlad responded and turned toward the door, leaving his ticket on the counter. For just a brief second, he was distracted by a woman wearing a light blue scarf that reminded him of a woman he was sure had been following him in New York City. Not possible, he thought to himself. A half second later he was stopped short by a poster on the glass door entrance that advertised helicopter tours from Westerly Airport.

"Where is this?" he asked, turning back toward the two behind the counter.

"On the other side of the airport...straight across the field. Take the access road around..." the young woman agent's voice trailed off as she watched the man named Chemenko hurry out the door.

Vlad headed towards his car but looked over the fence across the field where he could see a red helicopter parked in front of a glass fronted building. He guessed it was about 500 yards away on the other side of the runway, just as the agent had said. He saw the nearby boarding gate through the chest high wire fence that led to a pair of New England Airline twin-engine prop planes neatly parked on the tarmac outside the ticket office. He made another snap decision and headed right through the unlocked gate.

He felt totally exposed as he walked quickly passed the planes and broke into a trot as he stepped onto the damp grass next to the runway. He picked up the pace as he realized he was committed. This was his way to Block Island! He could hear and feel the squish of the standing water that had accumulated from the day's rain as he moved toward his new travel plan.

For Stoney Bullard, the morning hadn't gone so well. The owner of Heli-Air Tours, he had to deal with two sicknesses. One was his helicopter and the other his chief mechanic. The Robinson R-66 five-seater was sitting outside the hangar in need of a checkup. The day before he had lost power momentarily with four tourists on board and was fortunate the engine restarted on the first try and their flight over Misquamicut Beach had ended safely.

He knew he was out of business until the mechanic could check the engine. The mechanic, however, had just called in sick. Stoney, a veteran fixed wing pilot with many military adventures under his belt, was new to rotary craft and did not have much confidence in the Robinson considering its unknown condition.

Plus, he knew the weather was going to keep him on the ground, even if the engine operated properly. Or at least so he thought. That's why he unpacked a spare fuel filter from the storage locker behind the Robinson's cabin, thinking he would tinker with the Rolls Royce engine. He heard the quick steps of someone running and looked up to see a man coming across the runway. Stoney put the filter in the back seat and stood by the copter watching the man run at him.

At fifty feet he pulled a gun out from his sport coat and pointed it right at Stoney. In his 74 years, 55 of which was spent flying around with the military and private security, Stoney had seen and fired just about every gun made by man. It was a hobby of his. However, this was the first time he had actually seen the MSP in person. He recognized it immediately from pictures. A two-barrel, derringer type pistol that used 7.62 mm SP-3 ammunition uniquely designed to minimize the sound it made when the trigger was pulled.

It was an effective weapon that propelled each of its two bullets at about 200 meters per second, powerful enough for close in combat. Stoney knew the gun had been standard issue by the Russian KGB since the early 70's and continued to play a role with the GRU when an operative needed effective and quiet deadly fire power, as in assassination attempts or personal defense.

"Don't move! I have to fly to Block Island right now!" Vlad yelled menacingly, aiming the gun right at Stoney's head from about six feet away. While Vlad had been working for years on disguising his Russian accent, a part of his plan to retire "upstate", he made no effort at that moment.

"If I don't move, don't know how I can help you, sir." Stoney said with a wry smile on his face. He had dealt with operatives and agencies before and was pretty sure this guy was working for something Russian.

"Ok, funny man, listen carefully. I want you to fly me to Block Island right now in this helicopter." Vlad nodded toward the bright red machine next to the two of them.

"Not this one, my gun happy friend. She's not safe to fly." Stoney calmly wiped his hands with the rag he was holding and tossed it through the open door of the helicopter. "You some kind of spy? KGB? Or whatever you're calling it this month."

Vlad moved with surprising quickness and caught Stoney's arm and twisted it around his back. At the same time, he brought the barrel of the gun up to Stoney's neck and pressed real hard. Vlad stood 6'1", a full head taller than the diminutive Bullard at 5' 6". The smaller man kept himself in shape, but he also felt it was better to bide his time, especially since Vlad had a gun.

"I want you to understand how sincere I am," the Russian spy said. "And how desperate! Now, climb in the cockpit and let's get underway. Do you understand?" He tightened his grip on Stoney's arms, twisting it so he could feel the pain in his shoulder.

"Look, spy guy, I'm sure you're desperate, but this 'copter is not fit to fly. Understand? *Ne moshet letat!* It shut off in midair yesterday and I was lucky to get it back here."

"How did you land it?" Vlad asked.

"Fortunately, it restarted up and I flew it home."

"Well, sounds like it works," Vlad said in a voice filled with sarcasm and menace. "We should do this, don't you think? Get in, start it and let's go. I must get to Block!"

"I'm telling you the chopper isn't safe! And look over your head, man! The ceiling is below minimums. How the hell am I supposed to see between the sky and sea?" Vlad looked up for a moment and then into the cockpit. He saw an iPad attached to the center console.

"That's a GPS, right?"

"So," Stoney did a slow pan from the GPS back to Vlad.

"No more delays, we must go!" With that, Vlad pushed Stoney Bullard into the cockpit, smashing him up against the doorway bulkhead. Stoney broke free of Vlad's clutches and took the opportunity to swing out with his left fist, but he missed. Vlad responded by firing the gun at him.

Stoney was surprised by the noise at first, or lack of it, then the pain that shot along his arm. The gun made a loud click rather than an explosive bang, confirming in Stoney's mind it was the MSP. The quiet bullet, however, launched from the chamber and grazed his right arm then crashed into the passenger seat on the left side of the chopper with a leather softened thud.

"You ass, you shot me!" Stoney moaned. By luck or by design, the bullet literally grazed his arm above the bicep, tearing his sleeve and leaving a crease of blood, as if a nail had sliced the outer skin, but not much deeper.

"You are lucky. Now move!" yelled Vlad with a push.

Vlad again pointed the gun at Bullard, but this time the gun was aimed back at his forehead. "The next one will be lights out, tough guy. Can we please go!"

Stoney held his ground for a second, staring down the muzzle, silently noting there was only one bullet left. He was still surprised Vlad had actually pulled the trigger. Patience being the better part of valor, he stowed his anger for another time and climbed up into the cockpit, took the righthand pilot's seat and began his pre-flight check.

Vlad jumped in next to him and kept the gun pointed. While Stoney was flicking switches, Vlad reloaded, replacing the spent bullet. Five minutes later, Stoney was ready to take off and he took one more look at Vlad and paused just enough to trade a stare that had the Russian tightening his grip on the pistol in his hand.

"Let's go, tough guy," Vlad said, acting like one himself, but his voice cracked and betrayed him.

Bullard gave him a small smile and applied power while moving the cyclic stick.

"Easy on the trigger and hold on, spy guy!"

In the manner that had suited him well all his life, Stoney Bullard went all in. He felt better handling the controls of even an uncertain machine than standing on the ground with some stranger pointing a gun at him. The sky was familiar territory for him.

The R-66 lifted off and immediately went into a nose down attitude as it accelerated forward. The Robinson's skids skirted a fence by only a few inches and then lifted over the trees lining the airport. In short order they crossed over the white sands of Misquamicut Beach, the speedo read 120 knots and the compass 150 magnetic as they headed toward Block Island about 100 feet above the dark gray waters of the Sound.

Vlad was initially unsettled by the dramatic movement and low altitude, but soon realized his pilot was only trying to scare him, not kill him. Whatever happened it was going to happen to both of them. He took a few deep breathes and glanced at his watch. He still had 40 minutes to meet his deadline. He focused on his breathing and started to review his next plan of attack.

Stoney ran through plans of his own but was soon totally focused on keeping the helicopter on course and out of the water which blended so well with the fog and low ceiling that it was nearly impossible to tell them apart. He kept his eyes dancing between the GPS, the altimeter and the line of color that separated the clouds and the sea.

thirty-eight

LILI'S HUNCH

Friday 1300

US report shows private security firms account for over half of intelligence community personnel. TEGI newest contractor for USIC, feeding at the trough. Already multinational clients. US & PeepsRepubChina? Whom do you trust? —SpyhakrF

When Lili Montczyk pulled into the Westerly Airport parking lot, she noticed a red helicopter flying low over the trees across the runway. She also noticed the black BMW that she had been following from New York City and breathed a sigh of relief. She had lost the Russian after he turned off the highway thanks to traffic and badly timed lights. Plus, she didn't even know the Westerly Airport existed until she drove by the entrance road.

She was a master of disguise, but she had also become a master of playing hunches primarily because she had to play them all too frequently. Her training from the Polish

Intelligence Directorate had suggested that hunches were at best a crap shoot. Better to perfect your spy craft and do what worked. That meant don't get lost and left behind when tailing someone.

As she walked toward the terminal, tying a white scarf around her head, her biggest fear was being spotted by the Russian, even though she was extremely confident he had not seen her over the last two weeks of her assignment. She liked to think of herself as the "Lady Ghost", always lurking on the distant edges of vision, but never really seen.

Her talents, unfortunately, had never been appreciated by her military bosses and she was drummed out of the Polish directorate after a year. The crowning moment was at a unit Christmas party when she had tossed a sergeant into a swimming pool, followed by a Christmas tree. Her defense that he had touched her inappropriately did not fly well with her superiors. She was out after a short hearing. But she was able to land a job with the private security firm TriEyesGroup Inc., known as TEGI, and in just six months had worked her way into a solid operative.

It was better than selling shoes and filing medical folders, two jobs she had tried in her short four-year career as a working girl. Only 24 years old, the last six months had been a joy working for the unseen contractor who communicated instructions by text and brief phone conversations. The Poles were never known for spy craft, but the new arrangement had broken many decades of old barriers. It seemed the Chinese found TEGI clandestine services a good fit for what they had in mind, which was a look at what this particular assistant deputy trade minister was up to day to day.

Then out of the blue, the US government had contracted TEGI only a few days ago, to follow the same person. Her bosses had no problem double billing for the same amount of work as long as the two adversaries didn't know they were using the same operative.

Lili didn't ask questions, she just took notes and filed reports by text every day. She immediately felt disappointment when she walked into the waiting lobby at the airport and didn't see her target. She was sure he was heading to Block Island. Why else would he have turned off and come this way?

"Can I get a ticket to Block Island?" she asked the young woman agent behind the counter.

"Sure thing, lucky lady! We just had a cancellation!" smiled the young woman. "The weather's getting better! Look like we'll be taking off in a short time!"

thirty-nine

Wet Work

Friday 1400

Stoney Bullard glanced at the altimeter at 150 feet and felt like an angel flying through cotton. The smoky mix of darker water with the brighter clouds and fog belied the reality that water would be like a wall if he flew into it. His eyes were still sharp at 20/20, but his brain started to feel the strain after ten minutes of flight. And then suddenly the shapes changed.

Distinct shapes, with clearer edges and once in a while different colors, formed in the mist below. It took a moment, but he realized he was flying directly over a fleet of sailboats racing in the Spring Series of the Off Soundings Club.

Dozens of sailboats ghosted along below him, their white decks covered by sailors in yellow, red and lime green foul weather gear. Spinnakers in red, white and blue flapped in slow motion mixed with foamy wakes trailing behind the boats. And then a vision occurred that is rarely seen and requires perfect timing but produces a moment that makes one appreciate mother nature.

Stoney saw the clouds ahead suddenly brighten and

in seconds the helicopter broke through the fog bank into bright sunshine. The sky was blue and the water below dark blue and two dozen more sailboats spread out in clear formation, stretching ahead toward the north end of Block Island. The east side of the island itself was visible in sand and greenery a few miles ahead. He shifted course slightly to stay in the sunshine, aiming across the northern tip of the island.

"They're heading for 1BI," he said to no one in particular, although Vlad Chemenko was still sitting there, the small gun still pointed directly at Stoney.

"What is 1BI?" Vlad asked, taken by the pretty sight ahead and thankful they were out of gray shroud of weather.

"Navigation buoy, the turning mark. They'll turn right around it and head for the harbor."

Vlad grunted and looked at his watch. "How much longer for us?"

"Five minutes," Stoney responded. "We'll come in from the north straight for the airport." He then turned to his intrusive passenger and asked him.

"Who are you planning to kill?"

"Kill? No one, I hope. Maybe you?" Vlad turned with a smile.

"Well, let me land first," Stoney replied. With the cloud cover gone, Stoney increased his altitude as they crossed over the lumpy grass covered dunes where the east and west sides of Block Island joined at the northern point. From the sky, the land looked like a bird's beak.

Several hikers were visible as the red helicopter zoomed past the iconic North Lighthouse. The church like stone structure, complete with tower and Fresnel lamp, had been sitting there since 1867, its flashing white light warning mariners about the sandy reef that stretched nearly a mile under the water to the north.

It was actually the fourth lighthouse built on the point since 1829. The previous three were built just a few feet above sea level, but too far off the shore and had repeatedly been washed away by the tidal currents and regular storms that tossed and turned the sandy terrain over the years. Block Island was an impediment to the flow of millions of gallons of water back and forth every six hours and the pressures and directional changes caused by the island's pork chop shape were the primary cause of the erosion that had been reshaping it grain by grain since it was carved in place by ancient glaciers.

Stoney didn't have time to think much about the picnic he had once enjoyed in the shade of the dunes a few years back with a special woman friend who had a thing for pilots, because as they crossed over the light's tower 250 feet below, the R-66 Rolls Royce engine skipped a beat.

He instinctively pulled on the collective to gain height while he still had momentum. The speedo continued to read 120 knots and the engine continued to run. But only for another 15 seconds, when it skipped a beat again and then just shut down completely as they crossed the northeastern shore at Clay Head.

That put them about two and half miles from the airport. With a dead engine, they weren't going to make it.

"Shit, my friend with the gun, you better hold on!" Stoney exclaimed in as calm a voice as he could.

He attempted a restart procedure but got no response this time. He knew there was no time for another and prepared for an emergency landing. He reached between the seats under the collective and pulled the lever to inflate the float pontoons affixed to the Robinson's skids. The sudden whoosh of pressurized air was satisfying to his ears and he focused on the beach ahead.

Auto rotation is a standard procedure for helicopters and

uses the momentum from the spinning blades to help slow the descent. The physics made it work even though it might sound counter intuitive. He pushed the collective down to flatten the rotors angle against the air and started looking for a landing spot.

Stoney often proclaimed that a helicopter has the same flying characteristics as a crowbar.

"If you drop the crowbar from a chopper that has lost power, the chopper will likely hit ground first!" he would laugh.

They descended in a semi controlled free fall and Stoney did what he could in the auto rotation, balancing momentum forward with a directional angle adjustment pointing the chopper's nose toward Crescent Beach just ahead and below them.

A handful of people were scattered along the beach, but none appeared to be aware that a red helicopter was falling out of the sky. About 30 feet above the water, Stoney pulled the cyclic back and flared the chopper, allowing the spinning blades to slow the descent slightly. A second later the machine dropped into the water with a big splash about 20 feet from the beach. It bounced forward and came to a stop floating on the four inflated pontoons at each corner of the skids.

Stoney looked at his passenger who appeared shocked they had landed safely, and he was not hurt. Vlad looked over and gave him a roll of the eyes and a nod. A silent nod of thanks.

"You did good, Mr. Pilot. I shall not kill you."

"Yea, well, thank you very much, but fuck you! I told you the chopper wasn't reliable!"

Vlad shrugged and pushed opened his door, hesitating for only a second before he stepped out onto the pontoons and jumped into the water. It came up to his waist and he pushed toward the beach, holding the small gun high above his head.

Stoney shut down the switches on the chopper cutting all electric power and thought about chasing after Vlad, but quickly realized he had a bigger problem. How to get his helicopter out of the water and how badly was it damaged with the sudden wet stop. The craft was still afloat, and the blades were slowing down, clear of the water.

On shore, a small crowd gathered near the edge of the beach, wondering from whence this mechanical intrusion had appeared. Vlad walked right passed them, eyes straight ahead, toward an opening in the dunes on the edge of the beach and the gray building beyond.

Sally Wren, the proprietor of the Beach View Bar, had been prepping her glasses behind the bar when she heard the helicopter's staccato chop approaching and then suddenly it was quiet. She looked out of the large picture windows of her establishment and saw the red machine steadily descending as if landing on the beach right in front of her.

"Oh my god!" she cried out. When something unexpected happens, most people respond by just standing stock shock still as they attempt to compute what just happened. Sally reacted that way, a glass suspended in mid-air in one hand and a dish towel in the other.

Petrika had just arrived at work and was coming out of the kitchen after hanging up her knapsack when she heard Sally's cry. She looked out the window herself and saw the red helicopter floating in the water.

"I will call Sheriff Bobby!" Petrika yelled to Sally. She turned around and went back to her knapsack to retrieve her phone.

In seconds, a man jumped out and waded to shore. She

watched him walk right up to the front porch and Sally went out to greet him.

"Are you all right?" Sally asked, still trying to accept the reality of what happened.

"Where is The Oar?" he shouted standing on the steps of the patio, his pants soaked. "I must get to The Oar!" he repeated. Vlad realized he was waving a small gun in the air. He smiled as if it was nothing to be worried about and quickly slid it into his wet sportscoat pocket.

Vlad stood there at the bottom of the steps staring at the women with the glass in her hand, expecting some kind of an answer. Petrika appeared behind Sally with her phone and punched in 911. She could hear the man muttering…in Russian.

Sally was still shocked that this man had emerged from the water and, apparently, from the sky. She also was somewhat unsettled as she tried to process why he was flailing a gun around.

"The Oar?" he repeated again.

After two rings, Petrika heard a voice on the other end. "911 Block Island. What's your emergency?" It was not Sheriff Bobby's voice, but the voice of his deputy, Patrolman Larry Collins, the newest of the three-man police force on the island.

"Hi, Larry, this is Pet over at Beach View. Ah, we have a helicopter crash in the water out front. Two men, but no one was hurt. One man is here now."

"A helicopter crash? At the Beach View." Collins answered precisely, as if he was writing it down. "No one hurt?"

"Apparently not, there is one man standing right in front of us." Petrika responded.

"Okay, we'll send someone right over. Thanks, Pet!" Collins rang off cheerfully.

At that moment, McGovern's Taxi pulled up. Win McGovern sat behind the wheel of the legendary red van his father had driven for the last 20 years, ferrying folks around the island. He had just dropped a fare on Mansion Road and saw the helicopter fall from the sky. That didn't happen every day on Block Island and he was curious.

Sally stepped off the porch and talked with the man from the helicopter. He listened intently as she explained with her arms how to get to The Oar pointing in different directions, turn by turn, sending him down Indian Neck Road, then a left and a right at the Fire Department, then around the bend left again after Payne's. She wasn't so sure he was getting it when the taxi pulled up. She stopped and simply smiled, "Win will get you there!"

"Need a ride, mister?" Win asked, overhearing his name. He waved the man in the soaking wet suit toward the van and started to climb in the driver's side.

"Win, come here!" Sally gestured to Win, calling him over.

"Careful, he's got a gun." Sally said quietly, almost in a whisper keeping one eye on the surprise visitor getting into the taxi.

"A gun?" Win said loudly, as if he didn't hear correctly. Sally nodded. "Well, that's gonna cost him more," the young man laughed and climbed in with seemingly not a care. He took one last look at the helicopter and drove off, making a U-turn to head north along Indian Neck Road.

"I called the Sheriff's office. Larry said they are sending someone," Petrika announced walking up next to Sally.

"Did you see he had a gun?" she turned to inform Petrika. "He was brandishing it around when he came up on the porch."

"A gun? I didn't see a gun," she said. "I did hear some Russian. Maybe he's a Russian. What's he doing here?"

"He had a gun. I saw it!" Sally confirmed. The two of them turned and walked slowly back up on the porch. Petrika stopped on the top step and looked back at the helicopter. It looked like the small crowd that had gathered were trying to push and pull the floating red machine toward the beach.

The intrusion to start her shift seemed like such a trivial thing compared to the thoughts she was having about Luke. She hadn't really stopped thinking about him since she left him at the lighthouse just over an hour ago. She was freshly showered for her shift, but could still taste him, feel him inside her, and realized she wanted more.

What nagged at her was the thought that the man, who Sally said had a gun, was heading to The Oar. And that's where Luke was supposed to be going as well.

forty

KEYS TO BLOCK

Lili Montczyk saw the red helicopter sitting on the beach at the tide line and knew it was the same one she saw leaving Westerly airport. She was sitting in a window seat several hundred feet over the island as the New England Airlines twin turbo prop lined up for a landing at the Block Island airport.

The sun had cleared 15 minutes after she bought her ticket and they would be on the ground in a minute or two. She had no idea why the helo was sitting on the beach and allowed second thoughts to creep into her mind that maybe her hunch that the Russian had to be on it was wrong.

She sent a quick text to her handler and advised that she was attempting to pick up the trail of Chemenko and was about to land on Block Island. "Great hopes of seeing him momentarily at Oar." was the last thing she typed. She hoped the handler wouldn't be too angry with her.

Five minutes later she stepped off the plane and into the tiny terminal lobby. Big enough for one counter and a few chairs. To the right was a doorway to Marty's Fly'n Grille, the equally tiny diner that offered good food and was open just about every day, even in winter. That's what the guy next to her on the plane had said.

He also told her about the unusual key box on the counter just inside the diner door. Marked "Keys", it contained sets of car keys for the locals and frequent travelers who left their cars parked in the lot next to the terminal. Their keys were stored in the box when they traveled off island and had them conveniently waiting when they returned.

Lili had never heard of such open trust among strangers, but after talking with the man, came to understand the locals weren't strangers so much, nor where they worried about losing their cars because there was no place to drive.

"Sheriff Bobby will track them down in a short time and then you have to deal with the Judge," laughed the man. "Not a big island. No place to hide!"

Lili made a new plan and stepped into the diner, looked over the pile of keys in the box and selected the distinctive logo of a Range Rover. Moments later, a few clicks on the remote fob had the lights flash on a blue one and she was underway, heading for The Oar. She felt confident her hunch was right that Chemenko would be there. The time on the car's GPS screen read 3:30.

forty-one

Fogarea

Rex Simpson's ego was bigger than his lifestyle and he felt like he was always trying to catch up. Even the fog on this particular Friday morning seemed to be holding him back as he looked south over Pine Island into Fishers Island Sound beyond. Calm, but foggy. June boating sucks around here, he thought!

Trixie caught his eye sitting on the bench seat at the stern of his 36-foot Chris Craft motor yacht and he smiled at her. They were not going far, just a couple miles to West Cove for a lazy day at anchor and at each other. But, a day on the water was always better with sunshine. The bloom was still on this rose, he thought, as he turned away from his mistress of two weeks and fired up his twin engines from the control panel in front of the helm station.

"Get the stern line, love," he directed her as he moved to undo the spring line amidships. Dock lines released, *Sassy One* floated free in her slip. Rex slowly fed it gas to slide her into the channel.

Suddenly, he caught movement off to the left, surprised

267

to see a man in a cowboy hat carrying a strange stick launching himself off the dockside storage locker, into the air and across the five foot gap between the dock and the boat, landing with a thump on the rear deck right in front of Trixie.

"Oh my god!" shouted a shocked Trixie, cringing deeper in her seat. "What the hell!"

The man landed on his two feet like an athlete and swung the stick in his hand like a baseball bat, then took a step and smashed it down with extreme force on the seat next to Trixie. He made eye contact with her and tossed a short smile, as if to say, do not move, I am in charge. He tapped her on the shoulder lightly to punctuate his intent with a sinister air.

Then he turned and took three steps to the helm station where Rex was standing, coming to grips with the sudden intrusion of this man who seemed intent on hurting someone. He couldn't help but wonder if that was indeed an Irish Hurley in the man's hands. For the briefest of moments, he smiled to himself for recognizing the stick from a charity event he had participated in several years ago as part of a work promotion. But, only for the briefest of moments.

Now his attention was divided between steering the boat and watching the man with the stick. His menacing manner froze Rex, for only the briefest of moments, before he shut down the throttles.

"Keep the power on, my friend!" demanded the intruder. "We need to get to Block Island as fast as possible. You understand me?" Rex complied and the boat began moving forward again.

Then the intruder swung the Hurley stick against the VHF radio sitting on the console, smashing the handheld microphone with enough force to pull the cable from the transmitter and send it flying onto the cabin deck scattered in four pieces.

Trixie jumped again and let out a sharp scream.

"Power on, now!"

Rex just looked at the crazy man with the stick but said nothing. He looked back at Trixie, his eyes wide, trying to convey a sense of confidence, but feeling rather intimidated inside.

"Okay, sir, Block Island," Rex said quietly. "Just stay calm, I'll get us there. I don't want any trouble."

"Good, we understand each other. I don't want any trouble either, but I promise you, I will bring it if you so much as deviate two degrees from the course!" McSamarlie put on his best snarl and held his Hurley threateningly close, slowly rocking it back and forth so it just touched Rex's shoulder with each rock forward.

They cleared the Pine Island bell at the marina entrance and Rex punched into the GPS the route to Block Island. He had made the trip several times and the buoys were already listed in order of their planned travel. A line appeared on the GPS screen to direct him eastward 9 miles along the north shore of Fishers Island, through the Watch Hill Passage and then a turn to the Southeast toward Block Island, a baker's dozen miles farther. Visibility was not good, but Rex added power as the speedo eased up to 15 knots. The radar antenna rotated, and the ETA read 1410.

An hour later they had cleared Fishers Island and were moving along at a good clip directly toward the New Harbor entrance on Block. Rex could see many targets on the radar a few miles to his East which he identified as the 100 or so sailboats in the Off Soundings Club weekend regatta well underway. That fleet would eventually be heading directly to New Harbor, but that was at least an hour or two away for them, especially in the light air.

Trixie had moved up to the wide helm bench next to Rex and felt protected with her boyfriend between her and the crazy man with the stick.

McSamarlie himself had resigned himself to the trip and was comfortable sitting on the stern bench, hat pulled low on his head, listening to the steady beat of the engines, hearing the rush of water past the inflatable dinghy hanging off the stern and watching the miles ghost past in the low ceiling and fog. He felt comfortable that he had put the fear of god in his captives and knew his savagery was never far away should they decide to try something.

He even allowed himself a moment of daydream dalliance and imagined sharing the young woman sitting next to the boat owner. That mixed well with his recent memories of his day and night with Rene' Sanderson, the crazy woman wild lady who had been the focus of his attentions the last 36 hours.

He understood Misha was not happy with his inability to find Lucky Lukey, and sheepishly admitted he hadn't thought to look on Block Island. He had clearly been distracted by Rene' but, be that as it may, here he was doing Misha's bidding again, heading to Block as instructed, on mission and this time it appeared he was going to be the main dude making the transfer.

"Now listen to me carefully, Mr. JMJ, this is very important," Misha had admonished him over the phone a short time ago. It was clear he wasn't happy not being able to reach him until this morning. "This Luke asshole has pissed me off once, and I won't tolerate it again. You have my permission to make him disappear once you get the package."

"Happily, shef," he had replied.

"But you must first get the chip! Do not hurt him until then," Misha had warned. McSamarlie was aware of

Misha's connections with the Russian Consulate but didn't pay much attention to the details. He knew there was big money in this job, but he was unaware of exactly who was Misha's contact and, frankly, didn't care. He was told that information would be provided when it was needed. Just get the chip.

He did relish the anticipation of encountering Lucky Lukey again. He liked saying his name out loud, almost turning it into a refrain from a song. He liked the way it rolled off his lips, the same lips that had been rolling around wild Rene'. Something about Lucky Lukey didn't settle well with JMJ. He seemed pliable enough when confronted with the Hurley stick, but there was a spark of defiance there that McSamarlie wanted to extinguish.

He looked at his watch and saw he was still ahead of schedule. Misha's call had come only a couple of hours ago, but he had smartly played his cards by checking out the Shenny Marina near Rene's house and had waited for the right moment to pounce on the departing boat called *Sassy One*.

He thought his plan to let someone else do the navigating and driving, someone who was familiar with the waters, was a better idea than just stealing a boat and figuring it out for himself. He looked at the couple huddled by the helm and was satisfied they were behaving as if they were just on a trip to Block Island.

Rex was not so comfortable at the helm. He was deathly afraid of something happening to Trixie or him but was also totally unhappy with an intruder just taking over their planned day. He thought of the equipment he had on board but, beyond the emergency flare kit, a small knife and some pots and pans, there wasn't much that could be used as a weapon. He teetered on the edge in his mind, balancing his anger with complacency. He had to do something, didn't he?

Doing nothing might prevent the stick man from hurting them while under way but, he wasn't sure what he might do to them after they got to Block Island.

He glanced at the radar screen again and noticed a new image about a mile to the East. It appeared it would be crossing their path. He looked carefully at the blip and realized it was two separate targets. He thought it odd that the two boats were so close together in these foggy conditions. A couple of minutes later, it dawned on him that he was likely looking at the radar pings of a tugboat and a barge. Still unseen in the thick white fog ahead, the two images were now clearly distinct on his screen.

He adjusted his course ever so slightly to the right thinking he would try to pass in front of the tugboat. McSamarlie didn't move and Rex was confident the change went unnoticed. Then he had an audacious idea that became his focus.

"Ah, excuse me. We are in the middle of the sound here; would it be all right if we put on our PFDs?" he asked calmly of his captor sitting on the stern seat.

James Michael Joseph McSamarlie didn't move, stared right back at Rex for a full 10 seconds and then nodded slightly.

Rex reached over and flipped up the passenger bench seat opposite the helm station and grabbed two orange life jackets from the storage space under. He handed one to Trixie who slipped it on, and he did the same.

"You want one?" Rex asked helpfully, holding up a third jacket.

McSamarlie just quietly shook his head and idly tapped his Hurley stick on the cabin floor in front of him.

"Tick. Tick. Tick."

"Tick. Tick. Tick."

Rex watched him tapping as if keeping time to some

unheard tune. The throaty rumble of the Chris Craft's engines was a constant presence that belied the calmness of the foggy day and practically obscured the sound of the wooden Hurley hitting the fiberglass deck. McSamarlie persisted with the beat, feeling it in his hands more than his ears.

Rex smiled thinly, turned away and glanced at the approaching tug and barge on his screen. He thought about what he was about to do. The wind and waves were down, the tide was running out, and the world seemed fairly benign, except for the fact that visibility was only about 150 yards. At 15 knots, *Sassy One* was covering about 10 yards a second.

On board the *New Jersey Sun*, the noise was not only deafening to the ears, but the rumble ran up through the deck boots of Captain Joe Wronoski and vibrated through his whole body. A pair of 1500 horsepower diesels pushed the 100-foot-long tug boat through the calmness at 6 knots. The speed was not very impressive until you realized 1000 feet behind the *New Jersey Sun* was a barge as long as a football field and half as wide, drawing nearly 20 feet of water and carrying 8000 gallons of diesel oil destined for New London's commercial fuel terminal.

A two-inch-thick metal cable of spun steel connected the two vessels. It was so heavy, it bowed in the middle despite the towing pressure of pulling a loaded barge through the water. At its deepest point it hung ten feet under the surface between the two vessels.

The captain had been watching the approaching vessel off to starboard on radar for several minutes, moving toward him at 15 knots, but angled to pass behind.

"She's closer than she needs to be," he muttered to his First Mate.

"What are they doing out here on a day like today?" the

First Mate answered. He looked up from the magazine he was reading and checked the radar and then looked off to the Southwest, seeing nothing but fog.

15 year's-experience working the waters between Boston and New York City had left the captain with the attitude that boaters wouldn't be anywhere near him if they only used half their brain. He was firmly convinced that most used only their other half.

"What is he doing?" he suddenly exclaimed. The target had shifted direction and was now aimed as if he was trying to pass in front of the tug.

Wronoski reach up and tugged on the handle of his ship horn and let loose with five long blasts. His First Mate looked up again from his reading and peered into the fog. Still nothing to see.

On board the *Sassy One,* the blasts from the tug's horn rolled out of the fog and surprised the hell out of McSamarlie. He stood up immediately and moved to the port side of the deck to stick his head out from behind the cabin. He saw nothing but that magical white grayness that could appear to be smoke, but wasn't as thick, didn't seem to be moving, yet was just as impenetrable. But it may just as well have been a wall, a seamless obstruction of vision that had no hard lines. It was a substance that had been perfectly named. Fog. No way to get or maintain your bearings other than to peer at the slight difference between the color of the water and the cloud of misty moisture droplets hanging above.

"What was that!" McSamarlie yelled to his captives, his hand firmly holding his cowboy hat on his head in the wind stream.

Rex ignored him, his eyes glued on the radar screen, as he pushed the throttles slightly forward to increase speed. He could see the blip of the tug clearly and he had made up his mind to bring *Sassy One* close by. It was a plan hatched in the isolation of fear and the need to do something, because he knew he could be a hero if he protected the woman by his side. Even if only to alert the tug of their distress.

"What are you doing?" McSamarlie yelled as he felt the boat speed up under his feet. He was torn between reaching for Rex and keeping an eye out along the side deck for whatever had produced the fog horn.

Now he could hear the rumble of the tug's engines, still lost in the fog, but coming closer. With no perspective, the sound gave off a grander scale than it deserved, as if it came from everywhere and filled the horizon. This was magnified by another five blasts on the horn.

And then the tug appeared, looking like it was hardly moving. It was big but did not cover the horizon. It was pushing a wall of water in front of it, its snout covered in shaggy knots of well used rope bumpers that cushioned the bow when it nudged up to docks or snuggled into the slot on barges that allowed the tug to push them from behind.

Trixie saw the tug and stood up from her position next to Rex at the helm. She raised her arms and started to move them back and forth across each other, a well-known signal of distress on the high seas.

Rex hit his own horn and got off five blasts before McSamarlie's Hurley stick came crashing down on his left shoulder and knocked him away from the horn button and the steering wheel. The boat kept moving forward at about 18 knots and it was heading directly for the middle of the tug boat, now about 100 yards away.

On board the *New Jersey Sun*, the First Mate saw the Chris Craft emerge from the fog, moving quickly and heading right for them. Both he and the captain reached for the horn at the same time and let off five blasts.

"This is gonna be bad!" the mate said, pointing out the

obvious. There are no brakes on boats, and it would probably be half a mile before the tug could stop, even in full reverse. The barge being towed behind would take another half mile, if the tug could maneuver to catch it. Plus dealing with the 1000-foot cable between them. The mate and the captain instinctively knew that wasn't going to happen.

The captain didn't touch the throttles, but the mate stepped out of the cabin and stood on the starboard platform to get a closer look. Now it was up to whomever was driving the Chris Craft.

For the moment, no one was driving. Rex and McSamarlie were in a struggle. Rex was trying to fight off the swinging Hurley stick and had managed to tackle McSamarlie to the deck. Trixie continued to wave and grabbed the wheel for the first time in her life. She had her driver's license but never had controlled a boat before. She saw the tug looming ahead and made a split-second decision to turn left to pass behind rather than try to cross in front.

It was the smart thing to do, because the turn took the boat in the opposite direction of the tug, passing starboard side to. However, the turn was a wide one, mostly out of control. Trixie looked up helpless at the man in a red hat with suspenders standing in the doorway of the little cabin on top of the tug. The *Sassy* One passed so close to the tug that it nicked one of the tire bumpers hanging from the side.

The boat lurched on contact and Trixie went flying, her hands off the wheel and she instinctively reached for something to grab to keep from falling to her right. Fortunately, she grabbed the throttle bars, pulling them toward her, shutting the power down to idle. Unfortunately, pulling herself back up, she grabbed the wheel, and that turned the rudder back to the right, sending the still moving boat into the starboard quarter of the tug.

Like a bathtub toy, the Chris Craft was bumped and

spun, the pointed bow momentarily caught between the tire bumpers and swung violently to the right, knocking all three on board to the deck. The tug continued to move away at 6 knots, and the Chris Craft started drifting backwards on the last bit of its momentum.

McSamarlie was the first to get to his feet and quickly recovered his Hurley stick which had fallen under the stern seat. Rex was dazed, fortunate his life jacket had absorbed a few blows, but was bleeding from one cut on the head which was unprotected.

Trixie was wedged between the console and the helm seat, on her knees, trying to stay hidden. An eerie calm descended on the boat, as the rumble of the tug faded into the distance to the West. It was already out of sight, lost again in the fog.

McSamarlie stepped quickly to the helm and pulled Trixie from behind the seat, tossing her toward Rex on the cabin sole. He checked out the console and saw the RPMs at idle. Still got power, he thought and glanced quickly at the two screens, one showing their GPS location with the blinking boat and the extended line that showed the route to Block Island. He noticed the big numbers that indicated they were 6.47 NM from the island.

The other screen showed the blips of the tug boat and the barge, one on each side of the middle of the screen. The middle of the screen where the *Sassy One* sat.

Then they all heard it from behind. The rush of a wall of water being pushed by the powerless barge, its forward movement the sole result of the 2-inch cable that was about 800 feet away connected to the back end of the tug. In what seemed like the blink of an eye, the submerged portion of the cable emerged from the water as the barge loomed out of the fog, the hawser clearly visible attached to a bridle of two cables coming from both sides of the barge's bow.

Sassy One was sitting directly over the cable and the wrapped steel ripped into the bottom of the plastic hull like a band saw moving at 10 feet a second, filling the air with a sickening crunch. The 36-foot Chris Craft was lifted out of the water, twisted to the left and jolted forward as it became hung up on the tow line. The cable wedged itself where it penetrated the hull and tipped the boat forward, the bow still in the water while the back end was up in the air.

McSamarlie went to survival mode and pulled his way to the starboard side stern cleat where a line held the 10-foot dinghy dragging behind the *Sassy One*. Normally used to get to shore from a peaceful mooring field, McSamarlie saw it as his only chance for escape. He looked at the front of the barge which loomed ten feet high 20 yards away. They were hung up and moving at the same speed. He realized if he jumped into the dinghy, the barge would likely overtake him. He would have only a few seconds to get the engine started and speed out of the way.

He pulled the dinghy as close as he could, ignoring the spray as everything was pushed through the water sideways. By stretching outboard, he was able to reach the small propane engine attached on the back and was pleased to see an electric starter switch on the handle. He reached for the key in the ignition, gave it a turn and pressed the switch. The engine sparked to life with a high whine because the prop was still out of the water.

With no hesitation, he dropped into the dinghy while simultaneously releasing the line on the cleat. The inflatable boat fell into the water and was pushed along by the hung-up Chris Craft. He landed in front of the engine, flipped the release mechanism and it responded. dropping the whining prop into the water with a satisfying 'S*plooosh!*'. The prop dug in and the whine turned to a comfortable gurgle. The dinghy's top speed was 15 knots and he twisted the throttle hard and used that quickness to get out in front of the *Sassy One* and then circled to his right to clear the evermoving barge's path.

As McSamarlie turned in the opposite direction of the barge, clear of its path, he saw Rex and Trixie hanging on to the seats by the helm. At that moment, the cable appeared to go slack, and the Chris Craft began to shift, sliding deeper into the water, still attached. He didn't see what happened next because the barge, like a fast-moving wall, obstructed his view. He continued to accelerate down her side in the opposite direction and crossed behind the barge, gauging the angle it was traveling and turned to what he thought was the course to Block.

The rushing sound of the water pushed by the barge changed tone slightly and a carefully tuned ear would have picked up the difference in sound as the tug's engines throttled back several hundred feet to the west at the other end of the slackening towline.

McSamarlie paid no attention as he peered into the foggy mist ahead. He fingered the leather strap on his Hurley slung over his shoulder at the last second and realized he was panting, and his heart was pounding like he had run the 100-yard dash. He liked to think of himself as a cool customer, but that was a close call. He smiled briefly feeling his hat still snug on his head then he searched in his soul for whatever homing instincts he had and focused on the next leg of his trip.

"The things I do for you, Misha!" he muttered out loud, the sound barely audible above the steady push of the tiny engine.

forty-two

THE OAR

Friday 1500

The flags stood out above the Boat Basin Marina in a lazy flap of stars and stripes, not quite stiff but close to breezy. For anyone sitting on the porch of The Oar overlooking the marina, the flags flew at an angle that presented the red, white and blue flush on. The famous bar on the south side of the New Harbor faced roughly north overlooking the water. 345 degrees magnetic to be exact and that meant the breeze was coming from around 245 magnetic. Typical south of west for a sunny afternoon on the Block.

The angle of the boats hanging at anchor was another key indicator of wind direction, but this day there were few boats in the harbor. They were either home making plans for a summer trip to come or in the Off Soundings Club racing fleet that was heading toward the island that very moment. The very sharp eyes could see the angle of the ripples on the water and tell the wind direction but, most of those talents were still out there in Block Island Sound making their way to The Oar.

Who cared about the wind direction? Certainly, the

sailboat racers who were drawn here, the explorers before them, the fishermen and the farmers and the seekers of adventures yet to be told. It was the wind that helped shape this pork chopped shaped chunk of glacial rock, sand and greenery sprung up from the sea seemingly in the middle of nowhere, a dozen miles off the coast of America. The satellite view shows Block Island as a pivot point of the broken coastline that is Southern New England from the wild curve of Cape Cod to the fractured land from New York City to Canada split by the Hudson River, making all of New England an island.

The wind was important to the island's earliest Native American inhabitants of the Narragansett tribe and to the handful of freedom seekers from Massachusetts and Rhode Island who landed in 1661 on the northern beaches in what became known as Cows Cove.

On this Friday in early June, the island was awakening from a quiet winter. The tourists had yet to arrive in great numbers, but the ferry schedules were up to date, the worker bees were prepping the hotels and restaurants and a final coat of paint was being applied to a wall, a door or a post.

And in the center of it all was a weather-beaten old building sturdy enough to support decades of partying visitors. Built in the mid 60's as a clubhouse for the Storm Trysail Club, it became a restaurant in 1967 and had been serving up doses of food, booze and fun ever since. Over 800 autographed, monographed, stenciled and painted oars, like you use to paddle a small boat, were hanging in the rafters and nailed to the walls, three and four deep. It has been suggested if the building's walls collapsed The Oars would keep the roof standing.

The Oar sat on a small hill overlooking the Boat Basin Marina and the New Harbor. Six steep steps up from the parking lot left you on the covered porch. The inside bar sat

20 with a few high tops and a full sushi bar. The windows looked onto the porch and the water. Underneath those windows waited bottles of liquor of every kind, making it one of the best stocked bars in New England.

The covered porch was the main attraction. It sat forty, with another 10 squeezed at the outside bar sharing the best view on the island. Picnic tables under umbrellas on the surrounding lawn added to the daily atmosphere.

The stories from The Oar were numerous and the memories forever. From mobsters to lovers, lost souls and found, escapes and captures, even sex in the bathrooms, all the craziness and all the players created the legend of The Oar.

George, the bar manager and leader of the band for a thousand years it seemed, didn't pay any attention to the colorful sights. It had only been twenty years for him, but the history was so engrained that he only thought about it during quiet moments of realizing how f-ing lucky he was to hold onto the job he had. He had seen it all before, designed the tee shirt and was more concerned about getting everything ready for the big tent party for the Off Soundings sailors outside on the lawn. They had over 100 sailboats racing from Watch Hill, over 600 racers, all scheduled to arrive around four, expecting the beer cold, the mudslides frosty and the shrimp fresh.

Over the coming summer he would herd over 100 bartenders, cooks, busboys, dishwashers and gofers, but today he had only half a dozen on the job. Just another typical early June Friday on the Block.

Joyce was excited behind the porch bar because it was her first big event, in fact her first day on the job at The Oar. She was shoveling ice, storing milk, counting Vodka bottles, cutting limes and enjoying the breeze that tickled her long black pony tail.

She added a shovel full of crushed ice to the mudslide maker as it slowly churned the popular frosty concoction that she heard was all the rage.

All that was missing was people. It was 3:00 and there was no one in the bar except for a couple of busboys telling jokes by the kitchen pass through window and old Sandy setting up his small sound system.

Sandy looked like the spawn of Santa Claus and a gnome after a drunken "night after Christmas" party, standing only five foot six, hair suite of bushy white from the top of his head, over his ears, down to his chin and beyond to mid chest. The mandolin he pulled from a beaten leather case foretold of some unusual entertainment in store for the sailboat racers.

Inside, the vets were watching TV. Bob Blue and Jammy had been tending bar at The Oar for six years and were, literally, barely awake.

George looked at his watch, waved his two busboys over and directed them to set up the crocks under the tent for the soon to come party. The five-gallon jugs, often filled with athletic juice, were soon to be filled with Dark N'Stormies, Mt. Gay tonics, Scotch and sodas, mud in your eye...and other concoctions that were trending for the sailboat scene.

This year a McCoy Coconut mix was on the menu. George didn't question. He just acquired the booze and prepped it.

Joyce leaned back against the back bar and stopped cutting. She was ready. Whatever might come.

And then it started.

Hae-Tae Se bounded up the steps of The Oar and stopped at the porch entrance. The tiny girl in black raised her dark shades and surveyed the scene. She was surprised to be the only one there. She slithered to the bar, light footed, like a cat sneaking up on a mouse, and grabbed an end stool near the rail closest to the harbor.

Joyce thought her black leather shirt and shorts with a beret a bit out of character for the locale. But then she remembered George's words.

"Everyone comes to The Oar, eventually. No surprises. No judgements. We serve everyone! Male, female and in between," he told her emphatically.

"Ice," the woman in black said simply.

Joyce couldn't help noticing her boots. Four-inch heels, over ankle lace ups with pointed toes. Sharp, even.

"I like your shoes!" Joyce offered cheerfully as she shoveled ice cubes into a plastic cup and slide it in front of Hae-Tae Se.

The tiny woman with the sharp boned face and soulful black eyes looked at her for a moment and then a thin smile of pearly whites spread across her lips.

"Not for you!"

Joyce was caught by surprise, her snappy comeback halted by the woman's abrupt turn to face the water.

"Don't' choke on the cubes," Joyce muttered under her breath as she turned away herself. Her attention immediately on a new face at the porch entrance.

Lucius Landow had not slept in 48 hours. Yet, his tie was neatly tied, his suit coat wrinkle free and his pants showed a single crease down each leg as if he had been dressed by a Kingsman 20 minutes before he showed his face at The Oar.

Agents in the field half his age could only dream of looking as sharp. His Beretta sat comfortably and unseen under his left breast pocket. The knife blade in his ankle holster was sharp and shiny. And the camera on his key chain would start a car with no one suspecting the video quality.

He was fresh off the ferry from Pt. Judith and all who

saw his traditional English Austin taxicab rolling off the *Jessica W* giggled and pointed at the classy marketing plan of whomever. Wouldn't "that Taxi" be "so cool" on Block Island. To hide in plain sight was his credo and his training. And for Lucius, this was to be his final mission. And he attacked it with the same passion he had attacked his first for MI6 some 40 years ago.

The fact his marching orders had come as a matter of chance just a day earlier were irrelevant to a man who had spent his life tracking, tracing, planning and executing the very best moments of British espionage.

And the very worst.

Lucius tapped his umbrella on the hard wood floor of the porch as a point of reference. He was here and he had made a decision. He would sit by the railing, at the far end in the corner so he could have the water at his back, but the room in front. A simple turn and he had all angles covered. Old school training.

Kyle the waiter appeared as soon as Lucius sat down and took his order.

"Tea and a Smithwick's," Lucius smiled.

"Sorry, sir, but no Smithwick's. Rhodey Red or 'Ganset on draft. Everything else is bottles."

Lucius turned at the slightest sensation of movement to his left and caught the eye of Hae-Tae Se as she shifted her position and looked directly at Landow. The same pearly toothed thin smile appeared on her lips.

For a moment, Lucius thought she might be flirting, but his training kicked in and he became convinced she was sighting.

His database-like mind failed to find a match, but he was suddenly put on alert. She would have to be watched.

"A Rhodey Red, please. Chill the glass if you would. Thank you."

Kyle noted, nodded and left. Lucius pulled his own black notebook from his right breast pocket and jotted a few thoughts. "Asian, black attire, thin, dangerous, beret. Oar, 1510 Friday the 8th. Dangerous shoes."

Landow had just stowed his pencil with his notebook when the sound of mirth drifted up from the front of The Oar a level below and at the opposite end of the room.

When Jack Bangerman arrived, his laugh usually warned everyone that he was coming. And the warning went out as he spilled from the VW Beetle convertible in The Oar parking lot.

"Thank you for the lift, ladies," came the unmistakable accent of a man who needed to shout rather than whisper.

Joyce could hear him from behind the bar. Later in the summer, she would not have pulled the peal of joy from the noisy afternoon, but this was a Friday in early June and the parking lot was empty, save for the newly arrived VW, a moped and an English taxi. The bar was not touched with noise and the harbor quietly awaited the turmoil sure to come.

And here came Jack, the happiest intelligence agent every to grace an Australian uniform and the most boisterous of lads to carry the battle flag of down under. If anyone knew an island it was Jack Bangerman.

And anyone who has survived a desert understands the power of resourcefulness and determination. Not to mention a lot of experience dealing with criminals.

Jack breezed into the open room and went directly to the pony tailed bartender and ordered a beer.

"Fosters if you please, young lady."

Joyce gave her sweetest smile and said, "No Fosters, my friend. We have Rhodey Red!"

"We want mudslides!" pipped up the two young woman

in tow behind Jack. He turned, smiled at them and turned back to Joyce with a gracious sweep of his arm.

"Mudslides it is, for all of us!"

"Three mudslides, coming down, sir!" Joyce laughed as Jack spun his finger in the air, indicating drinks around. She went to work preparing the frosty, creamy concoction that had become a part of Oar lore.

The two women grabbed stools at the far end of the bar opposite Hae-Tae Se. Jack stood between them and did a quick scan of the room, noting the petite woman in black who was staring out toward the water. He took in the sight himself, with the flags flying and the water and sky bright as a chamber of commerce day. So much for the fog, he thought. He had already ordered his pilot to move the plane from Montauk to the Block Island airfield and stand by.

He then eyed the impeccably dressed chap in three-piece suit sitting in the far corner and immediately connected him with the taxi parked outside.

"Like out of a bleedin' movie, don't you guess?" he muttered to the women next to him.

"He's absolutely darling!" gushed the brown haired one to Jack's left. The two women caught Lucius' eye with their giggling and waved at him in return to his raised tea cup.

Jack gave him a two fingered salute in acknowledgement.

Lucius was delighted to hear the friendly Australian accent and watched the three intently. He felt an immediate sense of connection with the loud man in the khaki field jacket and pants. He was sure he saw a slight bulge under the left shoulder and wondered if the Aussie was packing.

He couldn't help himself as he wrote a note in his book and sipped on his tea. He was interrupted by a sudden crash and he looked up in time to see a young woman sprawled on the floor at the bottom of the two step drop at the porch entrance. The woman's large handbag was spilled open showing an assortment of scarves and other pieces of clothing, sunglasses and cosmetic packets. One pair of sunglasses skittered across the floor and stopped at the feet of the petite lady in black sitting at the end of the bar.

The Aussie Jack Bangerman spun around from his conversation with his two companions and immediately offered a hand to help the woman to her feet. They also stepped closer and offered their concern.

"It's okay. I'm okay!" the fallen young woman exclaimed, apparently unhurt, except for her pride. She stood up with a hand from the blond Aussie and smiled at him.

"So stupidly clumsy I am!" She seemed more inconvenienced than embarrassed, thought Lucius, and then she strode purposely to the end of the bar where she picked up her sunglasses, exchanging a blank stare with the lady in black who didn't move from her position, except to turn her head toward the sound of the commotion, then back to the view of the water as if it all meant nothing to her.

A moment later, the young woman had reclaimed her spilt possessions and settled into a chair at a table against the inside wall under the windows of the inside bar, opposite where Lucius was sitting. She smiled again at everyone as she reached for a menu presented by Kyle, the young waiter.

At that moment, Joyce served up three mudslides to the Aussie's entourage and everyone reached for their drinks. Quiet returned to the porch with just the occasional clink of a halyard clanging against a metal mast from the marina, the flapping of the green cloth that covered the harbor side railing of the open end of the bar and a giggle or two from the threesome at the bar slurping their vodka, Kahlua and Irish cream liqueur concoctions.

Lucius studied the young woman who had made such a dramatic entrance, noting her age in the mid 20's, dressed in loose fitting clothes over her slim body. A scoop necked shirt in blue under a patterned blouse with an orange tone gave her a summery look, over brown comfortable slacks and what appeared to be sensible shoes. She could probably run, thought Lucius.

He stopped in mid-thought and smiled to himself. Relax, you English dog! Enjoy the view of the day and stop cataloging the world! He took a long sip on his Rhodey Red, sat back in the plastic chair and picked up the menu in front of him. You are retired, my friend! Enjoy it!

Lili Montczyk held her menu in front of her face but didn't see any of the dishes offered. She was totally upset with herself and her clumsy entrance. She had charged up the stairs at The Oar's entrance, worried she was late for whatever events were to happen and fretting over missing her mark. Then totally surprised when she didn't see Vladimir Chemenko on the porch, she missed the two-step drop and toppled into a swan dive.

She slowly caught her breath and wondered what happened to Vladimir. She gazed around the room over her menu and noted the older well-dressed gentleman in the left hand corner by the open railing, the petite woman in black who had stared right through her sitting to the left at the end of the bar and the threesome at the other end of the bar, apparently getting along spectacularly based on the frequent peals of laughter and animated conversation.

She also saw into the harbor and noticed that a line of sailboats had appeared. She counted half a dozen in a well-spaced line, their sails stowed, motoring toward the mooring field. She followed the line back to the harbor entrance where many more were approaching. She couldn't help but smile at the beautiful sunny sight of blue water filled with sleek boats and a placid harbor in a place she had never been to before. Definitely better than selling shoes, she thought.

Her view was suddenly blocked by young Kyle appearing in front of her to take her order.

"Iced tea, unsweetened," she answered pleasantly and thought how innocent he looked with deep brown eyes, blond hair and an athletic physique fitting for someone in their early 20's, as yet unspoiled by the spoils of living. She watched his tight ass as he walked away to get her drink, but Vlad's appearance in the main entrance brought her back to reality.

She made a conscious effort to not react and pulled out her phone and started scrolling through her emails. Out of the corner of her eye she watched her target move easily down the two steps and drift over to a table in the middle of the room, just two away from where Lili was sitting. She was sure his eyes were burning a hole in her, but he seemed to sit down without noticing, facing toward the bar. She could see part of his face from behind and when she looked up, he was scanning the room in front of him, not looking at her.

She realized this was a close as she had been to him since she had started tailing him two weeks ago. That first encounter had been in Bryant Park where she watched him retrieve a package taped under a table. She had been on the other side of a hedge in the middle of the park, hidden less than 15 feet away. It was a thick, letter sized package that she assumed held either a stack of money or many folded pages of some type of report.

She remembered following him to the park but had to duck down a path when he suddenly turned around as if looking for her. She grabbed a seat by the hedge, trying to figure out where he might go, and was surprised to see he had walked down the street and entered the park from the opposite end, only to walk directly to the table just on the other side of the hedge where she sat.

It was the first hunch that paid off for her and boosted

her confidence like nothing she had experienced before. The appearance of the bartender in front of Vlad brought Lili back to the present place and time. She listened to their exchange without looking.

"A mule, please," Vlad said to the smiling pony tailed bartender.

"We have lots of mules, sir," was Joyce's friendly response. "We have Moscow with ginger beer, French Mule with wine and olive juice, a Block Island Mule with Fishers Island lemonade and..."

Vlad cut her off with an expression of disbelief on his face.

"French Mule, with olive juice!?" he asked, shaking his head in disgust. "Make it a Moscow Mule, please."

"Coming up, sir!" Joyce cheerfully responded and headed off to the bar to prepare the drink.

About 100 yards away, across the parking lot of The Oar and hidden behind the outbuilding that housed a storage room and a grocery store selling sundries from sunglasses to twinkies, lotto tickets to tee shirts, Bob Smoot and Bob Smith hunched forward in their seats inside the FBI's surveillance van. The dual monitors showed the porch of The Oar and the seven individuals who had showed up in the last 15 minutes.

"Who is *this* guy?" Smoot asked again. So far, he had not recognized anyone who had arrived at the famed bar. Sitting in New Haven and New York City, other agents huddled around remote feeds of the camera image coming from the surveillance van and transmitted over Skype.

Agent Heslin in New York spoke up. "That's Chemenko, Vlad Chemenko! He's a spy handler from the New York consulate. What the hell is he doing here?"

"I'm going to suggest he might be Yevtechnov's final

contact," Agent Moore answered on the open audio channel, watching from New London.

"Has to be," agreed Heslin. "But why is he showing his face now? Agent Restin, you on line?"

Agent Will Restin was sitting in a black SUV parked outside Misha Yevtechnov's palatial home on the corner of Dexter and Shore in Brighton Beach, Brooklyn, right on Sheepshead Bay. He was filling in for Agent Smoot on the Yevtechnov stake out detail.

"Nothing happening here, sir. We've got the house in view. Yevtechnov returned here from the Avianka Restaurant about an hour ago. No one has moved since and we can see Yevtechnov's car behind the gate."

Another voice cut in on the open channel.

"Agent Heslin, this is Jennifer in New Haven. We have facial recognition coming up now on Jack Bangerman and Lucius Landow. The Aussie is ASIS and Landow is MI6, retired."

"The Brits and the Aussies? What the hell?" Heslin muttered. Two photos popped up side by side with ID information from the USIC database on a second monitor in the ops room. Heslin turned to US Attorney Hadley Carlson sitting to his right.

"What are they doing here?"

"I have no idea," she responded.

"Well, someone get on the horn and track down these guys' bosses and find out if they are on vacation or just messing up the works!"

"Val, are you on?" FBI Agent Moore called over the intercom.

"Vanallison here," came the recognizable voice. She was crammed in the surveillance van outside The Oar with Martin, Smoot, Smith and Antoine Barskow.

"How about you get inside and chat up this guy Bangerman. Find out what the hell he's doing here."

"Ok, Seamus. On my way."

She pulled off her headset, stuffed it into her purse and stepped out of the van. Agent Martin grabbed her by the arm as she left.

"Be careful," he offered her.

"Always," she said with confidence, smiled at his concern and stepped out of the van and through the back doorway of the grocery store, walked down the aisle past the bread shelf and a freezer case filled with ice cream. Without stopping, she grabbed a small bag of Smartfood and dropped two dollars on the counter in front of a young clerk who did a double take, trying to figure out from where this small woman had appeared.

Vanallison walked out the front door, looking like a summer tourist in tan shorts, a white t-shirt under a light blue jacket, complete with sunglasses, slacking her hunger with some finger food.

She almost bumped into a tallish man in a curled cowboy hat with some type of stick hanging over his shoulder who was walking up from the marina docks immediately to her left. He swerved to avoid her but didn't stop walking, hell bent on heading into The Oar.

Suddenly, he did stop and turned to her with a grin on his face and a look of apology.

"I'm so sorry. I didn't see you. I'm trying to meet a friend and I guess I'm just not paying attention," he said.

"No harm. No problem. You heading to The Oar?"

"I am. After you, please. Be my guest." The man with the stick gestured with his right arm and let her go in front of him.

"I'm James," he offered as friendly as pie.

"Val," she responded and turned to climb the six stairs

that led up to the porch of The Oar. James Michael Joseph McSamarlie watched her climb ahead of him, noticing an irregular bulge in the small of her back under the summer jacket she wore. He then focused on the pleasant shape of her shorts as she climbed the steps.

forty-three

OLD WOUNDS

Spy stories die slow and hard. They eat at you, consume you, even destroy you. Learning to let go becomes easier as the original moments drift off into the cloud of age and ambivalence. The emotions simmer, awaiting the trigger that awakens skills long at sleep. —SpyhakrF

When Vladimir Vladovich Chemenko entered The Oar, Lucius Landow choked on his Rhodey Red. He recognized him immediately despite the 20 years since their last encounter. It was a face that would live with Landow forever and he used all his will to stay in his seat and not leap for Chemenko's throat.

Simply put, Chemenko was long suspected as the Russian operative who had poisoned Oktyabrina Gulkina, the only woman that Lucius Landow had ever loved. A Russian journalist and defector, Oktyabrina was an international critic of the Russian Federation and its KGB spawned President. Her stories appeared in British and German newspapers, cataloging acts of viciousness that included abuses of power, theft of state funds, sexual improprieties and murder.

Her stories were born of her hate for the men who were destroying her Mother Russia. Sadly, the one story she could never write was about her own murder. One afternoon she was poisoned by an Asian extract of gelsemium in her tea. Sadly, Landow himself served the tea in his own kitchen while entertaining the journalist during their year-long affair. A partial fingerprint keyed a ten-year investigation by Landow who followed trails of evidence that convinced him Chemenko had broken into his home and slipped the poison extract, known as "heartbreak grass", into the glass cannister that sat next to the stove filled with loose leaf Earl Gray.

The Russians were apparently unhappy with aa MI6 termination operation that Landow led during the chaos of the 1990's. Two KGB associates of Chemenko were eliminated in that op. The poisoned tea was apparently meant for Landow in retaliation.

He opted instead to drink a beer that day and had carried a level of guilt for years. As well as his own lust for revenge.

The Russians, of course, denied any involvement, although Landow unearthed back channel chatter indicating there was no remorse for the death of the woman defector who was a journalist thorn in the side of the Federation.

After ten years, the trail went cold, Chemenko was promoted to the US consulate while Landow went to the Far East desk for the remainder of his MI6 career. And now, he was sitting three tables away in The Oar on Block Island.

Landow made a conscious effort to sit perfectly still, as he was trained to do when observing what was happening around him. Lucius had not noticed any discernible reaction when Chemenko glanced his way as he first stepped onto the porch. Yet, he had every reason to believe that Chemenko, a

Russian trained spy, had the same control over his emotions as a British trained spy.

After Chemenko gave his drink order, Landow watched Vladimir look at each person in the room, clearly assessing his environment. He looked twice at the young woman sitting to his right along the wall that backed against the inside bar. She in turn stayed buried in her phone's screen, intently scrolling through some depth of the internet.

After several minutes, Lucius could feel the shackles of his training loosening. Twenty years and suddenly the man of his nightmares, the focus of his anger, long buried, suddenly unearthed, sitting right in front of him! His reasons for being at this place at this time were erased in an instant. There was only revenge on his mind. He would not let it rest. He could not.

He slid his chair back and stood up.

He walked purposely to Chemenko's table, pulled out a chair and sat down. Chemenko reacted slowly. "Does he recognize me?" thought Lucius to himself. But, Chemenko said nothing, just turned his head and looked at the crisply attired Brit suddenly sitting at his table.

"If the devil were to slip into my home, I suspect I would feel like I feel right now," Lucius Landow whispered to Vladimir Chemenko.

The Russian looked around the room with a slow turn of his head, making a big deal of his scan. He then looked directly at the Brit.

"This is now your home?" he asked, a thin smile on his lips.

"I am of the belief, sir, that you are the cause of much pain in my life," Landow continued to whisper, ignoring the apparent sarcasm from Chemenko, now convinced that Vladimir indeed remembered him. "And I sit here, contemplating the pain I can inflict in your life."

"And yet, through all the pain, we both sit here very much alive and smiling," Vladimir said slowly, unaffected by Landow's sudden appearance and his angry tone.

And then Valarie Vanallison appeared at the porch entrance with a bright step. She made her way to the bar, intentionally cutting between Jack Bangerman and the two girls to his left.

At 5 foot 2 inches, a shock of curly black hair and an athletic figure, Valarie always turned heads when she walked into a room. As an NCIS agent she felt the need to be serious when confronting suspects and witnesses, to let them know she was all business. But, through her lifetime, she had been blessed with a radiant, toothy grin and apple cheeks. When she lit up her smile, she lit up a room with a delicious innocence that belied the fact she was carrying a Glock in the small of her back, had a badge in her pocket and a pair of handcuffs in the small handbag that hung from her shoulder on a thin strap that reached to her hip.

She was undercover, so she turned it on. Everyone stopped to watch her bounce into the room. She slipped onto a barstool with a curt "Excuse me!" and stretched her hands in front of her on the bar, as if claiming the space for her personal enjoyment.

"Mudslide please, top shelf!" she asserted in the direction of Joyce, the bartender busy making Vladimir's Moscow Mule.

"You got it, sweetie," came the reply as she tossed a big smile at the diminutive dark-haired newcomer.

Val turned to the tall blonde man next to her and met his gaze. "You look like you just came in from the bush!" she giggled.

"And you appear to have ridden in on a unicorn," Jack Bangerman retorted. He stuck out his hand. "Name is Bangerman. Jack Bangerman."

Val was caught by surprise, because in her rush from the surveillance van, she hadn't thought of a new undercover name. Should she use her own name? "Reed, Helen Reed." The name of a distant aunt was all she came up with on the spur of the moment.

"Hello, Helen Reed. You have a delightful smile!"

"Thank you, Jack Bangerman. You're not from around here, are you?"

Jack's eyes wandered around the room before he answered and Val's followed, looking at the seven folks who she had been watching from inside the van.

"I'm going to guess no one is from around here, Helen Reed."

He was certainly right about that. A Brit, an Asian, a Russian, an Aussie and 3 unknown ladies. And no one could tell where the mandolin player was from.

She laughed and nodded her head. "Well, here's to being here if not being from here!" She reached for her mudslide just as Joyce slid it in front of her and the two toasted.

"What brings you to Block Island?" Jack asked. She laughed inside. That was supposed to be her question.

"Meeting a friend at The Oar. It's an annual thing. How about you?"

"I guess I'm on a bit of a walkabout, getting away from it all for a short time."

"Are these your sisters?" Val asked, nodding toward the two women who were chatting on the other side of Jack.

He laughed. "They're my ride!"

She nodded and took a long pull on the straw in her mudslide. Then she spoke quietly, as if talking to the glass, but loud enough for Jack to hear.

"You know, no matter how hard you try to escape, it seems there's always someone watching."

She ended by looking right at him, then looked over her

shoulder turning her eyes toward the ceiling in the back corner. He took her lead and followed, both of them staring at the camera Smoot had installed in the corner of the rafters the night before.

Young Lili couldn't help but notice the new woman at the bar and when they both turned, she thought they were looking at her. She buried her face in her phone again, instantly realizing they were actually looking over her head. A moment later, after they turned away, she snuck a look at the ceiling to her left and spotted the tiny tube-like device unobtrusively stuck at the corner of the rafters, hidden among the oars hanging there.

At the bar, Jack turned back to the woman who called herself Helen Reed. They held each other's gaze for a few seconds and Jack turned back to his mudslide, offering her a slight nod of understanding.

"Saw that shortly after I came in. Are you the director?" he asked.

"Noooo, just one of the bit players. You've got pretty sharp eyes."

"Well, shucks, ma'am, you know when we're not busy chasing kangaroos and giving the Aussie salute, we are pretty keen on technology," he said in a mock dumb voice.

"Aussie salute?" she asked.

He flashed his hand back and forth in front of his face, like he was swatting flies.

She laughed. "Got it!"

She smiled at him, admiring the handsome face, blonde hair and blue eyes. She had never met an Australian before and like what she saw. He fit the image of a character in a movie and she thought that would be a good approach to take with him.

"You know, my director isn't interested in having any Australians in this movie. Know what I mean?" She couldn't help noticing how handsome he looked and had to turn away to keep her concentration. She wondered if they could make another movie and include him in it.

"Sure, I'll just rage on here with my girls. I'll stay out of the way until something happens." He smiled warmly at her and raised his glass.

At that moment, James Michael Joseph McSamarlie, wearing his crushed and curved cowboy hat, appeared from the inside bar, pausing at the top of the landing that led down to The Oar's main porch. He scanned the open area and found no one he recognized other than that small woman he bumped into at the entrance. Luke was nowhere in sight, so the man in the hat with a weird stick on his shoulder sat down at a hi top on the small upper porch so he was overlooking the entrance to his left and the porch to his right. Then he waited.

forty-four

THE EXCHANGE

Friday 1630

Eyes on the ground still matter. Eyes in the sky online. Be it in Moscow, DC, Beijing, or Block Island. Law enforcement has to see and hear. Your spy is on the manhunt with close up access as net closes on man with the sub secrets. We're mobile and patched in. Keep your cell nearby for updates! –SpyhakrF

"Where the hell is our guy?" Agent Moore asked, muttering to himself. He turned to the small group of technicians assembled in the monitor room of the New London FBI office. Unlike the more permanent operations rooms he had seen in New York, Moore oversaw a piecemeal set up of three monitors, two radios, twin fanned PC boxes under the table and a big ass router.

"Jennifer, can we get some eyes in the sky. I thought the drone was going up!"

"Stand by, Seamus!" Jennifer responded, sitting at the

keyboard that controlled their comms and accessed the internet databases that had become an essential part of every investigation.

She picked up her handset to contact Master Chief Petty Officer Riley Cadwin of the USCG First District Southeastern New England. Cadwin, a Coast Guard instructor stationed at the Academy in New London, was alone in Charlestown, sorting out some video glitches coming from the drone called "Old Eagle Eyes" by the small crew that still knew how it worked.

"Picture coming in a sec, Jennifer! Just another sec."

"Damn legacy crap!" Riley muttered to himself as he flipped a switch that keyed the video format to the right frequency. The snowy monitors in New Haven, New London, New York and on Block Island in the FBI surveillance van suddenly started transmitting High Def color. The radio signals controlling the drone were limited by line of sight and Old Eagle was already about 15 miles away, well over the horizon. So, he needed to keep it flying at about 1000 feet.

"There he is!" exclaimed Antoine Barskow, squeezed in the back of the van behind Smoot, Smith and Martin. He had worked hard at keeping his mouth shut, delighted to feel a part of the operation, but it had not been easy. His mind was racing between what was supposed to happen and what might happen.

He felt immersed in the thrill of the stakeout but didn't want to spoil his welcome. When the drone video popped up, he saw Luke immediately walking past Dead Eye Dick's restaurant on Payne's Wharf.

"He's coming in along the beach!" he pointed out at the monitors.

"I see him," Smoot acknowledged. "Old Eyes, target on

Payne's dock area. The guy in blue denim, khaki pants, wearing the knapsack. Keep him centered."

"Got him," came the response from Master Chief Cadwin at the drone controls. He maneuvered the joystick slightly and commenced a wide left-hand turn, the camera mounted under the drone's nose twisted on its gyro ever so slightly to stay centered on the man walking casually along the road toward the pier.

On the ground, Luke thought he heard a light buzzing overhead giving way to an image of a flight of bumble bees in the distance. He stopped and looked up, shading his eyes with his hand, but saw nothing in the clearing blue sky. At 1000 feet, the drone was virtually invisible, despite its white and orange Coast Guard paint scheme. The tilt rotor design with twin tail sections was a miniature version of the Army's V-280 full size tilt rotor transport. It was the prototype of the Techtron UAV built in the late 80's and still flying after all these years. It had a wingspan of 14 feet and had been modified with a Hi-Def camera and gimbal assembly in the nose.

After a second, Luke surmised the bees were probably a drone and was both surprised and pleased that the FBI had gone to that extent to ensure the mission would work. At least they could watch whatever chaos was about to follow, he thought. He realized again he was likely to be at the center of that chaos.

Just a few feet before the pavement gave way to the wooden pier of Payne's Dock, Luke ducked behind the marina pump house and stepped onto the beach. He allowed his memory banks to distract him, thinking another time and another day he would have kept going straight, would have felt the wood of Payne's Dock under his feet and got drunk at Mahogany Shoals among the boats, boaters and his friends who found comfort at the well-used bar just a few hundred feet away.

But not today.

He forced himself to reach into the breast pocket of his denim shirt and click the pen microphone recorder transmitter Antoine had given him that morning.

"This is your connection to the mother ship, my friend," Antoine told him, flashing his usual toothy grin. "Hell, M is probably listening in."

"I thought she was dead," Luke had deadpanned, referring to the actress Judy Dench, who ended her iconic role as the head of MI6 in the James Bond movies by dying in *Skyfall*.

"She will never die in my eyes," the Bond nut had deadpanned back at him. "Besides, this M is Moore. Seamus Moore, FBI."

"Not Roger Moore?" Luke continued with their Bond game.

"Shit, man. Wake the fuck up!" Antoine stopped smiling and grabbed his buddy by the arm. "This is the real deal. Today! Moore is your ticket out. Make the exchange, let Misha know you're ready to help him and then get out."

They were sitting in Luke's jeep at the top of the stairs that led to the Southeast beach 200 hundred feet below, next to the lighthouse hideout where Luke had spent most of the week. Antoine was there to put the Luke cooperator plan into action. Their Wednesday night phone call had convinced the FBI that Luke wouldn't work with anyone else but Antoine.

Luke had agreed cooperating was his only way out although, he was still not ready to reveal his hiding location. He didn't trust anyone, not even Antoine. Call it a last resort defense, brewed from a mindset that he was not ready to give up complete control of his destiny.

"I'm not telling you where I am," he had explained to Antoine. "I've pretty much blown up everything else in my life, give me this one last position. One last out."

"You got nowhere to go," Antoine had said quietly.

Luke looked at his buddy and smiled.

"So, you're my handler, right?"

"Sure, I guess so." Antoine answered sheepishly. They looked at each other and both burst out laughing.

"Real spy shit, my brother! Just what you wanted!" Luke had heard enough over the years of their friendship to know Antoine's dreams and hopes. They always thought they would never be more than that.

They shared a fist bump and for just a moment savored the reality that one of them had reached a portal in life.

And Luke realized he had also reached a portal, as unintended as it might be.

"So, where are you going to be all day?" Luke asked.

"Hanging in the surveillance van with the FBI guys. I'll see you at The Oar, I promise."

"Hey, leave the jeep near the ferry dock with keys under the rear bumper," Luke requested as they said goodbye. "Wait a second."

He reached in the back seat and pulled out his Jackie Robinson souvenir bat. The worn wood was smooth to his touch and he easily strapped it to the side of his backpack where he had carried his camera tripod so many times before. He waved to Antoine as he drove away in a cloud of dust.

The hint of buzzing overhead brought Luke back to here and now, and he stepped onto the beach and headed toward The Oar just a few hundred yards ahead, leaving behind the thoughts and memories of the last five days of his life. Most of it by his choosing and, like all the choices he had made before, whatever happened would probably be mostly out of his control.

He laughed as he walked past the kayaks and dinghies pulled up on the beach line, most attached to cinder blocks so they wouldn't float away at high tide. Such a simple technique to fool mother nature. It was apparently illegal to anchor off the beach, but not to anchor on the beach. He laughed to himself.

Life was not a straight timeline nor was it a pendulum. It was a circle and it seemed that he moved on the circle, even as the circle was spinning itself. And other circles with other people and other moments were moving around him. Sometimes they connected, overlapped and merged with each other. Sometimes they spun off on their own. Always moving, changing and even repeating as the circle came around again.

"All my life's a circle, sunrise and sundown..."

The old Harry Chapin song drifted through his mind as he walked. Then he thought of Petrika, as fresh as the sand under his feet. She was part of the circles and they had connected. Where would that take them?

He had walked this beach many times before with friends and by himself. Now it felt like the first time. He realized he didn't know its name. If it even had a name. Regardless, it was a part of his experiences as a sailor, a part of what he had come to love about Block Island, what made it such a comfortable place. A place to escape. This time he had run to Block Island to hide. And he realized that was not an escape from anything.

He focused on The Oar up ahead, with the green umbrellas dotting the lawn and the gray, weather beaten shingles lining the sides and the open-air bar dissecting the building. He saw the pony tailed head of the bartender and trudged forward unsure what was to happen next.

Inside, James Michael Joseph McSamarlie quickly checked out each of the patrons in the bar. No Luke, but he smiled at the young woman sitting along the inside wall and she smiled back. He was able to catch the eye of the thin Asian woman in the black outfit sitting at the end of the bar and they traded smiles too. Hers was especially inviting and caught him off guard with its toothy openness. Is she interested, he thought rather shamelessly to himself?

He remembered a time when he was 16 and had said no to a young girl who was ready to give herself to him. They were laying in a wooded area in early evening, comfortable on a bed of leaves and pine boughs, but somehow the words, "I can't accept the responsibility," came out of his mouth.

That was more than two decades ago, and he regretted it still. He had not uttered those words again and was happy to be called a hound dog by his friends. And enemies. Sex drove him and he hung on for the ride. What else was there for a roustabout tough guy who made his living as muscle for a mobster?

The Asian turned away and JMJ shifted his attention to the Aussie at the bar who was proving to be quite the entertainer. The three women surrounding him giggled, laughed and on occasion shrieked with joy as they traded stories. They drank their mudslides and seemed to be the only ones in The Oar who weren't waiting for something. Or someone.

And then it dawned on JMJ that he knew the man sitting with the old guy in the middle table. The two of them had been talking quietly but earnestly for several minutes. The guy on the right with the decidedly British accent he did not know. But the guy on the left was Vlad, the Russian from the consulate on 93rd Street. JMJ had seen him once before talking with Misha on the Boardwalk at Coney Island.

"What the hell is he doing here?" McSamarlie said to himself.

"Don't you sit there with righteous indignation and tell me your double 0 license to kill is sacrosanct and above the laws of most moral men. You Brits are so lost in yourself you don't see the world as it is...only as you want it to be and if it's not in your image, you want to obliterate it!" It was Vladimir in a raised voice, apparently goaded into a loud reaction by something Lucius said.

"We know right from wrong!" Lucius responded, also with a raised voice. "You Russians only know what you think is right!"

"I had a mission. I had a job to do! And I lost two comrades. It was the right job for me!"

"You made it personal. It wasn't a job."

"You killed first! They were working men, doing their jobs and you decided, no, your precious Queen decided they deserved to die!"

"My Oktyabrina did not deserve to die!"

"Oh, she deserved to die, alright! And so, did you!"

Lucius snapped, pushed back his chair and stood up, drawing his Beretta from his shoulder holster and pointed it at Vladimir. The Russian spy responded immediately, knocking over his chair as he stood up and from his still damp suit pocket, he pulled the small, two-bullet, MSP pistol, and pointed it directly at Landow.

"Whoa!" came the reaction from Jack Bangerman at the bar. Like everyone else on the porch, the increasing loud argument had drawn their attention. When Jack saw the guns appear, he reached for his own and pulled it out.

Lili ducked quickly under her table, reaching into her bag for a small revolver and watched intently in a defensive crouch.

Hae-Tae Se sitting by the edge of the porch deftly pulled

a knife from a hidden compartment built into the heel of her left shoe. She poised her body by the rail, ready to drop over it should the gun posing turn into shooting.

"She did not deserve to die!" Lucius shouted. It was a desperate cry driven more by grief than anger.

"No one deserved to die, my friend! We were just doing our jobs!" came the reply from Vladimir, in an intense yet, softer tone, as if understating the foolishness of it all.

Valarie Vanallison thought about the Glock tucked in the small of her back but decided to hold off for a second. She shifted slightly on her bar stool and moved her hand to her side, ready to draw if necessary. She didn't want to give away her cover just yet even though she was the only authorized law enforcement agent in the place.

McSamarlie watched quietly and somewhat amused from the two-top, even as he calmly unslung his Hurley stick from over his shoulder. The carved stick of ash would not stop any bullets, but he was ready to strike out at any attempted attack on him.

For a split second there was quiet. Then the unmistakable sound of a pump action shotgun being cocked broke the tension. It came from right in front of McSamarlie where George, the long-time manager of The Oar, stepped out of the inside bar with a 12 gauge in his hands. He pointed the shotgun at the two men in the middle of the porch.

"Now listen to me. This is The Oar! No gun play allowed! Do you understand?" He spoke in a loud, authoritative voice and had everyone's attention instantly.

The Russian and the Brit looked at the big shotgun 15 feet away, then at each other.

"Seamus, we have a problem," came a voice over the headsets in New York, New Haven and New London. It was Smoot, the FBI surveillance guru in the van behind the grocery store just a hundred feet from the action inside The Oar.

The dozen agents, techies and analysts who had just been bug eyed glued to their screens watching the gun play in The Oar listened to Smoot's interruption.

"I can see the problem," Agent Moore said impatiently.

"No, Seamus, check the drone video feed," Smoot directed. All eyes switched to the aerial view of The Oar and the surrounding area. There was Luke about to step up from the beach to the lawn between the big white tent that was the center of attention for the sailors coming in from their race. And on the other side of the tent was the flashing blue lights of a red and white Ford Bronco careening along the dirt road that connected the Ganset Hotel and The Oar parking lot.

"It's the friggin' Sheriff!" Moore muttered. He could see that his surveillance operation was about to go off the rails. "We failed to mention this op to the locals, didn't we!" Moore turned to agent Martin, who sheepishly shook his head and kept his eyes on the screen.

"Dammit!" Moore snorted. "That's on me! Shit!"

Sheriff Bobby Jackson had been sitting in front of the Post Office a few minutes earlier catching up on the latest from Francois Demuniez when he received a call from Jammy, one of the bartenders at The Oar.

"Sheriff, I was talking to Francois earlier today and he told me about your long night. Too bad about Freddy, hey?"

"Yea, Jammy, did *you* see Freddy last night?" the Sheriff had asked.

"Nah, didn't like him much, but sorry he's dead."

"Yes, Jammy, we're all sadden. What do you know?" Sheriff Jackson rolled his eyes at Francois and mouthed Jammy's name. Francois nodded.

"Francois says you'all were looking for some Asian chick in black?" Jammy asked.

When the Sheriff interviewed Freddy's buddies Thursday night after the body was found, he had added a woman in black to his list of persons of interest, which prior to that had included only the guy that Petrika knew. The boys said she drove away with Freddy on the back of a moped. That was the last time he was seen alive. This morning, Aldo, the local baker and moped king, reported one of his bikes was missing from his rental fleet.

"Well, she's right here."

"Right where, Jammy? You at work?"

"Yah, I'm at the bar like usual and she's sitting outside. On the porch. Been here a few minutes I guess."

"Really? She's there now, you say?"

"I'm looking at her right now through the window. She's hot! Want me to talk to her?"

Sheriff Bobby Jackson couldn't help but smile. Jammy was a good guy, but not the sharpest tool in the box. He poured a good drink and more than a few for himself.

"Jammy, you tend bar and just keep an eye on her. I'll be right there!"

On the porch, Vlad the Russian and Lucius the Brit slowly lowered their weapons and slid them inside their respective hiding places.

They slowly sat down, and Vlad said in a near whisper, as if a child in the classroom getting in one more word without the teacher hearing, "I was just doing a job!"

Lucius was still angry, but calmly, grimly nodded his head in understanding.

"What crap jobs we had!" he grunted.

"We have!" answered Vladimir. "I just want to get on upstate. Saranac Lake. Retire and hide!"

"I'd just like to forget," Lucius added quietly.

At the bar, Jack Bangerman the Aussie, relaxed and holstered his weapon, slipping it smoothly under his left armpit. Valarie Vanallison, sitting next to Bangerman, took a deep breath and couldn't help but cast a look of relief toward the camera hidden among the oars at her fellow agents watching.

No one seemed to notice Lili had put her gun away as well and returned to her sitting position against the inside wall. She sat quietly, intently watching the two men in front of her. She reached into her bag and pulled out a blue sun visor and slipped it on her head.

George, standing two steps above the assembled group, nodded his head in satisfaction and lowered the shotgun which had been pointed at Vlad and Lucius.

"Thank you, gentlemen! Not here!" was all he said in stern admonition and turned to put the shotgun away behind the counter by the entrance. An entrance that suddenly became very busy as multiple events started to happen.

First, a couple of sailboat racers name Lenny Cane and Jan Franson reached the bottom of The Oar's stairway, walking with a sense of confidence a few feet ahead of another group of three sailboat racers. A casual observer might not notice any urgency in the movement of this group, but there was a real sense inside each of their lizard brains that drove them to this spot at this moment.

Despite several hours of boat for boat competition on the water, despite having just docked their boats at the Boat Basin, despite already having downed a couple of beers, they were still racing on land. Lenny and Jan held the distinction of being the first two racers from the Off Soundings event for the last three years running to get to The Oar and order the first mudslides of the hundreds that traditionally would follow for the afternoon and into the evening.

The three behind them were from another boat and were trying to overcome their 2nd place finish on the race course by being the first to get to the bar. These five represented the first two boats of 114 boats to finish the Off Soundings Club Spring Series race from Watch Hill to Block Island. An event that had been going on for over 80 years.

An event where bragging rights were important, in a trivial sort of way, yet where moments like this took on the importance of a national crisis. Importance that can only be explained by fellow sailboat racers.

And up the steps came Lenny and Jan only to pause at the top when they heard the blip of a siren and turned to see the red and white Ford Bronco with the name 'Sheriff' emblazoned on the side, come to a scrunching halt on the sandy pavement in front of The Oar.

Out popped the Sheriff, followed by Francois from the passenger side, and into The Oar they rushed, sweeping right by Lenny, Jan and the others. George was surprised as well, happy he had tucked the shotgun out of sight.

Sheriff Jackson nodded to George.

"Looking for someone," he said curtly and crossed to the top of the steps overlooking the porch area. He immediately spotted the black clad Asian woman sitting at the end of the bar not 20 feet from him.

Hae-Tae Se at first didn't move. She had replaced her knife in her shoe and was sucking on ice cubes intent on watching the Russian and the Brit to her right.

Sheriff Jackson stepped purposefully down the steps and across the room, ignoring the three ladies and tall blond guy at the bar.

Lucius Landow, still seething at the comments of Vladimir Chemenko, slipped away from Vlad's table and returned to his original seat by the railing and watched the Sheriff march in. While his anger seethed internally, he couldn't help a glimmer of recognition appear with the tall man in the floppy fishing hat walking behind the Sheriff.

Sheriff Jackson stopped right in front of the woman in black, blocking her in against the bar and the porch railing overlooking the marina. At that exact moment, Sandy the white-haired musician picked up his mandolin and began to play. It was time for his gig to begin.

And his gig was to pull from his eight strings and ten fingers a unique mix of Irish jigs and nautical whimsey, enough to paint a sense of fun in the background for the partying sailors. The fact that not everyone was partying just added to the color.

"Hello, Miss. I'm Sheriff Bobby Jackson, mind if I have a word with you?"

"What you want from me?" came the response.

"I was wondering if you could tell me your name?" Sheriff Jackson smiled, but he couldn't get out of his mind the pointed shoes he had noticed as he walked across the room toward her.

"My name is Hae-Tae Se!" she pronounced carefully.

"You staying on island, visiting, Miss Hat See? I haven't seen you about," he told her. He gave her a wry smile.

"I am waiting for somebody," she answered truthfully after a moment's pause. She smiled back, flashing her toothy whites at the policeman. Her eyes were focused on the growing commotion behind him as more sailors started to arrive.

At least a dozen had gathered by the entrance and were patiently waiting for George and the waiter Kyle to direct them to tables. Others pushed toward the bar. The first group, led by Lenny and Jan, had already lined up two deep just behind Jack Bangerman and his group. They created an opening and Joyce took their order allowing them to successfully hold their title of first to the finish line, first to the bar.

Sheriff Jackson turned to look behind him and also saw things were getting crowded. He wondered if he should move the interview outside, but there were sailors now everywhere coming from the docks and spilling onto the lawn and entering the big tent nearby. The party was definitely on. The mandolin music hit full chord and the buzz on the porch built.

"So, tell me. Do you know a Freddy Fritz?" Sheriff Jackson asked, watching intently for her reaction. He had to raise his voice as the quiet of the early afternoon was now gone.

"Freddy?" responded Hae-Tae Se, the name rolled out of her mouth as if she had not only heard it before, but likely spoken it as well. The Sheriff picked up the familiarity and pressed the question.

"You know him, don't you? Where were you last night, Hat See? You were with Freddy, yes?" he pressed.

"Fred-dy." She tried to suppress any memory of the angry sex they had enjoyed the night before when her need for satisfaction had targeted Freddy because he was there. And was willing, right up to the moment of release when she had plunged her blade into his throat even as his hands tightened painfully on her own throat. The blood lust was too strong to suppress. For a moment she liked that his lust seemed to match hers.

And then Luke walked up the steps of The Oar and stood at the entrance and smiled. The place was crowded, sailors were everywhere, just as he had planned. Been here, done this, he thought. Except he was always with the sailors, not on a mission from hell to somehow save his butt. He looked around for a Yankees hat and was surprised to see the curled cowboy hat of James Michael Joseph McSamarlie sitting at the two-top just a few feet in front of him.

McSamarlie was looking directly at him, a smug smile on his face and he held it until Luke reluctantly walked through the crowd and sat down across from him.

"I told Misha I didn't want to see you again!" Luke spat out, clearly expressing his distaste at the vision of McSamarlie sitting there.

"I don't give two shits what you want, Lukey boy. I'm here at Misha's orders, so you might as well deal with it." He patted the angled handle of his Hurley stick hanging from the tabletop. Like everything about McSamarlie, thought Luke, it was totally out of place, especially in The Oar on a Friday afternoon with a crowd of sailors on a path to intoxication.

"So, have you got it?" McSamarlie asked, looking directly at Luke. He grabbed for the knapsack sitting on Luke's lap. "Is it in here? Let's go, I want to get out of here! This place is turning nuts"

Luke pulled the bag back then reached in and revealed the silver travel mug where he had stashed the tiny chip. Just like that, he thought to himself. Hand it over and be gone? He knew that wasn't going to be the case, at least not immediately. He had still one more card to play.

"What assurances do I have that you will keep your stick in your pants, Mr. J?" he asked.

McSamarlie rolled his eyes. He leaned in closer across the small circular table and looked right in Luke's eyes.

"I don't like you, Lukey boy. Never have, from the moment you walked into the House of Cards, Mr. Big Shot Card Shark with your kick ass girlfriend and that never-gonna-lose smug look on your face."

Luke sat back, surprised by McSamarlie's intensity.

"Well, how's that working out for you, asshole? You crawling to Misha with your life in a travel cup? And your girlfriend?" He paused with a sly grin on his face. "I can tell you she is still kick-ass!" He grunted in a sexually satisfied way that cut right into Luke's brain.

"Fuck you!" was all Luke could muster. The mention of Rene' stung for a moment. He pulled the travel mug with the chip inside back against his chest.

McSamarlie reached for it with his left hand and grabbed Luke's arm. They struggled for a moment, but JMJ let go. He sat back, not willing to cause a disturbance just yet.

"Come on, Lukey, hand it over!" McSamarlie suddenly played the reasonable one, his tone reflecting a willingness to get the deal done. "This is why we're here. You get your life back - I get the football!"

Luke looked around at the crowd. He nodded at a familiar face but couldn't place his name. Then he spotted Antoine lurking inside the bar just next to the sushi display. He tried to focus on the reality of what he was doing here. He was pissed that McSamarlie got to him so easily. He tried to imagine the FBI agents listening to the conversation someplace nearby.

"Okay, you're right. I give you the chip and I'm even, right?"

JMJ nodded with a thin smile. He put his hand out. Luke couldn't tell if he expected to shake hands or was demanding to have the travel mug placed in it.

"Hand it to him!" Agent Moore shouted, watching on the monitor in New London, as if Luke could hear him. "Make the transfer, damnit! Agent Martin, get ready to move in. I want that cowboy in custody if he takes the chip."

"Tell Misha there might be more where this came from," Luke said. "Next time I have to deal directly with him. Him only."

Luke pushed the travel mug across the table to JMJ just as the crowd around the bar sudden surged outward. A high-pitched scream pierced the room, cutting through the mandolin music and the loud chatter. It wasn't a scream of pain as much as one of determination, more like the ignition of an explosion.

"Whiskey Tango Foxtrot!" yelled the sailor Lenny Cane as he was pushed backward. Luke felt a cool liquid splash on his face, even as he and JMJ grabbed at the silver travel mug.

The source of the commotion was the Asian woman called Hae-Tae See. It was she who had let out the blood curdling scream!

The Sheriff had attempted to handcuff her, and she was not having any of it.

"Miss, I'm going to have to take you to the station house and continue...," he said, but she suddenly bent over from her stool, grabbed her right shoe and exploded upward with her left elbow into the crotch of the Sheriff. She followed with the sharp point of her heel, meeting the Sheriff's head as he doubled over from the elbow to the balls.

The sharp heel connected right in the Sheriff's ear and his stagger from the first blow was completed as he collapsed to the floor.

Without hesitation Hae-Tae Se bolted through the crowd toward the exit. The first couple of sailors crowded around the bar were pushed aside and the others cleared a path as the tiny woman shot through them. Their movement created a human ripple of disturbance across the bar. The sailor named Lenny Cane, with mudslide in hand, was pushed backward and he collided with Luke and McSamarlie who had their hands on the silver travel cup with the chip inside at the two-top at the other end of the bar.

Lenny's mudslide went flying, the white creamy liquid splashing on Luke. McSamarlie grabbed at the travel cup as their planned simple transfer had turned into a personal free for all. He was able to pry it from Luke's fingers, but the cup bounced on the table and went flying into the crowd where the sharp eyed, gymnast reflexes of DPRK trained assassin Hae-Tae Se plucked it out of midair with her right hand.

She had seen Luke enter while the Sheriff was questioning her and never lost sight of what her goal was in traveling to The Oar. Get the chip. Execute. She broke out of the crowd, her bloody shoe in her left hand, and leaped over the handrail on the steps, launching herself into the parking lot. She never stopped running.

Right up until she collided full body with the red pickup truck owned by Sally Wren of the Beach View Bar driven by Petrika Rushevski. Pet's timing was accidently perfect as she came to a halt next to the Sheriff's Bronco just as Hae-Tae Se leaped into the parking lot. The force of the collision knocked the small assassin for a loop and sent her shoe one way and the silver travel cup, with the chip inside, the other. Hae-Tae Se rolled to the left off the hood of the truck and the silver travel cup flew right into the driver's side window, missing Petrika's head by inches.

Stunned but still conscious, Hae-Tae Se crawled to her feet and started to stumble away, cutting through the opening in the parking lot fence that led to the large party tent where the sailors were getting down to business. Agent Ed Martin was coming across the parking lot from the surveillance van when he saw the collision and he was the first to chase after her. He followed her into the tent and caught up to her, tackling the young woman near the drink crocks set up on long tables in the middle.

The Aussie ASIS agent Jack Bangerman was next to arrive and lent a hand securing the feisty woman who was still struggling. He had come to The Oar on a hunch and a whim. He wasn't sure who was who, but he had been trained to be a good guy his entire career. When someone runs from the police, there's usually a bad reason. He knew it would be sorted out later, but his first instinct was to chase the runner as soon as she bolted away from the Sheriff. And he held onto her legs on the ground as Agent Martin slapped on a pair of handcuffs.

"Bangerman, ASIS," he announced to Martin. They pulled her to her feet, and he flashed his ID just as a bloody Sheriff Jackson limped up to them holding a black pointed high heel shoe in his hand. A crowd of sailors, red cups in hand gathered around trying to figure out who was crashing the party.

"Australia, eh? Bit off the beaten track, I would say." Ed Martin nodded to him. "I'm NCIS."

"That your partner in there, the cute one?" Bangerman asked his thumb pointing toward The Oar.

"That's Valarie," Martin nodded again and smiled.

"And who the hell is this?" Bangerman asked, pointing at Hae-Tae Se.

"Not sure where she fits in yet," Martin said.

Sheriff Jackson looked at Agent Martin's badge on his belt and took Bangerman's ID for a closer look. He looked at both of them, surprised and grateful they had intervened.

"What the hell is Australian intelligence and NCIS doing on Block Island? Oh, shit. That sub thing. You here for that?"

Martin nodded. Bangerman said nothing.

"Okay. Saw the BOLO, but I got other things going. She's a suspect in a murder last night of a local boy," explained the Sheriff. He raised up the shoe in his hand and showed the two agents holding his suspect the small knife tucked in its sheath on the heel.

Hae-Tae Se smiled, standing but still groggy, kicked out with the leg that still had a shoe on it. The Sheriff easily stepped aside and deftly grabbed the leg and ripped the other shoe off. It also had a hidden blade in the heel.

"You, young lady, are not from around here, are you?"

He shook his head admiring the unique shoes and then gestured toward the parking lot.

"You guys mind taking her to my car. I'm kind of busted up here."

Jackson was dripping blood from his ear and his crotch was still a center of pain from Hae-Tae Se's elbow.

"No problem, Sheriff," answered Martin and led Hae-Tae Se back toward the parking lot. The sailors who had encircled them in the commotion watched as they led her through the tent, then returned to their partying with a new wrinkle to their storytelling.

forty-five

THE CHASE IS ON

Friday 1630

NCIS REACT squad locked and loaded. 4 units across US give Navy own SWAT teams. Firepower and mobility the goal to protect NCIS agents and the public. New Commander says bad actors will be met with deadly force. Newport unit out of Quonset Field. Chatter hints action soon. Test or real? –SpyhakrF"

Vlad watched the chaos fifteen feet in front of him and didn't move from his seat until he saw the woman in black grab the silver travel cup right out of the air. Then he lost sight of it again in the crush of bodies.

When the Sheriff limped after the woman, Vlad jumped up and ran to McSamarlie's table. JMJ was pushing and shoving with two sailors who had taken offense at the pushing and shoving caused by Hae-Tae See when she broke through the crowd. JMJ's knack for using his Hurley stick always pushed buttons that turned tepid issues into hot ones. The sailors felt his wood after the two had knocked him from his chair and the fisticuffs flew.

Vlad pulled the two sailors away and helped McSamarlie get up.

"Do you have the chip?" he asked, his quiet voice betraying the anger he felt realizing his holy grail was out of reach for the moment. Another plan down the drain.

"Fuck no, the bitch in black grabbed it! Lukey shithead just couldn't do it simple and easy! He had to go fucking around."

"Who the hell is she?" Vlad asked.

JMJ just shrugged his shoulders and picked up his Hurley stick. He was fighting his anger, the pain in his shoulder from hitting the railing in his fight with the two sailors and the fact that it had been a trying day doing the bidding of his boss Misha.

"Where is that asshole, Luke?" McSamarlie seethed. He pounded the Hurley stick on the table.

Then he looked at Vlad. "What the hell are *you* doing here? Did Misha send you?" Vlad looked at McSamarlie for a split second and answered curtly.

"Misha doesn't *send* me."

They exchanged a silent stare and JMJ understood. Vlad reached out and touched the Hurley stick, holding it against the table.

"The cops are here, maybe the FBI. You must be calm, walk out and get away from this place. No antics, no anger. Just walk away like you are part of this sailing crowd. Maybe get lost in the tent over there. We'll figure this out, but we have to find the chip and most important, avoid the authorities." Vlad spoke in his father-knows- best tone of voice.

JMJ looked around the porch and saw the sailors had quickly returned to their story telling and mudslide drinking. The two he had battled were mumbling but had no apparent interest in continuing the fight. The mandolin music continued in the corner. JMJ saw the Brit still sitting near the railing but didn't see the young woman who had been sitting by the inside wall.

And no Luke. He nodded at Vlad and they turned and walked toward the exit.

Lucius, meanwhile, watched from his seat, scolding himself for losing his cool earlier. His breathing was back to normal but, he wasn't ready to make any move just yet. His analytical brain worked through what he had just seen transpire between the Sheriff, the young girl in black and the sailors. He again noticed the elderly tall man in the fishing cap who had come in with the sheriff but was now sitting on the bar stool where the woman in black had been sitting. He was focused on a full-sized cellphone in his hands.

The man suddenly turned and looked right at Lucius and a smile of recognition appeared on his face.

"Landow? You English fop! Is that you?"

"Demuniez!" he responded. "It is I, indeed!"

Sure enough, his initial sighting was correct when Francois entered the porch with the Sheriff. It triggered a memory cell from days gone by when he spent a week working with a French agent of the *DGSE* identifying a cell of Chechnian rebels posing as members of Greenpeace who laid out an elaborate scheme to blow up the Eiffel Tower. Lucius and Francois were on the team that identified the primary players and exposed the ruse.

He had not seen him in 20 years and the two shook hands like distant relatives long separated.

"Never far from the action, my friend, are you?" laughed Francois.

"You seem closer to it than ever!" returned Lucius.

"I'm mostly just a watcher these days," Francois smiled

and sat down. "So, are you part of *this* adventure? That why you on Block Island?"

"I'm watching for some friends. And wandering," Lucius answered.

"Then you'll love this," Francois said and showed the large iPhone in his hand with what appeared to be an overhead shot of a parking lot. Lucius immediately recognized his taxi parked against the building and realized he was looking at an aerial shot of The Oar.

"Where are you getting this?" he asked in amazement.

"The FBI has a surveillance team in place. I hacked the signal." He looked at his old friend and smiled. "That's what I do these days."

"SpyhakrF?" Lucius pointed at him with a grin at his revelation.

Francois nodded noncommittedly as he punched buttons and the signal changed to the interior shot of The Oar. They could see themselves in the corner of the shot, heads bent over the handheld screen. Then it switched to outside again showing a commotion around a red pickup.

Lucius's eyes were glued to the screen, even as his mind came to the full realization that his role in the game of spying was over. It was all digital, portable and beyond his skill set. The Beretta under his arm seemed so quaint and obsolete.

Francois pointed at the obvious English taxi sitting out of place in the parking lot showing on the tiny screen.

"Tell me that is yours," he laughed.

"My Chariot of Retire!" Lucius laughed back.

"Well, my old friend, good luck with that! Me, I must go and see what's what. The whole world might be watching!" Francois looked at Lucius and gave him a curt nod, as if their connection many years ago was a solid, professional one, but not one for tears. And then he was gone, leaving the Brit sitting there, alone with the noise of partying sailors and a gnome-like mandolin player.

At that moment, outside, Antoine and Luke stood at the back exit of The Oar. When the rumbling at JMJ's table started, Antoine jumped out from the inside bar and pulled Luke through the doorway, past the sushi bar and down the back stairs. Luke protested all the way because he saw the silver travel mug in the hands of the woman in black heading the other way.

"Let the Feds take care of it, let the Feds get it," Antoine repeated as they came out at the other end of the parking lot. They could hear a commotion by the front steps and looked around a bush to see a red pickup attracting a crowd.

"Which ones are the Feds and who is the girl in black?" Luke was asking. He watched Agent Martin and a tall blond guy in a khaki jacket running after her into the tent. "Who are those guys chasing her?"

Luke turned to Antoine, a near panic look on his face.

"What am I supposed to do now?"

"Things have gone a little sideways, Luke. Seems like the Brits and the Aussies are here and there's a Russian, probably with Misha's guy, cowboy hat."

"McSamarlie, that asshole!" Luke spat. He looked at his friend as they crouched down by a hedge along the building.

"And I don't know who the girl in black is. I don't think anyone does," Antoine continued.

"Just great!" Luke laughed, although he didn't think anything was particularly funny at the moment.

"She grabbed the chip!"

"If we get back to the van, behind that building, I can get you out of here and you can turn yourself over to the Feds." Antoine realized as soon as the words were out of his mouth, Luke wasn't going to react well.

"Fuck that! I'm not turning myself over to the Feds when the chip is still on the loose."

He began to wonder how many people knew he was here and how many wanted the chip. It never dawned on him that the rest of the world knew about his theft. Then he saw movement through the rear window of the pickup.

"Holy shit, it's Petrika!"

He didn't hesitate for a second, breaking into a sprint to cover the 75 feet to where she had stopped the truck. Her head disappeared for a second as if reaching on the seat for something. He pulled up to the passenger side window and looked in just as she lifted her head and saw him.

Her smile drove right into his heart like a flash of sunshine. It was one of the happiest he had ever seen. He threw open the door intent on throwing his arms around her. Time and place seemed irrelevant except she was right there and was clearly glad to see him.

Then he saw the silver travel mug in her hand. It had somehow ended up in the truck! At that moment, there was movement in the tent as two men escorted the woman in black toward them, followed by the Sheriff in uniform, holding a towel to his head.

Luke grabbed the travel mug and looked at Petrika.

"Pet, we have got to get out of here right now, go, go, go!"

She responded like a pro, dropped the truck in reverse and accelerated backward, spinning the tires on the sandy pavement. She came to a stop inches short of a row of mopeds lined up along the building and spun the wheel, accelerating past an unusual English taxi, and onto the access road away from The Oar.

As she spun the pickup around, Luke looked back to see James Michael Joseph McSamarlie coming out of The Oar. To Luke, it appeared as if they made eye contact because JMJ pointed right at him with his Hurley stick. The gray bearded man next to him was older and Luke did not recognize him, but they appeared to be together.

"Go! Go! Go!" was all he said to Petrika.

They sped out of the parking lot, up the access road and out to the main road a couple hundred yards later just as another red and white police car turned down toward The Oar.

"Go right. Right! Right!" Luke yelled. He looked at the officer in blue, a young man maybe 25, driving the red and white with the big letters New Shoreham plastered on the side. The driver glanced at Petrika, surprised to see the young waitress from the Beach View Bar behind the wheel of Sally Wren's pickup.

"That's Larry!" she smiled.

"A cop, right?" Luke laughed.

"Yes, Bobby's summer help! He's nice boy."

"Yea, well, we'll see how nice he is when they catch up to us."

"Who is chasing us?" she asked innocently.

"No one yet, but I have a feeling everyone will be coming soon." Luke sat back in the seat and let out a deep breath. He opened the silver travel cup and pulled out the small clear plastic container that held the microchip with the SLACLONET 1000 Operating and Calibration Manual digitized in its entirety. Information that was going to change the course of submarine warfare.

Of course, the world wanted this secret! He never thought they would be *here*. Russians, Asians, cowboys, FBI!? Who else?

He looked over at Petrika, the Russian girl he now knew for about 24 hours and who had changed the way he felt about himself.

"How in the world did you know to show up when you did?" he asked.

"It felt like the right thing. This man came out of the helicopter waving a gun and he was a Russian and I thought he was one of the people who you had to see and I didn't like him much and I thought it wasn't my affair, but..." she paused and looked at him and smiled.

"I was worried about you, so I come see."

"To my rescue! Thank you." He didn't even care there was a helicopter involved!

"Right place, right time, right?" she laughed.

He laughed too and reached over and touched her leg gently. He was smitten, he realized. And he was afraid.

"Take the West Side Road to the lighthouse. We're going to have to come up with a plan to stay out of sight. I'm sure they're coming. Misha's guy is not going to let me get away."

She nodded, intent on driving the truck. "I'll use Black Rock Road," she said.

A moment later she turned to him and asked with a trace of concern in her voice. "Who was that girl I hit?"

"I have no f-ing idea who she was!" he responded, shaking his head. He looked at Petrika and shrugged his shoulders. Then he smiled, finding comfort that she was with him on this adventure.

forty-six

THEY ARE COMING

Friday 1700

"Did she grab the chip?" Seamus Moore was shouting again into the monitor in the New London op center. In the commotion at The Oar the pockets of scuffling had obscured some of the action from the view of the wide angle camera tucked in the rafters. It looked on the monitors like a rugby scrum as the tiny Asian in black ran out of the bar.

"She grabbed it, for sure!" came Smoot's voice over the headsets.

"She doesn't have the travel mug." It was Agent Martin's voice on the comms contradicting what the others were saying.

"She got hit by a truck. We've got her in custody, but there is no chip, no travel mug. Just nasty, pointy shoes!"

"I need eyes, people," Seamus barked into his microphone. "Where the hell is the drone? Jennifer!"

The monitor picture shifted from the grassy lawn with picnic tables next to The Oar to the parking lot next to the tent. The drone started a left-hand turn and zoomed in on the movement of the red pickup truck as it backed quickly away from The Oar and sped off on the access road.

"They got her!" Smoot announced as the woman in black known as Hae-Tae Se was led out of the tent between Agent Martin and the Australian.

"That's the truck that hit her!" yelled Martin pointing as the red pickup pulled away.

"And there's the Russian and cowboy guy!" Seamus announced. "On the stairs!"

Jennifer directed the drone operator to zoom closer.

"Vanallison, you got your ears on?"

Agent Vanallison had removed her comm earpiece before going into The Oar, since it was likely not something a pretend tourist would wear.

"Just on here now, boss. Had the ear piece out inside."

"Good. You stay with the cowboy and Russian. Blend back, watch where they go."

"Got it," she answered. She was about 10 feet behind them at the top of the stairs. The crowd of sailors had returned to normal focus after the momentary excitement caused by the woman in black. Vanallison hung back as most of the movement was coming into The Oar, except for her two targets who were at the bottom of the stairs heading out.

Vlad had his eyes focused on finding the silver travel mug and watched the Sheriff supervise the other two men as they placed the woman in black into the Sheriff's SUV just as another red and white police car pulled up. The silver mug was not visible on the ground or in anyone's hands.

JMJ was focused on the red pickup racing away up to the access road. He watched it turn right onto the main street and speed away.

"We need to get after that pick up. That's Luke and I'm

thinking where there's Luke, there's the chip." He grabbed at Vlad's arm.

Vlad continued to scan the area, fruitlessly searching on the ground in front of him for the silver travel mug. Nothing. Then he spotted a familiar face. He grabbed JMJ's arm and led him toward a blue Range Rover parked 50 feet away.

Lili Montczyk had slipped out of The Oar at the moment the pushing and shoving began. She figured there was only one way out and what ever happened, her target would be coming to her, so why not wait in the car. Besides, the earlier gun play had seriously unsettled her, and she wasn't ready to play hide and seek with bullets.

And now, her throat went dry as her hunch played out again. Vladimir Chemenko and the cowboy walked right up to her car. Vlad had a smile on his face as he walked to the driver's side window. He couldn't help but notice she had a different colored scarf around her shoulders than she had while sitting next to him in The Oar. Yet, her face was eerily familiar.

"Young lady, pretty exciting in there, wasn't it?" Vlad offered in a friendly tone.

Lili just nodded her head. The passenger door opened and JMJ sat himself down next to her, the Hurley stick leading the way. He had a "don't mess with me" smile on his face.

"I'm afraid we are going to have to get to the ferry as soon as possible," McSamarlie said quietly.

"So, we'll need to borrow your car," Vlad added from the other side.

He slowly pulled his hand from his jacket pocket and revealed the MPS handgun with the two quiet bullets loaded in the chamber.

Lili responded immediately with a smile, grabbed

her shoulder bag and stepped out of the car. "Yes, yes, I understand. Take it. It's not even mine!" She laughed nervously and stood aside as Vlad jumped in and started the engine.

Vlad took one last long look at her, as if trying to memorize her features, and then drove out of the parking lot and gave chase to the red pickup.

NCIS Agent Vanallison stood by the bottom of the stairs and reported to Agent Moore.

"Seamus, targets are in a blue Range Rover and heading off to the west. Same direction as the red pickup."

"Jen, get me eyes on their vehicle! Blue Range Rover!" Seamus ordered.

"Listen people, we have multiple targets. Ed, you stay with the Asian woman, find out what you can. Fill in the Sheriff on whatever he needs to know."

"Got it, boss. Ah…what about the Aussie? He's on our side." Martin smiled at Bangerman as they stood by the Sheriff's SUV.

"Ah, shit! See if he can round up some transportation for Val." Seamus could see Jennifer looking at him out of the corner of his eye in the ops room.

"What?"

"You are going to want to see this," she said pointing to a separate monitor. She hit a button and the frozen video from the drone started moving. It was from a few minutes earlier and showed the approach of the red pickup to the front of The Oar. The angle was not a great one coming from the water side, but the long shot clearly showed a black clad woman suddenly appearing from under the roof line over the stairs, take three steps into the parking lot and slam hard into the red pickup as it came to stop right in her path.

"What the...stop it, go back," Seamus commanded.

"You saw it, right?!" Jennifer exclaimed.

She played it again, slightly slower, and upon her body slamming into the truck, a black shoe shot out of the left hand of the woman and the silver travel mug shot out of the right. The shoe landed on the ground. The travel mug landed in the cab of the truck.

"Son of a bitch, Luke still has the chip! Okay, so that's good, right! We have the football."

"Yea, but the Russian is after it. Looks like they're a few minutes behind, but they are heading in the right direction and there's really no place to go."

"Get me the REACT team at Quonset. Where's that map of Block?" The NCIS Rapid Emergency reAction Counter Threat team was on standby at the Army base just 30 miles north in Rhode Island.

He grabbed a map that came right out of the tourist rack at the New London Travel Information Center down the street from the FBI office. Agent Moore looked it over carefully.

"Okay, initial target will be the airport, but we have lots of space on the south side. Let's get the drone focused on the red pickup and we'll make a decision while REACT is in the air. Tell the squad to launch and head to Block."

Meanwhile, young Lili found a seat along The Oar's walkway wall that bordered the parking lot. She pulled out her phone and contacted her TEGI handler with a brief text.

"Target paired with UNK. Pursuing PKG."

She then stood up and walked among the half dozen mopeds parked along the wall. She found the one she wanted and casually straddled it, turned the key left in the ignition and puttered off without a glance backward.

At the same moment, Jack Bangerman came out of The Oar holding the keys to the VW bug he had driven up in with the two girls. He waved to Agent Vanallison and they jumped in and sped off to join the chase. They passed Lili on the access road and Val took a good look at her as they passed.

"Who is this woman?" she asked.

"She was in the bar. Made a big entrance, for sure!" He laughed, then added seriously looking at Vanallison. "Also pulled a gun at the big drawdown."

"I think she's in this chase. Seamus, you on?" she switched on her mic.

"Go ahead, Val" came the reply from New London.

"We have a young woman, the girl who was in the bar along the wall, actively involved. Don't know who she is working for. She's on a moped."

"Yea, well, looks like we have a full court press. We have a visual on the red pickup and the Russians are close behind. They're going south and not too many places they can go. Suggest you take Center past the airport and maybe intercept them at Cunneymus."

Val looked at her new found friend the Aussie. She smiled.

"You have any idea what he's talking about?"

He just shook his head. "Came by boat. Don't know the streets. May just as well follow the dust in the air."

"Me, too. Let's turn left here. I think the airport's up this way."

Seamus Moore was annoyed that his surveillance operation had blown apart. He had been doing this long enough to understand not every op goes as planned, but He was angry they had not been aware that others would be interested in what was going on with the stolen information. And they would show up on Block island. He turned to US District Attorney Hadley Carlson.

"Hadley, what do you want to do here?"

"With no transfer, we don't have a deal with Parmelian," she said. "The Russians haven't done anything yet, that we can prove. He's the thief. Yes, he's cooperated with us, but nothing's happened."

"They showed up. They took his bait. They expected to get the package." Moore didn't want to sound like he was defending him, but that's how it came out.

"I'm sorry he got himself into this mess, but he broke Title 18. If we can't put the real bad guys away, he's the bad guy."

"I suppose we could just sit back and cover the exits and wait for everyone to show up. At the ferry or airport or stealing a boat. You have to get off the island to make it all work."

"We also have to get the package back before it lands in some enemy's war chest."

Moore watched the monitor of the drone visual on the red pickup truck. It was racing in a cloud of dust along the southern end of the island.

"New London ops, this is REACT One, we are airborne."

The crisp military voice cut through the room in the FBI operations center in New London.

"Copy that, REACT One. This is New London ops. Block Island Airport is LZ." Jennifer's voice responded equally as crisp.

"Copy that. Block Island Airport LZ. ETA 10 minutes."

Under that dust cloud, Luke watched Petrika handle the pick up like a race car driver. She spun the wheel confidently as they slid off Black Rock Road onto Snake Hole Road and bounced through the puddles of the uneven surface. Rarely used, it was basically the only way to get to the summer homes that lined the south side of the island. Million-dollar hideaways with a view of the Atlantic Ocean and not a penny spent on road improvements. You weren't there unless you were hiding from something or someone, thought Luke. But he knew this wasn't going to be a hiding place today. Just a delaying place.

The bushes grew to over fifteen feet tall in many places and the dirt road became more like a trail, meandering in and out of the cover overhead. More than once they had to edge off the side of the road crushing through the greenery to avoid deep, water filled ruts that would scrap the axle of even the toughest off-road vehicle.

He had thought about this during the last few days hiding in the lighthouse cellar. What he could do if they came for him. Not much was his educated opinion. The impetuousness of going to the island on Tuesday locked him into the difficulty of getting off the island. It didn't seem to matter then, but now....

Regardless, anything was better than turning himself over to the FBI. When Antoine said that, he went off the rails. Slam the door on that concept!

"Once we get on Mohegan Trail, we'll pull in by the stairs to the beach," he told Petrika. "Pull in real close."

A moment later Snake Hole Road turned sharply north away from the cliffs and they returned to pavement. She spun the truck onto the main perimeter road on the south side of the island. A quarter of a mile later they were in the dirt lot where the tourists parked to visit the beach below the Mohegan Bluffs. She bounced over a painted two by four meant as a parking guide, crashed down the narrow walkway with branches on both sides and drove another 50 feet right to the top of the 141 stairs that led to the beach below.

Luke left his door open and ran around to her side. He gave her a hug.

"You are a great driver!" he exclaimed.

"Like a tractor, but more fun!" she laughed.

"This way," he said and grabbed her hand and led her

away from the truck and the stairs. A path appeared and they followed it to a viewing platform that overlooked the rocky shoreline. He slipped over the rope boundary in front of the platform and onto a smaller path that led into the head high brush. The water below was as clear as the edge to the cliffs was hidden by the leaves.

She followed him without protest as they crashed along what soon narrowed to a one-foot wide meander through the greenery. At times there was no path, just less resistance against the branches and leaves of the Multiflora Roses and Northern Arrowwood that swarmed the area. Growing to over ten feet, like weeds on sandy soil that redefined fertile, the flowers momentarily hid them from view.

They pushed on for about 500 feet, then the path just stopped. Luke paused for a moment to get his bearings, and then pushed straight on through a bush and came up against the fence that surrounded the property of the Southeast Lighthouse. Luke paused again to bask in all its late afternoon western sunshine glory. A monument to man's ingenuity, a literal beacon of guidance for mariners and a symbol of memories forever etched on Luke's mind and the minds of thousands more. Except, this monument was on a trailer like platform with wheels and was surrounded by a construction site and a trail of dirt that led from its original home site just 50 feet from the cliffs.

"Honey, we're home!" he turned to Petrika with a big smile. He hopped the fence, helped her over and they ran together across the open field like targeted soldiers hoping against hope the snipers were not watching.

Someone was watching. The venerable "Old Eagle Eyes" drone was still flying.

"Got them," reported Jennifer as they emerged from the bushes by the lighthouse. She had been on wide view finding it easier to track the Range Rover with the two

Russians. She just caught their movement on the edge of the frame, tiny figures emerging from the brush.

"The Range Rover has found the pickup. Two subjects by the stairs, two more heading for the lighthouse," Jennifer reported.

Agent Moore and US Attorney Carlson watched and waited. They both knew there was little they could do. But Moore grabbed the mic in front of Jennifer.

"REACT One this is New London ops, change of LZ. Redirect to Southeast Lighthouse. Do you copy?"

"Copy, New London. REACT One to Southeast Light."

"Smoot, this is Moore. Time to pack up and move yourself. Work Spring Street toward the Southeast Lighthouse. All targets are there."

"Copy that, New London. Spring to Southeast Light. We're moving."

Vlad and JMJ in the Range Rover passed the Mohegan Bluffs parking lot before doubling back when nothing showed up at the Lighthouse site where the big sign promoting the soon to come museum was the most obvious activity.

They pulled deep into the parking lot and found the red pickup. Vlad jumped out and immediately went to the top of the stairs.

"They're going to the beach! That will lead them to the harbor up north and then a ferry." He ran down a few steps to the first landing and looked down, unable to see any movement.

"I'm not sure," replied JMJ. He was surprised by the animated Vladimir, gray beard and all. He himself was 20 years younger and still had no desire to attempt the stairs. He couldn't see the bottom, just the wind turbines a couple of miles out and the endless ocean rolling in toward the shore. A vastness he couldn't contain. He liked to limit his thinking to just a few feet beyond the reach of his Hurley stick.

"I'm thinking they stayed up here. Look over there." He pointed at the top of the Southeast Lighthouse, the light tower with its Fresnel lens showing over the green bushes that extended several hundred feet to the East.

Vlad looked at the light and then at the beach.

"Ten minutes. I'll go down, you go that way. If you find nothing, call."

He held up his phone and turned down the stairs. He had no idea how many steps down, but he knew there were just as many up. Still, he pressed on. He was driven by Konstantin, by Saranac Lake and by the immediate desire to get the job done.

JMJ headed off down the narrow path around the observation deck and into the brush. He was hoping Lucky Lukey was at the end of his search. Oh, yea, and Misha's chip.

forty-seven

Hiding Again

Luke and Petrika sat next to each other catching their breath in the cellar of the lighthouse where they had earlier consummated their budding relationship. They both listened intently for any noises above the slatted ceiling. He enjoyed feeling her close to him and again marveled at how quickly and comfortably she had filled a void in his life.

"This is an adventure you have taken me on, Luke Parmelian," Petrika said with a big grin. "Who are those people?" she asked again.

Luke looked sideways at her and smiled back. He reached into his knapsack for the silver travel cup that held the chip with the SLACLONET 1000 details.

"They all want this thing," he said, turning it over in the dim light from the small camp lantern. He opened the top and held the clear plastic case between his fingers, the tiny microSD card sitting harmlessly inside.

Petrika wondered how so much could be inside so little.

"The cowboy is Misha's guy, the Russian mobster. McSamarlie. I don't know the bearded guy with him."

"He's Russian, too. I heard him when he came from the helicopter on the beach. I am sure he is government. GRU."

"Great. I guess I shouldn't be surprised."

"Do you think they will find us here?" she asked.

He looked at her and laughed to himself.

"I heard a funny story about this place, when the big hurricane of '38 hit," he started quietly in a way of answering her question.

"Hurricane of 38?"

"Big ass storm, worst in decades around here. The wind was so strong it was picking up stones from the cliffs and slamming them against the windows of the lighthouse. Breaking the glass."

"Ouch!"

"The light keeper and his helper grabbed frying pans to protect themselves when they had to run out to try to save one of the small buildings. Next morning, all the buildings around the lighthouse were demolished, turned into piles of wood."

"Some storm, yes!"

"Yes, but one building was still standing through the night. The outhouse they used for a latrine!"

"*Otkhoshee mesto.*"

"Yea, what she said. The shitter!"

Petrika laughed.

"Well, that didn't seem right, especially since the keeper and his helper were sick of having to walk outside all the time to take a crap! So, they knocked it down themselves!"

"Ha!"

"So, when the government inspectors came to survey the damage after the storm, they agreed it was time to install indoor plumbing in the lighthouse. A benchmark in history! Proving once again, that trickery works!"

She laughed and gave him a playful shove.

"Is that a true story? Or just a story?"

"Stuff of legends, my sweet lady!" Luke laughed. "Just

like I'm hoping trickery will keep them away from here." The truck parked by the stairway to the beach was maybe enough to send the Russians on a wild goose chase. He expected the Feds might have seen them running toward the lighthouse. The sense of relief was not great, comparing jail to a beating. The lesser of two evils, and all that.

"So, we huddle and cuddle and wish them away."

"Pass by unseen, right?" she agreed.

He leaned in and kissed her softly on the lips. She responded and they shared another moment, pressing their lips together in full acceptance of the other, come hell or high Russian holy hell!

And it came with a creak of a board a moment later. Petrika heard it first and opened her eyes and turned to listen closer. Luke put his finger to his lips. Then they heard a rap of wood on wood and footsteps along the dirt. Their moment was over when Luke stood up and reached for the Jackie Robinson bat still hanging on his pack.

"You stay here until I come back," he whispered to her, touching her cheek. His mind clashed. One moment anger for putting her in this position, the next understanding that she had chosen to follow him.

He crept into the other room and stood at the base of the stairs. He could clearly see a pair of legs walking slowly back and forth through the crack in the plywood cover. The Hurley stick of JMJ was visible hanging by his side. Luke knew what he had to do. The confrontation was upon him.

He moved to the lower steps and poised the bat in his hands ready to swing. McSamarlie could be heard with a low, taunting chant, "Lukey boy. Lukey boy. Oh, lucky Lukey boy, time to meet the Hurt-ley mon!"

The legs stopped at the trap door and Luke braced himself. McSamarlie pulled hard on the cover to reveal the steps into the abandoned lighthouse cellar. He didn't expect

Luke to come charging up the stairs with bat in hand, like a rhino in heat.

"Mother fuckerrrr!!" Luke shouted and burst out into the open and was able to get off the opening salvo, a mighty right-handed swing with the bat that connected with the Hurley and sent it flying.

JMJ lost control of the Hurley but swerved to avoid the left-handed swing that came next, aimed at his midsection. Even as he swung, Luke moved away from the opening in the ground and pulled back from his opponent. He immediately regretted giving ground, but the solid connection with the Hurley had surprised him as much as it surprised McSamarlie.

McSamarlie pivoted away and moved to pick up his stick which had landed on a box of shives and stakes used to position the lighthouse on the massive trailer where it now sat. He retrieved it and turned to look for Luke, who had moved between two other boxes. The two men moved among the debris and construction crates until they came out next to the box truck that was parked by the bluffs. Then they both attacked.

The carved ash Hurley and the round maple baseball bat are two different species designed for the same purpose. Smash a ball a mile. The crack of the two hardwoods connecting in mid-swing echoed off the nearby brick edifice originally built in 1875. An ancient sound in a modern moment.

McSamarlie was quick and handled his Hurley like a lightsaber, whacking left and right with alternating twists of his wrists, swinging the flat blade so the edges struck Luke's round bat. Luke immediately felt overmatched by JMJ's aggressiveness. He backed up step by step with each blow, even as he twisted his own bat side to side to deflect the blows.

"You likin' this, Lukey boy!?" gloated a confident McSamarlie as he pressed the attack. "All you have to do is give me the goddamn chip and I'll spare your ass!"

"No way! Not today!" Luke retorted. He pulled his bat back just as McSamarlie took another swing. The expected crash of the two sticks was replaced by a "swish!" as the Hurley swung through air. Momentarily pulled one way by momentum, McSamarlie was open to an attack on his right side which Luke exploited with a backhanded swing.

It connected, though with half the power had it been a right-hand swing. Still McSamarlie winched in pain as his ribs felt the sting. Luke pulled his bat back and reloaded for another swing, but McSamarlie dove to Luke's right and rolled, expertly slashing out with his Hurley and catching Luke behind the right knee.

That pain was excruciating, driving Luke down as his knee collapsed. The previous bruises from his night of card games nearly a week ago magnified the contact. While Luke was down another blow across his shoulder blades did the same. He was knocked to the ground, flat on his stomach. For one split second all he saw was the ocean below as he landed at the edge of the bluffs. The sandy cliffs seemed to fall away directly to the rocks and foamy waves finding their way on shore.

But, enough sightseeing. Luke knew he was in trouble and rolled over, bringing his bat up just in time to deflect a downward overhead smash from McSamarlie. Luke kept rolling, three times, away from the cliff and the slashing Hurley kept missing him, landing on the dirt harmlessly.

He rolled to his feet and took up another defensive posture. McSamarlie pressed the attack again with a renewed fierceness. The bat and the Hurley pounded against each other. Luke was totally on defense and McSamarlie was getting in some blows against Luke's hands and arms. He fought the pain and kept swinging back.

Suddenly, the Hurley connected dead on, knocking the Jackie Robinson special out of his hands and it went flying toward the cliffs, bounced once and disappeared over the edge.

"Oh, man! My dad gave me that bat!" was all Luke could say at the moment he went defenseless.

McSamarlie was surprised for a split second and looked at Luke with a smile.

"Last call, Lucky Lukey boy. Give me the fucking chip!"

He pressed the Hurley into Luke's chest, just as he had done that first night. He kept at it, pushing him back. Somewhere deep in Luke's consciousness, amid the flames of fear, he was sure he heard a familiar sound from somewhere out to sea.

"I'm not a traitor, asshole. Tell Misha the Feds are coming for him and he's not getting the chip." Luke didn't know where the bravado came from, but he was totally defenseless, his hands unable to counter the pressure from McSamarlie's push on his chest. He stumbled backward to his knees, just as McSamarlie reached high over his head to unleash a blow to the back of Luke's neck.

A mix of sounds filled his dulled hearing. One, the staccato chop-chop-chop of a big motor beating the air and then, two pops, like firecrackers, and finally a thud on his back. That brought a sharp pain, a flash of white light and the world just fell away.

forty-eight

THE BLUFFS

Petrika Innesova Rushevski tried to stay hidden as Luke had requested, but she really wasn't that kind of woman. Her curiosity was endless, and it was only a minute after she heard the cracking of wood against wood overhead that she stuck her head out of the cellar of the Southeast Lighthouse. She was surprised to see her new found man in a sword fight with a guy in a cowboy hat. But they weren't wielding swords.

She could see it wasn't going so well for Luke. He was backing up and seemed outmatched by the other man who was flailing away with an unusual club, smashing time and again against Luke's baseball bat. She moved up the stairs and behind a crate as she watched the battle rage toward the cliffs.

She saw Luke fall once, then roll over and she feared for him. She ran toward the two. Then the bat went flying and Luke was defenseless.

She screamed.

"No! Stop it! No! No!"

She kept running toward them, fearful for her downed man and glad she had thrown her knapsack in the truck with the little Springfield XD S 9 mm, taken from its hiding place in her apartment just an hour ago. Now she didn't hesitate to use it when she saw Luke in grave danger.

Without stopping, she raised her left hand and fired two shots.

The shots rang out, the sound almost lost in the mechanical noise of the helicopter that suddenly appeared from below the cliffs and flew directly over her head. Her attention was on the flat shaped stick the man in the cowboy hat had unleashed at her man and the crumpling of two bodies as the blow hit Luke. He went over the edge and disappeared, but strangely, so did the other man, knocked out from under his cowboy hat, which went flying upward for a second before it followed them both down the cliff.

Petrika ran to the edge, shocked by what she had done.

The brewing chaos of a storm drove the water before her, a random pattern of nature appearing so regular from up here, she thought. No beginning, no end, only endless strips of white foam stretching across the blue green sea, rolling relentlessly to the rocky beach below, depleting their power in a splashy crash and then meekly sliding back into the churning sea with a bucket of sand. Was the sole purpose of this display to return the land to the sea? She wondered in a flash as if a lightning bolt zapped across her brain.

The wind tugged at the blonde strands encircling her cherub face, spilling them across her blue eyes. The gun in her hand was heavy, more from strangeness than weight. She knew how to hold a gun, but it tugged on her shoulder, threatened to upset her balance and send her tumbling down the sandy cliff, too. The feeling was real, even as her feet stood firmly on the grassy edge.

She couldn't believe he was gone.

Her fingers tightened in her other hand, grasping the cool silver cylinder that was to blame for it all. She didn't want anything to do with it, but she clung to it firmly. It was Luke's and she had grabbed it from the cellar, knowing he would want her to protect it.

And suddenly, she was shoved hard by a man who rushed up from behind and grabbed at the silver cylinder. She turned and struggled, but he roughly knocked her down, sending the cylinder to the ground. He grabbed it, turned away, and wrenched open the screw top. He found nothing inside.

"*Trakhni menya!*" he shouted. His disappointment was genuine. He turned to Petrika who was on the ground unhurt but pissed.

"*Mydak!* Asshole!" she shouted at him. Then she recognized the gray beard wearing the gray suit that was soaking wet last time she saw him.

"You are the Russian! Government, yes!" she accused him.

Vlad was surprised to hear her call him a "*mydak*". A goat in Russian.

"You are Russian, too?" he asked in surprise. "What are you doing here? Where is the chip? Did he have it?" He pointed over the edge of the bluffs not ten feet away. He walked right to it and looked down.

Petrika picked herself up and joined him, but afraid to look herself. She was happy Luke had apparently taken the chip from the mug. Trickery!

She thought happily of the first time she had looked over this bluff and seen Luke's surprised but smiling face looking back up just fifteen feet below her. She didn't expect the same greeting when she finally focused on the sandy sides of the steep cliff wall below her feet and the striations of sand, rocks and brush that had built up as each section of the bluffs pulled loose from the land above and slide down toward the water. Over the centuries, irregular piles had grown to create an angular mosaic of upheaval with sharp edges at the high points and soft crevices at the low.

A sense of finality overwhelmed her as she focused below her feet. She was surprisingly calm and spoke with an intense sadness to the man beside her, unsure if he was the enemy, or a friend, but in the least, a fellow Russian.

"Он был моим другом. Я думаю, что убил его," she said quietly in their native language. "He was my friend. I killed him,"

"Ну, ты убил кого-то," was Vlad's response. "Well, you may have killed somebody."

He recognized JMJ lying halfway down the slope, motionless and splayed out in an unnatural position as if he had free fallen while asleep, unable to make even the slightest effort to protect himself. He was face down, his head toward the water, his cowboy hat resting on the dirt above his feet.

Petrika's heart skipped a beat. She did not see Luke anywhere on the slope.

"Tolka odin!" she blurted out. "There's only one!"

Then the voice of authority filled the air followed by boots scraping on the dug-up dirt.

"Stand right there! Do not move! Put your hands in the air!"

NCIS Deputy Commander Roger Moscater of the REACT team shouted the commands. The two Russians standing on the cliff turned to see four armed soldiers in flak jackets, helmets and automatic weapons pointed directly at them. Vlad could see two other soldiers searching the grounds to his left.

"Miss, please put that gun on the ground," shouted Moscater, gesturing with his rifle. He waved another soldier forward and he walked carefully up to Petrika. She forgot she was holding it and gave him a small smile as she handed it over. He checked the weapon and unloaded it, sticking it in his flak vest. He then gently grabbed Petrika by the arm, pulled her away from the edge of the cliff and stood her against one of the construction crates.

He gestured to Vladimir and motioned for him to join her, which he did. Another soldier came up and went through their pockets.

"Vladimir Chemenko. Russian diplomat, I see. Deputy Trade Minister. What are you doing here on Block Island?" the Commander asked after looking at the diplomatic passport pulled from Vlad's pocket. He recognized the small MPS revolver and nodded to Chemenko.

"Nasty little weapon. Don't see these much anymore. KGB, right?"

"There is no KGB!" Vlad answered, rolling his eyes at the over used, out of date moniker American's insisted using to capsulate the entire culture of the Russian nation. Then he glanced at Petrika.

"I am consulting with my fellow countryman about the beauty of America. And maybe future employment at the consulate."

Petrika gave him a sharp look, but kept her mouth shut.

"Do you have ID, miss? A passport? Something more than your small gun?" the Commander asked, gently but sarcastically.

"My passport in my bag, down there." She gestured toward the Lighthouse sitting up on its massive trailer.

Commander Moscater waved to one of his men to check it out.

"Commander, you'll want to see this," said the first soldier who had taken Petrika's gun. Moscater walked over to the edge of the bluffs where the soldier was standing and looked down to see the body lying upside down about 100 feet below them.

"Okay. That's one. Where's the other one?" he asked.

The Commander switched channels on his radio.

"New London ops, this is REACT One. I have two in custody and two missing. Both missing apparently off the cliffs. Shots have been fired. We will need a recovery op ASAP."

There was a moment of silence, then the radio crackled.

"REACT One, New London ops, copy. Two off the cliff, two in custody. Did you find the package?"

"No package. We are searching the area," replied Moscater.

"Copy that, REACT One. We have a unit on the way to your location right now. Can you execute recovery?"

"We will need help," Moscater reported curtly and then turned to his two captives.

He walked back to them and gave a long stare before he spoke. An agent handed him the silver travel mug which was empty.

"Soooo, anyone ready to tell me what happened here? How about you Vladimir Chemenko?"

"I wish to speak to my embassy as soon as possible before I make any statements," Vlad said with a smug look on his face. He believed strongly that despite all the issues Russia and America faced in the political arena, the rules of diplomatic immunity were sacrosanct and the worst that would happen to him was deportation back to Russia.

That thought did cast a dark shadow on his plans to retire "upstate", but at the moment, standing on the edge of the bluffs of Block Island with American guns pointed at him, that was a mild disruption.

"Mr. Chemenko, we have what appears to be a dead man over the cliff. Doesn't that mean anything to you? Do you know how he got there?"

Chemenko shook his head. "Embassy, please."

"How about you, young lady?" Commander Moscater asked just as he was handed the backpack by the young agent sent to retrieve it.

"Looks like someone's been living down there," said the agent. He had a look of disbelief as he handed over her passport. "Found blankets, beer bottles and a lantern."

Commander Moscater looked at the passport. "Petrika Rushevski? How about it, Petrika? What's been happening here?"

He couldn't help but be impressed with her blue eyes and gazed into them.

She looked right at him, trying to determine how important her next words were. She felt like he was a friend and would listen to what she had to say. However, she wasn't so sure Luke wanted her to tell the truth. Most of all, she wondered if Luke was, in fact, still alive. Should they be looking for him if he was hurt? Or should she hope that he gets away if he was not hurt? And did they even know it was Luke?

"Petrika?" the Commander persisted, quiet but firm.

"I protect my friend. He was attacked by the man with the funny stick. I scare him with the gun."

"You shot at him? Which one?" the Commander asked.

"The one in the hat," Petrika answered.

The chirp of a police siren turned everyone's attention toward the roadway and the front gate. The familiar red and white Bronco of Sheriff Bobby Jackson's paused for a moment as the lock was opened and then a small caravan of vehicles entered the grounds of the Southeast Lighthouse.

The Block Island Fire Department's utility vehicle pulled out from the line and drove up just short of the cliffs. Three men got out, walked to the edge of the cliff for a quick look down and then went about setting up a rope and pulley system with a stretcher to retrieve what they expected to be two bodies from the Bluffs.

Sheriff Jackson was soon joined by NCIS Agent Vanallison who arrived with Jack Bangerman in the borrowed VW bug. The FBI surveillance van also parked in the small circle of vehicles. FBI agent Bill Smoot joined Vanallison, Jackson and Commander Moscater from the REACT team.

Antoine jumped out of the van as well and took a few steps toward the group before he was stopped by one of the REACT agents.

"Far enough, son. Hang right here, please!"

"Where's Luke?" he asked but got nothing but blank looks in return. Everyone was standing still, listening on their headsets to Special Agent Moore setting the marching orders.

"The Russian diplomat, Chemenko and the girl are to be detained for questioning. Retrieve the bodies and everyone returns to the Police Complex so Agent Martin can sort this all out."

"Vanallison to the airport, you're on watch there for Luke," Moore continued. Then he gave out an audible sigh. "And you may as well bring the Aussie with you."

"Roger that, he's my ride," responded Vanallison.

The petite NCIS agent and the tall Aussie smiled agreeable to that mix and jumped back in the VW bug and headed off.

"Smoot and Smith, you've got the ferry dock. I want video on everyone who gets on. Next ferry in 30 minutes. Move out now!"

"Commander, can you send the chopper along the beach, follow the bluffs north?" Moore continued.

Moscater questioned his pilot standing nearby, with a thumbs up or down. The pilot took one look at the black clouds overhead and gave a thumbs down. A crack of thunder punctuated his gesture.

Moscater turned to two of his men and pointed along the beach. They got the message and headed off toward the stairway.

"Lucky us," said one of the men. "We get to walk home." "In the rain," said the other and they broke into a trot.

Agent Moore sat back in his chair in front of the multiple screens in New London, feeling disconnected from the action. He looked over at Jennifer and shrugged his shoulders.

"Any other ideas?"

"The marinas, Seamus. He knows the sailors, maybe a private boat?" she offered.

Moore nodded and got back on the radio directing the REACT One team to cover the three marinas in the New Harbor.

"Commander, try to have your men keep a low profile," Moore smiled.

"Copy that, New London."

Commander Moscater couldn't help but laugh. He imagined his flak jacketed, automatic weapon toting team trying to blend in at the docks filled with sailboat racers who had just spent a day racing and were full into an evening of drinking. He waved to Agent Smoot and in a few minutes three of his team were loaded in the surveillance van and headed off to another tedious task of searching and hoping their target was going to show his face.

And then the forward edge of the dark clouds that had been forming in the southern sky played their opening card with a gust of wind that quickly reached 25 knots. That was followed by rain drops in a light sprinkle but soon opened up into a classic Block Island summer thunderstorm.

Petrika was helped into the back seat of Sheriff Jackson's

Bronco next to Vladimir Chemenko. She felt empty, fearing the worst for Luke, and still surprised by the chaff of the handcuffs around her wrists.

As the Bronco pulled out of the Lighthouse grounds, Vlad recognized the young woman who had been sitting at The Oar from whom he had stolen the Range Rover. She was sitting by the side of the road on a moped, a scarf over her head attempting to protect her from the rain. She watched the police activity through the fence. He suddenly remembered he had seen that same scarf on a woman in Bryant Park.

forty-nine

Luke Gets a Ride

Manhunt continues for missing chip, missing geek, missing sub secrets. Two in custody, one dead and one MIA. Old friends and new friends still in the game. FBI has lock on Block. Or do they? Russian and DPRK ops busted. —SpyhakrF

Tortured was the word that came to mind as Special Agent Seamus Moore watched the action on the Mohegan Bluffs from the Coast Guard drone flying at 1000 feet over the south end of Block Island. It reminded him of some horror film with skeletal fingers reaching out from the surface of the vertical cliffs, the boney sharpness on top descending and morphing into soft piles of sand at the bottom and ending in the foamy ocean as it endlessly pushed onto shore and then retreated and repeated.

Like the unaware frog slowly boiling in a pot of water, the island was changing every moment, but no one could see it.

The drone view zoomed in suddenly and focused on the still figure of James Michael Joseph McSamarlie. He filled only a third of the screen and was lying on the western slope half way down one of these boney fingers of sand and rock. He apparently had not moved since he fell there.

"That is definitely Yevtechnov's muscle guy," Moore announced to those listening in the ops room in New London. The Hurley stick nearby the positive identifier. He was still mystified that the second body of Luke Parmelian had not been found.

He had ordered the drone to sweep along the cliffs to the East and North, but nothing had turned up. The western setting sun mixed with the approaching storm to cast shadows across the crevices and obscured entire sections of the terrain. Efforts to get closer were limited by Old Eagle's inability to drop low enough for a closer look. Ducking below the bluffs would block the signal and the operator sitting in the small control room in Charlestown would lose control.

After ten minutes of looking, compounded by the thunderstorm's building force, and growing concern on his ability to control the drone as voiced by Chief Petty Officer Cadwin, Agent Moore ordered 'Old Eagle Eyes" back to base. He had to pin his hopes of finding Luke to the ground team searching along the beach.

Rumbles of thunder ripped across the southern sky and stirred Luke awake. He opened his eyes to wet gusts of wind as the southeastern air flow carried the rain up the slope and right into his face. He could see the black clouds overhead but, his view was partially blocked by a boulder under which he had slipped.

He felt a tremendous pain in his left shoulder and his left buttocks. The shoulder pain came from the final blow of the Hurley delivered from McSamarlie. The buttocks from the slide he took down the sandy cliffs. He tried to move, but his right leg was jammed under the boulder. He looked down and saw blood on his right knee. He slowly twisted his body and after a few seconds was able to extricate his booted foot. Every movement was painful.

He lay back and took several deep breaths. He looked over his head to the top of the bluffs and realized he had fallen on the eastern side of one of the finger like spines that came out of the earth, sliding down a sandy slope into a deep crevice, then under the rock which was half exposed, its other half buried in the spine.

He figured he had fallen straight down about 20 feet, then hit the sand that lessened the angle of the slope. He couldn't help but think of the legend of the Niantic Tribe, who lived on Block Island in the 16th century and defended their land by forcing the invading Mohegan Tribe off the bluffs. He had survived!

He was thankful for his khaki pants and denim top which helped camouflaged him against the sand, rocks and shadows.

Then he realized he had to move. The rain was falling harder and he was driven by the image of the helicopter that buzzed right over their heads as he battled with McSamarlie. The good guys had arrived, but they were after him.

He felt the back of his leg and found his pants ripped open. His hand came back in red, blood from a large gash across his hamstring muscle which had apparently absorbed his slide down the slope. He ignored the pain, ignored the blood and gingerly edged his way down the sandy slope about 80 feet to the beach below.

He glanced over his shoulder towards the top of the cliff, but his view was blocked by the spine. He thought he saw the face of some monster embedded in the mix of earth's spillage. A couple of notches for eyes, a slit for a mouth and an outcropping for a nose and one for a chin. He tended to see faces among the shadows and angles whenever he looked at amorphous shapes. He was silently glad that part of his brain still seemed to be working.

Then he started to walk along the beach. He his legs and ankles seemed intact and handled the movement and his weight. That pleased him. He walked maybe 100 yards and had to stop, panting.

"Breathe, you idiot! Breathe!" he commanded himself. He began walking again, forcing his breath in a steady rhythm. The beach surface was irregular, sometimes smooth, hard sand, sometimes rocks and in a few spots the water came right up to the rocks and the sand was soft and spongey, his feet sinking and slowing him down as he plodded along. He soon passed Sand Bank Cove and then Cat Rock Cove.

He had studied the scalloped shape of the Southeast corner of the island in preparation for sailboat races, where a foul tidal current often forced boats in close to shore to keep up their speed. Now he had as close up a look at the shoreline as he could ever want and mentally ticked off the curves as he turned north. A dull ache filled his entire body, but he pressed on knowing this was the only way out.

After three-quarters of a mile, he stopped by Green Hill Cove and considered climbing off the beach. The bluffs were lower there, not as steep, covered with more foliage and he estimated he could get up it, walk through the backyards of the widely scattered private homes on top and join Spring Road that ran along the East side of the Island. He also realized the roadway was likely to have eyes on it.

He stayed along the beach and after an hour of trudging along, he stopped and leaned on a boulder sitting a few feet from the water's edge and rethought his limited options. He was sure the FBI were chasing him, or at least waiting for him, because there were only three ways off the island. By ferry, by plane or by private boat. His car was at the ferry landing just around the bend ahead at Old Harbor. It was useless to him because he would never be able to get on the ferry. Surely there was someone waiting for him there. Maybe even Antoine on the lookout!

He considered hiding in one of the small cargo containers, but the dock was open, and the freight moved on and off at the last minute. That complicated things. Nowhere to hide!

The airport was so small he couldn't smuggle a sneaker off island, much less himself in all his beat-up glory. One airline, eight passengers at a time in small twin prop puddle jumpers. He would need a pretty good disguise.

He considered one of the sailboats that had come to race for the weekend with the Off Soundings Club. There were over a hundred scattered on moorings and at the Boat Basin or Payne's dock. He knew a couple dozen owners personally, certainly well enough to get a ride back to the mainland. They still had a day of racing ahead on Saturday and he didn't have any time to waste.

Then he heard a laugh from far away, carried by the southerly breeze. He peaked over the rock and saw movement behind him where the last scalloped spine from the bluffs ran down to the beach. Two men in blue uniforms and helmets, rifles slung over their shoulders, searched the beach, following the path he had just taken. He ducked behind the rock he was resting on and then began to move, crab like, away from them, angling up the slope as he went.

It was a painfully hard scramble because the sandy bluffs were now only a few feet above the beach, but the sandy soil had been replaced by rocks dumped as a protective barrier against the waves. He made it on top acquiring a few more dings and scrapes on his hands and knees. He walked on the pavement a couple hundred yards until he reached the cover of the brush around Spring Pond. He hugged the foliage, ducking in and out as openings appeared and made it to the sewage treatment plant just behind Nichols Park overlooking Old Harbor's downtown.

He crossed Spring Street near Weldon's Way and found himself only one block behind the main downtown district. He skirted behind Aldo's Famous Bakery and through several backyards, coming out behind the Library. At one point, he grabbed a towel hanging from a porch railing at a rental cottage and wrapped it around his waist. At least his ripped pants and bloody leg were now hidden.

Dodge Street was not too busy, but the rain had stopped, and folks were back outside, heading for their nightly dinners and drinks among the harbor restaurants. At one point an old English taxi drove by his hiding spot, a nattily dressed older man driving with a young couple in the back. He couldn't help but smile.

"That's a neat marketing idea!" he thought.

He crossed to the Blue Dory Hotel and slipped down the driveway toward the grassy dunes sitting next to the Yellow Kittens overlooking the south end of Benson's Beach. He crouched among the greenery unseen and looked around.

There were no sudden movements or unusual activity. The beach near the Surf Hotel had a few folks watching the last rays of the sun as it poked through the gap between the dark clouds that had moved off to the northwest and the Connecticut shore. Cars moved on Dodge Street behind him and Corn Neck Road right in front of him.

He listened intently for any buzzing noise overhead. Nothing. Then he saw it. The red helicopter sitting at the edge of the water in front of the Beach View Bar. He suddenly understood what Petrika had been talking about earlier in the day. And he suddenly understood whose helicopter it was.

He started running toward the beach.

At that moment, Stoney Bullard understood that he

really did not like the smell of aviation fuel, even though it was the lifeblood of his flying career for over 50 years. He especially didn't like the smell of it on his hands and clothes, which currently stank of that very thing. He had been tinkering with installing a new fuel filter and finally felt satisfied that all the seals were sealed, and all the bolts were bolted.

His ailing mechanic had led him through the process by phone and it was now time to test it out and get the hell out of dodge. While the curiosity factor was high a couple of hours ago when the red Robinson R-66 fell out of the sky, most folks had lost interest. And there's nothing like a Block Island thunderstorm to shift tourists' attention. Even the one police officer who turned out to investigate had left over an hour ago on another call.

So, Stoney's task now was to shoo away the handful of people still hovering around the helicopter so he could start it up.

"Watch the tail rotor, folks. It will hurt you like nothing else!" he shouted cheerfully, waving his arms at the blade in back. He was like a barker outside a circus tent, but warning everyone to stay back!

"Need everyone 50 feet away. Gonna' get noisy and breezy! Back up, please, thank you, sir. Up on the roadway would be just fine. Go watch from the porch of the bar right across the street. Be safe. Have one for me! Thank you! Thanks! Let's get this thing going!"

He moved to the righthand door just as Luke ran up to him with a towel around his waist and a big smile on his face.

"Mr. Bullard. Stoney, it's Luke. Parmelian!" Luke greeted him like a kid who hadn't seen his uncle in years.

"Luke? Well, fry my shorts, Luke! How you been, boy?"

"Just great, Stoney!" Luke answered.

They shook hands just like they had done ten years prior when they had first raced a sailboat together with a fellow named PJ McDonough. Palm to palm, grab the thumb, hook the fingers, fist bump.

"You out here racing?" Stoney asked.

"Nooo, been busy doing some other stuff. Got myself in a bit of a jam and, well, I'm wondering if I might be grabbing that helicopter ride you promised me a few years back." Luke gave him a wide-eyed stare that was more of a plea.

"Well, shit, Luke, I'm not so sure this is the moment you want to ride, not in this thing. Just had some issues, as you might guess by my landing zone here." Stoney smiled, looking around.

"Hey, if it's a bad time, I understand, but I really need to get back to the mainland."

Stoney looked at him for a moment.

"You in some kind of trouble?" he asked quietly.

"Well, if I stay here, tonight, there might be some trouble. My options are kind of limited."

"Not good."

"You once said if your options are limited, pick one."

"I said that?" Stoney laughed, shaking his head. He looked at the helicopter and then back at Luke.

Stoney Bullard was a brave soul, confident of his abilities on a boat, in a car or in the air. He had many miles and hours of each under his experienced bones. His veteran eyes had seen a lot more than most. He was known to follow the rules and known to make his own when he thought it necessary. That approach to his life had worked so far. He took one look at the sky and turned to Luke and smiled.

"Okay, Lukey boy, we have a small window here. Jump in let's see if this puppy can fly."

Five minutes later the turbine spun up and the rotors began to turn. The sand kicked up as Stoney throttled up the RPMs and that moved even the most curious back. With a flick of his wrist, he pulled on the collective and the red machine rose off the sandy beach about 30 feet, tipped its nose forward and headed out over the water, non-stop for the mainland of Connecticut.

As the horizon of lights on shore appeared over the northern end of Block Island, Luke thought about Petrika, the way she smelled, the way she felt and the way she had changed his life. It dawned on him that no matter how far he tried to run away, he would always be running toward her.

He reached in his pocket and wrapped his hand around the clear plastic case that held the microchip. There was still much to do.

But first, he really needed a drink.

fifty

THEY ARE STILL COMING FOR YOU

Friday 1800

The handcuffs came off easily and Petrika gave Sheriff Bobby Jackson a big hug when he finished removing them. He was embarrassed in front of the Feds who had taken over his office at the public safety complex where Ocean and Beach Avenues converged on Block Island.

"No charges at this time, but you will have to stay on Block until the investigation is finished," he said seriously looking down at the cuffs in his hands. He couldn't help but give her a big smile when he looked up. It had been that way from the first time they met.

"That is good, yes! I stay on Block Island and not in jail," she smiled. "*Spasiba bolshoi!* Thank you so much!"

The decision not to press charges had been made jointly by the FBI and DOJ. Agents Moore, Heslin and Dixon in concert with Attorney Carlson hashed it out quickly. DNI Miller joined them on the phone line, feeling enough pressure from the White house after the failed efforts to recover the chip. He wanted to take a direct role in the planning.

"This Russian waitress did nothing wrong that I can see, but she is still our best connection with Luke. If what she says holds, he'll surely try to contact her," says Carlson. "We'll need someone to stay close and keep a watch on her."

"Whose budget will pay for that?" asked Agent Moore wryly. He laughed. "I guess it doesn't matter. We have to do it."

"We have the budget," DNI Miller jumped in. "I know a guy. We'll keep her close. We've also got this Antoine kid. He's working Luke's friends to keep an eye out."

"He did good. I told him we'd help him fill out his application to join the government services," Agent Moore laughed. "He wants to apply to the CIA."

"Good. We can make that happen," DNI Miller chuckled.

"We have one less mobster to worry about with McSamarlie out of the picture. It's time to put more pressure on Yevtechnov," piped in the voice of Agent Heslin in New York. He was handling the RICO investigation into the Brighton Beach crew.

"We are close on the fruit financial forensics," said Carlson.

"Time to upset the apple cart," laughed Heslin.

"And one less spy. The president has ordered Chemenko expelled and he will be out of country in a day or two, so he is not a factor now." It was Miller again. "At least until they put someone else on the case. They still want the chip. You can be sure of that."

"The Asian woman has not been cooperating. Agent Martin believes she's North Korean, but right now she has a murder charge to deal with in Rhode Island and the Providence Plantations. We still don't know who she really is." It was US Attorney Carlson. Hae-Tae Se had several passports, but her actual country of origin had not been determined since they were all fake.

"The Sheriff wants her out of his jail as soon as possible," laughed Carlson.

"Let Rhode Island state troopers take her in custody to Providence, but keep Martin talking to her until she lawyers up," DNI Miller. "Keep working on her modem encryption. Find out who ordered her after the chip."

"Copy that, Harold," said Agent Moore. "I think we all agree. Get the chip and get Yevtechnov off the streets. Two different worlds, but we are the lucky ones who get to clean up both of them."

There was general agreement and the principals rang off, each turning their focus on what they needed to do to get the job done.

Monday Morning 0800

DNI Miller shaking the USIC alphabet tree with high level BOLO for one Luke Parmelian. He continues to elude manhunt for stolen Top Secret Sub Chip. Escape from Block leaves agents scratching heads. Quiet has returned to island for the moment. Summer tourists arrive next. Your spy blogger on double alert now that action has touched home. Not over yet! –SpyhakrF

EPILOGUE

Misha Yevtechnov liked to paint when he was unhappy,
and the brushes were out this night. The death of JMJ was a
shock. Though he never liked bullies, JMJ was one himself
and that's how he died, albeit doing Misha's bidding, as he
was supposed to do. Misha accepted no blame, paving over
any emotion with the need to be the *shef,* who understood
the cost of business. It was a nasty business for sure.

He dipped his brush in the red paint and focused on
the gums of the horse with the bit in his mouth, the teeth
bared in full gallop, a moment of joyful exertion perfectly
captured on horse number 14 on the ScreamTown at Coney
Island carousel sitting under the parachute jump at the end
of the Riegelmann Boardwalk.

Then the phone rang.

"Hello?" he answered, curious who would be calling
him at 2 o'clock in the morning.

"Misha, it's Luke. How are you this morning?"

The voice was unexpected.

"Luke! Well, this is a surprise! You are alive?"

"Very much so. I have the chip. It's at the cage. Right now."

"The chip? Well, a pleasant surprise…" but the line was
already dead before Misha could finish his thought.

He stood up and carefully placed the cap on the paint
can on his portable work bench and wiped his hands. He

then gave a gentle tap on the head of the horse he was working on and spoke to it as if it was a living creature.

"Don't go anywhere. I'll be right back."

The amusement park was deserted as Misha walked the 100 yards to the Sling Shot ride. Only the work lamps cast pools of light among the steel, wood and plaster structures that sat quietly along the boardwalk. The shouts of laughter and fear were missing, on pause until the sun came up and another summer day welcomed the world to play.

Misha was firing little arrows of anger in his mind at Luke. Damn him for hanging up on me! Then he saw the envelope sitting on the molded seats of the cage. He was excited. The failure of JMJ and Vlad had left him without his hoped for $100,000 windfall from the chip. He had received a mysterious inquiry from a Chinese firm about it, but he had no chip to sell. Now, it was in his hands. A sudden rebirth of his idea to add another ride!

He looked inside and there it was, tiny, simple and his ticket to ride! He stashed the envelope in his pocket.

"This is not for the children," came a voice in the semi darkness off to his right.

"Luke?" he asked peering into the darkness.

"It's all about the pot, Misha. You boiled it for everyone else. Until now."

"Luke. Wait. Look, forget about the money. You've paid up!" Misha opened his arms as if he was offering a hug. He stood up in the cage just as Luke pressed the button on the control pedestal.

The powerful magnet under the cage released and the bungee cords attached to the sides unleashed their stored-up energy and shot the cage into the air. Misha was slammed back into the seat. His first thought was the safety bar locked open over his head.

"oohhh…" was all he muttered.

At the top of the flight, the cords went tight, the cage expended all inertia and stopped, only for the briefest of seconds, at the apex of its flight. Then it dropped. The sliding door across the front of the seats, however, remained open and Misha kept going for only a few more feet, launched by the thrust upward until his inertia was also used up.

For a moment, Misha saw the grandeur of his creation before and below him. It was a resurrection of the venerable old amusement park in which he took great pride. He loved to make the people scream with joy.

And then he screamed, too. His scream filled the air along the beach but did not end in joy. Only a thump on the boardwalk he loved for so many years. A boardwalk stained with crimes for the very last time.

The next morning, FBI agent John Heslin from the New York City office in charge of the RICO investigation of the Brighton Beach *Slova Golovi* crew was called to the scene and found an envelope in the pocket of the dead mobster Misha Yevtechnov.

"I have the chip," he reported by phone to Agent Seamus Moore in New London.

"Great work, John!" Moore responded.

Later that morning, on Block Island, Petrika Rushevski was introduced to a new waitress at the Beach View Bar by owner Sally Wren.

"Petrika, come meet the new girl. She'll be working with you for the rest of the summer!"

"Hello, you can call me Pet. You have come to the right place and at the right time! It's gonna be fun!"

"Hi. Nice to meet you. I am Lili."